The Human Heart
Stories of Love and Life

by Billye Grymwade

Published by Puma Press
116 Blackburn Place
Ventura, California 93004-1255

Prepared for printing by Mehle Printing, Inc.
2250 Craig Drive
P.O. Box 6157
Oxnard, California 93031-6157
www.mehleprinting.com

Cover Design by Penny Henschel

ISBN: 0-9742649-1-1

Printed in the United States of America

10 9 8 7 6 5 4 3 2 1

Dedicated to my daughter and son-in-law,
my favored critics.

INDEX

THE GRYMWADE COLLECTION

OF

SHORT STORIES

BRENDA

As soon as I set foot on U.S. soil again, that morning the ship docked in Oakland, me, Private James Beck, and all my buddies--some of us Marines and the rest of us Swabbies--took off in different directions. There was a paper in my pocket that told me I could take thirty days leave, so I went straight to the bus station and bought a one-way ticket to Moss Landing, California.

I hadda feeling, even when I got on the bus right away, that I should've gone straight home, back to Custer, Nebraska. But to pass up Fred's little widow without a "gosh-I'm-sorry," or without a "I-knew-him-before-he-died," was unthinkable. Something told me inside my gut that I shouldn't go buttin' in to somebody else's life, but all the rules of good manners and what my Mom used to call good breedin', plus my natural curiosity about ol' Fred's little wife, pointed me in her direction. So I put my hat on the rack and settled down for the three-hour bus ride to go see my dead buddy's widow.

I had already caught myself daydreaming about Mrs. Lowery long before we left Nam. In fact, a few times I had waked up in the morning to remember that I had dreamed about her in my sleep, too. Come to think of it, I had daydreamed about her and nightdreamed about her a long time before Fred got it with the land mine. Only reason I had any kind of dreams about Corporal Fred Lowery's little wife was because he used to brag on her so much in a way that made a guy wish he'd known her, too. Maybe wish he'd known her before the guy that married her knew her.

Fred used to show us her picture now and then. The wallet-size photo was pretty much worn out around the edges, on the corners, and across the face of it, too, but you could still make out the eyes and nose and the mouth a little bit, and the neck. She had a gorgeous neck. She looked like she might've been blonde, but you know how it is in a photo with shadowy lighting and all that wear and tear of the photo from a lot of handling.

Besides, a woman can be blonde today, red-head tomorrow, and brunette next week. Didn't matter whether I could see how she looked or remember her face or hair or anything like that anyway because what I dreamed about mostly was her body--how she looked stretched on the sand at the beach, how she looked perched on a white stallion of the merry-go-round at the carnival, how she looked snuggled up next to you in the front seat of your car while you drove down the road, how she looked curled up under the sheet while she waited for you to undress.....

I took off my uniform jacket and hung it on the hook near my seat. Mind you, I never went through those motions with the girl, 'cause I never met her before in my life. I dreamed those things about her because those were the things Fred used to describe about her. Those and a lot of other things.

He used to gab on and on forever about his little girl, he sometimes called her. He talked about everywhere they ever went and everything they ever did. And how they did it. You'd think a guy would get sick of hearing the same old stuff over and over, but Fred was different. We figured the way he went on about it and the way his voice got low and almost emotional when he told about their great times together, we figured he was really in love with the gal. There was no doubt about it in my mind, anyway.

I checked my watch and the timetable and figured I'd get to Mrs. Lowery's late enough that they'd be all through with lunch but not so late that I'd be interfering with their supper time. Great. I could pay my respects and get in my say about Fred and be on my way, all in an hour or less.

Fred had already told us that his father-in-law operated a little place on the Coast, just a few miles above town. It had a cafe and bar with an apartment overhead, a couple of gas pumps, a two-story wing of motel rooms, three cottages, and a little store.

I asked the bus driver if he knew that place, and he said he did. In fact, bein's how I was in uniform and a stranger in the state, he made an unscheduled stop and dropped me off at the place where Fred Lowery's widow was staying. She and Fred used to live in one of the motel rooms, and they both worked for her dad. But after Fred went overseas, she moved back into the apartment to live with her dad.

I found Mr. Hayes in the cafe, working the counter, and I introduced myself and told him why I had come--to pay my respects to Mrs. Lowery and tell her about Fred. He welcomed me like a son.

"Well, well, Mr. Beck. Come in, my boy, come in!" He came through the counter break and put an arm across my shoulders. I looked around. There was only one customer at the counter having coffee and a donut, but he wasn't paying any attention to us. I smiled at Mr. Hayes.

"Come on out to the patio. We serve outside sometimes, when the weather's nice. We've got a big pepper tree that makes a nice shade for the whole patio. Want a cup of coffee, son? Or maybe you'd like to have a drink? Bar's not open yet, but we can fix something for *you*, Mr. Beck."

"Oh, no, thanks, Mr. Hayes. I really wouldn't care for anything. Not just now, anyway. But thanks all the same."

"Well, whatever you say, son. You stay put here, and I'll go get my little girl. She'll really want to see you and talk to you, especially when I tell her you knew Fred. She was pretty broken up, you know. I'm real glad you came today. I'll get my little girl now. She'll be right down."

I watched him disappear around the corner at the back of the cafe-bar building. It gave me a weird feeling to hear him refer to his daughter, Mrs. Lowery, as his little girl. Just like Fred used to do.

It was quiet, businesswise, but there was a distant muffled roar that made me wonder, so I investigated. I took off my uniform hat and tossed it onto one of the tables. I walked toward the back of the patio where there was a low, rough stone fence. When I got to the fence, I could see that it served as a barrier for the top of a steep decline down to the beach. It was the surf that was making the dull roar.

To my right was a redwood gate and just beyond that was the back of the cafe-bar building. Mr. Hayes must've gone up those outside stairs to get Fred's widow from the apartment.

My mouth suddenly went dry, and I began wishing I did accept that drink. Even a sip of hot coffee would have been some relief. I strolled along the edge of the patio next to the stone fence, away from the building. Then I could see the cottages. They were farther down the decline to my left and almost on the beach. There were two of them on a ledge. I couldn't see the third cottage.

Fred used to talk about that third cottage, the one not visible from the main building. He used to talk so much about how he and his little gir--

"Mr. Beck?"

I whirled around to see who had called me. "Oh, yes! Miz Lowery?"

She nodded. It was her all right. It had to be. Looked kindof pale, though, and frail, too, like she'd been sick or something. I guess the news of Fred's death had left its mark. I know it've done the same thing to Fred if it was the other way around--if she had been killed, and he had survived. He'd've been pretty sick, too.

I tried to stop staring. My tongue had gone bone dry and frozen stiff.

"Mr. Beck," she said, in that small delicate voice of hers, "won't you sit down?" She walked to an iron bench near the fence. She sat on it, facing the fence. I walked over toward her, but I didn't want

8

to sit next to her. That is, I didn't want to sit next to her right away. I stood in front of her, then leaned against the stone fence in back of me. I finally loosened my tongue and forced the air across my voice box.

"Miz Lowery, I don't know how to begin." Stupid Blockhead, I called myself. I had three hours on that damn bus to think about what I was going to say to this poor little thing, but all I had done, I realize now, was dream about her. In fact, I had more'n two weeks on the ship to think about what to say to her because long before I even boarded the ship, I had made up my mind to look her up, to tell her about Fred, to offer my sympathy.

But she was so frail! I wasn't sure she could take it, and I was beginning to wish I hadn't come. Lord! What am I doing here?

"I gather you've come to tell me about Fred, Mr. Beck. If so, I want you to know how grateful I am that someone who knew him has taken the time and trouble to come by and tell me about him. You're very kind, Mr. Beck, and so very thoughtful."

"Oh, no, ma'am, I'm not all that. I mean . . . Look, Miz Lowery, if this isn't a good time to talk about Fred--"

"It's as good a time as any," she said. "All I know is that he was killed, and that it was a land mine, and that it was near a bivouac area. A letter from your company commander said he was not engaged in combat at the time it happened. Another letter from a chaplain was polite and sympathetic but not exactly informative."

She stood up and came over to the fence next to me.

"Were you with him, Mr .Beck? Were you with him when he--"

"Oh, yes, Miz Lowery. I was with him, all right. It's a miracle I didn't get it, too, it was so close. Honest to God, ma'am, I don't know how it missed me. I--"

I really didn't want to start out by telling her the worst part, the part about how Fred's foot was missing, and his arm was riddled into fragments, and the forearm was hanging from its elbow. God a'mighty! I wisht I hadn't've come here.

"Anyway, Miz Lowery, I really didn't want to tell you about that just yet. Later on. What I want to tell you first is why I decided to come here."

She turned around and faced the sea. Her shoulders were so close to mine, the motion of her turning around sent a fragrance from her light brown hair into my nostrils that made me think I was in heaven. It was a delicate scent--delicate like her. That threw me off my course, too. I swallowed hard, then my mouth was dry again.

"You see, Miz Lowery, Fred used to talk about you so much! He talked about you and him so much that after awhile, we all felt like we knew you as well as he did."

She turned her head toward me and had a puzzled look in her eyes. She looked back at the sea when I began to speak again.

"Yes, ma'am, he told us all about how you and him used to go bowlin' in town, go dancin' in Salinas, go to the movies at the drive-in. Oh, you kids were somethin' else! A guy'd think you were sweethearts instead of married folks, the things you used to do at the drive-in!"

She looked at me again, sharply.

"I mean--the neckin' was all he told about, at the drive-in."

She looked down toward the beach, then turned away and began to walk toward the tables.

"Oh, I'm sorry, Miz Lowery, I shouldn'a gone on like that. It was personal, and that shouldda been private 'tween you and Fred."

"No, Mr. Beck. It's all right, really it is." She looked pathetic standing there alone with the empty tables and chairs around her. "Please go on about Fred."

"Oh, yeah. Well, as I was sayin', Fred was always talkin' about you. I mean *always*. But we never got tired listening to him. We never got bored, even when he repeated some of the stories. We never got sick of listening to him because--and this is the God's truth--he was so blind-dumb crazy about you. That's right. We could tell, the way he talked about you and the way he always referred to you as his little girl, his gal, his little soul-mate. We knew how much he loved you, and I guess that's why we never got tired of hearing him go on because he was so honest about it, and so open about it, too. That's why I had to come and see you. We . . . I felt like I already knew you, just from Fred talking about you all the time. And he never got tired of reminiscin', either. We must've re-lived with him every wonderful minute you and him ever had together. It wasn't just the movies and dancin' and bowlin'. There were the picnics, always down on the beach and up a-ways--"

She moved away from the tables and came back to the fence but not close to me this time. I moved down beside her and looked down onto the beach with her.

"And then there were the times you and him used to go into the third cottage."

"The third cottage?" She didn't take her eyes off the beach.

"Yeah. The one you can't see from up here. Which way is it? Up to the right?"

"Yes," she said without any feeling, without expression. "It's to the right, and beyond the first point. There's a small, quiet cove back there. It's excellent for swimming. And for picnics. It's private."

"Yeah. That's what Fred used to say. Quiet and private. And you and him used to stay at the cottage whenever it was empty. One look at the reservations cards, and you could tell whether it'd be occupied and when and for how long.

"One time, he told us about how you spent three nights in a row, together and alone. It was heaven, he said. You both came up to work in the day and eat lunch up here. But the rest of the time, you took supplies down there, ate breakfast and supper there and stayed the three nights. Boy, he said those nights at the cottage were some of the happiest times of his whole life. I believe it, Miz Lowery. I swear I believe it. He told us how--"

She walked away from me again and stopped near the gate. It looked like she was hanging onto the gatepost, for dear life, maybe. Her knuckles looked whiter than ever. I walked over next to her again.

"Honest to God, Miz Lowery, I don't know why I'm sayin' all these things to you. They are personal, and maybe they shouldda been private and maybe Fred shouldn've told us so many details. But I swear to God, Miz Lowery, what Fred had for you and what you had for him--those things between you were the greatest! You oughtta know how Fred really and truly felt about you. He said not one time but a thousand times, I bet, that no other woman in the whole world could satisfy him the way his gal could. You know what I mean, Miz Lowery?"

She lifted her head a little and fixed her eyes on the surf and slowly nodded to tell me she knew what I meant.

My gosh, I wisht I had the nerve to put my arm around her, she looked so helpless. Maybe if I just put my hand on her arm----She let go of the gatepost, though, and turned away from me and walked real slow back into the middle part of the patio, through the tables, and up to the big pepper tree. She leaned her forehead against the bark. It was too far away to talk to her from the fence, so I went through the tables, too, and stood near her and the tree trunk.

I was beginning to feel I'd better wind it up and get on my way. There was just one little thing, though, that I had to tell her-- just one more thing. It was important. She had to know this one part. It was the last thing Fred said before he went.

"One more thing to tell you, Miz Lowery, before I leave, and then that'll be all." She nodded once.

I went on. "Well, you see, after the mine exploded, it took us a second or two to collect our wits. Then we looked around to see what had happened. And I saw Fred first. I yelled for the corpsman, and I ran to Fred. I couldn't pick him up, or anything like that. But I knelt down beside him and spoke to him to see if he was conscious. He tried to answer me when I called his name. He groaned a little, and he tried to get up. But I pressed against his shoulders, ever so gently, 'cause it didn't take much to keep him from moving. And he relaxed and stayed still and quiet on the ground. I spoke to him again and asked if he hurt anywhere. He shook his head and shut his eyes tight and groaned again. I said, 'Fred? Fred, say somethin' to me. Please, Fred!'. . ."

That godawful lump filled up my throat again--the same one I had that afternoon Fred got it. I tried to push it back down with a swallow. I tried to go on with the story.

"Oh, Miz Lowery, you got no idea what it did to me when he said his last word. You'll never know how his last word came from his lips and went through me like a knife! Yes, ma'am, his last word was just a name. He was thinking of you to the very end because all he said when he answered me was, 'Brenda' . . . and then just once more he said it . . . 'Brenda?' . . . and then it was all over."

I tried to look at Mrs. Lowery when I finished, and it was then I saw her fists squeezed real tight and pressing against her temples. I felt awful for making her feel bad. But I had to tell her because I figured it'd mean so much for her to know that her dead husband thought of her at the end and only her.

I started to put my arms out to bring her around to face me and maybe let me comfort her. I barely touched one of her shoulders when she straightened up suddenly and quickly stepped away from the tree and away from me. She turned and, with tears sitting in her eyes, ready to spill over, she spoke to me in a voice so even and unstrained, and almost cold, that it kinda scared me.

"Mr. Beck, you've been very helpful, more than you know, by coming here today and telling me about my husband. I want you to know how much I appreciate it, and I thank you for all that you've done. If you'll excuse me?"

She turned and quickly walked across the patio, through the gate, and out of sight. How long I stood there after she left, I haven't any idea. I couldn't make up my mind about going into the cafe to say goodbye to Mr. Hayes.

Just as I had decided to pick up my hat, though, a convertible car drove up into the parking area at the front of the patio and cafe building. It drove up with a screeching stop, spitting up the gravel, and stirring up a cloud of gravel dust. I wouldn't have paid anymore attention to it but for the fact that a gorgeous creature opened the driver's door and jumped out. She pulled her long blonde hair out of her eyes and called to me as she came floating through the tables, her handbag on one arm, a package of mail in her hands.

"Hey! Where'd you come from? You're about the cutest Jarhead I've ever seen! Haven't you been served yet? You gotta go inside, place your order, and then the waitress brings it out to you. Where's my sister? She usually serves outside. Oh, well, I'll take care of you myself in a minute. My sister!"--

She hunched her shoulders once, then let them drop again. She tossed the mail on a table, the same one where my hat was. Then she took a pack of cigarettes out of her handbag. I lit her cigarette with my lighter.

"My sister!" she went on. "Such a baby. Been sick off and on for a long time. In and out of the hospital, too. I even gave up my job in San Francisco to come back here and help out, just because she was sick so much."

She took a deep draw on her cigarette and blew out the smoke like a big sigh. She went on.

"Then, when she got word about Fred--he was her husband, a Marine, just like you. When she found out he'd been killed in Vietnam, well, that was a real setback! Have to do all my work and more'n half of hers. I'll be glad when she pulls out of this slump. My dad's always babying her. She may never make it."

Mr. Hayes must've heard us outside. He came out of the cafe and joined us.

"Oh, hi, Dad," the blonde doll said to him. "Didn't you know we had a customer out here?"

"No, honey, he's not a customer. He's a guest, a very special one. Let me introduce you. Honey, this is Private James Beck. He knew Fred in Vietnam. Mr. Beck, this is my other little girl, Brenda."

# # #

13

MUSIC HATH CHARMS

The bookstore in Hollywood ran the display for six weeks. It was a display for Uriella Hamm's first novel, "Right of Way."

The book was immensely successful. Uriella was able to make some major changes in her life. She quit her job as a Data Entry Operator, and she began to write her autobiography. She moved out of her low-rent apartment in Port Hueneme, California, and into a high-rise apartment building in Santa Monica, across the street from the beach. She bought a new car, she began to have her hair done professionally each week, and she hired a housekeeper to do the cleaning and some of the cooking.

Uriella's life style changed very little otherwise. She continued to walk two miles every morning, to read every evening, and she continued to witness a concert, a play, an opera, a ballet, or a musical at least once a month--alone. She continued to keep in touch with her family, a son and a daughter, both out of town, by calling them each week. She also had a granddaughter, Bob's child. He was separated from his wife and in the throes of a divorce. He had custody of his daughter, Sandy. Jenny and Ben, Uriella's daughter and son-in-law, had no children.

Life went on as usual for Uriella until one Saturday afternoon in February when she attended the matinee performance of a musical at the Shubert Theater. She fell in love--head-over-heels, wildly in love. It was only the third stirring of interest in a man that she had experienced since her marriage was dissolved ten years earlier.

She had faced the fact many times in her single life that she simply was not attractive to men. They rarely noticed her; therefore, there were virtually no men in her life. She convinced herself that it did not matter. She liked living alone. Many times, however, when she would be out in public for lunch or dinner, or to attend one of the monthly functions, she wished she had a companion.

By Tuesday, after doing some heavy thinking and some careful calculations, Uriella had made up her mind. She bought another ticket for the following Saturday's matinee performance. After the last curtain call, she drew herself up, gathered her purse and program, and headed for backstage.

In spite of the general pandemonium, she was able to spot the actor who had intrigued her, a young man with long brown hair, dark eyes, and a glorious baritone voice. He was of medium-to-tall height and had a stocky physique.

Uriella approached him and asked, "Royce Howland?"

"Yes," he answered.

"Loved your performance. Love your voice."

"Well, thank you."

"Enough small talk," she said. "I have a proposal to make to you."

"Is it some kind of job?" he asked.

"In a manner of speaking. Yes."

"So, what is it?"

"Is there a place we can go for some privacy?"

"Sure. I'm about to go get a bite to eat before the evening performance. You'll join me?"

"Indeed," she replied.

He led the way from backstage and out the theater, across the concourse, and into a health-food restaurant. They sat down and the waitress brought them menus. Royce closed his menu and said, "I already know what I want."

"What are you going to have?" Uriella asked.

"Chilled cucumber soup, a tuna salad, and water," he replied.

"Sounds good to me. I'll have the same. I'm into health foods, too."

The waitress left the table.

"Now," said Royce, "what's up?"

Uriella took a deep breath and began, "Marry me, Mr. Howland, and in one year we'll get a divorce, and your settlement will be $500,000. We'll sign a pre-marital agreement, of course, to guarantee you that amount."

Royce was startled and uncomprehending. He looked at her with a frown and said, "You want to 'buy' me?"

"So to speak. Where else can you earn that much in one year?"

He emitted a low whistle and said, "Nowhere. Not at the rate I'm going right now. And besides, I haven't anything lined up for when the show closes next month."

They ate their light meal, chatting about the show, the weather, and local politics. When they had finished, they stood up and Uriella took a card from her purse and handed it to him.

"Call me when you've decided, one way or the other. And please....don't keep me just hanging."

"Okay," he said.

"I'm a writer, and I'm at home most of the time, after a two-mile walk early each morning. And except for Friday mornings when I get my hair done and shop for groceries, and on Sunday mornings when I go to church."

"I'll remember that, Miss Hamm, and thank you."

Throughout the remainder of his break between performances, Royce was plagued by the proposal Uriella Hamm had made. He thought about its outrageousness, its kookiness, and its blatancy. His thoughts dogged him throughout the evening performance, the rest of the weekend, and into the beginning of his day off, Monday, when the theater was dark.

Royce tried to remember what Uriella looked like: She was a Plain Jane, if ever he had seen one, with strange blue-green eyes. She had white hair in the front, gray at the sides and medium brown at the back; she wore glasses; she was average height; and maybe she was just a shade on the chunky side, but just a touch. He even asked himself, "What would it be like to be married to an older woman?"

* * *

Uriella went home after the musical and settled in to a waiting status. She wondered at her own audacity, and she wondered what action Royce Howland would take as a result. She waited.

On Monday morning, Royce called Uriella. "Shouldn't we have a date, or something?" he asked.

"We should," she answered. "How about lunch today?"

"Right," he said. "Today's my day off. However, I couldn't take you somewhere fancy. I'm almost broke."

"Not to worry," she said. "My treat."

They met at Perrinos. After they had ordered, Royce said, "You know your scheme is crazy, don't you?"

"Absolutely," she answered. "That's what makes it ever so attractive."

"That and the money," he said.

"Of course." She added, "So, you have been thinking about it, I gather."

"I sure have, but doesn't the age difference bother you?"

"Not if it doesn't bother you," she answered.

"What is our age difference, anyway?"

"Well, you must be around 23 or 24."

"Twenty-five."

"And I'm 60. That's . . . . a 35-year difference."

"Whewee," he exclaimed. "I thought you were about fifty."

"Thank you for the compliment."

"Where would we live?" he asked.

"In my apartment. Would you like to see it this afternoon?"

"Sure. Why not?"

After lunch, he followed her in his Toyota to her apartment building, met her in the underground garage, and they took the elevator up to her floor. Upon entering the apartment, the first thing Royce saw was the grand piano in the living room. He walked straight to it and sat down on the bench. He placed his hands on the keys, then withdrew his hands. He looked up at Uriella and said, "I forgot my manners. May I?"

"Certainly. Please go ahead."

He played a few bars from the musical he was appearing in. He stopped and emitted his low whistle. "Man, the tone is perfect."

He got up from the bench and with boyish enthusiasm, walked to the wall of floor-length windows in the same room and looked out at the view. Another low whistle. "With that piano and this view of the ocean--man, I'd have it made."

Uriella said, "I've noticed you don't smoke. That's a plus. Neither do I."

"I know. If I'm going to make a living with my voice, I have to take care of it."

"I suppose you drink alcohol?"

"Not since I began eating health foods. I figure, again, if you're going to take care of your entire body, go all the way."

Uriella emitted a small sigh of relief. "I'm glad to hear that."

"So," he said, "if we have any minor differences, I guess I could live with that--for one year."

"Does that mean you accept my proposal?"

He looked through the window again, and after a few seconds, he said, "What the hell? Yes."

She smiled. He smiled, and then his face clouded over. He said, "Wait a minute. What if I were already married? What would you have done about that?"

"I take it you're not married."

"That's right."

"Well, I would have waited the six months for you to get a divorce so that you could marry me."

He laughed."You had it all figured out, didn't you?"

"Exactly."

Uriella walked to the couch and sat down. Looking up at him still standing at the window, she said, "However, I haven't found out if you have a girl friend. That, too, could be a complication."

He sat in a chair opposite her and said, "I don't have a steady girl friend. I date once in a while. Hardly ever the same woman twice. I'm free as a bird."

"And you'll continue to be free, even after we're married. All you have to do is be nice to me."

"I can handle that."

"So," she said, "I guess that means we're engaged."

He looked at her quizzically and asked, "Should we set a date?"

"How about next Monday, your next day off?"

"Sounds okay to me, Miss Hamm."

"Call me Yuri."

"That a nickname?"

"It is."

"Okay, Yuri."

He got up from the chair and sat down next to her on the couch. He put his hand under her chin and turned her face toward him. He kissed her. He said, "There. That makes it official."

* * *

The following Monday morning they signed a pre-marital agreement in the office of Uriella's attorney. Her daughter and son-in-law, Jenny and Ben, came down from Ventura to witness the marriage at City Hall. It was late afternoon when they left City Hall, and the four of them went to dinner at the Bonaventure Hotel.

When dinner was over, Jenny and Ben left for Ventura, and Uriella and Royce retired to their room at the hotel.

While Uriella undressed in the dressing room, Royce undressed, put on his terry cloth robe, and sat on the bed to watch television.

Uriella left the dressing room wearing a peignoir only. Royce looked at her and drew out a long, low whistle. He turned off the television with the remote control.

"Yuri," he said, "you are one good-looking woman! Why do you hide behind glasses? Why don't you wear contact lenses?"

"Because I can't stand the idea of a foreign object sitting on my eyeball." She shuddered.

"And what a figure, for a woman your age. Not bad. Not bad at all."

Uriella, encouraged, lay across the bed with her head in his lap. She felt the hardness under her head. She smiled, pleased with herself at the knowledge that she could excite a man--a young man at that. There was no question in her mind that she would be aroused. She knew she would be and she was.

* * *

By Tuesday afternoon, Royce had moved out of his furnished pad and had moved into Uriella's apartment with a stack of clothes, a guitar, and two boxes of music.

When the show closed in March, Royce received a phone call from one of his old music professors in Los Angeles. The professor had suffered bad health, a heart attack, and needed someone to take over his classes for the remainder of the semester. Royce accepted.

The last class was in June. For the following three weeks, Royce studied parts for four operettas so that he could go to St. Louis for the Opera-Under-the-Stars season.

Uriella accompanied him to St. Louis and found an apartment to set up housekeeping while they were there for the summer. She had bought a laptop and rented a printer, all compatible with her equipment at home, so that she could continue work on her book.

By September, they were in San Francisco. Royce had an offer to appear in another musical. He spent two weeks preparing for the role. Uriella was with him there, too. This time they lived in a hotel.

Royce did not have very much opportunity to think about his relationship with Uriella because he was so busy since their marriage. But now and then he took time out to reflect. He realized that Uriella was a quiet and unassuming person, all the more remarkable considering the outlandish proposal she had made to him in February, and which he accepted.

He noticed little things like dressing and undressing, putting away the dishes, brushing her teeth, and putting the car in gear--all were done with grace, like a ballet. She moved slowly but deliberately. When she walked, she glided.

Whatever city they were living in, Uriella always went to church on Sunday mornings. She invited Royce to accompany her one Sunday, and he did. He discovered that it was nondenominational and that the entire congregation sang a capella. There was no choir and no soloist. Sometimes he was invited to sing a solo at other churches, all Protestant churches. He would finish his solo, then rush to Uriella's congregation and join her there. He sang bass and listened to Uriella's tenor in the male octave. Her range was limited. She could barely reach F below middle C. She could not reach E. When that occurred in the hymn, she made up a higher note that would harmonize with the other parts.

Royce sang for the sheer joy of it. Singing a capella was a special treat. Uriella was not an accomplished musician, as he was, but she had a passion for music that matched his. While he actively participated in music, she was, by and large, merely a spectator. She had an almost perverse liking for bagpipe music, a liking which Royce found difficult to fathom. Uriella explained it was a throwback from her Scottish heritage.

Uriella's car radio was always set to a "listenable music" station. She listened to it in the apartment, too. Every now and then, if Royce were with her, she would announce, "That's a favorite of mine!"

Politically, they were similar. He was moderate right; she tended to be a notch beyond moderate right.

Royce loved the way Uriella gave him back rubs. When he'd come home from a performance, wired up and tense, she would massage his temples, neck, shoulders, and back until he was relaxed and nearly asleep.

Royce enjoyed looking at Uriella in the wind. The wind blew a wisp of hair down onto her forehead. It gave her a rakish look and that was the only time he was reminded of the one rash thing she did in her life--propose to him.

* * *

Every morning before breakfast, while Uriella walked her two miles, Royce jogged his five miles.

Uriella had one brother, deceased, and no sisters. She had few friends and only a small number of acquaintances. Royce noticed that she wrote letters to more friends than what she had in Santa Monica. They were far-flung friends: they were in Maine, Florida, Michigan, Arizona, Colorado, Louisiana, Texas, and New Jersey. She also wrote to cousins in Texas, Arizona, and Kansas.

Any parties that Uriella and Royce hosted or attended were business-related parties. Uriella's children and grandchild visited her from time to time. Royce was amused to be stepfather to two children who were older than he. He delighted in the company of Sandy, his step-granddaughter.

Occasionally, one or two of Royce's college buddies came to see him at the Santa Monica apartment. Uriella often made lunch for them and sat with them, listening to them talk. Royce seemed to be bilingual. With his contemporaries, he spoke one language. With Uriella, he spoke another language.

* * *

During the first seven months, Uriella had ample opportunity to think about their relationship. She adored Royce. She had been apprehensive about whether their sex life would be satisfactory, remembering her disastrous first marriage sexual experience. She needn't have worried. It was completely fulfilling, so different from her first marriage. From the beginning, Royce seemed to know what to do for her and whatever he did, it was most pleasing to her. She

21

kept thinking that sooner or later he would do something to irritate her, but it never happened, except for the snoring. If he slept on his back, he snored. She was totally enamored of him.

Uriella was accustomed to seeing Royce dressed in various costumes when he was on stage, but his at-home garb usually consisted of Levis, T-shirt, and athletic shoes.

The usual clothing for Uriella, at home, was a Muumuu. Her street clothing were all designed by her and made by her Filipino dressmaker. All her clothes were plain and hung loosely from the shoulders. For streetwear, she never varied her hemline.

Royce was such a boy, she thought, but what did she expect, with his being almost young enough to be her grandson? It did not matter to Uriella, however, because every aspect of their life together these past seven months was delightful. Even Royce's playing contemporary music at home on the radio surprised Uriella. Although she abhorred the loud and raucous hard rock "non-music music," as she called it, she found herself listening to the beat. That caught her ear's attention.

Wistfully, Uriella regretted that they had already passed the six-month half-way point. But, an agreement is an agreement.

Uriella's birthday was in October, while they were in San Francisco. Royce woke up early that day and ordered coffee, juice and croissants from Room Service. He had finished showering when Room Service arrived. He woke up Uriella and kissed her on the cheek and then gave her her birthday present, a small box.

"They say good things come in small packages," she said.

"You'll see."

She unwrapped the paper. It was a cassette tape.

"It's unmarked," she said.

"Go ahead. Play it," he urged.

She put it into the cassette player and started it.

"That's your voice!" she exclaimed. "And it's one of my favorite songs. Oh, Royce, it's lovely. I like it!"

"Wait 'til you hear the rest, Yuri."

They listened to the remainder while they ate their breakfast.

"Royce, you've recorded all favorites of mine. Eight songs, four on each side. Oh, Royce, this is the nicest birthday present I ever received in my life. Thank you very much, dear."

He glowed at her pleasure. "You're welcome, sweetheart."

"This must explain all those extra 'rehearsals' you've been attending the last couple of weeks."

"It does. I was rehearsing, all right, but it was at a recording studio, not at the theater. And it was great fun doing that for you. Believe me, Yuri."

"I'm truly touched, Royce. Thank you again."

She kissed him on the cheek. He turned his face toward her and kissed her on the mouth. The joy of having pleased her was immeasurable. Royce remembered what she had done for his birthday in April. She paid off the balance due on his Toyota.

* * *

As Thanksgiving approached, they discussed what to do for that day. Should they stay at home, or go to his mother's and father's home for dinner in Redondo Beach? Uriella's children were involved with dinner at their father's home in Ventura.

Uriella dreaded going to Royce's parents' house because their reception of her was cool. She couldn't blame them. After all, if they were looking forward to grandchildren, as they surely were, it was not going to happen. Uriella remembered, however, that Royce's parents were not aware of hers and Royce's arrangement: one year of marriage and then it would be over.

The mother was almost insulting most of the time. The father was downright indifferent. Royce was aware of those upcoming unpleasant conditions and agonized over the prospect of spending the day at his former home.

As it happened, outside events provided a solution for them. Royce's show in San Francisco closed, and he was called to New York to fill in at an off-Broadway theater for an actor-singer who had sustained a sprained ankle. Uriella went there with him. They stayed at a hotel. Thanksgiving was an intimate dinner in their hotel room before the evening performance.

The same question arose for what to do and where to go for Christmas. Uriella supplied a solution for that. She reserved space for the two of them on a cruise to Acapulco. It was peaceful and Royce realized he had needed the rest. He hadn't taken a vacation for three years.

The cruise was his first, and he was seasick. But Uriella steered him to the clinic where the ship's doctor gave him an injection and pills for the remainder of the cruise. Then Royce was all right.

He asked her, "Yuri, you are so lucky not to get seasick. It's awful!"

"Well," she said. "I have a confession to make. I get seasick while the ship is still tied up at the dock. I have to take something before sailing and again every 24 hours during the entire cruise!"

He smiled. He was not alone, after all.

By January they were back in Los Angeles. Royce was studying for an act at a nightclub in Las Vegas. He said to Uriella while at the piano, "Next month is the end of our year."

"I know," she replied."I try not to think about it because I feel I will be devastated when you leave."

His dark eyes penetrated her soul. She wondered what was on his mind. Finally, he spoke again.

"Yuri, I don't want to leave."

"You don't! But . . . what does this mean?"

"It means, Yuri, that I have come to enjoy the having someone do my laundry, cook my meals, clean up the place, the grand piano, the view. But more than that, Yuri. It means that I have come to care for you very much." He fingered the music on the rack on the piano. "I love you."

There was a significant moment of silence while she gazed at him. "Royce," she said softly, "you've never said that before." She walked to stand behind him at the piano bench.

"Neither have you," he said. "But I love you just as I feel you love me, Yuri."

"Oh, darling, I do love you. More than I can express with mere words." She hugged him, and he kissed her soundly.

"But you want the money, anyway, don't you?"

"Yes, Yuri, I do. But I don't want us to be divorced. How can we do that?"

"Simple," she said. I'll give you the money and then we'll sign another contract."

"What contract?" he asked.

"Well, I have to protect myself against your taking the money now and then filing for dissolution later and claiming half of my remaining assets, according to the state's community property law."

"Yuri! I wouldn't do that!"

"Maybe not, but there must be a contract. Do you understand?"

"Sure. I guess so."

* * *

In February Uriella and Royce appeared in her attorney's office again. They signed a second contract in which Royce waived all financial claim in the event of a divorce or upon Uriella's death. Then Uriella handed him his check for $500,000.

The first thing Royce did with his money was to buy a new car, a LeBaron (because he liked Uriella's Fifth Avenue so much). The remaining money he invested in tax-free municipal bonds and used the interest for income. He had gone to Uriella's investment counselor who studied his financial needs and wishes and advised him how to invest. Royce began paying some of the living expenses they incurred, in Santa Monica, for traveling, and while living in other cities.

"It was time," he said, "to stop being a kept man."

* * *

In the next five years they managed to take a cruise every year, in the spring or in the fall, depending on Royce's schedule. He "worked" the cruises, performing as an entertainer for the ship's shows, singing several nights during the cruise. It was not work for him. It was play. He always took the seasick pills to keep him well for each cruise.

On the first cruise during which he "worked," he said to Yuri, "Honey, be sure to come to the performance tonight in the Starlight Lounge."

"Of course I'll be there–with bells on–but why are you asking me specifically to do that?"

"You'll see. Just try to sit fairly near the front row, first seat off the middle aisle."

"Well," she said slowly. "Okay. I'll be there."

At the performance that evening, Royce sang "Music of the Night" from "Phantom of the Opera." And close to the end of the number, microphone attached to a lapel, he walked through the audience. He stopped at Uri's seat, reached down for her hands and raised her up to stand before him. He then took her face in his hands and kissed her soundly.

Uri was thrilled that he would incorporate his kissing her into his act. The audience went wild, and at the conclusion of the number, there was thunderous applause for the unexpected ending.

* * *

Back in Santa Monica, one night Royce came home from a performance in a musical and sat down in a chair in the living room, across from Uriella on the couch.

"Yuri, I've had it!" he exclaimed.

"Had what?" she asked.

"I've had it with the women on the set who keep trying to go out with me alone. It's one thing to be with them at a cast party, or whatever, but I'll be damned if I'll go out with them alone!"

"So, what brought this on?"

"This one aggressive female has been making a play for me for weeks. I've had it! I can't shake her."

"You could go out with her, you know. I'm not holding you back."

"I know that, Yuri. But you've got to remember, I don't want to go out with other women. I'm more than happy to stay with you when I'm not at work."

"I appreciate hearing that, Royce. However, that doesn't solve the problem with the one girl."

There was a silence between them. Then Uriella said, "You could tell her what you just told me."

His face brightened. "By God, I could. And I will."

The strategy worked. The woman never bothered Royce again. Neither did the other women in the cast. The word got around. The strategy worked at other times, too, with other women who hung onto him and begged him to date them.

* * *

Most of Royce's work was done in Los Angeles, but one year he and Uriella went to London for him to perform in a musical. While in Europe, they visited Paris, Rome, Madrid and Lisbon.

One day in Rome, while they ate lunch at an outdoor café, Uriella watched the young Italian women flirt with Royce, openly. She said to him, "I want you to promise me something, Royce."

"What is that?"

"Statistically, you will outlive me by a considerable number of years."

"So?"

"So, I want you to promise me that when that happens, you will re-marry soon and start a family."

"Yuri, I don't want to talk about it."

"We must, Royce. Promise."

"I'm not sure I even want children."

"The desire will come, probably later. Be sure to marry someone who wants children and wants them right away."

He nodded his head. "Okay. I promise. But I don't want to talk about it anymore."

The extra travel broadened horizons for both of them. They returned to Santa Monica refreshed and stimulated.

* * *

The years found them going to Chicago, Detroit, Houston, Atlanta, and Cleveland. They returned to New York on several occasions. There was always work for Royce in New York.

During one stay in New York, Uriella and Royce went to a late dinner at a supper club with her publisher and his wife, Mr. and Mrs. Bledsoe, and his niece, Paula, an attractive young woman of 22.

There was dancing after dinner, and Uriella said, "Royce, why don't you ask Paula to dance?"

"Sure," he said, and he and Paula moved out onto the dance floor.

"Look at him," Uriella said to Mrs. Bledsoe. "He's a natural!"

Mrs. Bledsoe asked, "Aren't you afraid to let him dance with someone so young?"

"What's to be afraid of? They aren't clutching each other. They have at least 36 inches between them!"

* * *

Uriella finished her autobiography, and it was published. She began writing a sequel to her first novel. She had worked up an outline for it some years before, and now she had only to flesh it out. It was published three months after they had celebrated their sixth anniversary.

They were in New York at the time, for Royce to fulfill a contract for making a video tape. They agreed, one morning, to meet for lunch during his break.

Uriella took a cab to the studio and waited in it for him at the entrance. While the cab was parked there, a truck rear-ended the cab.

Royce left the entrance just at that moment. He ran to the cab and peered into the back seat.

"Yuri!" he cried. "Are you all right?"

She did not answer. He opened the back door and entered the cab. He put his arms around her.

"Yuri!"

She opened her eyes and said, "Royce . . ." "Promise." . . . . . "Prom . . . . . . "

The cabbie shouted, "Somebody call an ambulance!"

Royce accompanied Uriella to the hospital. She died on the way.

Later, at the hospital, the intern on duty explained: "Your wife did not die from injuries incurred during the accident. The accident triggered a heart attack. That was what she did not survive."

* * *

Royce completed his contract in New York and flew back to Los Angeles. He, with Jenny, Ben, and Bob and his daughter, held a memorial service for Uriella. She had been an organ donor and, in her will, had arranged for the cadaver to be donated to a medical college.

Uriella's attorney informed Royce that she had changed her will two years ago in that she made Royce and Jenny and Bob co-heirs to her estate. Royce now had more than a comfortable income. But he kept on working doggedly.

Royce was desolate and wasted. He grieved for Uriella for months. He worked harder than ever to try to forget. He could not forget her because he dreamed about her nearly every night and thought about her every waking hour.

After a year of driving himself into near exhaustion from work, moving from city to city, he took a break and re-evaluated his life. He knew he was tired and decided he was tired of the constant moving from city to city, from show to show. He brought out his teaching certificate and applied for a job as music teacher in a junior high school in Loma Vista, California. It was a relief from the hectic schedule he had kept since Uriella's death. Teaching music was what he had trained for, after all.

He continued to sing, however, as soloist in various churches in and around Los Angeles. One Sunday in a church in Hollywood, he was singing a solo. Near the end of his rendition, he saw a young woman that caught his attention. She was in the second row. She looked exactly like Uriella did in her pictures and snapshots he had seen of her in her old albums.

Royce suddenly remembered his promise to Uriella.

He left the church building and waited at the front of the building until the service was over. He was not quite sure what he was going to say to her, but he knew he must speak to her and somehow get to know her.

He saw her approach. She recognized him and smiled at him. She extended her right hand to him. He took it, and they shook hands.

"Loved your solo," she said. "Love your voice!" She paused for a moment, then continued. "I'm Helen Bertram, and I see on the program that you're Royce Howland. How do you do?"

Royce was still tongue-tied but finally managed to respond.

"How do you do? And thank you . . . for the nice compliments." He felt like a teenager, hesitating and stammering. But he went on. "I, uh . . . . I'm going to get a bite to eat. Would you care to join me?"

"We-l-l-l," she said. "I don't know. I'm into health foods . . ."

# # #

THE BANK ACCOUNT

First National Bank, Clairson, Iowa

Check No. 0001; Date, March 3, 1923; Pay to the order of Dr. J.C. Morrow, M.D.; Amount, $35.00; Memo, delivery of son Wm H. Letterman; signed Jason W. Letterman

Louise Pinkley, age 16, made her first entry on a bookkeeping machine at the bank. Mr. Newell, the bank manager, had hired Louise at a young age because she passed his test for all applicants at the bank: she proved to be honest.

Louise was still in high school, but she was able to work from 3:00 p.m. (closing time at the bank) until others left work at 5:00 p.m. Not only was she honest, but she was diligent and reliable. A bank manager could ask for no more than that.

Check No. 0002; Date, March 31, 1923; Pay to the order of Elsie McGillicuddy; Amount, $10.00; Memo, Nanny's wages; signed Marie Letterman

Check No. 0003; Date, April 30, 1923; Pay to the order of Elsie McGillicuddy; Amount, $10.00; Memo, Nanny's wages; signed Marie Letterman

Check No. 0004; Date, May 31, 1923; Pay to the order of Elsie McGillicuddy; Amount, $10.00; Memo, Nanny's wages; signed Marie Letterman

The months wore on, and Louise found herself following the life of the infant William Letterman. She often fantasized about the infant, ensconced in his lofty home atop the only hill in Clairson. What was he doing now? Who was changing his diaper? Who got up in the middle of the night to comfort the crying baby? She had two younger brothers and one little sister. She knew that her mother did all those things for the younger children. Louise thought about that. "She must have done it for me, too."

Check No. 0022; Date, March 3, 1927; Pay to the order of Clowns, Inc.; Amount, $8.50; Memo, Billy's 4th birthday party; signed Jason W. Letterman

Check No. 0104; Date, March 3, 1928; Pay to the order of Clairson Bicycles; Amount $12.00; Memo, bicycle for Billy's 5ᵗʰ birthday; signed Jason W. Letterman

Louise Pinkley was now 21 years old, of legal age, and by now women had the right to vote. It was a big thing for Louise, the right to vote. She was on the bank's payroll as a full-time employee, now that she was legally an adult. Mr. Newell also gave her a promotion.

For three months, Newell had Louise spend her lunch hour with one of the tellers (a different one each day) to learn the ropes. Since the end of World War I, he got into step with the rest of the nation and began to allow women tellers into the bank.

After the three months of training, Newell put Louise at a teller window. She felt as though she had come full circle, even though her secondary job at the bank included still doing the bookkeeping-machine entries, after her teller-window duties were finished each day.

The promotion included a small advance in pay. Very small. By 1929, the country was in an economic depression that threatened many businesses, large and small, and small banks across the country. But First National at Clairson held on.

Check No. 0336; Date, March 3, 1930; Pay to the order of Hobbs Department Store; Amount, $5.00; Memo, pair of shoes; signed William H. Letterman

Two weeks before this check showed up in the bookkeeping department, Louise served at the teller window a seven-year-old boy, Billy Letterman. His dad was turning over the account to the boy, standing by, watching him and coaching him.

Billy was a darling boy, so polite, so respectful, and so grown-up acting! Intelligent, too. He signed the account cards, and from then on, the account was his to use as he pleased. Louise, however, with her 23-year-old common sense, wondered how wise it was to turn over a checking account to a lad only seven years of age.

Of course, the father was the one making the deposits into Billy's account. It was clear to Louise that Mr. Letterman had weathered the storm of the depression without undue worry. The money kept coming in.

Check No. 0758; Date, July 15, 1938; Pay to the order of Boy Scouts of America; Amount $20.00; Memo, Boy Scout summer camp; signed William H. Letterman

Check No. 1067; Date, November 1, 1941; Pay to the order of Pontiac Motors; Amount $150.00; Memo, Pontiac sedan; signed William H. Letterman.

So, Louise, mused, the Letterman boy Billy bought himself a new car. She was aware that it was new because Pontiac Motors handled only the new models.

Check No. 1068; Date, November 3, 1941; Pay to the order of Mary's Flowers; Amount, $2.50; Memo, orchid for Becky; signed William H. Letterman

Check No. 1069; Date, November 3, 1941; Pay to the order of Hillcrest Restaurant; Amount, $11.75; Memo, dinner for two; signed William H. Letterman

Check No. 1070; Date, November 5, 1941; Pay to the order of Mary's Flowers; Amount, $4.50; Memo, corsage for Marian; signed William H. Letterman

Check No. 1071; Date, November 5, 1941; Pay to the order of Manson's Dining Room; Amount $13.89; Memo, dinner for two; signed William H. Letterman

Check No. 1072; Date, November 5, 1941; Pay to the order of Cash; Amount $5.00; Memo, cash; signed William H. Letterman

"What is this boy doing?" Louise asked aloud but to no one in particular. It would not be professional to discuss bank customers' spending habits. She had her own suspicions: cash for booze? "Good Grief! He's only a boy!" And, the county was dry.

Check No. 1073; Date, November 6, 1941; Pay to the order of Clairson Police Department; Amount, $15.00; Memo, DUI ticket; signed William H. Letterman

"Drunk driving . . . already? What is this world coming to?" This Louise said to herself. Foolish boy. Where did he go wrong? she thought. She felt bad, too, because the last time he came into the bank, he was so grown up and so handsome! She reddened at the thought. "What am I thinking? I'm 16 years older than that boy!"

Check No. 1090; Date, December 8, 1941; Pay to the order of Shamrock Bar; Amount, $45.00; Memo, going-away party for boys enlisting; signed William H. Letterman

In February of 1942, Bill Letterman showed up at the bank to say goodbye to Mr. Newell and to all the tellers. He was resplendent in an enlisted man's Army uniform. He had completed basic training and was headed for advanced basic training. He had been drafted.

"I don't know when I'll be back. I hope I get a furlough after advanced basic training. If not, I'll be on my way to serve as cannon fodder. Ha ha ha ha." It was a hollow laughter. And no one else laughed. Louise walked up to him, put her arms around him and gave him a "sisterly" squeeze. Already his shoulders and arms were hard as a rock. "Lots of tennis and bowling," she thought.

Surprising himself and Louise as well, he hugged her back more vigorously than she had hugged him. She ducked her head, feeling her face turning beet red.

Check No. 1104; Date, March 3, 1942; Pay to the order of Pearson Hotel Banquet Hall; Amount, $75.00; Memo, birthday bash and booze!; signed William H. Letterman

Check No. 1105; Date, March 4, 1942; Pay to the order of Margaret Tillson; Amount, $100.00; Memo, ??????????; signed William H. Letterman

"Well!" exclaimed Louise to herself. "What in the world was THAT all about?" Obviously he celebrated his birthday, and, also obviously, he spent the night with a girl. "Oh, my goodness!"

Check No. 1106; Date, March 4, 1942; Pay to the order of Greyhound Bus; Amount $6.29; Memo, transportation back to the post; signed William H. Letterman

"Oh, my goodness!"

Check No. 1107; Date, March 8, 1942; Pay to the order of Lester Black; Amount, $25.00; Memo, lost a bet for when we leave for overseas; signed William H. Letterman

"Oh, good Lord!"

Check No. 1108; Date, March 30, 1942; Pay to the order of Spike Monroe; Amount, $65.00; Memo, gambling debt; signed William H. Letterman

Check No. 1109; Date, May 8, 1945; Pay to the order of The American Red Cross; Amount, $1,000.00, Memo, Because of VE Day; signed William H. Letterman

Check No. 1110; Date, September 2, 1945; Pay to the order of Feed the Children of the World; Amount, $1,500.00; Memo, Because of VJ Day; signed William H. Letterman

Check No. 1111; Date, October 15, 1946; Pay to the order of Mark Hopkins Hotel; Amount, $90.00; Memo, 2 nites on the town; signed William H. Letterman

Check No. 1112; Date, October 29, 1946; Pay to the order of Best Motel, Amount, $16.00; Memo, last night as a soldier; signed William H. Letterman

Sergeant Letterman got off the train in Chicago, then took a bus to Clairson. The whole town turned out to greet their local hero. The high school band, in full regalia, played martial tunes as the bus pulled in and as Bill appeared at the door of the bus.

He was embarrassed and wished everyone would go away. He saw his parents. They made their way to him, and they greeted him with hugs and kisses. And tears. All of them, Bill included. Looking at the crowd and listening to the band, he kept thinking, "I don't deserve this." Aloud, he said to his father, "Can't we get out of here? This is making me crazy!"

"Of course," said the father, and they pushed their way through the crowd to their chauffeured vehicle.

"Hello, Harry."

"Welcome back, Mr. Letterman."

"I want to ride up front with you."

"Yessir!"

"No, no, Harry. I'm just a sergeant."

"A very important sergeant, sir. I see you aren't wearing your medals."

"No, sir. I don't deserve them."

"Tsk!"

Louise Pinkley was in the crowd that joyous day. The bank closed just to greet the WWII hero. She saw him from afar, at the outer edge of the crowd. She thought that he looked ten times as handsome as the day he left. Handsome and what else?......Weary?

She was close enough to the Letterman limousine, however, to hear the exchange between Bill and the chauffeur.

Then Bill, the sergeant still in uniform, saw Louise.

"Excuse me a moment, Harry. Go ahead and help my parents get into the limo. I want to have a word with Miss Pinkley."

"Yessir."

A withering look from Bill, and Harry said once more, "Tsk!"

"Louise! You came to the bus station in all this madness?"

"Couldn't help myself, Bill Letterman." She threw her arms around him; he returned the favor, squeezing her more than she thought she could stand.

Bill said, disengaging his arms and backing away from her, "Oh, Louise, Louise! It's great to see you! I cannot thank you enough for all those cookies and brownies you sent me overseas. And, I apologize all over the place for never writing you to thank you for your goodness and faithfulness to a GI overseas--me."

"Shoot! It was nothing. Not compared to what you were doing. And I can only use my imagination."

Skipping over the comment, he changed the subject with, "How did you get my address?"

"From your mother, of course."

"Of course." He regarded her for a moment longer, then asked, "Can we drop you off somewhere, Louise?"

"Not really, Bill. I'm due back at the bank, just in the next block, as soon as the excitement here at the bus station levels off. But thanks very much."

"You're welcome." He got into the front seat while his parents sat in the back. They drove off.

Check No. 1113; Date, October 30, 1946; Pay to the order of Harold Smith; Amount, $1,000.00; Memo, for a WWI veteran; signed William H. Letterman

"Master Letterman!" said Harry, lapsing back into addressing Bill as a boy. "What is the meaning of this check!?"

"You're a veteran, and now I'm a veteran, too. I know what you went through in WWI. If the government doesn't reward you, then

I will—with this pitiful amount. It doesn't come near what you're worth, Harry, for your part in World War I. I know. I was there for the next big one. Believe me, I know. Take it Harry. Use it wisely. Or foolishly. It's up to you."

Check No. 1114; Date, November 11, 1946; Pay to the order of Veterans of America; Amount, $1,000.00; Memo, in memory; signed William H. Letterman

Check No. 1115; Date, November 12, 1946; Pay to the order of Presbyterian Church; Amount, $1,000.00; for the mission work; signed William H. Letterman

Check No. 1116; Date, November 12, 1946; Pay to the order of Food for the Homeless; Amount, $1,000.00; for the homeless; signed William H. Letterman

Like a story opening up in front of her, Louise could see an enormous difference between the Bill Letterman before the War and the Bill Letterman after the War. Sensing more proof of the changes in Bill Letterman to come, she scrutinized even more carefully than ever each canceled check as it came into Bill's bank account.

Check No. 1210; Date, January 5, 1947; Pay to the order of Iowa State University; Amount, $257.98; Memo, books, dues, fees, tuition; signed William H. Letterman

Check No. 1211; Date, January 5, 1947; Pay to the order of Elmhurst Apartments; Amount, $65.00; Memo, rent, 1st month; signed William H. Letterman

Check No. 1212; Date, January 5, 1947; Pay to the order of A&P Grocers; Amount, $86.57; Memo, food for pantry; signed William H. Letterman

"Ah," Louise breathed to herself. "So this is part of the changes."

Check No. 1213; Date, February 5, 1947; Pay to the order of Elmhurst Apartments; Amount, $65.00; Memo, rent, 2nd month; signed William H. Letterman

A phone call in March from a stranger (Louise thought it sounded like Bill) who said, "Louise, do not use my name. Say 'Yes' now and then, or 'Okay.'"

"Okay," she said, really recognizing this caller to be Bill.

He continued. "Louise, I'm in trouble–maybe. Can you look up a canceled check of mine back in 1942? A check to a Margaret Tillson. I think it was for a hundred dollars. It was just before I shipped out for the South Pacific."

She remembered it. Clearly. "Yes," she said. "I think I can pull your statement out of the file cabinet with no trouble at all."

"Great. Go ahead. I'll wait."

"Okay."

She went directly to the pertinent file cabinet and straight to the statement in question, finding the entry for a check to Margaret Tillson. She took the statement back to her desk.

"You still there?" she asked.

"Yes."

"I have the statement in front of me."

"Can you retrieve the canceled check and take it to the photo shop and get three photo copies to mail to me, as soon as possible?"

"Yes. But . . ." she almost said "Bill." Then she continued. "What is this all about?" dreading the asking, dreading even more the an-swer. She had a disturbing premonition.

A distinct pause before Bill said, "The Tillson woman is black-mailing me for child support. Says her five-year-old boy is my son."

"Incredible!"

"I know. My attorney is already at work, getting photocopies of the birth certificate from the state's bureau of vital statistics, getting a mimeograph copy of my orders to go aboard the troop ship, with the reporting endorsement."

"Sounds as though he's done this before."

"True."

"Good luck?"

"Thanks, Louise. I owe you big time."

"No, you don't. Just don't let this . . ." She stopped. He didn't want her to use his name, here in the bank. Telling him not to let this trouble interfere with his studies should be done at another time, in another place.

"I won't," he said, understanding what she left unsaid. "Goodbye, Louise. And thanks again."

"You're welcome, sir. Goodbye."

Check No. 1221; Date, April 28, 1947; Pay to the order of Patrick

D. Mulhaney, Atty.; Amount, $650.00; Memo, attorney's fee; signed William H. Letterman

In early May 1947, Bill called Louise in the evening at her apartment.

"Louise! It's me, Bill."

"I'd know your voice anywhere! What's up?" Bill never called her at her apartment. Never called her anytime at the bank, other than the one mysterious call about the Tillson woman and her baby.

"I'm calling you at your apartment because you're entitled to an explanation. . . ."

"I know," she answered.

"Yeah. You know why, don't you? Well, here goes. Mulhaney, my attorney, visited Margaret Tillson and leaned on her pretty heavily–figuratively, that is."

"Yes."

"He had your photocopy of my canceled check; he had a photocopy of her baby's birth certificate; and he had a copy of my orders to go aboard the troopship with the reporting endorsement. What it all added up to is this: The 3-4 March 1942 time period was the only time I was with Tillson. My ship left on the 31st of March. The baby was born July 1, 1943!"

"Then you couldn't . . ."

"That's right. No baby is seven months late. Some babies are late, but not that much, and it's usually a case of miscalculation of when conception took place. She didn't have a leg to stand on! Mulhaney told her she was lucky I didn't sue her for harassment! Which I may yet do! . . . His words, not mine."

"It'd serve her right!"

"I guess."

"So it's over?"

"Yes," he breathed. "Thank heaven! And thanks to you, Louise, for your help. Like I said, 'I owe you big time.'"

"It's my job, Bill."

"And a marvelous job you do, Louise. I admire you so much."

"No. I admire YOU for your focus on education. I think it's outstanding!"

He laughed. "You sound like my old Unit Sergeant, back in my Army days." He chuckled. "Outstanding!"

"Good night, Bill. I'll be so happy when your last semester is over."

"Me, too, Honey. Good night."

More checks followed in the next two years, every one of them for university and independent living costs.

Check No. 1299; Date, August 30, 1949; Pay to the order of Ames College of Medicine; Amount, $1,550.78; Memo, books, dues, lab fees, tuition; signed William H. Letterman

Louise now knew where the boy–man was headed: to be an M.D. She was so proud, she was about to burst. The young man, having pulled through his difficult teens and having served honorably in the military during wartime, was preparing for a life of service to mankind. No other way to describe it. She was SO PROUD!

Check No. 1386; Date, June 3, 1951; Pay to the order of Denny's Restaurant; Amount, $72.76; Memo, end-of-the-school-year celebration with the guys; signed William H. Letterman

Louise was closing up her cash box, receipts totaled, cash balanced, when a customer approached her window. It was Bill Letterman.

"As I live and breathe! Bill Letterman! Congratulations on finishing another year of college!"

"Yeah. You would know about that, wouldn't you?"

"Pardon my lack of professionalism, but I couldn't help myself, seeing you here in the flesh!"

"Louise," he said, "you have any plans for dinner . . . tonight? I just got into town, and I have to leave in the morning."

"What's going on, Bill?"

"That's what I want to tell you, at dinner. How about it?"

"Of course! I'd be delighted!" Delight was far less than what she really felt. Euphoric was the word!

They got into his Pontiac. "Still driving this heap?" she asked herself, certainly not aloud.

He drove the "heap" to Manson's Dining Room. Upon arriving, Louise moaned, "Oh, Bill Letterman, I'm not dressed for this fancy place!"

"Believe me, Louise. You're fine. Just fine. I'm proud to be seen with you in public."

They were seated, they read their menus, and they ordered. "So," she said, "what's up?"

"I want to tell you first, Louise. Haven't even approached my parents on this yet." He took a breath, then continued, "I'm being called back into the Army, Louise, to serve in the Medical Corps in Korea."

"Good Lord! WWII wasn't enough?"

"Apparently not. But the bright side is this: I'm committed for only two years of the 'police action' in Korea. After that, I can come back to the U.S. and continue my medical studies. I'd still be eligible for the VA benefits."

"Well," she said. "That sounds wonderful on the surface, but haven't you been in combat enough? It isn't as though you're an Army career man."

"First of all, I've had too much education to go back into the enlisted ranks. I'll have to attend OCS. I'll be one of those infamous 'Ninety-Day Wonders'! If I'm lucky, I'll be assigned to a big Army Hospital in the city. If I'm not that lucky, I'll be a member of a MASH. "

""What's that?"

"A field unit, mostly surgery and recovery until the patient is able to travel to the hospital, for the most serious cases. I wouldn't be able to practice, of course, not having a medical degree, but I'd probably be assigned some administrative job."

"Well, I never!"

The salad was served. The meal continued.

After dessert and coffee, he wrote a check. Smiling, he said, "Would you like to see a check before it gets canceled?"

"You jest!"

Check No. 1387; Date, June 5, 1951; Pay to the order of Manson's Dining Room; Amount, $65.00; Memo, dinner with a Princess; signed William H. Letterman

"Darn!" she exclaimed, when she saw the Memo on the check.

"What?"

"I'm always turning red when a real compliment comes my way!"

He smiled some more. "And that would be and should be all the time."

She turned redder than ever. And loved it!

Bill drove Louise to her apartment building. She wanted in the worst way to invite him into her place. But she hesitated. She decided against it. She had no idea why!

"Thank you, Bill, for a wonderful dinner and a more wonderful evening."

"You're more than welcome, Louise. I wish it could have been more than dinner. So little time before I have to leave."

"I know."

He leaned across the seat and kissed her. She kissed him back. She opened her door, quickly got out of the car, and ran into her building.

He smiled. He said to himself, "She's still unmarried at age 44. Would she wait for me until I get back . . . again?"

Check No. 1388; Date, July 7, 1951; Pay to the order of The American Red Cross; Amount $1,000.00; Memo, Because; signed William H. Letterman

Check No. 1389; Date, July 9, 1951; Pay to the order of South Korean Relief Fund; Amount, $1,000.00; Memo, Because; signed William H. Letterman

Check No. 1390; Date, July 31, 1951; Pay to the order of The Orphans of South Korea; Amount, $1,000.00; Memo, Because; signed William H. Letterman

Check No. 1391; Date, August 22, 1951; Pay to the order of MASH Officers Club; Amount, $150.00; Memo, contribution; signed William H. Letterman, 2nd Lt., USA(R)

"But Sir," said the bartender, a corporal, to Lt. Letterman, while accepting the check from him. "You don't even drink! . . . Not here in the O Club, anyway."

"So be it, Corporal. Others do, and for their own reasons, find solace in it."

Scratching his head, the corporal said, "Yes, Sir . . .?"

Check No. 1430; Date, August 30, 1953; Pay to the order of Coronado Hotel; Amount, $55.00; Memo, overnite, incl. phone call; William H. Letterman

Louise smiled when she saw this check. That phone call was from Bill . . . to her, wanting to know if she were still at the bank, still living in Clairson, not making any sense of it all, as far as Louise was concerned.

He phoned her again, this time from Shepherd Air Force Base, near Chicago.

"Louise! I'm coming home . . . again!"

"I'm so glad, Bill."

"I'm trying to get a bus out of here to . . . somewhere . . . so that I can catch another bus to Clairson. Wait for me?"

"Wait for you? Of course I'll wait for you Bill."

"Just wanted to make sure, Louise. I've missed you. A lot."

Check No. 1431; Date, September 3, 1953; Pay to the order of Mary's Flowers; Amount, $40.00; Memo, dozen red roses; signed William H. Letterman

Looking at the canceled check, Louise remembered that she had read the card that came with the dozen red roses, delivered to her at the bank: "For the red-faced rose of my life." No signature. She asked herself, "What in the world does this mean?" She received a phone call while still at the bank.

"Tell me you're free for dinner tonight!"

"Of course, Bill," she said, recognizing his voice immediately."Now I know. You sent the roses, didn't you?"

"Ah, I see you figured it out. I'm going to make you the most red-faced you've ever been in your life, Louise. Guaranteed."

He waited a beat. Then he said, "I'll pick you up at the bank at five. That okay with you?"

"You'll never know how much okay that is, Bill. See you then."

She pondered if she should go home during lunch and change into something more fitting for dinner. "No," she mused, "I don't want to look TOO obvious."

Dessert was over, coffee was served. Bill said to her, "Louise, I want you to know that I've already made arrangements to start the fall semester back at Ames Medical. Be there at least another two years. I'll be a full-fledged doctor by that time. But then I have to serve a two-year internship, no pay, probably. Just a room and meals."

"It's a long haul, isn't it? she asked. "Especially with the two-year break in education while you were in Korea."

"Indeed! It'll be a good four years from now before I can begin a practice. And, Louise, when that time comes, I want you to be my wife. Can you wait that long?"

Check No. 1432; Date, September 6, 1953; Pay to the order of Hillcrest Restaurant; Amount, $23.79; Memo, She said yes; happiest day of my life; signed William H. Letterman

Bill was too busy at med school to write to his parents and to

Louise. So, he called them and her once every week.

Same thing during his internship. The hours were horrendous! And, he had chosen a prestigious hospital. The greater the hospital's reputation, the smaller the pay. Or, in Bill's case, as he had predicted: no pay at all. Only the gratuitous room and meals.

Never mind that, he thought. His father continued to support him for his other needs. There was always money in Bill's bank account. He wanted for nothing, except time.

Check No. 1559; Date, October 2, 1955; Pay to the order of Louise Pinkley; Amount, $50.00; Memo, Happy Birthday to the sweetest ever; signed William H. Letterman, M.D.

After he wrote the check, he asked himself, how could he be so lucky all these years? And, in the offing, a wedding.

Louise began attending classes at the local community college. She said to herself that she needed to bring herself up to speed, if she were going to be a doctor's wife!

Check No. 1612; Date, June 15, 1957;Pay to the order of Manson's Dining Room; Amount, $122.45; Memo, celebration; signed William H. Letterman, M.D.

Louise smiled as she saw the entry on Bill's statement. He had taken his parents and her to dinner at the high-fallutin' restaurant to celebrate the end of his internship.

Later that evening, when they were alone in her apartment, Bill said, "Darling, Now we can make serious plans for our wedding. Where shall we start? Big? Small? Somewhere in between? You name it!"

"Oh, Bill, I cannot believe you still want to marry a woman 16 years your senior. This is madness! I'm 50 years old! I should not start having children at 50, even if I am still capable of it!"

"I know, Sweetheart," he said lovingly. "I waited so long to be able to support you, without my father's monthly contributions. But do NOT worry about an age difference, and do NOT worry about whether you should have children." He took her in his arms. "I have a plan for us to have children, scads of them!"

"What kind of nonsense is that?"

"How's your Spanish, Sweetheart?"

"And what in the world does that have to do with anything? I had two years of it in college. Foreign language was a requirement, and

I chose Spanish. Already had one year of it in high school."

"Fortuitous!" he exclaimed. "Let's sit down, darling. And I'll tell you why we're going to need to speak and understand Spanish."

They sat on her couch, holding hands. He began. "I'm being considered for a slot in a children's clinic in Bogota, Colombia. I'm thinking seriously of accepting. Actually, I'll be groomed to take over the clinic when the current director retires in another year."

He squeezed her hand and said, "So, what do you say, Louise? We'll have lots and lots of children! From the clinic."

Louise was speechless except to say, "Darling . . .!" and to give him a more-than-adequate kiss.

Check No. 1619; Date August 10, 1957; Pay to the order of Bridgeman Dept. Store; Amount, $219.50; Memo, trunks and suitcases; signed Louise P. Letterman

Check No. 1620; Date, August 24, 1957; Pay to the order of Avianca; Amount, $558.63; Memo, one-way air fare for two; signed William H. Letterman, M.D.

# # #

Frank Newman, his wife Alice beside him, drove his car through New York City and onto the expressway to Kennedy Airport. They were going to meet their daughter Sally, who was returning from her four years at the University of Brazil in Rio de Janeiro.

Sally was returning with her fiancé, Riichiro Barbosa. They had met on campus at the beginning of her junior year and as he had begun his graduate studies in engineering.

Lean and graying, Frank was a successful ad man. He had spent the World War II years in the Navy and went to college on the GI Bill afterwards. He had taken his young family to Rio during the fifties while he worked for a cosmetic company based there.

Alice kept her gray hair covered with a champagne blonde color. The lines around her eyes were just beginning to form, but she was still attractive.

"I can't believe Sally's coming home to be married," Alice said a little ruefully." We no sooner have her back when she'll be gone again."

Frank said, "Of course, Chicago's not very far. We'll see them often."

"Perhaps."

At the arrival gate in the airport, Frank and Alice watched Sally wave excitedly to them. Her light brown hair touching her shoulders, her hazel eyes shining, she ran up to them and hugged and kissed them joyously. Then she introduced Riichiro who stood behind her.

"Mom, Dad, this is Riichiro. We can call him Richard--that's probably the English equivalent to the Japanese Riichiro."

Richard had been left as a foundling at a Tokyo orphanage when he was about one week old. Barbosa was the family name he had taken when he emigrated to Brazil. A wealthy philanthropist, a Japanese woman, brought a dozen teenage Amerasian boys to São Paulo in 1964 to start a new life there.

"How do you do?" he said with a mixed accent.

"Welcome to America," Frank greeted him.

Alice said to him, "We're both happy to meet you, Richard. Welcome."

Sally and Richard had already cleared customs and immigration. They and Alice stayed with their baggage while Frank brought the car to them from the parking garage.

Back on the expressway, headed for the city, Sally talked incessantly about their flight, Richard's new job in Chicago, and their wedding plans. She showed them her ring.

"For an engagement ring," Sally said, Richard gave me this one that belonged to him."

Richard explained: "It was tied on a string around my neck when I was taken in at the orphanage. When I was fifteen, the orphanage director removed it from his safe and gave it to me to keep, and I began wearing it then."

Frank couldn't see the ring because he was driving, but Sally described it from the back seat as she showed it to her mother in front of her.

"It's a golden eagle on a round base of black onyx, and there's a diamond in the center of the eagle."

Frank pulled off the expressway and drove onto the city streets. He stopped for a traffic light.

"Now let me see that ring, Sally," Frank said. She put her hand across his shoulder, and he was able to get a good look at it before the light changed. "Very nice," he said.

When they arrived at the apartment, Alice and Sally went into the kitchen to prepare a late lunch. Frank and Richard were alone in the living room.

Frank took a deep breath and said, "Richard, you cannot marry my daughter."

Richard blinked in surprise at the unexpected announcement. Had he done or said something wrong already? Could it be racial prejudice? Finally, Richard asked, "Why?"

"Because," Frank replied, "that ring you gave Sally . . . was mine."

# # #

THE HOMECOMING

Pamela sat in a chair in front of the TV in her apartment's livingroom in New York City. Two packed suitcases and a tote bag stood next to the table near the door to the apartment. Her purse was on the table.

Another planeload of freed American Prisoners of War from Vietnam was due to arrive at Floyd Bennett from the Airlift Wing in Schenectady, New York. She watched them carefully, looking for Brian.

Brian Miller, her husband of six years—actually, for only the first two years because after that time, as an active reservist of the Army National Guard, his unit was transferred to Vietnam. Soon after he began his tour of duty there, he was captured and was a prisoner of war for four years. She looked back at the day they were married. Was it a century ago? It seemed like it.

* * *

Only her brother and her sister-in-law witnessed the wedding, held in a judge's chambers. Pam still possessed the photo that was taken of the four of them. Both the men were in uniform. Brian, a 2nd Lieutenant in the Army; Pam's brother, a Lieutenant (j.g.) in the Navy.

As soon as the photo-taking was finished, the four of them went to a hotel dining room in the city for a wedding lunch. Afterwards, the Navy Lieutenant and his wife left for the airport to return to his duty station at Great Lakes, Illinois. Brian and Pamela retired to their room in the hotel.

* * *

By the next morning, Pamela knew, with a certainty, that the marriage was getting off to a bad start. She was not sexually fulfilled. She had heard about faking it, but declined to go that route. So false. Brian was abusive, verbally, filled with his own satisfaction, blaming her for being frigid.

* * *

The first prisoner of war alighted from the aircraft. Photos were flashed, motion picture cameras whirred. The Army Captain, still wearing his prison garb, was interviewed. He answered a question or two. He made a brief statement. Then he was free to be greeted by his wife and two children.

The second prisoner of war appeared at the doorway, squinting in the sunshine, looking around him, happy and glad to be home again.

47

His wife ran to him as he left the bottom step.

Pam watched each one and counted them.

* * *

Thankfully, Brian did not want them to have children while he was on Active Reserve Army duty. And *she* did not want to raise children without a father in the home, and, truth be known, she did not want to raise children while married to a man like Brian. Brian, the super-hypochondriac, the hater of hypocrites, the perfectionist, the demander of perfection from everyone else, but especially his wife. And yes, Brian, the sadist, enjoying the act of making other people squirm in discomfort with scathing and snide remarks, and sneers.

* * *

She watched the tenth man alight from the aircraft. Tall and gaunt, thinning hair, emaciated. He seemed to be met by his mother and father. He looked almost as old as they.

So did Number Eleven.

Number Twelve was next. He limped down the steps, past the TV journalists and the cameras, and proceeded as quickly as he could manage, to his wife who was holding a baby.

A baby? Pam wondered, Just how long was this Number Twelve man imprisoned?

* * *

Well, Pam thought, at least she kept herself pure, not taking those kinds of risks during Brian's absence. It wasn't because she was faithful in her heart—only in her behavior. There were a few times when she was sorely tempted to be intimate with another man during those four years Brian was imprisoned. But the one thing that kept her from acting on those feelings was a time-worn, basic rationale: Fear. Fear of an untimely pregnancy.

* * *

Number Thirteen came into view. She wondered, How many are on this plane, anyway?

Number Fourteen, Fifteen, Sixteen. Now they were all a blur to her. She was not noticing who did what and who met whom. Seeing them come off the aircraft tended to make her wonder at the tortures they experienced—every one of them. The lack of medicines, only impure water to drink, no proper shoes to walk in; a slab of concrete to sleep on.

It's a wonder Brian didn't take his own life, he was so enamored with his creature comforts and often ranted about euthanasia and assisted suicide.

Wait. There he was, Number Twenty-one, looking exactly as he did the last time she saw him. He was not emaciated, as others were, and he was not limping, as others had done. He strode self-confidently, and arrogantly, looking into the crowd.

He might be looking for me, she said to herself. It suddenly occurred to her that he would no longer have his key to the apartment. She went to the door, unlocked it, then returned to her chair. It was only a matter of time before a confrontation would take place. She must steel herself for it.

She continued watching the remaining prisoners of war leave the aircraft. When the last one alighted and met his family, she looked at her watch. An hour to go, she surmised, before Brian would find a cab and arrive at their apartment.

Their apartment? For now, yes. But not for long.

* * *

There was a demanding knock on the door. Pam looked at her watch. Her timing was correct. It had to be Brian, thinking the door would be locked (they lived in New York City, for heaven's sake!). She called out, "Come in. The door's not locked."

The knob turned. The door was flung open as if an insistent gust of wind had blown it open. "Just like Brian," she thought. It was he.

He came through the door like a tiger attacking its prey. "What the hell do you mean, leaving the door unlocked—in this godforsaken city? And, *why* the devil weren't you at the airport to meet me? Everybody had someone to meet him. But no. Not me. You couldn't get your fat bottom side off the chair to meet me?"

She began to cringe . . . already . . . at the blast of recriminations, charges and blamings. She caught her breath, tried to smooth her emotions, and said, "Be glad I am even still here in the apartment. In case you didn't notice, I have two suitcases and a tote bag packed and sitting by the door. And, by the way, I am not fat-bottomed. *Flat*-bottomed would be more accurate!"

He looked down at the luggage. He slammed the door shut. "And what the hell does this mean?"

"I'm leaving you, Brian."

"That's it? You're leaving me, just like that? After all I've been through, this is all you have to say to me?"

"It is." She got up from her chair.

He got in her face, gesturing with both hands and arms. "You bitch! You can't do this to me!"

"Oh, yes, I can. Get out of my way. The least I could do was to stay long enough for you to come home and for me to tell you, face-to-face, before I take off."

"I said, 'You can't do this to me!'" He remained standing where he was, in front of her. You owe me an explanation! And I demand it. Right now!"

She thought, of course he demands an explanation. So, here goes. "Think back, Brian, to the first two years we were married. Before you left for Nam.

"All that rotten name-calling. The insults, day after day. And the humiliations—in front of my family and yours, in front of neighbors and friends. *That's* the explanation. What more do you need?"

She stepped aside to go around him and head for the front door. She would call a cab from the doorman's office in the lobby. Not from here. No way.

He sneered, "You know you'll lose all your military-dependent benefits the minute you step out that door!"

"I will not! It won't happen until *you* get a divorce and on the date it becomes final."

"You can't survive out there without the benefits: medical, commissary, base exchange! You can't survive without *me!*"

"Watch me!" What Brian did not know is that Pamela had saved a good portion of her generous salary, plus all the dependent's monthly checks over the four years he was in the Service. With each thousand dollars amassed, she invested—heavily. She had a comfortable income to tide her over while she looked for an apartment and decided on which new employment to accept in Washington, D.C.

She continued. "Just to make it easy on you, when you file for divorce, and *if* you file, I'll be sending you my new address. I'm going to Washington, D.C., where I have two job offers. I merely have to make up my mind which one to accept."

"You're damn right I'm going to file for a divorce! You won't get another penny out of me!"

"Excuse me, Brian. State law says otherwise, in many cases. And so does federal law."

"I'll see you in court, by damn!"

"No, you won't. I'm not even going to contest it. You're on your own."

She had a second thought. "By the way, there are groceries in the kitchen cupboard and fridge, enough to last you for a week. *Then* you're on your own."

She reached the door, opened it. She shouldered her purse, from the table beside the door, picked up the two suitcases and the tote bag. "Good by, Brian."

He lost it. He ran to her. He threw his arms around her. "Pam, Pam, Pam! I'm sorry I yelled at you! Please don't leave me! *I* can't live without *you*!"

"Too late, Brian. You wrote this ticket–this scene–during the first two years we were married. It was bound to turn out this way. You were and still are unbelievably overbearing, pedantic and dictatorial. I cannot live out the rest of my life under such circumstances, certainly not with you!

"Oh, and by the way," she said. "Here's my door key. I won't be needing it. Not any more."

* * *

Before the divorce became final, Pamela received a telegram from the Army, informing her of Brian's death by suicide. She was then informed that her widow's benefits would take place as soon as administrative action was completed. She would be notified.

She said to herself, still looking at the telegram: "You did it, Brian. As I always knew you would do it, eventually. Thank you, Brian for doing it before the divorce was final. Thank you, Lord, for my hard-earned freedom from the nagging thorn in my side. And forgive me if I do not mourn his death. It's a blessing . . . for everyone whoever knew him."

Folding the telegram and inserting it into her shoulder bag, she opened the door of her Washington, D.C., apartment and stepped into the hallway. Closing the door behind her, she went to her new job. It was a fabulous job at NASA Headquarters.

And life was fabulous, too. . . . now that the homecoming was over, really over.

\# \# \#

THE HOSTAGES

It was early in the 1950s. World War II was over, and the nations began picking up the pieces. In America, defense industries stopped making ammunition, rifles, jeeps, tanks, armored cars, fighter planes, bombers, and warships; they began making fertilizers, washing machines and dryers, trucks, automobiles, recreational motor homes, new and modern trains, commercial aircraft and sleek sailing craft. The production of uniforms went back to "civvies"-- suits and dresses. A plethora of housing tracts dotted the country outside cities all over the nation.

Katie Sorenson, 25, single, and a sometimes-published writer, received an unusual phone call from her uncle, Captain Sven Sorenson, U.S. Navy (Retired). "What's up, Uncle Sven? And where are you? Did you actually get a telephone up there in the woods of the Rockies?"

"No, Honey. And we hope we never do. The radio is sufficient for our needs. Except, in this case, I needed to reach you to talk to you personally. Didn't want to write a letter, either. So I'm using the phone down at the general store in Thornview. You know, the nearest village?"

"So? I ask again, what's up? Anything wrong? Is Aunt Nettie okay? And are you okay?"

"She's fine, and I'm just fine, too. What I'm calling about is to ask you if you are free to come here to our place and stay for the winter. We'd like to have a house sitter while we're gone on our around-the-world trip. What say?"

"Uncle Sven! Are you kidding? I'd *love* to house-sit for you! You have everything anyone would need, with your basement freezer and cold-storage rooms, with the radio gear, and I assume you would be leaving your car for me to run into town for groceries . . . before I get snowed in?"

"Of course! But we need to make certain of one thing, Katie. Are you sure you won't get cabin fever all by yourself, all winter long?"

"No way, Uncle Sven. I'm a writer, remember? And I can use the isolation to great advantage!"

"Then it's settled? Can you come out at the end of next month? That'll give you several weeks to take care of affairs at your end."

"You bet I can! Uncle Sven, I'm thrilled to pieces with your invitation!"

"Good girl! We'll meet you in Reno. I'll send you an airline ticket right away."

"Thanks, Uncle Sven. I'm truly looking forward to the adventure!"

* * *

Katie was medium height, ash-blonde hair and green eyes. When she walked, she floated with regal grace. Being an author, she had very little contact with the general public. When she looked back on her short life, she had had few–no, *very* few–dates. That never troubled her because she was so engrossed in her work. Only her mother was troubled: 25-year-old daughter and no husband in sight? No grandchildren? Ridiculous! Impossible!

One week after Katie's arrival at Captain Sorenson's self-sufficient mansion in the mountains, she was settled in and checked out on how everything in the house operates, especially the radio and the generator. The radio would be her sole contact during the entire stay. She drove her aunt and uncle to Reno to catch a plane for the port city of the ship's beginning its world cruise.

She drove back toward the mountain house. The first snowfall was coming down in fluffy flakes. So she made a hasty stop in Thornview to pick up one last batch of groceries before the mountain became snowed in. Sam Jenkins, owner and operator of the general store, greeted her, remembering that Captain Sorensen had introduced her to him before the Captain and his wife left on their extended journey around the world.

"Howdy, Miss Sorensen! Makin' one last trip before the big one, are you?"

"Yes, sir! One last touch with civilization before the snow closes off the one roadway from the house to your store. And, Sir, I'd be pleased if you called me 'Katie.'"

"Only if you quit Sir-ing me, Miss Katie!"

"Done! Do you happen to have any bananas in the store, Sam?"

Sam snorted in spite of himself. "Oh, Miss–I mean, Katie. I can sure tell you're not from 'round here! We get bananas maybe two times a year, in the summer only. No, we do not happen to have any bananas in the store. Wrong season! 'Course, bananas can be delivered here from the valley, but they're a lot more expensive in the off-season months, coming originally from Central and South America."

"Of course! Silly Me. I had no idea it would be that different here in a mountain community."

Sam helped her take the last-minute groceries she had purchased out to the car, and before they said goodbye to each other, Sam reminded her to be sure to call him on the Sorenson's radio if she needed help for anything at all.

* * *

She was delighted to see the snow coming down, knowing that by morning, upon awakening, the mountain outside her bedroom window would be covered with it. A virtual fairyland. Beautiful. Breathtaking. And the silence to go with it. Wonderful.

These carefree thoughts filled her head as she drove from the village to the house, 1,500 feet higher up the mountainside. She parked the car at the front of the house to unload the groceries, and she would put the car into the garage later. She picked up the two grocery bags, keys in her hand, and juggled it all while she put the house key into the front-door lock.

A further struggle to get the door open, still dealing with the two bags of groceries and the keys and the door. She kept her eyes downward, watching where she was going. *Don't want to stumble, break a leg, or something stupid like that.*

Once over the threshold, she looked up. A man stood in the hallway in front of her, pointing a gun at her.

* * *

Not the time for panic, she thought. But in spite of that, her breathing was shallow, heart pounding thunderously.

"Are you alone?" he asked.

"And if I'm not?"

"Please," he said, earnestly, "just answer the question. We'll find out soon enough, anyway."

"We?" she asked.

"Les is guarding the back door and the door into the garage."

She took a deep breath. "Could I just put down these bags of groceries? They're getting heavy."

"Of course. Carefully."

"Of course," she said as she eased one bag at a time onto the floor. *No point in throwing something heavy at his weapon. The other man would come to assist him.* "Now what?"

He smiled a half-smile and, lowering his gun, said, "Now we wait and watch for someone else to come up the road. This is the last house on this road, isn't it?"

"What if it is, and what if it isn't?"

"Don't play games with me, Miss. We've had our eye on this place for ten days. We saw you, the old man, and old woman get into the car with all that luggage. Going to be gone for a long time, we figure. How come you didn't go along?"

She was silent.

"I see," he said. "Have an argument with your old man, or the old woman? Both?"

More silence.

Calling toward the kitchen, the man shouted, "Les! Come on in here. In the front hall."

Les, a bumbling kind of oaf, charged into the hallway. "How come, Boss?"

"This lady seems to be alone. So stop watching the garage and put her car in it. Then find a position at a front window here in the house and watch for a car or cars to come to the house from the road."

"Okay, Boss," Les answered, giving Katie a long and appreciative look.

"Your keys, please?" the man asked.

She felt like throwing them at him, but she held back a moment. Then she handed him the keys.

She broke her silence after Les passed her in the hallway to go outside to move the car. She said, "So, do you have a name other than 'Boss'?"

Motioning with his gun for her to precede him, they headed for the kitchen. He said, "Sit." He pulled out a chair for her, then he pulled out a chair for himself, across the table from her. "Yes," he said, finally. "I have another name: Tate Taylor." He was almost six feet tall, sturdy but not particularly muscular. His blondish hair contrasted nicely with the tinge of his face. The gray eyes looked a hole through her.

She, frowning, said, "That name sounds familiar."

"It should. A few years back I went to prison. It might've been in the papers."

Shivering, she asked, "Are you a murderer?"

Indicating contempt, he said, "Hell no! I could *never* be that!"

"So," she continued to probe, "did you rob a bank?"

"Not exactly. I robbed a corporation by embezzling a bundle. A big one."

"Ah. Now I remember. The Plano Investments Company."

"That'd be it."

"Yes," she confirmed, "it was in the papers."

"Now let's get down to your name. Must be Sorenson because we saw it on the mailbox. You the daughter?"

"No. Niece."

"What does your uncle do?"

"He's a retired Navy Captain."

"Well, that explains the ramrod-straight back . . . and the conservative clothes."

She said, "I see that your own clothes are not exactly flamboyant—dark blue suit, white shirt, subdued tie, black shoes, black socks."

"You take it all in, don't you?"

"Yes. I'm a writer."

" Well, don't let the clothing fool you. Mine and Les's clothes are obtained 'on credit.'"

"You mean *stolen*, don't you?" She said heatedly.

"I repeat: 'on credit.'"

"I'm sure!"

"And let's get back to your name. The Captain is your uncle on your dad's side, or mother's side?"

"Dad's."

"And what comes before the Sorenson?"

She hesitated.

He cajoled, "Come on. We're going to be in this for the duration of the winter. We might as well be civilized about it."

"You call embezzling 'civilized'?" she said, leaning forward from the chair back.

"You're getting off the subject. Your name, please?"

She slumped back in the chair. "It's Katie." She looked at him, imploringly, "What's going to happen to me?"

"That's more like it. And thank you. Now let me spell out what's it's going to be like while we're all here, snug and cozy in this beautiful mountain home. Les and I have checked out the entire house. Heated garage. No telephones. A transmitting radio and receiver. A generator for all your electrical needs. We saw the modern cold rooms in the basement: one for frozen products; the others maintaining certain temperatures to preserve foods that can't be frozen successfully. Very clever. Very handy. From the looks of the supply of food, we won't run out until after spring. Well after Les and I have left this place."

"Ah. You *are* going to leave? Well, I can't wait for that to happen!"

"Not so fast. You'll do all the cooking and the kitchen stuff. Les and I will do the cleaning. Each of us can do his own laundry. We've had ample experience in prison for all that."

"I'll believe that when Hell freezes over!"

"You'll see. Just be patient. That a fair deal? You cook; we clean."

* * *

It was time to start dinner. Tate recognized that his stomach was churning. He and Les had grabbed a few items from the fridge to eat while they stood watch, before Katie arrived. They had lived out of their vehicle with groceries they had purchased 100 miles away. They slept in the car, taking off their outer clothing to sleep in their underwear and with blankets. A nearby stream provided the water for washing up and for washing out some of their clothing. They spent ten days watching the Sorenson house, nearby, and at the same time, maintaining the ability not to be detected from the house.

Tate began the chore of doing his laundry while Katie cooked and while Les maintained his watch at the front of the house.

"You have any laundry to put in with mine, Katie?"

This is so weird, she thought. "Put my clothes in with yours? Not likely!"

"As you wish," he said with that same half-smile she had seen earlier.

* * *

By nightfall, Tate told Les he could leave his post. The snow was already up to the bottom of the first-story window sills. For the first night, they would stand watch in two shifts. On the second day, Les would sleep in the day while Tate stood watch; then, Tate would sleep at night while Les stood watch. They would maintain that schedule throughout the internment.

Katie breathed more easily once she learned that Tate would be the day watch, while Les slept. And Les would be the night watch, while Tate and she slept. Les made her skin crawl. *Why doesn't that happen with Taylor? Curious.*

* * *

Tate Taylor took the first shift to stay awake on this first night. He said to his partner, "Okay, Les, like we said earlier today, you take a break before the first watch for tonight, and I'll call you later to take the watch for the rest of the night.

"Okay, Boss." He look a bit confused. "You want me to sleep on the couch?"

"No, Les. Our talking, Miss Sorenson and I, would keep you from sleeping easily."

"Huh?"

"Sleep in the bed of the room you chose earlier."

"Oh, yeah. The room with the wild animal pitchers."

"That's the one. Good night, Les."

"G'night, Boss." He went upstairs.

Katie wasn't sure what to do. Her insides were still shaking. She felt extremely uneasy and vulnerable. She decided to try to find out more about her "captors." She asked Tate, "What was Les in prison for?"

"Assault and battery. He almost killed a man."

That information made her more uneasy than before. He could see that such information affected her negatively. "He's pretty much okay now, though. The prison psychologist gave him a clean bill of health. According to Les, he was really ticked off when he beat almost to death the guy that had been tormenting him."

"Lord," she said, "I hope he doesn't get riled while the two of you are here."

"Don't worry. He depends on me to think for both of us. I never taunt nor tease him. He'll be okay as long as that doesn't happen."

"I'll certainly remember *that!*"

"You'll be all right, Katie. I'll see to it."

She gave him a look of gratitude and wondered. *This embezzler has guaranteed my safety, and I have to believe him? Well, there's no recourse. Damn! Why did this have to happen to me?*

She asked Tate, "So, did you and Les get a parole . . . and break it? And now you're on the run?"

"Not quite. We escaped from prison and practically waltzed our way up here to your ideal spot for hiding out. We'll wait for the breakout business to cool down."

"Do you mind telling me how you managed a breakout? Obviously, it wasn't with guns blazing."

"You got that right! We, or I, messed up some telephone wires, leaving only the warden's line free. He sent for a telephone-repair crew. Les and I were waiting near the site where we knew they'd be working. We overcame the two repairmen, gagged them, removed their clothing, tied them up and put them into a closet."

"You abandoned them?"

"Well, not exactly. We left them unhampered enough to work their way to the door, where they could bang on it with their feet and be rescued."

"How nice of you . . ."

He ignored the barb and continued. We put on the repairmen's work fatigues. We got into the truck, and simply drove out the prison gates. No questions asked. "

"Did you repair the mischief you had done on the telephone wires before you left?"

"Are you serious? Of course NOT! Just before we left, we messed

59

up the Warden's line, too. It gave us some leeway for getting far enough away to go undetected, unreported, and unpursued."

She said, half-admiringly, "Sounds as though you thought this out very thoroughly."

"I can take that as a compliment?"

"A left-handed compliment, I believe."

He gave her his half-smile.

She then made the comment, "How did you and Les ever pair up? You're so different from each other."

"Brain and brawn need each other. It's an unusual man that can have both. Les and I are symbiotic. He needs me. I need him."

"And," she pushed on, "how did you get your clothes--on credit?'

"Ah, well, that took a bit of creative planning and inventive maneuvering. I did have a buddy–an old Army buddy, as a matter of fact–who came to see me a few times, once a month. I didn't tell him how much I had embezzled . . . a tidy sum. However, the prosecutors in the case never did know how much it was, for sure; and the company's bookkeeping people were too confused to come up with a firm figure.

"So, my buddy–who will remain nameless–and I concocted the plan. He would buy clothing, garment bags, suitcases, toiletries, etc. Then he would put it all into a large locker at the airport–which will also be nameless."

"Of course," she said with a shrug. "So how'd you get a key for the locker?"

"He put it in the back of one those magnet key holders and slapped it against the inside of the left front fender of the truck."

"How could he do that, not knowing which truck was going to the prison?"

Again, the half-smile. "My buddy was a dispatcher in the telephone repair department. He knew when and where each and every truck was going. A stroll out to the lot where the trucks are parked, and he installed it in exactly the right truck. He did the assigning of the trucks each day, for Pete's sake."

"Didn't you stand out at the airport, with the telephone repair uniform on?"

"Not really. The uniforms were nothing more than khaki trousers and shirts, with a logo patch on the chest. A small one."

"And the car?" she asked. "That, too, is 'on credit'?"

"Of course. Just like the clothing. You see, this buddy who helped us from the outside knows he'll get paid. Our plan had to work, and so far it has. When I retrieve my assets–which will . . ."

"Be nameless," she filled in.

"Exactly. When I retrieve the assets and turn most of them into cash, I'll mail to my buddy an unregistered, uninsured package (so as not to call attention to it) containing the cash I've promised him for helping us escape."

"What a neat story," she said, almost sarcastically. She was not smiling.

But Tate was . . . his half-smile.

* * *

Just before Katie went to her room for the night, she asked one more question in this intricate puzzle: "How did you and Les get into the house?"

"Well," Tate said, "among his other abilities, Les is a renown lock picker."

"I might have guessed."

He said, "And you would have been right."

An hour after Katie turned in, Tate went upstairs to waken Les to start the last half of the night shift.

"Wake up, Les. Time for your turn."

"Wha'?" He was slow to wake up.

"Come on, man, let's move your stumps and get you downstairs. I've made a fresh pot of coffee for you."

"You did? Gee, thanks, Boss." He was on his feet and on his way to the kitchen.

* * *

The days and nights went by without incident. Except for one thing. Katie managed to sneak into the radio room to try to make an outgoing call: S.O.S. She couldn't get the radio turned on. Nothing worked. A voice behind her startled her. It was Tate.

"It won't function, Katie. I've removed a vital part. It's well hidden. Don't try to look for it. You won't find it."

"How on earth did you know what to remove?"

"I was in the Signal Corps, Army, during the War."

"I see," she said. "And that probably explains how you were able to mess up the telephone wires–really good."

"True."

It was two weeks later when, lying in her bed and wondering what to do about the radio, she remembered that Uncle Sven had told her where he kept spare parts to the radio.

The next day she found a space of time in which Tate was occupied with listening to the radio in the living room, while Les slept

61

in his room upstairs. She went to the basement to the work bench and pulled out the top drawer. She hunted and hunted for anything that resembled a radio part. She lost track of the time. Again, a voice behind her startled her.

"There's no substitute in there," said Tate. " I've removed it and hidden it, as well."

She slammed the drawer back under the work bench, frustrated and mad as a wet hen. "Damn!"

He approached her and placed a hand on her wrist, the one nearest him. "Don't be so hard on yourself, Katie. You're very smart. You knew where to go to look for the missing part, or its replacement."

"That's no help, to me, anyway!"

"Come on. Let's go back upstairs. There's nothing you can do about the radio."

* * *

That day wore on. Les appeared for the dinner hour. The three of them ate more companionably than they did at the beginning. After running the dishwasher and wiping down the stove and refrigerator and sweeping the floor, Katie was dead tired. She announced to the two men that she was going to her room and would be there for the night. Tate would not retire until later, he decided.

Some time after she fell asleep, Katie heard something from the downstairs. It was music, piano music, that had awakened her. *Is Les listening to that kind of music on the radio?* she wondered. It was a piano for certain, and, after listening more carefully, she realized that it wasn't the living-room radio. It was "live" piano music!

What time is it? Almost midnight! This is so unusual, I better investigate.

The house had cooled down. She put on her winter robe. She left her room. She never was locked in, from the beginning of her being held hostage. Down the hall she went to the top of the stairs. From that point of the house she could distinguish exactly where the piano music came from: the music room that Uncle Sven arranged for Aunt Nettie when he designed the house after his Navy retirement.

That cannot possibly be Les playing the piano! She came down the steps slowly, carefully, silently. At the bottom of the stairs, Les was not visible. She turned right, into the music room. There he was, Tate, playing a beautiful, haunting Chopin.

Still moving slowly, she walked up to Tate, approaching from behind him. She stepped around the piano and leaned on it, facing him.

Then he saw her. He stopped playing.

She said, softly, "Where on earth did you learn to play like that?"

The half-smile again. "I was trained since age 9 to be a concert pianist."

"Incredible," she breathed. "What happened?"

"The War," he said simply, not smiling.

"Pity," she said still softly.

"I suppose so. After discharge from the Army I had to get a job. Piano became my pastime. My favorite pastime. Still is."

"But you've been here for how long? And I never heard you play before tonight."

"Haven't played before tonight."

She moved around the piano and sat on the bench next to him. "Please continue."

He placed his hands onto the keyboard, began to play once more, the half-smile returning to his face.

When he had finished that piece and two more, he stopped. He took her left hand, turned it over, and he kissed the palm. It was a tender moment. It touched her deeply. She almost smoothed his hair with her other hand. But something held her back. She stood up, withdrew her hand from his, and went swiftly up the stairs and back into her room.

His half-smile never left his face until she had disappeared out of the music room. Leaving the piano, he stepped into the living room and said, "Good night, Les."

"Good night, Boss. See ya at breakfast."

"Yes."

* * *

At breakfast the next morning, Katie came downstairs late. Tate had already fixed breakfast, and Les was just finishing eating. He retired to his room upstairs for his sleep period.

"I'm so sorry I'm late," she said. "Is there anything left for me to do?"

"Only for you to sit down, and I'll serve up your breakfast." He turned to the stove. Tipping his head slightly toward her, he asked, "You all right?"

"Yes." A beat passed. "No."

"You sick?"

"No. I just couldn't sleep after I came back upstairs. After I left you in the music room."

She saw the half-smile forming. She blushed. She hadn't intended for him to connect his kissing her hand with her wakefulness for the rest of the night. But he had.

She changed the subject. "I really and truly liked your piano playing last night. It was so lovely. You play professionally. So naturally. As though the instrument were made just for you."

"A very pretty speech. And I thank you," he said, with a slight bow toward her before he sat down to have another cup of coffee while she ate.

* * *

The day wore on. Lunch was served and eaten. Les appeared for dinner. They ate mostly in silence. There was nothing to talk about, but Katie did venture to ask Tate, "You going to play again this evening?"

"If you like."

"I like."

Les made a face. Then he left the dinner table to start his laundry. Tate and Katie sat on the piano bench while he played, nonstop for an hour. It was a private concert, for her enjoyment only. At the end of the hour, he said to her, "I"m going to give you Brahms' 'Lullaby' to help you sleep tonight."

"How sweet."

She got up from the bench and stood behind him, both hands resting on his shoulders. At the end of the lullaby, she leaned down and kissed him on the temple. He stood up, walked around the bench, took one of her hands in his and led her upstairs to the door of her bedroom. He opened the door and motioned for her to enter.

Katie suddenly couldn't breathe properly. It was ragged. She wasn't sure what was going to happen next. Tate put his hand on the doorknob and closed it behind him as he left her room and went down the hall to his own room.

* * *

The private piano concerts continued. Tate inserted a semi-classical piece now and then. Katie usually sat on the chaise-longue in the music room. She had the distinct feeling she had reached heaven. The music was heavenly. The ambience was heavenly. She looked at Tate Taylor with an entirely different viewpoint. He was an amazing man. It struck her oddly that when he took her up to her room that one night, he let her into her room, then closed the door and went straight to his own room. *Strange. He could be a married man, for all I know! However, he wears no wedding ring. That doesn't always mean there is no wife in the picture.* Finally, she decided that Tate Taylor was a true gentleman, embezzler or no embezzler.

Suddenly, she noticed the music had stopped, for he sat onto the chaise-longue by her feet. They gazed at each other for what seemed interminable minutes. Then he stood up. He reached for both her hands and brought her up from where she sat. He kissed her lightly. Then more aggressively. She kissed him back.

"I've wanted to do this since the first moment I saw you coming through the front door with those two ridiculous bags of groceries in your arms." No half-smile was visible. He was dead serious.

"I didn't know."

"Know it, Katie. And believe it."

"I don't know what to say. I'm so confused."

"It doesn't matter." He took her by the hand and led her from the music room. "Come, Katie." Together they climbed the stairs, slowly, deliberately. Arriving at her room, he opened her door and, again, motioned for her to enter. Then he followed behind her.

With the door still open, he said, "I don't have any protection for you."

Without faltering, she answered, "And I have none for me, either."

"But you know I want to have you. Here and now."

"As I do you."

He kissed her once more, with her heart-felt response, arms clasped without constraint, bodies pressed tightly.

"Good night, Katie, Darling."

"Good night, dear, dear Tate."

* * *

A perceptible change had taken place between Katie Sorenson and Tate Taylor. An undefined relationship. Wanting without achieving. But Les was totally unaware of the dynamics between the other two. If anything, he began fantasizing impossible dialogues and scenes with Katie. Had Tate known this was happening in Les's mind, he would have taken steps to persuade him to think otherwise.

Unknown to either Tate or Katie, Les was a simple soul, never dreaming of bringing his fantasies to life. As long as Katie paid him no special heed, Les was strictly a hands-off kind of man. Les was dense; he had no idea that Tate and Katie had a relationship, one that was very special to both of them.

* * *

As winter wound down, toward the spring thaw, she began to

worry full time about what would become of her. Would they kill her? Would they bind her and leave her to be discovered eventually? Were Tate's amorous attentions just an act? . . . to keep her off guard? What???

There were no answers. She wondered if Sam Jenkins were having disturbing thoughts that she had never contacted him during the big snow. No way of knowing, one way or the other. The mind-boggling wondering and worrying were getting to her already taut nerves–two strange men in the house.

Would Tate and Les leave in the night? Tate not saying goodbye? She couldn't visualize such insensitivity. Not from Tate. Again, was he just acting? She honestly didn't think so.

The worrisome hours went on and on.

* * *

The eaves began dripping water from the melting icicles. The snow was wet and had begun subsiding, settling. It had snowed all the way to the second story windows, at the beginning. But now it had begun to let the weak sunshine come through the top half of first-story windows.

Tate stood in front of a living-room window, watching the melt-ing snow and ice uncover their hideaway, inch-by-inch. *Soon we will leave. Very soon.* Then he saw a sight in the front yard that made him freeze: a white bearded man on snow shoes came trudging up the driveway.

"Kate!" he called, almost in panic. "Come quickly! In the living room!"

She came from the kitchen, running to him. "What is it, Tate?"

"Do you know who that is? A guy on snowshoes?"

She peered through the window with him. "Looks like Sam. How in the world did he get up here?"

"You do know him?"

"Yes!"

"Open the door to talk with him. Do NOT let him in. Tell him the house is a mess. Tell him anything but not that you're being held hostage! Do you understand me?"

She looked at him with alarm. She nodded.

"Please, Darling. Do not let him in. We're too well entrenched to pick up everything and get it out of sight before he gets here!"

"I got it. I got it." She watched Sam get closer. Then she opened the front door and called to him. "Sam? Is that you, Sam? How on earth did you get here?"

Stopping to get his breath, he explained that the snow plow had come up the private road, but couldn't get onto the driveway. So he drove up as far as the driveway, put on his snowshoes, and, he said, "Here I am!"

"Oh, Sam, I wish I could invite you in for coffee, but the house is a terrible mess! I've been writing and writing, and papers are all over the place!"

"That's all right, Katie. Just thought I'd check on you. We hadn't heard from you all winter long. We got worried about you."

"That's nice, Sam. And thank you. But everything's fine."

"Okay, I'll be on my way back to my truck on the road. S'long."

"So long, Sam." She almost began to close the door when she thought of something more to say to him. She'd take the chance, Tate standing behind the door, his weapon pointed at her. "Sam?"

"Yes'm?"

"Could you bring me some bananas the next time you come up?"

Tate stiffened.

"Bananas?" Sam was thinking wildly. Then, as calmly as he could, he said, " Why, sure thing, Katie! See ya." He trudged on down the driveway and out of sight.

She closed the door.

Tate rasped: "What the hell was *that* all about? Bananas? What were you telling him?"

She took a deep breath. He had plenty reason to be suspicious. It was an off-the-wall thing to say to a visitor that she couldn't invite into the house. She explained, "Sam knows how much I love bananas, knows they don't last long, even in cold storage, and freezing does weird things to them. So, that was a way to let him know that I'd be ready for some more bananas when the chance arises. Indeed, if I had *not* asked about the bananas, he would have probably been suspicious."

She mentally crossed her fingers. Would Tate go for it? Would Sam get the message that something was awry here at the house? Then she physically crossed her fingers for the lie and for good luck.

* * *

Tate woke up Les and told him of the visitor whom Katie fended off with the story about a messy house. "We have to pack and stay packed until the snow is melted enough for us to get out of the garage."

"I gotta pack now, Boss?"

"Yes. Now!"

"But we ain't goin' no place yet."

"True. We still have to be ready to leave suddenly, quickly. Someone has already walked to the house on snowshoes. The road is cleared by the snowplow as far as the driveway. If that man can make it to the house, so can someone else, anyone else! Come on, Les! Start packing!"

Nerves were on edge since the Sam visitor came so close to entering the house. Katie stewed and stewed about the final outcome. Would they force her to escape with them? Become a hostage in their getaway as well as snowed in with them, in the house all winter?

Tate sensed her dis-ease. His packed suitcase was beside the kitchen door to the garage, Katie watching him as she cleared the lunch dishes. Les was up earlier than usual, also packing his suitcase. Their schedules topsy turvy. All because Sam put in an appearance.

Katie spoke first. "So, while I was a hostage all winter long; both of you were hostages with me. You couldn't get out if you'd wanted to."

"Yes, we were all hostages. You're right about that. God, Katie, I hate like the devil to leave you!"

She mentally breathed more easily. *So, they are not taking me with them, I think.* She was torn at the thought: she did not want to lose Tate with the threat of his being found here. If only she could go with him. *But that would be a fool's errand! He's a man who'll be on the run the rest of his life! I can't handle that!*

What to do? What, in heaven's name, is going to be the outcome?

* * *

Tate, after their preparations for fleeing were completed, realized they needed not only to be strong for the escape from the mountain, but they needed to get their rest, without exception! He and Les got back onto their schedule: Tate sleeping at night; Les sleeping at day. They slept only on the couch in the living room, fully dressed and ready to take off in a hurry.

Katie dearly missed the piano interludes. She missed Tate, for he was distant, distracted, and alert at the same time for trouble. The waiting for the inevitable was almost too painful to bear. She had come to care for Tate fiercely.

The time raced by. Tate watched the snow level get lower and lower. Katie did the same but with apprehension. At times she was opposed to having him leave. Then she knew he had to move on.

He had said to her one night, before she went to her room, "You know, Katie, I cannot take you with us. But I promise you with every part of my mind and body that I will send for you. I can't tell you from where–mostly because I haven't worked that out yet. Thought about it? Yes. A lot!"

"You'll send for me?"

"That's what I said. It'll take some time to get passports, visas, tickets, a house, some servants and such. But when that's all ready, I will most certainly send for you! I love you Katie, with all my heart and soul."

She threw her arms around him, almost sobbing. "I love YOU, Tate. So much it makes my heart ache, knowing we'll be separated. I can hardly bear it!"

"I know, Katie. I know." He stroked her hair gently, gently.

* * *

None of the three could have foreseen what was to come, as it actually played out. Tate and Les were ready to leave the next day, early, so that their traveling through Thornview would not be noticed by late sleepers, at least.

Everything was ready. Nerves were taut when the unexpected happened. First they heard a strange noise. Tate identified it immediately–a helicopter. He tensed to see if it were going to pass overhead and keep on going. It did not. It hovered in place, then landed on the remnants of snow on the front yard.

At the first loud speaker's blaring blast, it addressed whoever was inside to come out. Les panicked. He ran for the kitchen, then out the back door. A voice shouted at him to halt. Les kept on going. He was shot in the back. He fell face down, blood staining the patchy snow.

Tate grabbed Katie, held her tightly, kissed her violently. Then let go. Slowly he opened the front door. With hands up, he tossed the gun to the side onto a patch of snow, and surrendered.

"Tate! No!" She was beside herself with sudden grief.

FBI agents jumped out of the helicopter, Sam Jenkins among them.

"Katie!" Sam shouted. "You in there? You all right?"

She appeared at the open doorway, waving. "Yes, Sam. I'm okay." Then she ran out, to Tate. Breathing with heavy gulps. Keening. He was handcuffed in front, not at his back.

Reaching him before he and the agents boarded the helicopter, she grabbed him and hung onto him for life. He pulled his handcuffed wrists upward, bringing his arms down over her head and behind her. They clung to each other. He sought her lips. She gave them to him. They kissed long and desperately.

"All right, Taylor. Time to go aboard," said Agent Larkins next to him.

Tate nodded and brought his arms back up and over her head, taking one last, long look at her. He wanted to remember every part of her face.

She murmured into his ear, softly, conspiratorially, "Contact me through Sam Jenkins at the General Store. He'll always know where I am. I promise."

He nodded once more. He understood. However much more time would be attached to his already unfinished prison sentence, she was going to wait for him.

He gave her one last half-smile. One to last her until she could see him again. It nearly broke her heart.

* * *

The newspapers were full of it: the capture of one prison escapee, an embezzler; and the death of the other escapee, an assaulter. Sam's ability to sense that something was amiss, when Katie had asked about the bananas, prompted him to call the Sheriff. The Sheriff, who had been alerted about two escapees' disappearing off the face of the earth, as it were, decided to contact the nearest FBI. It took only 20 minutes to activate the helicopter. The stunning capture, the runner's demise, and the dramatic rescue of the hostage made good copy for a few days.

Tate Taylor got five years added to the six years he had already served on a ten-year sentence.

Six Years Later
Chicago, Illinois

Katie Sorenson, now 31 years old, had gained some mild fame with the publication of two more books.. Her faith in seeing Tate Taylor again had waned. She struggled to try to forget him, forget his tenderness and sensitivities, forget the music of his life, forget all about him. But she found it impossible.

Tate had been released from prison a year ago. But no word in any form had come from him.

Just as she had almost written him off altogether, the phone rang.

"Hello?"

"Katie?" Her heart skipped a beat–no, two beats. She recognized the voice instantly.

"Tate! Where are you, Honey?"

"Sweetheart, you know I can't tell you that, but watch your mailbox carefully. I'm sending you a one-way ticket to join me. I'll have a gray limo waiting for you at the airport. You'll find it all right. It'll be the only one there."

"How do you know that?" she asked.

"Trust me, Katie. It will be."

"How will I know what to pack?"

"Pack everything! Gotta end this soon, Honey. I love you–as much or more than I did before, when I could say it to you in person.

"I know your airline and your arrival date and time. From the moment you get on the plane, I'll be taking care of you, taking care of everything for you. Don't disappoint me, Darlin'."

"That'll never happen, Tate."

"Bye, Honey. See you soon."

"Goodbye, Sweetheart."

* * *

Five days later, Katie was on board a South American airline that took her to Quito, Ecuador. She found the gray limo, just as Tate had said she would. The driver, through broken English and gestures, insisted she count all her luggage as he put it into the trunk. Then she entered the limo. He was there, inside. The limo windows were tinted; that hid him from public view.

Tate put his arms around her and embraced her soundly. He looked fit. The prison pallor was gone.

They kissed each other hungrily while the driver started the engine. Then she said, "I had no idea you'd be here, meeting me at the airport."

"Wouldn't miss it for the world!" Then he told the driver, in Spanish, to proceed.

"Where we going?" she asked.

"To get married–in a little village outside the city. Miss Katie, will you marry me?"

"Oh, Kind Suh, Ah'd be thrilled to death to marry you!"

They laughed. The limo pulled into the traffic.

While driving through the city, Tate gave Spanish instructions once more to the driver. The limo turned into an industrial type building, in the middle of what otherwise seemed to be a commer-

71

cial neighborhood: banks, department stores, specialty shops, cafes, churches. Tate indicated that Katie should get out of the limo with him. Tate and the driver removed all luggage and transferred it to a smaller, older automobile.

"In you go, Honey." He held the passenger-side door for her.

"Yes," she said as she ducked her head and got in. Wondering why they were doing such a transfer, she immediately came to the conclusion that Tate was still running. Then he spoke to the driver, still in Spanish, and handed him an envelope. The driver entered still another vehicle and waited until Tate and Katie drove away first. When they had departed from the building, onto a different side street, the driver also took off–through the way they had originally come into the building.

"May I ask," she said, "how long have you known Spanish–and so well?"

"You may ask. In prison, of course."

"Might that not be a clue as to the general direction of where you're going–after release from prison--for any law enforcement agency?

"It might. However, everyone of us in prison taking classes signed up for Spanish. Who knows? All for the same reason? I don't think so."

"I remember you once told me that the courts and the corporation never knew exactly what assets you had stolen nor how many."

"True. And they won't know until the paper trail peters out in the Caribbean, in Europe, in Asia, in Australia. None in South America. It'll take decades. The Bureau will have so much personnel turnover during those years, no one down the line is going to have a clue where the money's being spent.

"I suspect," he continued, "that the main reason they gave me only one extra year above my ten-year sentence was to begin chasing me and to find out what corporation assets I stole."

* * *

In half an hour of city driving, they reached the city's edge and proceeded into the countryside. She asked, "How come we have to go to a little village to be married?"

"So that we'll be more difficult to find."

She paused a beat. That explained the transfer to a lesser car. "You're still on the run, aren't you?"

"Just making sure."

They rode in silence for a mile or so. She asked, "How do you know we're not being followed this very moment? You made a phone call to me at my apartment—telephone statements, mine, telephone bugs in my place, postmark of the envelope of an airplane ticket—"

"Not to worry, Honey. I drove to another South American city to phone you. Traceable, yes, but to the wrong city and country. I mailed the ticket to my 'employee' in Houston, and he forwarded it to you in another envelope with the Houston postmark."

"You're 'employee'?"

"The same one who helped Les and me escape."

"I see."

"Then," he said, "just in case you had been followed all those years, I had to take further precaution at this end when you arrived: I stayed in the gray limo with tinted windows; we changed cars inside a building in heavy traffic; and here we are on our way to get married."

She shivered. "You really think I've been followed all that time?"

"They'd be crazy if they didn't.

"Meanwhile, we're going to have a rip-roaring honeymoon. It's all planned. We'll be going to 'The Middle of the World,' 'Avenue of Volcanos,' the Latacunga Indian market, Riobamba, 'Devils Nose,' the Todos los Santos ruins, Cajas National Park, and we'll end up in Guayaquil, largest city in Equador. We stop there for a rest. I've already rented a small apartment. A male servant is already installed and waiting for our arrival.

"After we've rested a few days, we pack up again—everything—in a different car, and we motor to Arequipa, Peru. We'll get lost among the high-rises. I've rented a penthouse. Hired a couple of house helpers. You'll love it, Honey. It has a piano." He paused for effect. "A grand piano."

"Oh, yes, Darling. I *will* love it!

The half-smile she remembered so well and had missed for years, appeared on his face.

After a while, he asked, "How do you feel about starting a family, Katie?"

"I am so ready, Tate! I'm 31 now. It's time to begin a family. No need to wait around."

"Exactly."

He squeezed her hand. The half-smile never faded during the next mile or so.

When we get married, you will become Mrs. Jose Montalvo. I had to have a new name, naturally."

She thought about that for several moments. Then, she said, "I see. I like the sound of it."

"Good."

A moment or so later, he said, "Of course, you will also have to use a different name for the marriage certificate."

"I will?"

"Oh, yes, to really throw 'them' off the track. They'll never find us with the names we're using."

"But I have no identification papers with a name other than Katherine Sorenson."

He pulled over to make a stop at the side of the road. He removed an envelope from his coat pocket and handed it to her. "Take a good look at this. It's your new identity: Celina Soares, from São Paulo, Brazil."

"I'm not so sure I can do this."

"You need to use it only for the marriage certificate at the church. Then you'll begin using the name of Celina Montalvo. But for now, take this pen and pad of paper and practice writing Celina Soares. That's all you need to sign when we get married. And one more thing. Say nothing in the church. If the priest asks you a question, I'll answer for you. Although Spanish and Portuguese are 80-percent alike, I'll convince him you don't understand him very well— because of his unusual accent. I'll tell him that. Thus, I can answer for you."

Hesitating a tad, she began writing. After five signatures, she said, "Okay. I have it down pat."

"Be sure you write that name and not the Katie signature."

"I will." She sucked in her breath. "Man, you think of every-thing!"

Then came the half smile.

They approached a small village. Tate pulled the little car up to the front of an inconspicuous, small village church. "It'll be simple, Honey. We 'll get married, take the certificate with us, and we're on our way again, to begin a fabulous honeymoon. Begin a fabulous life." He sat in the car for another moment before getting out and opening her door.

Tate turned toward her . He asked, "It *was* the bananas, wasn't it?"

She looked squarely into his eyes and answered, "Yes."

He sat there, facing forward again, not moving. Then, the half-smile returned.

* * *

Washington, D.C.

Agent Larkins said to his superior, "We tracked the Sorenson woman to Quito, Ecuador, Sir. Our local agent watched her deplane and get into a gray limo with tinted windows. A dead giveaway. Good chance Taylor was inside. However, she and Taylor seem to have gone underground. The agent lost them in heavy traffic. But we'll keep trying. Taylor probably has a new identity. That's the only way he could get out of the country without our knowing about it. He's smart and slick. And he knows it. What he doesn't know is that we've tracked the woman since the day he went back to prison. He was bound to send for her when the coast was clear."

The superior officer said, "That scene you described to me when Taylor got picked up at the mountain home was a classic: the woman hanging on to him for dear life. The kiss! They were an item! Of course he'd send for her!" Then, he asked, "Is there positive proof that Taylor and the Sosrenson woman never knew each other before she was taken hostage?"

"No, Sir. But everything points in that direction: that she never met him until he and his partner took her hostage on the day of the snow storm."

"Do you have anything to add to your report?" asked his superior. "We still don't know where he stashed his assets. We still don't know if they've been cashed in. We still don't know how much money is involved. We're not even sure *what* assets he took. Plano Investments never gave us anything substantial to go on. All we know about him is where the woman has led us to. And that was a big plus. At least we're reasonably sure she's with him."

"Yes, Sir, we can assume as much. Our Quito man has the pictures of Taylor that show a much younger man, but he should be able to spot him easily. He also has more recent photos of the woman."

Larkins took a deep breath. "And, Sir, I have nothing more to add to this report."

"You might go to Quito, join the agent there, give him your input, and fill him in with all the intelligence we've gathered at this end. Work together to find Taylor and Sorenson."

"Yes, Sir."

"Taylor has already paid his debt to society, with the prison time, but he still has to fork over the money from the sales of the stolen assets."

"Yes, Sir."

"Probably spent a big part of it already. Being on the run is costly."

"Yes, Sir."

Switching subjects, the superior officer said, "Do you have bags packed, like all agents are supposed to do? And are you ready to leave on a moment's notice?"

"Yes, Sir.

"I'll start the paperwork now."

"Yes, Sir."

* * *

Three months later

"Honey," Katie said to Tate. "I've never been on a cruise before! This is fabulous!"

"Neither have I, Katie. I hope you'll like Santiago. It's our next home."

"I can't understand why we had to move again, this time to Chile. You know something I don't know?"

He looked out across the ocean, took her hand in his, and, still regarding the ocean, said, "It's not something I know, Darling. It's something I feel. I have to listen to feelings . . . when they get weird."

"Is that why you booked this cruise? Even though I'm already three months pregnant?"

"I wrestled with that fact over and over in my head. I've acted on the feeling that we're being hunted again. No, not again . . . yet.

"With a cruise to another country, under still another different set of names again, and getting off at Valparaiso but not flying back to the port of departure, we can slip into Santiago and set up housekeeping again. We'll stay in a hotel until we find the right apartment. Shop for another grand piano. Interview prospective employees. And then, just to make sure–really make sure–we'll change identities again, before moving into the apartment. Then, we'll locate a reliable doctor for you.

"That should do it up nicely, Katie/Celina/Rosaria/Josephina."

"Yes, indeed, Tate/Jose/Rufino/Juan. Good grief! At this rate, we're going to run out of names for our baby!"

"I'll think of something," he said.

She turned to face him fully. "I know you will."

"Now," he said, "it's time for another Spanish lesson. You're picking it up quickly and nicely!"

"Muchas gracias, senor. 'Stoy muy felize."

He gave her his most endearing and precious gift for her: his half-smile.

THE MEDAL

She felt somewhat nervous about putting their three children on an airliner for Florida, to travel alone. Lora Nelson looked at her 15-year-old Glenn and decided he was dependable enough to be in charge of the two younger children for this journey. Lonnie was 7 and Julie was 5. So what if the flight were all the way from Los Angeles to Tampa? Glenn can handle it.

There, she told herself for the 100th time: *Glenn can handle it.*

Lora and her husband Alfred accompanied the children as far as the boarding gate. They were among the first passengers to be called to board Flight 67. A flight attendant met them at the gate and helped them get settled in a bank of seats to accommodate five passengers. Julie on the aisle, Glenn in the middle, and Lonnie next to him on his other side. Glenn was a good-looking teenager, exuding self-confidence (and a measure of importance), with hazel eyes and brown hair. Taller than his dad already. Lonnie was a skinny little kid at 7, but showing signs of filling out eventually, and certainly stretching to be as tall as his big brother. He, too, was a brown head, but with brown eyes, like his Dad. Julie, at 5 years, was already a heartbreaker, blessed with blonde hair and blue eyes, like her Mom.

Al and Lora returned to the check-in desk. He said to her, "Should we go on home now? They've already boarded."

"I don't think so," she answered. "We've both been in aviation, in the Navy, and we know how sometimes a flight gets delayed for takeoff. We should be here to stay with the children, in case they have to get off and wait for the flight to be called again."

"Good idea," he said. Then, covertly, he said into her ear with a lowered voice, "Do you know who that is beside you?"

She turned to look at the man next to her: a black man, she had heard his speaking to the airlines clerk, without listening to him. She gave him more than a glance, studying the face.

"Haven't a clue," she said to Al.

"Sure you know who it is. It's the black actor, Brian Trent."

"Oh, yes! I see, now. Sounds as though he's going on this flight."

"Right. He's trying to get a non-smoking seat in First Class."

"Should be no problem. New ruling: no smoking anywhere on a commercial aircraft."

* * *

Brian Trent had watched the mother and father escort the three children, obviously their own, as far as the gate. Then he saw the parents come back to the check-in desk. Meanwhile, he learned, eventually, that all commercial aircraft are non-smoking now. *What a relief! Can't stand to be around that smoke anymore!*

Takeoff was smooth. Brian settled in for the long Red-Eye flight, brushing off the flight attendant's insistence that he have a drink. Last thing he needed. What he needed was to go to sleep. Try to get some rest. This was supposed to be a vacation, wasn't it?

* * *

The sounds of a commotion in First Class awakened Brian suddenly.

"What's going on?" he asked his seat mate, an older gentleman.

"We're being skyjacked! Keep your head down!"

Brian instinctively slumped downward in his seat. His own safety overpowering him in an instant.

His next thought was, *What about those three children that got on by themselves? They must be scared to death! I don't think they're in First Class. Must be in Cabin Class.*

He craned his neck back and forth, wondering where the skyjacker or skyjackers were. He asked his seat mate.

The gentleman said, "There's one guy in the cockpit with his gun. I don't know if there are others back in Cabin Class."

That's a big help. Sort of. He made a decision. Foolish, probably, but he had to follow through because of his fears for those unaccompanied children.

He unfastened his seat belt, he stepped in front of the seat mate and into the aisle. He approached Cabin Class carefully. The skimpy aircraft curtain was not closed. Moving very slowly, he approached the partition between First Class and Cabin Class, hiding behind the curtain now pulled back almost to the partition. He could see a man farther down in the aisle, his back toward Brian.

Searching quickly and wildly, Brian spotted the three children only five rows away. He moved cat-like to the aisle seat where the little girl sat. He leaned across her and spoke to the teenage boy.

"I'm Brian. I'm going to help you out. Tell your little sister I want to sit in her seat, and she can sit on my lap."

Swiftly, Glenn processed the instruction and unfastened Julie's seatbelt, waking her, calling her by her name, and at the same time, explaining to her that this man is going to help them. Glenn pulled Julie over onto his lap and held her there until Brian got into the seat she had just vacated. Brian took her from Glenn's lap and onto his own and strapped the two of them together.

Julie was too sleepy to notice what was going on. She leaned back against the black man's chest and went back into a deep sleep.

Brian said to Glenn, "How you all doing? Okay?"

"Yes, sir. Okay. A little scared, but we're okay."

"That's good. What's your name?"

"Glenn." Pointing to Lonnie, he told Brian his name, too.

The little boy was wide awake and obviously terrified. He was old enough to understand "skyjacking."

Brian reached across Glenn, put his hand on Lonnie's arm and said, "Hang in there, Lonnie. We're all going to come out of this okay. Don't worry."

Unfortunately, Brian honestly did not feel the reassurance he gave Lonnie. Neither did Glenn. He, too, was plenty scared, as he had already indicated to Brian.

Checking his wristwatch, Brian realized they were just an hour away from Tampa. Where were they really going? Cuba? That would be his first guess. His mind's wandering came to a screeching halt.

The other skyjacker, the one Brian had seen the back of, as he made his way to the children, was standing next to him, Julie on his lap. "What's going on here? You were *not* in this seat earlier!" His accent was heavy. Menacing.

"I came back from First Class to be with these children. They're traveling alone."

"Just don't move again. You hear me?"

"I don't need to be told twice. You are pointing a big cannon at us right now."

"Shut up, *boy!* "

"That tears it!" Brian exploded. He almost came out of his seat. With Julie in his lap, he curtailed his immediate reaction to being called "boy."

The skyjacker yelled at Brian. "I said, 'Shut up!' And . . . don't give me no heartburn. You hear me?"

Brian closed his eyes, clenched his teeth. Slowly he nodded his head. The skyjacker moved on.

* * *

Glenn said, "Whew! That was a close one!" He looked more carefully at Brian and asked, "Brian? Aren't you Brian Trent, the actor?"

"That's right."

"I saw you in 'The Irreconcilable.' Awesome, Man!"

"You liked it?"

"You bet I did!"

"Glenn," Brian said, wishing to change the subject. "I'm working on a plan. I'll need your help. You with me?"

"Sure, Brian! What're we gonna do?"

"First," said Brian, "do you think there's room for both Lonnie and Julie in one seat?"

"Oh, sure! Then what?"

"It's just a thought, actually, but maybe we can pull it off. Let's get Julie into the seat with Lonnie and buckle them in together."

"Okay, said Glenn. "Julie, honey, wake up for a minute. We're going to move you again. Sorry, Julie."

It didn't matter to apologize. Julie was out of it, never knowing that she was being moved once more. The two younger children were secured in the one seat, together.

The skyjacker returned, walking to the rear of the aircraft.

"What's next?" Glenn asked.

"First things first. Isn't there at least one other skyjacker on the plane? Say, for the other aisle?"

"Sure, Brian. But he walked to the back of the plane a long time ago and hasn't appeared again. Not like the guy in this aisle."

"Gone a long time? What do you suppose that means?"

Glenn said, "I don't know. Maybe the guy's airsick."

"Airsick! It'd serve him right!" A pause. "We should be so blessed!" Then, "Here's the plan, Glenn: Next time our guy comes up the aisle again, I stick out my foot suddenly and trip him. If we're lucky, he'll lose his weapon. That's where you come in. You get out of your seat as fast as you can and make a dive for the gun. Meanwhile, I'll sit on him and hold him down. If we're lucky again, other men around us will help me subdue the skyjacker. Main thing is, you grab the gun. Got it?"

"Got it!"

"Be alert. Could happen any time now."

"Sure thing," said Glenn. "Where d'you suppose the flight attendants are?"

* * *

What Brian and Glen didn't know was that the other skyjacker was indeed airsick. Locked up in the head, he was on his knees, puking out his guts into the commode. Then he sat on the deck, his back to the locked door. Helpless. And useless.

And the flight attendants, as they discovered later, were gagged and bound and stowed in the aft pantry.

* * *

Brian tried to remain as calm as possible. It was difficult. He was so pumped up!

They did not have long to wait. Brian kept looking over his left shoulder as inconspicuously as possible. Glenn kept an eye on Brian, ready to make *his* move.

Then it happened. The skyjacker approached from behind. Suddenly, Brian stuck his left foot out into the aisle, tripping the guy. He sprawled, landing in an ungainly heap, losing his weapon in the aisle, ahead of him. Brian was on top of him instantly. Glenn moved quickly, stepping hard on the back of the head of the skyjacker. It stunned him momentarily, giving Brian a chance to pin the skyjacker's arms onto his back.

It was so easy, Glenn grabbed the gun and turned to point it at the skyjacker.

As Brian had hoped for, three men immediately unbuckled themselves and came to Brian's assistance. One man took off his necktie, and they tied the skyjacker's wrists together. A lady passenger offered her long scarf, which was used to tie his ankles together.

The three men sat on the skyjacker as soon as Brian got up and took the gun from Glenn.

"Good work, Brian! Good thing you stomped so hard on the guy's head. It gave me an edge over him."

Glenn blushed. He said, "What you gonna do next, Brian? Do you need any more help?"

"Don't think so, Glenn. Next part's going to be messy. I have to confront the skyjacker in the cockpit. Keep loose, Man. Staying with your little brother and sister is the best thing for you to do right now. Thanks for your help, Friend!"

Glenn blushed again.

Brian noticed that the third skyjacker had not appeared in the other aisle yet. At least, not in their section of the plane.

Brian walked the distance forward toward the cockpit, assuring passengers on the way that the one skyjacker was down, and he was on his way to the one in the cockpit.

Reaching the locked door of the cockpit, he took a deep breath. Then he pounded on the door, saying nothing, and hoping the skyjacker inside would think the pounding was being done by one of his partners.

It worked. The door opened slowly. As soon as the skyjacker saw the black man with a weapon in his hand, he withdrew his own weapon from the side of the pilot's head, and tried to point it to Brian. Brian shot first, close range, upper body, killing the skyjacker instantly.

Blood all over the cockpit, all over the pilot and co-pilot, and covering Brian's shirt front.

The pilot, almost too stunned at the outcome, took his eyes off the instruments long enough to determine who had made the fatal shot. Seeing the black man, he recognized him instantly.

"Good job, Mr. Trent!"

"How do you know who I am?"

"One of the flight attendants told us you were on board."

Brian asked, "Where we headed?"

The pilot answered, "We *were* headed for Havana, but we're already changing direction for Tampa."

"Got enough fuel for the extra miles?"

"Sure thing. Excuse me, while I announce the news to the passengers."

"Yes, sir. Does Tampa know what's going on?"

"You bet! The co-pilot's already on the horn, ordering police and ambulances."

"Can all the people in Tampa who are meeting your passengers be alerted to what's happened?"

"Of course, Mr. Trent."

"Good! I'll go back to the children."

"You got children?"

"No. I just adopted three of them, after the skyjacking started."

"What?" asked the pilot.

"See you later, Sir. Just get us to Tampa, all in one piece!"

* * *

There was still the mystery to be solved--of the missing third skyjacker. Brian moved into the other aisle and carefully made his way aft. He asked passengers along the way if they knew where the other skyjacker was. Three passengers, seated near one of the heads, told him they saw the skyjacker go into that head . . . . a long time ago. Never came out.

Brian tried the door. It was locked. Taking a credit card from his wallet, he maneuvered it into the narrow space between the door and the bulkhead. Little by little, he slid the bolt away from the slot. He tried to push the door inward, but the door was jammed by the body of the skyjacker, still sitting on the deck, passed out. . . a threat to no one. With help from two of the nearby men, they, with Brian, managed to move the body forward and onto the toilet, making room for the door to be opened fully. Again, as with the first skyjacker, passengers contributed clothing to tie up the man while he was still out of it all.

Brian searched the skyjacker's body for a weapon, found it, removed it, and gingerly carried it back to the cockpit. The pilots could dispose of both the skyjackers' weapons, after landing.

* * *

Flight 67 landed safely at Tampa International Airport, a tad late. The media were on hand to greet the passengers, especially the hero, Brian Trent. He was besieged with questions: "How did you come up with the idea to overcome the skyjackers?" "How did you know *how* to overcome the skyjackers?" "Where did you learn to handle a gun?"

Answer: "I been in a lot of movies. That's where the idea came from. Also, I learned how to attack an unsuspecting perp, and I learned how to handle firearms–also in the movies. And, before my movie career, I had learned a lot in the streets."

Glenn, Lonnie and Julie were met by their distraught grandparents, who were thankful that they were unharmed, but alarmed at Glenn's part in Trent's plan to re-take the aircraft back from the skyjackers.

* * *

One year later, Brian's press agent informed him that a phone call from the Department of Defense revealed that the Secretary wishes to present a medal to him for uncommon bravery displayed on that Flight 67 from L.A. to Tampa. He outlined the details of flying him to Washington, D.C., military vehicle to the Pentagon, escort to the auditorium, introduction to the Secretary of Defense, rehearsal of the ceremony, the actual presentation, a photo session, lunch, etc., etc.

Brian said, "Sounds like a lot of nonsense to me." He had a thought, then said, "No, wait. Tell the Secretary's assistant, or whatever he or she is, that I'll do all that providing they give the same benefits to the Nelson family and bring them to the ceremony. All of them."

"Whatever for?"

"You'll see. Just do it. And if they won't go along with my request, forget the medal!"

Brian realized he was acting like a spoiled movie-star brat. But he didn't care. He had his reasons for making the request. So be it!

* * *

In three months' time, the finalized plans were put in place to honor Brian Trent for his bravery in the headline-making skyjacking of Flight 67 from Los Angeles to Tampa. The Secretary of Defense, at a special meeting in the Pentagon, presented the medal for bravery to Mr. Brian Trent.

Also present were the Nelson family: Mr. and Mrs. Alfred Nelson, Glenn, Lonnie, and Julie. They had been invited upon Brian's insistence.

Before the presentation, Brian again exerted his "star" status by insisting that Glenn be placed to his left and that Lonnie then Julie be positioned to his right. He didn't care where the parents stood. The Secretary's aide did as the popular Brian Trent directed.

At the ceremony, Brian accepted the medal on a ribbon which was placed around his neck. After shaking hands with the Secretary, he removed his medal, turned to his left to face Glen, and placed the medal for bravery around *his* neck.

While the attendant crowd of invited guests applauded, Brian gave Glenn a big bear hug. He said into Glenn's ear, "Thanks, Good Buddy, for being there when we all needed you." Glenn smiled grandly through the hug and the message. He didn't even feel strange with the show of gratitude from the big movie star, Brian Trent. But, anyway, Glenn blushed.

The next day, newspapers around the nation featured the story about the big movie star's giving his medal for bravery to the young teenager who had assisted him in overcoming the skyjackers. Television journalists in the field badgered Trent for interviews, followed him everywhere he went. Brian Trent couldn't elude all of them, but when pressed for a statement, he declared over and over that the boy deserved such a medal as much as he did himself.

With that declaration, Trent's popularity soared upward more than ever. He was riding high. He was flushed with such success and . . . the movie offers piled up to keep him working for years.

All because of a medal . . . . . and its disposition.

# # #

THE WIDOW

Sarah Bowman was widowed when she was 43 years old. She and her deceased husband Ned Bowman, when they married each other, began running his father's lemon grove in Southern California. The elder Bowman had been ready to retire.

Their son and daughter were already out of the nest. Ned Jr. had two more years of college before graduating. He was studying to be a mining engineer. Nellie had just finished college and married her high-school sweetheart. They lived 70 miles away in a Los Angeles suburb.

There was a family meeting, after the funeral, to make a decision about the ranch. Who would run it? Should Ned drop everything and come home to do that job? Should Nellie persuade her husband Bob to move back to Santa Paula where she could assist with the office work—as she had done for her Dad before she left for college? Ned Jr., himself, had worked hard on the ranch since he was 12 years old until he left for college.

Sarah had a thought and made a suggestion: The ranch foreman, Juan Gonzales, could run the ranch until some more permanent arrangement showed itself. Gonzales came to the ranch as a boy of 10, looking for work to augment his mother's inadequate stipend doing housework and laundry. Sarah felt sorry for the boy and had persuaded Ned Sr. to take him on as an errand boy at first, then as a general helper in all the various chores of a lemon ranch.

Juan eventually worked his way up to assistant foreman, and then to foreman, which he held until Mr. Bowman's demise. Sarah knew he could handle the working affairs of the ranch, needing to call on her only for an occasional crisis decision. She could do that easily because when her husband was alive, he always kept her apprised of the problems and decisions and deals regarding the ranch.

Juan Gonzales was an honest and hard-working employee. And because he had worked on the ranch for so many years, he was almost like family.

He was not precisely like family, however, because there was that fine line between the landowners and the land workers. The differences were always there. Always would be there, as far as either landowner or land worker knew.

* * *

Sarah Bowman had a very fair complexion with dark brown hair (a premature streak of gray hair beginning at left of center of her forehead) and eyes as blue as the water of a mountain stream. Her stature was medium height with strong arms and pretty legs. Her arms were strong from helping with some of the ranch chores at the beginning of her married life with Ned, on his parents' property.

After Nellie learned to type in high school, she and Sarah had worked together in the office over the years. Sarah could manage by herself until they might hire an office manager sometime in the future. The office was in a room at the back of the house. To the side of one wall there was a small bathroom, which also opened into an anteroom off the kitchen

Sarah's pretty smile had been her most endearing feature. She used to smile a lot but had closed down when she lost her husband in death.

The man now in charge of ranch management, Juan Gonzales, noticed that Mrs. Bowman's smile was missing. He, of course, said nothing about *that*, but especially to Mrs. Bowman.

Juan was also of medium height, sturdy physique, well muscled. His hair was a shiny black, almost curly, but not quite. It went well with his expressive brown eyes, looking warily ahead and flashing with fire when riled. That did not happen often, however, for he was slow to anger. He seemed to have a perpetual suntan.

* * *

"Juan!" Sarah called. "The water bill for last month seems a bit high. What do you think that's about? And have you noticed it?"

"Si, Senora. My Mahder, she say da same t'ing. Da rates, dey go up."

"Of course. There should have been a notice about it beforehand. I probably opened up the envelope and dispensed with the notice without really reading it. Thank you, Juan."

"Si, Senora. Joo are welcome."

Juan began to leave the kitchen where they took care of most of the ranch business. Sarah said, "You have enough food at the bunk-house? I didn't get extra groceries for you last week."

"Ah, si, Senora. We have plenty! T'ank you veddy much!"

She said, "I really appreciate your hard work and management, Juan. You do a wonderful job."

He tucked his head, feeling that his dark complexion was turning beet red. "Si, Senora. T'ank you veddy much!" he said again. He fled before he embarrassed himself by letting her see how red-faced he had turned when she gave him such a nice compliment.

* * *

The weeks and months went by. The lemon trees were topped,

the cuttings left on the ground for nutrition. Lemon-picking crews were hired. The irrigation system was utilized every three weeks for three days running. The aisles between the lemon-tree rows were cultivated to get rid of the weeds. The broad-based ditches for drip water from trees were cleared out. Maintenance had to be done for the wind machines, which were a replacement for the old smudge pots. Underground irrigation pipes had to be dug up, inspected, and repaired. The frost alarm needed to be tested on a regular basis.

Running a lemon grove was not an easy job, nor was it a job for the lazy. All the time, something needed to be tended to.

* * *

The year of El Niño arrived in Southern California. Heavy rains, pounding rains, flooding everywhere in the cities and small towns.

Sarah's house was built on an incline, near the foot of a mountain, but not at the foot. Debris collected everywhere there was an obstruction, such as the house itself, the trucks in the back yard, the bunkhouse, the sheds, the lemon tree trunks. On an especially bad night, Juan and Sarah stayed up the entire night, maintaining a flood watch for the property. Juan supervised the other workers' attempt to clear the collected debris before flooding could occur on the property.

Sarah kept the coffee pots going all night. Sometimes she donned rain gear and went outside with a heavy-duty flashlight to see how the work was going. Juan shooed her back into the house, mostly for her own protection. She could have stumbled over debris that had not ever been there before. He feared for her safety.

When daylight came, their world was still wet with spurts of the heavy rainfall interrupting the lesser rain showers. Everyone was exhausted, but the clearing of debris could not stop. Juan sent half the workers to the bunkhouse for breakfast and a short nap while the other half continued to work. Then, when the first shift arrived back into the grove to continue working, Juan sent the second shift to the bunkhouse for the same treatment.

Sarah noticed that Juan had divided up the work force and that he did not take a break himself. Once more, she donned her rain gear and sought out Juan, scolding him for not taking a rest. He insisted he must stay with the others. She insisted he come into her house and have breakfast.

Juan resisted, claiming he could not dirty her nice, clean kitchen.

"Then take off your boots at the back door and place them next to mine."

He obeyed. He looked at the two sets of boots on the back porch, touched by the familiarity of it. Then he stood in the kitchen, where he had conferred with Sarah many, many times, discussing ranch business. But, at this hour, on this fretful day, he felt terribly out of place.

"In the next room, Juan, there's a cot. You catch forty winks while I make breakfast for both of us."

"Forty winks, Senora?"

"I'm sorry. 'Forty winks' is an expression meaning a short nap."

"Si, Senora." But he did not move. Take a nap in the Senora's house? Unheard of! he thought, in Spanish.

But now Sarah was taking him by the arm and leading him to the cot in the next room.

"Now, lie down and take a short nap, like I said. I expect you to do this, Juan!"

"Si, Senora." He really did not want to do this in the Senora's house. It was unseemly! These thoughts in Spanish racing through his head. But, on the other hand, he was dead tired. So tired that he lay down on the cot and went to sleep instantly.

Sarah smiled.

She stopped in mid-cracking the first egg. What seems so different so suddenly? she asked herself.

She said aloud, "I smiled. I do believe I smiled," she said softly to herself. "That felt so good."

Half-an-hour later, Sarah wakened Juan. "Breakfast is ready, Juan. Wash up in the little bathroom next to the anteroom. Then come to the kitchen and sit at the table."

Groggily, Juan stood up. He looked at his La Dona, Sarah, and he couldn't believe what he saw.

"Senora, you are smiling again!"

"I am?" It had already become comfortable, realizing she smiled all through the breakfast preparations.

"Si, Senora. I be happy you smile again."

"Well, Juan, truth be known. I'm happy I'm smiling again, too!" Her smiled broadened even more so. "Go wash up, now. Then come to the table. I've made pancakes. I hope you like pancakes."

"Ah, si, Senora!" he said joyously. He was liking this tiny change of relationship. The pancakes smelled inviting!

* * *

At last the rainy season was over. Most of the debris was cleared from the property. What could be used for outdoor fires was piled high near the back of the bunkhouse. The workers still liked to make their own outdoor fires for warmth and for most of their cooking. Otherwise, the bunkhouse had a small kitchen with running water, electricity and gas.

A plus had come out of the storm: more firewood was collected, not bought.

* * *

Juan was bone weary from the exhaustive work of keeping the Senora's property free from flooding. He lay down on his own bunk, still unbelieving that he had slept earlier the day before on La Senora's small bed next to her kitchen. Still unbelieving that he had taken breakfast with her in her own house! Yes, he was tired, but he was too elated to drop off to sleep immediately--from thinking about the beautiful smile of La Senora. It had come back. It had come back to give him so much pleasure--just to see her smile.

However, there was still much work for all the hired help to neaten up the property everywhere. Boring, back-breaking work, bending over to pick up all the limbs and logs and trash that had rolled with the mud down the mountainside and onto everyone's property.

Finally, Juan was able to announce to Sarah that the job was truly finished.

"All ees back to what eet used to be, Senora."

"Oh, thank you, Juan. So much extra work. All because of El Niño!"

"Si, Senora. I glad eet ees done!" He waited a beat. Then, "And, Senora, I t'ank you for to make the coffee for everyone all night long. And for to make my breakfast. Eet was . . . how you say? 'Deleecious'!"

The pretty speech was worth the effort. It brought on La Senora's lovely smile. Juan beamed back at her.

"You're entirely welcome, Juan. I am such a lucky woman to have you and all your men to do so much extra work and to do it so well!"

"Si, Senora."

She put a hand on his forearm and lightly squeezed it. "Bless you, Juan. You've been my rock."

"Senora? I have bean jore rock? How ees dat so?"

She made a small sigh. "There I go again. Talking in metaphors!"

"Senora?"

"What I mean is, I call you my rock because you are solid, steady, strong. And you are always there when I need you."

Again, Juan was beset with turning red at a compliment. "Senora, joo are too kind! But I like what I hear."

Her smile widened more. He was bedazzled by it.

* * *

A few days later, Juan appeared at the back porch, rapping on the kitchen door. Sarah knew it was he because the kitchen was where all their conferences took place.

"Senora?" Juan said as she opened the back door and motioned for him to come into the kitchen.

"Yes, Juan, come on in. What is it?"

"Senora, forgeeve me. I have come at bad time. Joo are having joor lunch."

"Doesn't matter, Juan." Before she asked why he had come, she had another thought. She said, "Have lunch with me, Juan."

"Ah, Senora . . . ."

"Wait. I know you're going to refuse. I don't blame you. I've never invited you to have lunch with me before. But I am as sincere as I can be when I say I want you to take lunch with me."

Juan was beside himself. He was invited to eat lunch with the Senora and told in the same breath not to refuse. "Senora. I do not see how I can refuse. T'ank you veddy much!"

"You can tell me what you wanted to ask or say–while we eat."

"Si, Senora."

She indicated to him where to sit at the kitchen table while she set another place for him. She chatted amiably as she put plate and utensils on the table. "You have to know, Juan, I eat dinner at lunchtime and lunch at dinnertime. It is the rancher's way."

"Si, Senora. Da workers, dey do da same t'ing!"

"Well, then, our schedules are in sync, aren't they?"

"'Een seenk,' Senora?"

She explained in sync to him, spelling the word along with the explanation. Juan listened carefully, mentally taking note, making the decision to remember what she told him.

"So, Juan. Why did you want to see me?"

He explained that one of the workers was sick, and Juan didn't know what to do for him.

After lunch/dinner was finished and dishes put to soak, Sarah accompanied Juan to the bunkhouse to see for herself what the problem might be. Juan set out ahead of her to make sure everyone was "decent" before she came inside.

The young man was surely sick with a raging fever, mumbling

weakly in Spanish. "What is he saying, Juan?"

"He t'inks he ees going to die and ees asking God to keep heem alive."

"Shoot! He's not going to die. Not on my watch!"

"Senora? Joor watch?"

"Sorry, Juan. I've used another expression. An old Navy expression my dear husband used to say, meaning nothing bad is going to happen while I'm on duty."

Juan was still puzzled, but said his usual "Si, Senora."

* * *

Sarah called her doctor, he came to the bunkhouse, he treated the young man, complimenting Sarah for putting cold cloths onto his forehead, and for giving him aspirin.

"Probably a case of the flu," he told Sarah. "Watch for more cases of it in the event it has a run among your workers."

* * *

The flu did take its toll but only upon one other person: Juan.

Sarah was so concerned about him that she had him moved into her house, onto the cot by the kitchen. She nursed him back to health, listening to his Spanish-ridden delirium, wondering what in the world he was saying.

Juan's assistant, Aurelio, now came to the house to confer with the Senora, but also to look in on Juan. He was soon convinced that Juan was getting excellent care. The Senora was babying him, so thought Aurelio. But he kept his counsel and did not convey that information to the other workers.

Juan's case of the flu was far more devastating than the first case, the other worker. His convalescence took longer. He was 'imprisoned' in La Senora's ante room, off the kitchen. She served him all his meals in bed, once he was well enough to eat again. She took his temperature. She kept a cold ice bag on his forehead. She bathed his face and shoulders and arms and chest with a cold damp cloth, letting the air cool down the heat emanating from his body. He didn't know how many days he was in her house before he realized she was bathing him. If he weren't so sick, he would have jumped out of bed and fled for the bunkhouse!

At the same time, he thought, he rather liked the little attentions she was giving him.

And Sarah liked doing it all for him. She had been worried to distraction about him at the onset of his illness.

When Juan was well enough to work again, Sarah released him from her care and sent him on his way. But first, Juan hesitated at the back door in the kitchen, before he left the house, wanting to express his gratefulness to La Senora. The very kind Senora. The most beautiful Senora.

"Senora," he began.

"Yes, Juan?"

"Senora, my Engleesh, eet ees so veddy bad. I want to say t'ings to you, but I do not know how to say eet best in Engleesh." An outpouring of Spanish erupted from him.

Sarah was bewildered. She caught a word here and there that she could understand: "heart," "confusion," "speak," . . . . "love"?

Now, she was thoroughly perplexed. She said to him, "Try, Juan, to say in English whatever you are wanting to say to me."

He hesitated for a long time. Then he began. "Senora. I speak from my heart. I am so–how you say? Confused?" She nodded. He continued. "Joo take care of me for long, long time. For dat, I love joo."

She smiled her broadest. She took his left hand into her right hand. "Of course, Juan. You are grateful for the care, which I was only too glad to do for you. You love what I did for you. Isn't that what you mean?"

"No, Senora. I love *joo*!"

Whereupon, he grasped her left hand with his right. They stood, enjoined in that way. He leaned into her smile and kissed her.

Sarah was shocked. She was flattered. She was trembling. Her heart raced so much, it nearly took her breath away. She thought, *What is happening here?*

She found herself doing something she had never dared think of doing. She was kissing him back! He released his hand from hers. He put his arms around her. She did not resist. She leaned her head against his shoulder. She had not known such peace–since before Ned had become ill and died.

"Senora," he said when he let her pull away from him. "What we going to do?"

"Nothing, Juan. Not until I sort out all this. I don't know what happened just now. And so, *I'm* confused!"

"Si, Senora." And he left.

* * *

Days passed before Juan came to her kitchen to discuss a problem with the irrigation pipes. He postponed it as long as he could. He was reluctant to face La Senora after his ungentlemanly conduct just before he went back to work, after his illness.

"Senora," he began. "I am sorry I keesed joo before I left joor house."

"Oh, Juan. Don't be sorry. I'm not! It was so sweet. It was so passionate!"

He thought he understood the word 'passionate' because it was close to the Spanish word. But, did he misunderstand? She is smiling. And smiling. Did she like it?

"Si, Senora. Eet was!" He ducked his head downward. "I come to talk about da iddigation pipes, Senora."

"Ah, yes. They are getting pretty old and some may need replacing."

They finished the discussion. They went to the site where earth had been dug up to expose the pipes for inspection. They discussed the pipes more. A decision was made. They began walking back toward the buildings. Juan did not turn off to go to the bunkhouse or shed. She realized he was accompanying her back to her house.

"Juan, you don't need to see me back to the house. I'll be okay."

"Si, Senora. What I weesh to do ees to make one more kees. If I may."

"We can do that right here, Juan. Out in the open."

"Joo would do *dat*?"

"Of course. Willingly. Happily!"

* * *

Juan knew in his heart that some of the workers–perhaps all of them–would witness his kissing the Senora . . . in broad daylight! And they did. *And* they teased Juan mercilessly. They put him through hell. But it was a kind of hell he ultimately enjoyed. Thoroughly.

Sarah, on the other hand, scolded herself as she made her way to the back porch and into the kitchen. *What was I thinking?! I must be out of my mind!* She continued scolding herself as she puttered around the house. She felt she must purge her thoughts by doing some hard housecleaning. But her cleaning lady took care of all that. Straighten the closets! Flip the mattress of her bed. Take down the drapes and send them to the dry cleaners. Take down the curtains and wash and dry and iron them and hang them up again. Do some filing in the office. Write checks. Anything! Anything to distract her from the amorous Juan!

Nothing worked. By bedtime, as tired as she was from the flurry of activity she set for herself that day, she could not go to sleep.

* * *

Another day passed. Another day of deciding what to say to Juan the next time she saw him. Deciding what *must* be said! The Juan thing was getting out of hand. She had to set things right again: landowner vs. land worker. They must stay separate entities, not connected.

It was all set in her mind how to let Juan down gently–as gently as she could possibly manage. She didn't want to hurt him, when all was said and done. He must be told that they could not continue with the crossing of the line–that line between landowner and land worker.

The next thing Sarah knew, Juan was knocking on the back door. She went to it and opened it. He spoke first.

"Senora, I have bad news."

"Something wrong at the ranch? A worker injured?"

"No, no, Senora. Eet ees personal."

"Oh, my goodness, Juan. What's happened?"

"My Mahder. She ees veddy sick. She want me to take her back to Mexico. To die. I must take her back to Mexico, and I must stay weeth her until she die. Eet ees my . . . how you say? . . ."

"You duty?"

"Si, Senora. I not happy to do deese. I not happy to leave you!"

Like turning on a light, Sarah saw this as an opportunity to postpone her prepared speech for him. Perhaps never having to use it. "Juan, I'm so sorry about your mother. What will I do without you to help me run the ranch?"

"Aurelio."

"Aurelio. Yes, of course."

* * *

The following week, Juan drove his mother to Mexico, using his pickup truck, meager baggage on the truck bed. Before he picked up his mother, he came to Sarah's kitchen only to say goodbye. He was so distressed with his new obligation, he did not even kiss her goodbye. Sarah understood.

As he drove out the back driveway to the main road, Sarah watched from her back porch. She had the quasi uncomfortable feeling she would never see him again.

* * *

Sarah called Ned, then Nellie, explaining the changes on the ranch (but not the change of relationship between her and Juan). Ned said his graduation was coming up in another month. He would come straight home and take over from Aurelio. He would stay as long as necessary to find and train a regular foreman as well as advertise for an office manager.

Sarah no longer needed to worry about any part of the ranch. Ned would take over.

And she no longer needed to worry about Juan. If she read the culture of land workers correctly, he would never return to the ranch, not even to the U.S.A. Sometimes, filial love and love of country could be stronger than a personal love.

Sometimes.

That uncomfortable feeling returned--that she would never see Juan again.

And she never did.

# # #

A MAN BEFORE HIS TIME

Lady Bess watched the tournament games from the sidelines with other members of the crowd, all guests of Count Mowbury. The Count held a tournament twice a year. Knights and spectators came from miles around to his castle for the festivities.

Sir Steven was the winner of the games at the end of the tournament, and Lady Bess noticed that but for an accident by a young knight, Sir John, he would have possibly won the tournament. Sir John had participated in the jousting segment, fell from his horse, and his head struck a rock jutting out from the grass. He was unconscious when the attendants and his page carried him off the field and into his tent.

That evening in the Great Hall before dinner, Sir John, fair and very blond with blue eyes, had recovered and was able to talk about his mishap with the other knights. They were standing in a group.

Lady Bess, also fair, with green eyes and chestnut hair, noticed Sir John from the moment he entered the Great Hall. She worked her way to that group and waited for a lag in the conversation.

"Sir John," she said,"you were nearly the winner of the games today. What a pity about the accident."

"Milady?"

"'Tis true. I watched you and you were a shoo-in for the winner but for your accident."

"Thank you, Milady. I am afraid you have me at a disadvantage. You know my name, but I know not yours."

"Lady Bess, sir."

"Lady Bess. . . . Lovely name, Milady. Would you do me the honor of allowing me to sit with you at dinner?"

"Of course, Sir John. I shall be delighted."

Lady Bess was unfashionably tall, nearly as tall as Sir John, but slim and angular. Because of his rigorous activities as a knight, Sir John was muscular and strong as a fortress. They made a handsome couple as they entered the dining hall.

At dinner, Sir John told Lady Bess about his home in the county to the south where his father, Lord Michael, presided over his estate, Landowill Castle. Sir John's oldest brother, Sir Richard, was being groomed to take over his father's position as Lord of the Castle. His second oldest brother, Friar Paul, was serving the Church to the North. Three sisters were standing in the wings, waiting to be mated with prosperous husbands. His mother was deceased.

Lady Bess told Sir John of her family in Buxhall Manor to the

East. Her father, Lord Sidney, managed his lands with assistance from his first son, Sir Ralph. His second son, Ronald, forsook the Church in favor of preparing to tutor the children of families in and around Buxhall Manor. One older sister had married the year before. A younger sister, Penelope, was still being tutored by Ronald. Lord Sidney's wife was also deceased.

Lady Bess's older married sister had been sent to Count Mowbury's castle the year before to seek a suitable husband and was successful. Lady Bess herself was visiting the castle for the same reason, but she did not reveal that fact to Sir John.

After dinner, the guests returned to the Great Hall for dancing. Sir Steven, the day's winner, was most popular with the ladies, young and old, but Lady Bess had eyes and ears only for Sir John. They danced every dance together. That did not go unnoticed by the Countess.

As Sir John accompanied Lady Bess to the door of her apartment, he said, "Next tournament, I am going to win. You can count on that, Milady!"

"Excellent," she replied. "I will be here when you return, and I look forward to our meeting again, Sir John."

"I shall count the days and hours 'til then, my good Lady Bess," he said, as he kissed her proffered hand.

* * *

Lady Bess stayed on at the Mowbury Castle as a guest, an arrangement made between her father and the Count. The weeks and months wore on and at last, the knights from the surrounding countryside began to arrive for the next tournament. Sir John was among the first. He sought out Lady Bess immediately. They greeted each other formally.

"Good day to you, Sir John. Was your journey pleasant?"

"Good day to you, my dear Lady Bess. No, my journey was not pleasant. It took too long. I could not get here soon enough!"

She smiled. He noticed.

The tournament began and once more, Sir John was a shoo-in to win each day's games, but in a face-to-face bout with Sir Malcolm, the latter dealt a blow with his sword to Sir John's right side. He fell to the ground, experiencing great pain, and much loss of blood. His page and other attendants ran to him on the field. Lady Bess stifled a cry of anguish. The castle surgeon had Sir John taken directly to the nearest wing of the castle--the harness and tackle room of the stables.

Sir John was placed on a table, and the surgeon began treating him. Lady Bess arrived, breathless, and asked the surgeon how serious was Sir John's wound.

"If I can stop the bleeding, the wound will heal, and he will be right as rain, in time," said the surgeon.

"What can I do to assist?" she asked.

"Pray, Milady. Just pray."

After the bleeding had stopped, the surgeon announced that under no circumstances was Sir John to be moved to his rooms in the contestants' wing of the castle. It would be too dangerous. His wound would need to be nearly healed before he could be moved.

Lady Bess installed herself in the tackle room in order to be his nurse during his confinement. A cot was brought in, her lady-in-waiting supplied linens and extra clothing, and it was three days before Sir John opened his eyes and surveyed his surroundings.

"Where am I?" he asked.

"On the road to recovery, thanks be to God," said Lady Bess. "Can you remember what happened to you?"

Sir John regarded his bandage, felt the dull pain, and understood. She placed her hand on the shoulder of his good side. He tensed.

"Did I hurt you?"

"Nay, Milady. On the contrary. Seeing you here beside me is good medicine." He smiled faintly and continued, "I was reacting to your tender touch; it affected me in a strange but an altogether thrilling way."

Squire Robert, his page, approached. "We have been here in the tackle room for three days, Sire, and Lady Bess has not left your side for a single moment."

"And, my dear lady," said Sir John, "I pray you do not leave me now."

* * *

In due time, Sir John's wound healed, as predicted by the surgeon, and he was moved to his rooms in the knights' wing. Lady Bess supervised the move, having her own things taken to her apartment, the cot relegated back to the store room. She continued to visit him in his room each day, taking all her meals with him, reading to him, telling him of the castle gossip, and some time after that stage of healing, Sir John was allowed to walk in the gardens, Lady Bess in attendance. Still later, he mounted his horse once again for an early morning trot. Lady Bess joined him for the daily morning rides that followed.

The rides became longer and longer in duration. They had picnics in the meadows, in the forests, and by the river. They took afternoon repasts together every day. They sat side-by-side at dinner every evening.

One afternoon, as they returned from a picnic lunch, a thunder shower descended upon them. They raced on their horses for the nearest shelter, the gazebo in the rose garden. They dismounted and, soaking wet, clothing saturated, entered the gazebo, laughing and shrieking with excitement.

Suddenly, they stopped laughing. They looked at each other as though it were the first time they had seen each other. He kissed her lightly. She put her arms around his neck and kissed him fiercely.

"John," she breathed.

"Bess . . . ."

That evening at dinner, Sir John announced to his hosts and their guests that upon his winning a tournament, he and Lady Bess would be wed. It was a surprise to no one.

* * *

Sir John was not strong enough to take part in the next tournament, but he began a vigorous program of practicing for the one following. Lady Bess sat patiently on the sidelines, watching him go through the exercises he designed for himself. She watched him hone his marksmanship skills with the lance, the jousting skills, and the swordsmanship skills. She winced whenever he took a fall from his horse. She applauded with "bravos" whenever he scored a win against his practice opponents.

By the time the next tournament began, Sir John was ready. To the sound of loud cheering and happy huzzahs, Sir John won the tournament.

* * *

Sir John and Lady Bess, with a retinue of knights, friends, squires, and ladies-in-waiting, along with a unit of guardsmen for protection, traveled to the north to the monastery where Friar Paul lived and labored. Sir John and Lady Bess spoke their vows of marriage to him, and there was rejoicing for three days for the newly wedded couple. Then the wedding party began its trek to Buxhall Manor for an extended visit.

The first night away from the monastery, Sir John said to his bride in their tent, "My dearest, I swear to you my undying love, loyalty, and faithfulness, in addition to my wedding vow. I love you so very much, my darling."

"And I give back to you ten times what you have sworn to me, my sweet knight."

After the traveling group arrived at Buxhall, new supplies were furnished for the remaining travelers to continue on their way, some back to Mowbury Castle, the others to their respective homes. The newly-wed couple remained at Buxhall.

Lady Bess's younger sister was thrilled with her new brother-in-law and dreamed of a knight in her future. Sir Ralph and Ronald, along with Lord Sidney, accepted Sir John as a proper and fit member of their family.

* * *

Six months later, a rider came to the manor from Sir John's home, Landowill Castle. Sir John turned pale at the news. The Duke of Borbid was marching from the south toward Lord Michael's lands to make war on Landowill Castle. Sir John was urgently needed to return and bring with him as many supporting knights as he could muster to assist them in fending off the Duke.

Sir John regretted having to leave, for there was strong evidence that Lady Bess was with child.

"You must come back to us, my darling. Fight well but come back to us," she said.

"Fear not, my love. Heaven and earth will not keep me away. I will return as soon as the Duke has been routed and sent back to his castle to the south."

"Goodby, sweet knight. I love you to the end of my days."

"Farewell, my wife, my love."

On his way to join his father and brother in battle, Sir John made a circuitous route through the countryside, enlisting the aid of all the knights he could find. They rallied around him, for the Duke of Borbid was an enemy to them all.

When Sir John and his band of supporters neared Landowill Castle, he could determine, through his scouts, that the castle was under siege. Approaching an outlying cottage in the woods, beyond the Duke's line of siege, Sir John, alone, entered the cottage and disappeared from sight.

A trap door in the floor of the cottage led to an underground passage into the bowels of the castle. Sir John was united with his father and brother. It was ascertained that the castle could hold out indefinitely, using the underground passage to bring in supplies.

But Father," said Sir Richard, "if we can hold out, so can the Duke--indefinitely! What good does that do?"

"You are quite correct, my son," Lord Michael replied. Turning to Sir John, he asked, "And what say you, John, on this matter?"

Sir John said, "Father, build up your stronghold here, train the serfs to fight, and let me return to my band of knights on the outside, beyond Duke Borbid's camp. At a pre-determined day and hour, we will attack the Duke from behind while you and your men attack from the castle. That will catch him off guard. We just may be successful in defeating the Duke, once and for all."

Lord Michael and Sir Richard agreed, and the three men set about formulating the plan.

* * *

The battle lasted only two hours. The Duke was vanquished and sent running back to the south with his straggling army. It was not without heavy cost, however. Lord Michael and Sir Richard lost their lives. Sir John sustained a serious wound--he lost his left foot.

The combined forces of Landowill Castle and Sir John's group of knights rested and re-outfitted. One by one the remaining knights took of their leave and returned to their respective homes or continued on to other quests.

Sir John received a note from Lady Bess, informing him of the birth of their firstborn, a son. He knew he needed to send a message back to her, but he was not sure about what to say. Finally, he began a letter to her:

"My dearest Bess, I regret to tell you that I cannot return to you as soon as I would like. Do not be concerned, my Love, but in the battle to send the Duke of Borbid on his way, my father and brother passed into that other world, and I have been wounded. The wound is not so that I cannot see, speak, or write, but I cannot walk for some time to come. I have lost my left foot. The convalescence goes well, thanks to the Almighty, but I am unable to return to you and the wee one. Stay well, my Love, until we are reunited. Your worshipful husband, John."

Lady Bess allowed the messenger to rest for two days, then she dispatched him back to Landowill Castle with a reply to Sir John:

"My darling, I cannot begin to tell you how distressed I am to learn of your losses. With our child, I am leaving Buxhall Manor to come to you at once. My place is at your side. Will Friar Paul be the new master of Landowill Castle? Your son and I will arrive as soon as possible, after you receive this message. I long to hold you in my arms and comfort you and nurse you back to good health. Pray for our safe journey. The Lord God give me strength and patience until I reach you, my sweet knight. Your adoring wife, Bess."

* * *

Sir John laid eyes upon his son for the first time when little Michael was five months old. Still abed with his healing stump, Sir John held the infant for long moments, gazing at him with wonderment.

"He's a tiny miracle, my Dearest," said Sir John.

"Aye, Love. "The miracle of life."

Lady Bess brought with her, besides their son, her brother Ronald, her sister, Lady Penelope, her lady-in-waiting, and a nursemaid. The cortege consisted of guards from Buxhall Manor to protect the travelers. After they had rested and re-supplied, the guards returned to Buxhall Manor.

Sir John informed Lady Bess that Friar Paul declined his inheritance to rule Landowill Castle in favor of continuing to serve God in the Church for the rest of his life.

"With the loss of my brother Sir Richard, I'm next in line," said Sir John. "I am now lord and master of my father's castle, lands, chattel, and serfs. Squire Robert is my legs, while I am abed, to run errands and deliver messages for me."

Lady Bess said, "And I will be your eyes and ears for you, reporting on all activities in and around the castle."

Based on her observations, Sir John could make decisions, and Lady Bess could see that they were carried out.

Ronald, at Sir John's suggestion, began to teach the children of the serfs how to read and write, as well as continue to tutor his own sister Penelope and Sir John's youngest sister Lady Ellen. Ronald noticed, early on, Lady Sarah, Sir John's middle sister. He wrote a poem for her every day. They were enamored of each other.

Squire Robert, meanwhile, was taken with Ronald's and Lady Bess's sister, Lady Penelope, and she in turn was taken with him. They met in the castle gardens every evening and exchanged stories about Buxhall Manor and about Squire Robert's aspirations for knighthood. He asked her to promise to wait for him while he departed to earn his knighthood. She promised, willingly.

* * *

Eventually, Sir John was fitted with a wooden brace, with leather straps, for walking. His blacksmith outfitted him with a special appliance that allowed Sir John's foot brace to fit into a stirrup, thus

103

enabling him to ride again, for short periods of time.

Sir John petitioned the Church to transfer Friar Paul to Landowill Castle to meet the spiritual needs of the residents there, and the request was granted.

By the time Lady Bess gave birth to their second child, a girl, Raquel, Ronald and Lady Sarah were wed with Friar Paul's officiating.

Sir Robert returned to Landowill Castle with his newly acquired title of knight. He asked Lady Penelope to marry him, and she consented.

With Sir John's program to have Ronald teach reading and writing to the serf children, some benefits surfaced. One boy offered to work as an apprentice to the silversmith, a craftsman who was married but had no son to whom he could pass on his skill. Another boy was selected by the chief scribe to assist him. Still another lad volunteered to work with the castle exchequer. Sir John realized that this took away some workers from the fields, but he saw the results as being an advantage because he did not have to import artisans and other members of his castle's staff.

Since Sir John was no longer able to participate in tournaments, he elected not to host them at Landowill Castle. He sought other means to burn off his energy. He turned to commerce. With his head gardener, he began to develop cuttings of the fruit trees from the castle gardens. In time, his orchards outside the castle became well known in the neighboring lands. Choosing the brighter lads from the reading and writing classes, he made them hawkers of his fruit. They took the apples, pears, peaches, and apricots to neighboring castles and sold each harvest at a handsome profit. Sir John then paid each boy for his efforts with a part of the profits.

Sir John and Lady Bess had two more boys, Sidney and William, and another girl, Gwendolyn.

* * *

When a serf's son, Owen, came into the castle for tutoring by Ronald, he saw, now and then, Lady Ellen, Sir John's youngest sister. It was not his place to speak to a lady of the castle, but his fantasies included doing just that.

One afternoon, as Owen left the classroom to go from the castle and do more work in the fields before dusk, he bumped into Lady Ellen, rounding a corner in the hallway.

"Begging your pardon, Milady!" he said.

Lady Ellen glared at him for a moment, and then she saw the dark eyes and dark hair and was taken aback. She noticed the coarsely woven clothing and recognized him to be a serf's son leaving the classroom for the day.

"Field Knave!" she exclaimed, and stalked off and out of sight. Owen blushed, fingered his worn-out cap, then went on his way.

The next day, Owen saw Lady Ellen leave the classroom just as he was entering. It was no accident that he had come early.

"Milady?" Owen said with a deep bow.

This time Lady Ellen blushed and skittered past him without a word.

Weeks later, when Owen had been chosen to assist the castle scribe, he was given clothes to wear befitting a young squire: linen and velvet. Furthermore, he was given the privilege of living in the castle, in a tiny anteroom off the scribe's work room.

Once again, Owen and Lady Ellen met in the hallway. "Milady," Owen said with a short bow.

Lady Ellen had to look twice before she recognized him in the new clothes. "Squire Owen," she said breathlessly, and continued walking away from him.

Owen was astounded. "She knows my name!" he breathed to himself.

They were both 14 years old. Lady Ellen began to make up excuses to visit the scribe. This did not go unnoticed by Owen.

It did not go unnoticed by the scribe, either. He reported it to Sir John, who, in turn, discussed the matter with Lady Bess.

"If it is a romance," said Lady Bess, "let it flourish."

"And if they should wish to marry?" asked Sir John.

"By all means, let them be joined," she retorted. "In time, Owen will become the chief scribe and hold a lofty position. He will make a suitable mate for Ellen."

* * *

A new age was dawning in Landowill Castle: A serf would be permitted to marry a noble lady.

Meanwhile, Lady Melva, Sir John's oldest sister, had designs on Thomas, the exchequer, an older man and set in his ways. Thomas was not responsive to her attentions as he felt uncomfortable, being a plebe. When it became apparent that Lady Ellen and the scribe's assistant, Owen, were to be wed, Thomas responded to Lady Melva more kindly.

Thomas grew bolder and bolder, and at last, on the day of the wedding for Owen and Lady Ellen, he sought out Lady Melva.

"Lady Melva, you would do me great honor if you were to marry me," Thomas said to her.

"My good man, think you not that my brother will disapprove?"

"Indeed not! He has already given one of his other sisters, who is your sister, Lady Ellen, to the serf's son, Owen, has he not?"

"Quite so," she answered.

"And I come from higher stock than that Owen boy. My father was an exchequer before me, and his father before him."

"Then," said Lady Melva, "I see no need to delay any further, my dear Thomas. Let us approach my brother immediately."

Friar Paul was not enthusiastic about uniting a patrician with a plebe for the second time, but Sir John implored him to perform the ceremony.

Sir John said to the friar, "My dear brother, our sister Lady Melva is not getting any younger!"

"So be it," said Friar Paul.

With one more sister to marry off and two daughters growing up, Sir John pondered how to bring prospective suitors into Landowill Castle. Hosting tournaments would have been a good source, but he could not bring himself to hold a tournament at his castle since his experience in real battle had been a painful part of his life.

"What can we do?" Sir John asked Lady Bess.

"Give a party," she said. "Give many parties and invite all the knights you have known and families from nearby castles. They have sons, you know."

"By the saints above, we will!"

* * *

Fifteen years after Sir John became master of Castle Landowill, he was widely known as the one-footed lord who profited from the fruits of his orchards and who broke the rules of society by teaching the serfs to read and write and letting two of his sisters marry commoners.

He was a man before his time.

\# \# \#

THE TEARS OF WAR

Corporal Rebecca Winslow, U.S. Army, was stationed in Heisburg, Germany. It was a small town but significant, crucial to the success of General Thayer's extensive plan to take over more enemy territory.

Rebecca, an average height Mid-westerner, with light brown hair and hazel eyes, did routine office jobs in the General's Headquarters in Heisburg. She and two other WACs were tolerated by the male enlisted members, but just barely. Their feeling was that the war zone was no place for women. That collective opinion was no problem for her. She had no desire whatsoever to be a true warrior, putting to use the Army's multi-arms-handling courses taken in basic training. She was satisfied to be as close to the "action" as this office afforded.

But fate, or destiny, had other plans for the WAC corporal.

It became necessary, one day, for someone to be courier for special orders to go to a forward encampment; a change of an attack plan was to be put in place. It turned out that the office had lost almost half the staff due to rotation. The men who were left in the office were far too valuable for one to be sent out as a courier. They were needed to perform the workings of the office. With the other WACs' reassignments' having sent them elsewhere, Corporal Winslow was "low man on the totem pole," therefore, she was selected to haul the courier pouch.

Rebecca did not have time to change into fatigues for the motorcycle ride to the forward encampment. Timing was eminently important; therefore, she held her skirt tightly around her legs and entered the motorcycle sidecar as gracefully as possible.

It was a good hour's ride to the forward position. Corporal Winslow delivered the courier package to a battle-weary Captain, coming out of his tent, giving verbal instructions over his shoulder to his clerk inside.

She waited for a possible reply. The Captain read the orders swiftly, then informed her there would be no reply. She was released to return to the motorcycle sidecar.

Incoming artillery blasts interrupted her departure. Before she got to the motorcycle, it literally blew up in her face. The vehicle and the driver were blown to bits. Other blasts fell all around her. She lay face down, sprawled on the ground, outside the Captain's tent, paralyzed with fear. Death and destruction were all around her.

When the artillery attack subsided, she arose slowly and surveyed the situation. The Captain was dead. Inside the tent, the Captain's clerk showed signs of being alive. She searched for a medic.

* * *

Sergeant Thomas Gear and his seven-man squad were pinned down behind a ridge. An enemy machine gun was entrenched in the next ridge ahead of them. The Sergeant had to lose only one man to determine what was happening. Searching their surroundings, he determined there was no way out except for a suicide run for the machine gun nest.

Wait. Oftentimes, that's what this war was about. Wait for something better to show itself: a better way, a better tactic, a better idea. The Sergeant truly needed a better idea. His squad nipped at the two-man German machine gun now and then. But the effort was absolutely useless. They were getting nowhere. He was running out of options. He had to make a move of some kind sooner or later.

While Tom wrestled with his indecision, he searched their surroundings once more. No trees for cover; too far afield to send one man to the left or to the right to pick off the nest. But an answer came to him "from above"? No, it was from their right side.

Rifle fire is what he heard. Three shots. The machine gun had stopped chattering sporadically. Indeed, it had stopped altogether. Putting his helmet onto the end of his bayonet, the Sergeant raised it slowly above the ridge line. There was no response from the enemy machine gun. Carefully, one by one, the men of the squad stood up. One rushed to the nest to find both German soldiers dead. Another rushed to the right to see what or who had disposed of the Germans.

The boy looked frail in his fatigues, no battle gear in sight. Only the rifle.

Private Alan (Pawnee) Wright stepped over the edge of the bomb crater where the boy stayed, seeming to be paralyzed.

"Come on up, boy. It's safe, now that you've wasted the Germans single-handedly."

"Sorry I missed on the first bullet."

"No complaints from us! You saved our hides! Thanks a lot, buddy," said Pawnee, whose nickname came from his ancestry: Alan Wright was half Pawnee, half Irish, with dark complexion, straight black hair, blue eyes. The blue eyes were bright and clear and sometimes searching. No one knew what they were searching for. But they were searching.

Such as at this moment, as he and the boy walked back to the ridge where the rest of the squad had climbed up onto, Pawnee thought the boy was awfully young to be soldiering in a man's war. They arrived at the ridge and joined the squad.

"This boy saved our skins, guys! We owe him big time!" Pawnee announced.

"Yeah." "Yeah." "Where'd you come from, kid?" "What's your unit?"

The "boy" took off his helmet. A collective gasp came from the men. This boy was quite obviously a girl! Bangs, straight hair cut to just below the ear lobes, glorious hair, they all thought. Not quite so tall as Pawnee who stood beside her. Pawnee himself was medium height for a man.

Sergeant Gear looked at the girl and asked, "What in the name of God are you doing out here? And what's your name?"

She answered, "I'm Corporal Rebecca Winslow, Headquarters at Heisburg. And, Sergeant, to answer your question 'what am I doing out here,' I'm embarrassed to say I'm lost."

The guys laughed heartily. The Sergeant grinned.

He said, "Suppose you tell us what this is all about? How did you get all the way from Heisburg? And why?"

She told them the story, from beginning to end. The ending was what fascinated them all the most. Back at the encampment, nearly everyone there was killed, a few injured. She was the only one not harmed. She could find no medic for the Captain's clerk. When she returned to him, he had died. She removed his battle fatigues and put it on herself. She found someone's rifle and checked the tent for ammunition and found it. She stuffed C rations in a pocket and a water container in another. She had no maps, not the faintest idea of which way it was back to Heisburg, but struck out anyway. And later, when she heard the machine-gun sounds, she threw herself into the nearby bomb crater, crawled up to the edge, and saw where the bullets were coming from, almost dead ahead, a bit to the right. She took aim, and fired.

Again, she apologized for the wasted first bullet.

"No need for THAT, Corporal. You saved our lives with the second and third bullets. That's what counts. Good shooting, Corporal!" The Sergeant was lavish with his praise. The men put in their two cents' worth, as well. She was overwhelmed with the comments. What now? She asked herself.

And that was exactly what the Sergeant was asking himself. What now? What the devil am I going to do with this female, who saved our lives? Since she didn't know how to get back to Heisburg, and was far too far for her to hoof it, especially alone, Gear decided she must come with them. There was no way out but to take her with them.

The Sergeant called for his radioman, to crank up the telephone equipment. Sarge had to report the loss of one man and give coordinates for the Graves and Registration Unit to locate the fatality.

Then they were headed for Breusch, a small town about ten miles ahead of them. There were at least three more hours of daylight. They continued their trek to Breusch before stopping for the night.

* * *

Pawnee stood the 2-4 watch; Iggy (Francis Ignatius Snyder) relieved him. At 0500, Iggy awakened the Sarge, who looked at the sky, just now turning light, then ordered Iggy to wake the others. Time to eat some rations and move on.

Iggy made the rounds: Tony (Anthony Malatti); Ziggy (John Ziegler); Willie and Eli (Willard Johnson, and Elijah Goad, friends since childhood, enlisted together at Jackson, Mississippi); and Red (James West, a redhead). Iggy wakened Pawnee last because he had been relieved of the night watch barely two hours ago.

The Sarge noticed that Becky (the squad gave her the nickname yesterday) was still asleep. Did Iggy think she didn't count? What the hell, he said to himself, I'll wake her myself.

Becky sat up stiffly, trying to flex her aching muscles. She missed her cot back at Headquarters. She wondered if she would ever see that place again. She felt like an intruder, a third leg. She would try not to be a burden. If there should be another day to get to Breusch, she would volunteer to do *something* to help out. Argh!

Camp was broken, and they continued the march to their mission. At noon, they stopped for their first break of the day. Although Becky was dead tired, she was still standing when she looked around and said to anyone, "What day is this?" She held her helmet by the strap, the bucket-shaped head gear dangling against her thigh.

Sarge answered, "September 3rd. Why?"

"This is my birthday. I'm 21 today!"

"Hey, Beck!" Tony shouted. "I got a present for you. Come on, guys, let's line up to give Becky a birthday kiss!"

Before she could protest, the line was formed, Sarge in front, Tony behind him.

The Sarge kissed her on the lips. Tony did the same. Red was bashful and merely brushed his lips against her cheek. Eli and Willie took turns picking up her right hand, bowing low, and kissing the back of her hand, each one wondering if he were doing it properly. Ziggy and Iggy, suddenly also bashful, brushed her cheek with a light touch of their lips.

Becky noticed, when each had taken his turn, that Pawnee had not been in the line. She looked around the group and found him off to one side of the group, sitting on a fallen tree trunk, cleaning his rifle, apart from the others. She walked over to him, stood in front of him and said, "Pawnee, aren't you going to give me a birthday kiss?"

Without looking at her, and without speaking to her, he placed his rifle against the fallen tree trunk. He stood up in front of her. He reached across to take her face in his hands. He kissed her like none of the others had. It was a slow, tender, long kiss that became more emotional. He removed his hands from her face to embrace her with his arms. She raised both her arms outward, let her helmet drop to the ground, then wrapped her arms around him.

The rest of the squad watched, amused at first. Strangely affected later, as they watched. Finally, one by one, they looked away, no one speaking, each one looking for some unnecessary chore to occupy the moments as they passed.

Rebecca and Pawnee ended the kiss. They looked at each other with wonderment, with a feeling that something new and magnificent had happened.

Sarge stood, watching, with hands on his hips. He looked wistful, but no one else noticed. Each of the rest of the men of the squad was touched in some way with the turn of events. This *was* an event, one to be remembered.

Pawnee picked up his rifle and led Becky a short distance from the group. Another fallen tree trunk was where they sat and talked quietly, each telling the other the big and little happenings of his or her short life. The attraction between them was instant.

Becky told him that she was born in Wisconsin, on a dairy farm. She knew a lot about cows, it turned out, but not very much about people. She had been engaged to be married to a high-school sweetheart, but he was killed while fighting the War in the New Hebrides. Then she enlisted in the Army.

Pawnee had a more forlorn history. Born in Kansas, he barely remembered his father, who had left the mother and four children and was never heard from nor seen again. Alan was the oldest child and soon figured out that the only way he could help his mother and brother and sisters was to enlist in the Army and send the biggest part of his pay, by monthly allotment, to his mother.

As soon as they had exchanged these meager facts of their lives, Sarge called the men together to continue their march. Pawnee took Becky's hand and led her back to join the squad. He picked up her helmet on the way and handed it to her. She put it on, then reached for her rifle, which was nearby, and shouldered it. They began the trek, single file. Pawnee moved to the place in front of Ziggy, Becky directly in front of Pawnee.

* * *

Sergeant Gear led his squad through the forest, instead of the road, in order to prevent their being detected by German patrols.

As they walked through the forest, Pawnee realized that he must not let his preoccupation with Becky keep him from being alert to whatever risks lay ahead of them. In the forest, they were reasonably safe. But soon, they will be approaching Breusch where real danger lurks.

In half an hour, the squad arrived at the outskirts of Breusch. The Sarge sent two men into the town to scout it for Nazi presence. They returned with a possible "negative" finding. The squad pushed a bit farther into town and entered an empty, shelled building.

Red was the squad radioman, and the Sarge asked him to get Headquarters on the line. He reported in and asked for further orders. After ending the radio contact, he took all members of the squad with him, except for Ziggy and Becky.

"Sarge," she said to him, "you don't need to assign a babysitter to me."

"No baby-sitting going on, Corporal. Ziggy is our 'safe' man. If he determines that the rest of us are wiped out, it's up to him to get back to Headquarters. He has to report what has happened. You need to get back, too, to report to your superior and tell him everything that's happened."

"Everything?" asked Pawnee.

The Sarge gave him an amused look. "Well, not *everything*." Turning to Becky, he said, "What about that, Corporal?"

"Yes, Sarge. Whatever you say, Sarge."

Addressing the others, not including Ziggy and Becky, Sarge said, "Let's move out!"

And they were gone, with Pawnee pausing to give Becky a "V for Victory" sign.

She smiled.

* * *

Becky and Ziggy waited, uneasily, for almost two hours before they heard irregular shooting in the streets. It made her heart jump up into her throat---not because she was scared for herself, but because she was scared for the others in the street fighting, namely Pawnee.

At last, the door was flung open. Tony was first into the room. Then Willie and Eli, assisting someone else to walk between them. Actually, they were half-way carrying him. Becky couldn't determine who it was, helmet on, head down. Whoever it was, he was wounded.

Willie and Eli put the limp body onto a table in the middle of the room. Becky went to him and saw that it was Pawnee.

Her worst fear had come true. "He's wounded!" she said to Eli.

"Yes, ma'am. Lost lotsa blood. Pretty weak."

"Oh, my God!" she breathed. She took his hand in hers. It seemed to affect him. He stirred and tried to speak.

"Becky?" He coughed, struggling for breath.

"Yes, Darling. I'm here. I'm here with you."

Pawnee was the only victim in the skirmish that the squad encountered farther into the town. Now Sarge was busy on the radio-phone, giving his report and requesting orders. Eli stood by, watching and listening to the exchange between Pawnee and Becky. Willie took him by the arm and led him a short distance away from the two.

Before they moved on, Becky turned to look at them and asked, "Is he going to be all right?"

The two men looked sorrowfully at her, each shaking his head, No.

"Pawnee . . . Alan . . . Please don't leave me, dearest. Please stay with me," she whispered.

He opened his eyes, saw her, recognized her, and smiled. "I love you, Rebecca."

"Oh, Darling. I love you so much, it hurts!"

"I know."

Alan (Pawnee) Wright breathed his last. He was gone.

Rebecca wept . . . and wept.

* * *

Corporal Rebecca Winslow had advanced to Sergeant by the time VJ Day was celebrated. She had been transferred to Fort Meyers, Virginia, and then to Fort Riley, Kansas. One afternoon, late, she had a visitor at her desk. She looked up from the files she was sorting.

"As I live and breathe! Sarge! What on earth are you doing here?"

He stole a swift glance at her left ring finger and saw that it was unadorned. "Looking for you, Beck. How about a change from mess hall chow and having dinner with me?"

"You don't have to ask twice! What time?"

"When you get off?"

"That'd be 1700."

"I'll pick you up then. Unless . . . you're all allowed to wear civvies off the post?"

"Yes, but we have to keep them in a locker off the post."

"Ah, well, in that case, I'll pick you up here, 1700 sharp."

"Yes, Sarge." She looked at the bank of ribbons on his chest. There were so many, she couldn't absorb them all. Then she saw the different rating badge on his arms, and she said, "Whoops, I guess I should address you as 'Master Sergeant!'"

"Affirmative!"

* * *

At dinner in a quasi-sophisticated restaurant, they stood out like two beacons, in their uniforms. She asked him, "When did you make that rarefied rank, Sarge?" She backed up. "I mean, *Master Sergeant.*"

"'Sokay, Beck, you can keep on calling me Sarge. I kinda miss it." He shifted gears. "I've been a Master Sergeant for only a couple of months now."

"I noticed that you got a Purple Heart. What happened?"

"Really minor, but major enough to get the Heart."

"I cannot even remotely fathom where you've been, what you've been through."

"Not wanting to bring up sad thoughts for you, Becky, but I have to tell you that the skirmish in Breusch was the worst event of my entire war experience!"

"It was for me, for sure, losing Pawnee. I still dream about him, in spite of the fact that our so-called 'courtship' was so short-lived."

"I felt and still feel so responsible for his losing his life," he said.

"Wasn't your fault, Sarge. You had a mission. Pawnee got the bullet. Could've been any one of the others, you included. Please, for my sake, do not feel responsible for him anymore."

"You mean that, don't you?"

She nodded vigorously.

She bolted the salad, ate half the steak, ate half the baked potato, and scarfed up all the vegetables. Then passed on dessert. Over coffee, she asked him how did he find her? They had never communicated with each other since she was returned to Headquarters at Heisburg.

"I have an old buddy in the Pentagon. He owed me some favors. I called in one, and he found you for me. I came here as soon as I could get a three-day pass."

"And," she said, squinting her eyes, "why would you want to do that?"

"I never forgot you, Beck. Sometimes I've had nightmares about that day Pawnee bought it, and we all had to stand by, helpless. I wanted to take you in my arms, then and there, to comfort you, but . . . . ."

"But what?"

"But . . . I don't know. Something, something stupid held me back. Stupid!"

"You're beating yourself unnecessarily, Sarge. Take it easy!"

"I can't, Beck." He looked at her seriously. "What I really wanted was to have you all to myself. There! I said it!"

"Sarge, I'm touched."

He gave her a faint smile.

"That's better," she said.

He went on. "Pawnee always had a look in his eyes–a look as though he were seeking something. Maybe for someone--someone to love. I think he found it, at last. You."

She was listening carefully, regarding him intently.

The Master Sergeant continued. "I feel as though I can't be a complete person, until I get you to look at me, one day, like you looked at Pawnee, after he kissed you on your birthday." He thought for a moment. "If only I could get *you* to look at me like you did at him."

Smiling, she asked, "Give me a chance?"

\# \# \#

115

THE TOUR GUIDE

Yuki Agara stepped off the train in a small station at the foot of Mount Fuji. She walked one block to the terminal that housed the bus tours for that area. She checked in for her first day at work without a "checker." A checker was someone from the tour company who had trained the tour guides. Yuki was on her own today.

Stopping in the ladies' rest room, she checked her hair, her lipstick, and her uniform. She liked her uniform: medium gray skirt, jacket, and a matching cap. She wore a vibrantly white shirt, open at the neck. She wore a large pin on her left lapel, with the tour company's logo and her name. Her shoes were medium-height heels, Navy blue. The shoulder bag matched the shoes.

She wondered, briefly, what her bus driver would be like. She hoped he would be pleasant and friendly—not surly and overbearing. One of her checking-out tours had such a driver. It gave her a shudder to think about it. "Here's hoping for the best," she said to herself.

She left the rest room and reported to the kiosk where the new tour guides gathered to get their bus numbers assigned. The drivers were already on board, engines started.

The supervisor walked Yuki to her bus, No. 114, and introduced her to the driver. "Mr. Hitori, this is Miss Yuki Agara, your new tour guide, beginning today." Facing Yuki, the supervisor then said, "And this is Mr. Akido Hitori."

"How do you do? And welcome to my magic coach, Miss Agara."

"How do you do, Mr. Hitori? Magic coach?"

"Climb aboard and see for yourself!"

Yuki was impressed with the formal/informal beginning . . . and relieved. She had some trepidation about starting out with a stranger. But already, she felt 'at home.'

A shadow passed over her as she thought, "I hope I don't forget my little speeches and the lyrics to the two songs we've been taught!"

The shadow passed as she glanced at Mr. Hitori in time to see him give her a thumbs-up sign.

"How American," she thought.

* * *

Speaking of America, she said to herself, I see that we have a little American family coming on board: father, mother, and two little boys. The father was very tall for Japanese vehicles, and he asked Yuki if he may sit in the front seat where his knees would not press against the back of a seat in front of him. Yuki granted him the request. The older boy sat with his father. The mother and the younger boy sat several rows farther back into the bus.

The bus was full. Akido pulled away from the bus parking area. Yuki began her first-ever welcoming speech. So far, so good, she mused. Something made her turn her head toward Mr. Hitori. He was smiling broadly at her, one eye on the road, one eye on her, it seemed.

* * *

"And now, ladies and gentlemen," speaking in Japanese, for that was the bulk of her passengers. The American family would simply have to watch the passing scenery. However, Yuki would, in some cases, relate a story here and there in English—for the benefit of the foreign tourists.

"I wish to tell you an ancient Japanese legend. It takes place in this area where we are traveling. A young Prince took a long journey, far, far away from his home. He encountered dragons and villains, but he was charmed by the gods in that he always overcame the enemies, no matter who or what they were. In this very same valley, the Prince halted his retinue to rest a few days before proceeding on the long journey still ahead of them.

"At the inn where he and his group stayed, there was a ravishingly beautiful servant girl. The Prince fell madly in love with her, and she returned with passion for him. The High Priest, who was a part of the Prince's traveling companions, spoke strongly to the Prince, warning him that this romance must come to a swift end. It is not fitting for a Prince to consort with a servant girl.

"The Prince paid no heed to the Priest and pursued the hapless servant girl with eagerness. He planned to take her with him when he left the inn, but it must be a secret. The Priest found out the plan devised by the Prince and pronounced a curse upon the Prince.

"In the middle of the night, the Prince rode from the inn, with the servant girl behind him on his favorite steed. Without his guards to protect him, they made good time through the valley. When the alarm went out that the Prince had stolen away in the night, the Priest pursued the lovers with the Prince's own guardsmen!

"The Prince and the servant girl encountered a band of thieves who slay the Prince and abducted the servant girl. The guardsmen, egged on by the Priest, had chased after the fleeing Prince and servant girl, only to find the Prince dead and the servant girl missing. Then the bandits returned to slay all the guardsmen and the Priest!"

"This valley where we are now traveling has a moaning wind blowing through it every night–the cries of the servant girl, who mourns for her beloved Prince."

* * *

At the lunch stop, Akido said to Yuki, "Will you take lunch with me, Miss Agara?"

"Is it permitted, Mr. Hitori?"

"Of course it is permitted. Tour guides and bus drivers are encouraged to get to know one another, to learn of their likes and dislikes, to be a compatible team for the tourists to be happy."

"High sounding to me, Mr. Hitori . . ."

"Miss Agara, if we are to be friends, we must be on first-name basis!"

"I am not accustomed to addressing someone I've just met by his first name."

"I will help you. Try 'Akido.'"

"Akido." She smiled in spite of herself, and he returned it. She said, "Now you try the 'Yuki.'"

"With pleasure, my dear Yuki. I liked the story about the Prince and the servant girl. True tragedy! Good riddance for the interfering Priest!" He slammed his fist into his other hand. "I never heard that legend before."

"I never did, either. But . . . true or not true, it's a lovely story to explain the nightly moaning winds in that valley."

They selected a restaurant and were seated together, away from their bus tourist passengers.

After they studied their menus and gave their orders, Akido said, "I also liked your song that you sang this morning. I hope you sing some more this afternoon."

"I will."

"I really like your singing."

They passed the lunch hour companionably. Yuki liked Akido's sense of humor. She liked his smile and his laugh. She liked it that he liked her singing. She liked much too much of him.

On the road again, Yuki began with the song she told Akido she would be singing.

> Oh, little maiden of the forest,
> Where do you come from?
> Oh, little maiden of the forest,
> Come to me. Come to me.

Oh, little maiden of the forest,
Why do you tarry?
Oh, little maiden of the forest,
Come to me now. Come to me now.

Akido was having a bad time trying to keep his mind on the driving, Yuki was so enchanting. He asked himself, where does she get these ditties? Why does her voice seem so sweet to me?

By late afternoon, the bus had returned to the train station from where it had started the tour. Passengers alighted, some of them passing a tip to him–everyone passing a tip to Yuki. He was not jealous. If anything, he was pleased and . . . something else. What was it? He was proud. Proud he drew a new tour guide so beguiling, so . . . he thought on this part for a moment. So alluring!

Yuki caught her train back to the city and to her apartment. Akido caught his train, the same as hers, to another part of the city. They rode together. She alighted before him. They said goodnight to each other.

That night, she dreamed of him, and he dreamed of her. She awakened the next morning, looking forward to another day on the tour bus. He awakened with warm feelings for the charming Yuki.

At the kiosk, Yuki reported to the supervisor who marked her present on her attendance chart. With a quickened step–and a quickened heartbeat–she approached Bus No. 114. Yes! Akido was there, and the engine was performing smoothly! She almost ran to the bus, once she had spotted his bus, him inside it at the driver's seat.

Breathlessly, she stepped into the bus to greet him. He smiled broadly and greeted her in turn. The tourists got on board. Yuki made a note of the number of tourists on the bus. She gave Akido the signal to pull out from the terminal. They were on their way.

Yuki told the same stories and legends and sang the same songs.

Akido thought he would never tire hearing them, Yuki's voice was so sweet, so pure.

They lunched together. They talked. They were almost late getting to the bus to open it up for the tourists to board again.

They returned to the train station for passengers to alight. Akido parked the bus at the terminal and joined Yuki for the train ride to their separate apartments. They dreamed about each other. They met the next morning and repeated the routine, never tiring of it, feeling fortunate to see each other every day except for their days off–the same days–only once a week..

Six months after Yuki joined the tour company, it was plain to her that she was truly in love with the Akido person. In the same breath, she brought up the thought that he surely was in love with her. That same day, after returning to the terminal, was the day that Akido asked if they could stop at the tourist's hotel near the bus terminal and the train station and engage a room, together alone.

Yuki had a moment of pleasure as she gave it a swift consideration. Then she was disappointed. Surely, by asking her to spend time in a hotel room with him, the act would cheapen the loving feelings they have for each other. This gave her pause—would he ask her to share a hotel room on the way home if he ever planned to ask her to marry him? She didn't think so.

She had doubts about their otherwise wonderful relationship. She refused.

Akido insisted, charmingly, of course. But Yuki was firm and refused once more.

"What am I to think, Yuki? That you do not love me?"

"And what am I to think, Akido, that you want me only for a moment of bliss and then go on about your usual business?"

"Would that it were not so, Yuki. I want you so desperately."

"Not desperately enough!" she retorted, and ran to catch their usual train. He did not follow her.

The next day was their day off. But the following morning, Yuki wondered how she could get on Bus No. 114 and keep her mind on her work. It wasn't easy.

Akido was barely civil. Yuki barely civil back to him.

Akido ached when she sang, he loved her voice so. He thought, "I cannot let this disagreement come between us. I must make amends."

Yuki thought, "I wish to the gods above that Akido had not asked me what he asked. I wish the abyss between us could be filled. That we could be good friends again. . . I wish that we could be lovers. Hi-eeee! That must not be!"

When the bus stopped for a lunch break, the tourists scattered in all directions, up and down and across the street to the various eating establishments. Akido said to Yuki, "Please, Yuki, let us eat together, as always. I wish to apologize to you for my bad manners of two days ago.

Yuki was so happy to hear his words that she, standing by his side, slipped her arm through his and leaned in toward him as closely as she dared, squeezing his arm as though she would never let it go.

That was enough of an answer for Akido. They practically

marched—no, ran—to the nearest restaurant and entered together and selected a table where they could be seated next to each other.

"Darling," he said. "I missed you so much yesterday, even though it was our regular day off. I missed you sorely!"

"And I you, dear one." Yuki beamed. Akido felt better.

* * *

The weeks and months passed. The two lovers, without ever consummating that love, continued to regale one another with endearments, to compliment each other lavishly, and to let their regard for each other grow into a passionate need.

Yuki began to wonder: Why does not the handsome Akido talk about marriage, after all this time of courting me during the tours? True, there is no courtship outside the touring hours. Curious. We have kissed, and it has been a heavenly experience! Not in public, of course. . . always behind a wall, in a maze, around a corner. I've seen Japanese young women with American male escorts, and they kiss in public, shamelessly! But Akido and I, we are Japanese and must obey Japanese social customs.

These thoughts plagued Yuki, night after night, upon returning to her apartment, alone. She wondered, each night, "What is Akido doing and thinking at this moment?"

* * *

It was the end of their work week. Yuki, on the tour bus, had sung her last song, related her last legend, her last story. She smiled at Akido. He was aware of her smile upon him, steadied his hand on the steering wheel, turned his head, and smiled back to her, openly.

Yuki, feeling warm love and a tinge of yearning, sat down in the tour guide's seat, behind the driver. The nagging thoughts plagued her once more: Why does Akido never ask her to spend their day off together? Is it up to me to be so bold and to ask *him*? Perhaps I will. This very day. At the end of the tour. Maybe on the train. Yes, that is what I will do.

* * *

At the end of the bus-tour day, Akido let all passengers off at the train station. Yuki told him, as the last passenger alighted, "I must tell my supervisor in the kiosk that the bus supplies are running low. I will join you at the train station, dear Akido.."

"Of course, darling Yuki."

She set off with glowing waves overcoming her body. That's what he did to her, she confessed.

After she conferred with the supervisor, Yuki walked from the kiosk to the train station. As she approached, she saw Akido standing with a woman, a stranger to Yuki. The woman smiled up at Akido and put her arms around his waist. He, without hesitation of any sort, gave her a big hug. He nuzzled her ear. The woman giggled.

What madness is this? Yuki asked herself. She approached the happy-looking couple.

"Akido, who is this?" Yuki demanded.

Akido broke away from the woman, looked strangely at Yuki, and said, "This is my wife, Ono. She came from the city today to surprise me . . . . ."

# # #

THE TYPIST

One day in May

Cindy Becker and Melissa Grant were co-workers at the Industry Insurance Co., based in Tarzana, California. Cindy was a receptionist; Melissa was a typist. She would, in other times, have been a member of a stenographer pool. But the department heads, branch heads, and division heads all had computers and input their own letters, memos, and reports. All that Melissa and the other typists had to do was pull up a document on their monitors, make corrections, and print out the final copies. Dictating a letter was outdated; stenography a dying art.

In due time, typists got a euphemism: keyboarder, or data entry operator, or input clerk. But in the end, they were still typists (using a computer keyboard instead of a typewriter keyboard). Melissa often thought, *Aren't euphemisms just great? But so pretentious!*

* * *

Cindy was pert, cute, flirtatious, and a lately-come-blonde young woman. Melissa was exactly the opposite: quiet, plain, shy, and a mousey brownhead. They lived in the same apartment building, three blocks from the company's building. They lived on different floors.

Other office personnel, both men and women, wondered what in the world did those two have in common? Melissa, herself, wondered why Cindy, so different from Melissa, insisted that they go to lunch together each day (except when Cindy had a lunch date with a boy friend); that they see a movie together (except when Cindy had a movie date with a boy friend); and that they go everywhere together (except when Cindy had a hot date with a boy friend).

Melissa noted that the boy friend was always a different guy. Where did Cindy get all that energy? She never had time to herself to clean her apartment, to cook a decent meal, nor to do her own laundry. She had time only to shop, date, and put herself together in the morning to go to work.

Cindy oftentimes asked Melissa to do her laundry.

Upon one of those occasions, Melissa said to Cindy, "You know, your asking me to do your laundry is getting a bit stale!"

"Aw, c'mon, Lissa. You know you love doing laundry!"

"Oh, sure. Mine, yes. Yours, I don't think so."

"Lissa! Don't be a poor sport! *Please* do my laundry this week. I'll make it up to you. Honest."

"Yeah, right." Melissa took Cindy's laundry bag reluctantly. She hated being treated like a servant!

June

A month later, Cindy realized she was wringing the life out of her friendship with Melissa; therefore, she planned an outing with Melissa and two men she had met only a week ago.

"Lissa! We're going to the Santa Monica Pier this Saturday. For the whole day! And with two really cute guys."

"Oh, great," Melissa grunted. "What about your laundry?"

"Forget the laundry. Saturday is the day to play. And we're going to have *fun*!"

"You know, Cindy, I really do have a problem with going out on a blind date, even if it is someone you already know."

"What's the problem? Bud's a nice kid. You'll like him."

"But will he like me? You're so bubbly, and I'm so quiet."

"Don't worry! Good grief, Lissa. You worry too much!"

Saturday

Early in the morning, Ray and Bud picked up the two young women in front of their apartment building. They took off in Ray's car for the Santa Monica Pier.

Ray and Cindy sat in the front seat; Bud and Melissa in the back. Ray and Cindy were already lovey-dovey, thought Melissa. Almost disgusting! Not safe to ride with that guy. He can't keep his hands off Cindy. Can't even keep his eyes on the road!

Bud was laughing with Ray and Cindy. It was a three-way bit of merriment; Melissa already felt like an outsider.

Ray parked his car, and they all alighted. They walked onto the pier. They rode the ferris wheel. They bought popcorn. They looked into all the shops.

The next thing Melissa knew, Ray and Bud, with Cindy in the middle were walking together, ahead of Melissa. She started to run to catch up with them.

She hesitated, then stopped. She watched them continue on without her. They seemed to have forgotten her, they were having such fun, the three of them. At last, they disappeared among the crowd, and she couldn't see them anymore. She stood alone, with people passing her from behind her and people passing her by going the opposite direction. She made a decision. She turned 180 degrees and began walking back toward the beach, the sidewalk and the street.

Melissa reached the street and waited at the bus stop. She boarded the bus she needed to get to another place on its route to make a transfer. She got off to wait for the transfer bus.

She sat on the bus-stop bench, put her face into her hands, and began to sob.

Suddenly, she felt a hand on her left shoulder.

"It can't be all that bad," a voice said to her.

Melissa stopped sobbing, wiped her face with her hands, and brought her hands down to her lap. She didn't dare move. The soft male voice did something to her. She couldn't explain it.

She said, "Oh, yes, it can!"

He squeezed her shoulder, then moved down to the other end of the bench, came back toward her and sat down beside her. She ventured a look at him. He was beautiful. Tall, blond, gray eyes, a bit on the thin side.

"Want to talk about it?"

"I'm not sure. I don't even know you."

"Sometimes," he said, "that's the best person to talk to–someone you don't know. Someone who doesn't know your friends and associates. Whatever it is, it'll not come back to bite you."

She said, wearily, "I'm not sure I know what you're talking about."

"Of course. I tend to speak in long and complicated sentences. My background; my training."

"And that would be?" she asked.

"We don't want to talk about me. It's you we want to talk about. Feeling better?"

"Oh, yes. Lots. And thank you."

"You are a lovely person, Miss ?"

"Grant. Melissa Grant. And you are?"

"Zack Blaine."

"How do you do?"

"Fine, and how do you do?"

She smiled. "Very fine."

"Good." He looked down the street. "A bus is coming. Will it be yours?"

"I don't know. I'm transferring onto No. 8."

"That's what I'm taking. May I ride with you?"

"I'd like that. Very much."

* * *

127

They chatted amiably as the bus made the stops on its route. The Zack person was most engaging. *Why in the world is he being so nice to me? We're perfect strangers!* Melissa was puzzled by it all. Puzzled, but in some way (which she could not explain to herself nor anyone else, had anyone asked), she was immensely pleased. This person, this man was making her feel very comfortable, very good. Very good about herself.

After almost 45 minutes of the bus ride, she said, "This is where I get off. My apartment is in the building on this corner."

"May I call you sometime, Melissa?"

"I didn't give you my number."

"Doesn't matter. I can find it. No sweat."

"If you say so. Goodbye, Zack. And thank you again for . . . . I don't know what I'm thanking you for."

"It's okay, Melissa. I get the message. And not Goodbye. 'So long,' Melissa."

He watched her as she got off the bus. He looked at the address of the apartment building as the bus drove by.

Melissa went straight to her apartment. She felt as if she were floating into the building, floating upward in the elevator, floating through her rooms. She had enjoyed the encounter with the Zack Blaine man, even if he did sideslip her question about his background and training. Strange.

Then she thought he had done that because he wanted to focus on her and her tears. Still, it was strange.

In spite of Zack's ability to lift her spirits, she thought once more about the fiasco at the Pier. *I have to face it,* she thought. *Cindy is popular; I am not! She's beautiful; I'm not even pretty.* This kind of thinking was getting her nowhere. Once again, Melissa Grant faced the fact that she was plain, perhaps even dowdy. No, not dowdy because she kept herself clean and ultra-neat. *Whatever possessed me to agree to going on a date with her and her two boyfriends? What a disaster!*

Then she thought of Zack Blaine again . . . and smiled.

* * *

After Zack said "so long" to Melissa, and the bus continued on its route, Zack waited for two blocks to pass, then got off. He crossed the street and waited for the next bus to go back to the transfer point.

Once there, Zack got off that bus, walked to his parked car, got in, and drove away.

* * *

Ray and Bud, with Cindy, stopped at the snack bar on the Pier to get some sodas. Ray suddenly looked around them and said off-handedly, "Where's Melissa?"

"Who?" asked Bud.

"Melissa! Where is she?"

Cindy was mystified. But not unduly concerned. "Maybe she's at the Ladies' Room."

"The Ladies' Room?" asked Ray. "That's a long way from here!"

Bud finally realized who they were talking about. He asked, "Should we go back to find her?" He said that half-heartedly. He showed no particular anxiety.

Cindy said, "Naw. She'll show up eventually. I'll have a 7-Up, Ray."

Sunday

Late in the afternoon, Cindy knocked on Melissa's door. Melissa opened it. Her face fell when she saw Cindy and wondered where did she get the guts to face her, after yesterday's humiliation.

"Where were you?" Cindy demanded.

"What do you mean, 'where was I'?"

"We looked and looked and couldn't find you. Where'd you go? We searched high and low and couldn't find you anywhere!" The lie came easily for her. "So where'd you go, Lissa?"

"Home. Where else?"

"Silly goose! You should have waited for us while we looked for you!"

"Don't call me that. I was sick of having the two guys hang onto you as if they were glued to you. I was sick of being ignored. Of course I came home!"

Cindy put her hands on her hips and demanded, "Did you do my laundry when you got back?"

"I did not!"

"Well, if you're going to sulk about yesterday, I wash my hands of the whole mess!"

"Is that all you have to say to me, Cindy Becker?"

"Hmmh!" She turned to go back to the door and left, slamming the door behind her.

Cindy returned to her apartment, saw the dirty-laundry bag, kicked it in its side, then lay down for a nap. She was dead tired. So much excitement yesterday. So much fun.

Tuesday

It was so easy. There she was in the phone book, "Grant, Melissa." No address. Then the phone number. Only one Melissa Grant listed. It was late evening. He dialed.

Melissa answered.

"Melissa? This is Zack Blaine."

"Ah, yes. I remember you!"

"How you doing since I saw you?"

"Great. I think I've rid myself of my so-called 'friend.' We had a real falling-out."

"Oh? That's too bad."

"No, it isn't. Good riddance! But I don't want to talk about that just now. How about you? How are you?"

"Very well, thank you. But I'll be a lot better if you were to tell me that you can meet me for lunch tomorrow. I remember your mentioning where you work. I know a café near there. The Rose Garden Café. Can we meet there at noon tomorrow? I hope you can! And do you know where it is?"

"Oh, sure, Zack. I know exactly where it is, and I'd like that a lot."

"Good, then. See you there tomorrow! At noon."

"Yes, Sir! Bye . . . I mean, So long."

He smiled at the telephone. "So long, Melissa."

Wednesday

At 11:45 in the morning, Cindy called Melissa on the phone at her desk. "Lissa, let's go to lunch. It's almost time to leave."

"Sorry, Cindy. I have a luncheon date with someone else."

Well! How can that be? She was wondering if Bud had made the date with Lissa. Then she thought better of it and dismissed the idea. "Somebody I know?" she fished for information.

"Hardly."

"That's it? 'Hardly'?"

"That's right, Cindy. And if you'll excuse me, I'm just on my way out now. See you at your desk."

Cindy looked at her handset, listening to the click followed by the dial tone. She didn't quite know what to think. Ten seconds later, Melissa passed her receptionist's desk. She waved to Cindy and kept on going. Cindy was truly baffled.

Zack was already at the café, seated in the reception area, waiting for Melissa. He stood up and went quickly to her as she came through the door. "It's so good to see you again, Melissa!" He picked up both her hands and squeezed them.

She squeezed back, surprised at herself for doing that. "Hi, Zack. It's good to see *you!*"

They were seated immediately. No waiting. They looked at their menus, gave their orders, gave up their menus. The waiter left.

"So, Melissa. How you doing today?"

"You wouldn't believe the fantastic morning I've had!"

"Tell me about it," he urged.

She went on to divulge some office gossip (okay for her to do that because he didn't know who she was talking about); she told about taking an exam toward getting a promotion; and she told about how her boss said she had made a very high score. Things were looking up.

"I can't tell you how happy I am for you."

Their orders were served.

At the beginning of a salad course, Zack plunged in with what he had been wanting to ask since he met her Saturday morning at the transfer bus stop. "Melissa," he began. "Can you tell me something about what made you cry last Saturday?"

"I can." She hesitated. "But I'm not sure I should tell you. Too personal. Too painful!"

"If it's painful, that's why you should share it with me. As for its being too personal, I guarantee you it won't go beyond me. I swear!" He thought better about that. He tried to amend it. "I mean, I would never, never, ever divulge another person's innermost feelings, her anguish."

They waited for the soup course to come.

She began. "I got separated from my girl friend and her two boy friends."

"So?"

She went on to explain that one of the men was supposed to be her date, but he, along with the two others of their foursome, ignored her completely–didn't even notice she had become separated from them–kept on going without a backward look, all three of them. "I felt miserable. I felt left out. I wasn't angry. I was . . ." she searched for a word . . . "I don't know what else I was."

"Disappointed?"

"That and more of whatever it was."

The soup arrived. It was very hot. Too hot to begin spooning it up and eating it.

He said, "I would like to meet this Cindy."

She blurted out, "Oh, sure! Of course you would! She's cute, blonde, and very beautiful!" She paused and then said, more softly, "She'll flirt with you. I know she will."

"I assure you, Melissa. That will not even phase me. It's you I'm interested in . . . . "

They began to eat the soup. He continued, "How about I accompany you back at work, and you can introduce us. It should be easy if she's a receptionist, as you told me the other day."

She nodded her assent.

* * *

"Cindy Becker, this is Zack Blaine."

"How do you do, Miss Becker?"

"Well, how's yourself, tall, thin and handsome?!"

Melissa mentally rolled her eyes, thinking: *here she goes–already!*

He ignored the greeting. Putting his hand on Melissa's arm, he asked her, "Is there an office policy that allows visitors at your workplace?"

"Yes. You want to see where *I* work?"

"Yes, indeed." To Cindy, he nodded, saying, "Excuse us, please?"

Cindy frowned as they walked through the typists' office door. Melissa barely revealed a tiny grin.

"This is it," she said to Zack.

"How many cubicles like this are there?"

"About fifty. All of us typists–or input clerks, if you like. Or data entry operators. Or keyboarders. Take your pick! At the outset, we're still typists."

"Looks as though this company spares no expense in outfitting each employee with all she needs. Very impressive! Even an extra chair in each space–for a visitor?"

"Yes. Would you like to sit down?"

"I'd better not. But thanks. I have a job to get back to, also!"

She almost asked what job that would be, but instead she said, "Thank you so very much, Zack, for the great lunch. I enjoyed it thoroughly."

"So did I. May I call you this evening?"

"I'd be happy to hear from you then."

He started to leave. She said, "Wait. I'll accompany you back to the elevator."

"Good."

They passed Cindy and waited at the elevator. She took his hand and said, shaking it, "Thanks again, for the wonderful noon hour." He held her hand with both of his. Then he bent down to put a light kiss on her cheek. The elevator arrived. He got on it. He waved to her just before the doors closed.

Cindy, watching them closely, sat with her mouth agape.

* * *

As promised, Zack called her that evening. She was pleased to note he did what he said he'd do. She couldn't say the same for most of the men she had dated–not, she reminded herself, that there were a huge number of them. A paltry number of them was more like it.

He said, "Melissa! I have two tickets for Saturday's matinee performance of 'Miss Saigon.' It's a re-production of the original. The reviews are good. Please tell me you can go with me!"

Saturday

When Zack rang Melissa's doorbell, she answered it, knowing who it would be. He was on time, arriving precisely when he said he would. "Come on in, Zack." With a sweep of one arm, she said, "This is my humble domain. Welcome."

"Lovely, Melissa. Just lovely. Very tasteful."

"Thank you. " She almost blushed. "Won't you sit down? I'd offer you a drink, but I don't drink alcohol. A Vernor's ginger ale?"

"What on earth is a Vernor's ginger ale?" he asked.

"It's time to try it. But don't breathe near the glass. Its fizz flies up your nose and makes you cough!"

"Pretty strong stuff!"

"You'll see."

* * *

Finishing their ginger ales, Zack said it was time for them to leave.

She felt wondrously marvelous. This was going to be an evening to remember, she was certain.

They left the elevator and headed for the street. At the main sidewalk, he turned to the right; she turned to the left. They stopped.

"Excuse me, Zack. The bus stop is this way."

"Excuse *me*, Melissa. I failed to tell you. I have an automobile. *This* way."

They giggled about that. But after he closed her door behind her, and then climbed into the driver's side, she said, "If you have a car, why did you take the bus in the city?"

"When I saw you on the bus-stop bench, crying, I left the car where it was parked to join you on your bus."

"Why would you do that?" She thought about it a tiny moment. Then, "You felt *sorry* for me?"

"Of course! Who wouldn't? You sounded as though your heart were tearing in two!"

He turned on the ignition, pulled out when the traffic had a break. They were on their way to the theater.

She was thoughtful. "Then, what did you do? Take another bus all the way back? To your car?"

"Yes." He stole a glance at her. "For you, Melissa. You were hurting. You needed help."

"And you were there for me, Zack. Thank you for that."

He smiled and, without looking at her (traffic was heavy), he put his hand onto hers and squeezed it. "You know you're welcome. It was my greatest pleasure of the day. Truly."

She smiled and turned her head away from him, tears welling up in spite of herself. She was so happy.

* * *

He took her to dinner after the matinee. They discussed the musical. They loved it. They loved the evening. They loved being together.

When he took her to her apartment door, she invited him to come in . . . for a cup of coffee. He accepted.

Seated together on the couch, she said, "Now then. It's time you told me more about yourself. Up to now, it's been all 'me, me, me.'"

"Where to begin?" he asked.

"Let's start with where you work and what you do. I haven't a clue what you do!"

He took a deep breath. He took another sip of the coffee. At last he said, "I have an office with desk and computer."

She nodded. "And your company? Your field?"

"No company."

"You have your own business?"

"Oh, no!"

"Well, then. What?"

He took another deep breath. After a significant pause, he looked at her. Finally, he spoke.

"I'm a priest."

* * *

A priest?!" Melissa was shaken to the core.

"Yes."

"How on earth do you explain the nice car, the fancy lunch, the elegant dinner, and the tickets to a popular and expensive musical?"

He answered, "My family is quite well off. They send me a generous check each month. They give me a new car every other year."

"And so, you bought the tickets?"

"No. A wealthy parishioner gave them to the Monsignor. He had already seen the original production. So he gave the tickets to me."

She was not only shaken, she was also dazed, bewildered. She thought, *I was beginning to fall for this man . . . hard! How foolish of me! What now?*

A silence fell between them.

At last, he said, "Oh, Melissa, I'm sorry if this news is unexpected. I'm so sorry. I really should have told you sooner–much sooner." He stood up. He said, "I best be going now."

He walked to the door of her apartment. She also stood up but stayed where she was. Her mind was whirling, wildly!

He reached the door and opened it, but before he went through it, Melissa ran to him and threw her arms around him, clinging to him more than she had intended.

He kissed her on the forehead.

Ah, she thought. *The kiss on the forehead kissoff! I was really beginning to care for this man. How stupid I've been. How could I know he's a priest?*

He removed her arms from around his waist. He walked through the door, closing it behind him.

The following November

Melissa answered her phone.

A voice asked, "Melissa?"

"Yes." Then, "Zack?"

"Yes, it's me. How are you, Hon?"

"What?! You haven't contacted me for five months! What's going on?" She was half angry; half apprehensive to hear from him!

"Darling, I'm phoning you from Sri Lanka. There's lots to tell you. Something to ask you."

"You have a nerve, asking a favor from me! Sri Lanka? What in heaven's name are you talking about?"

"Honey, I've left the priesthood and I've left the Church. It's been chaotic while I've been making those changes. That's mostly why you haven't heard anything from me.

"Meanwhile, I've been accepted into a nondenominational church here in Jaffna, second-largest city in the country. I'm undergoing extensive training before I get reassigned back to the States. I have an apartment furnished with everything I need, with one exception. You." A pause. Then, "Melissa, will you marry me?"

There was silence.

Quickly, he continued. "Take two months to get ready to come here. You can get a passport in L.A.; you can get a visa at the Sri Lankan Consulate in L.A. Put everything in storage except your favorite treasured items. Come as soon as all that is done. Please, Darling. Come to me here and marry me. The apartment needs a woman's touch–your touch, Melissa."

Still silence. "And I could use a really good typist, Honey!"

More silence. "Melissa, I'm sending you air tickets today. Tickets for a flight in two months. Please, Darling, say you'll come and marry me!"

He began to experience some anxiety. Her silence was unnerving. "Melisa! Say . . . something. Please."

"Zack . . ."

He broke into her hesitation with, "It's someone else, isn't it? You've found someone else!"

"Yes," she breathed.

"I knew it! I shouldn't have waited so long. Serves me right!"

She said, "It's not what you think."

"And what does that mean? Darling what can I do to make it up to you? What can I do to make you change your mind about the guy? Whoever he is."

She repeated, "Zack, it's not what you think."

"What? What're *you* talking about?"

"It's not another man." A pause. "It's a little girl. I'm in the middle of the process to adopt her."

Now the silence came from his end.

"Did you hear me?" she asked.

Finally, he answered, "Oh, yes. But, Honey, I don't believe it! What's this all about?"

"Bonnie has had a terrible and tragic life for a six-year-old. Her mother was murdered by her father, which she witnessed, and he's in prison."

"Good Lord!"

"And not only would it be traumatic to take her to a strange country, I'm not sure I'd be allowed to do that. Not for a very long time, anyway. The Agency has already ordered psychiatric counseling sessions for her. That'll be rather extensive. Years, perhaps.

"Zack, I'm all she has, other than an elderly great-aunt who can barely take care of herself, let alone herself and a little girl."

"Melissa!" he wailed. "Melissa. What am I going to do? I need you desperately."

"Not so desperately as Bonnie needs me."

"I'm devastated, Darling. I need your help, and want you with all my heart."

"You may want me, yes. But after waiting so long to contact me, and after all that's said and done, I think that what you *really* need . . . .is just a typist."

# # #

THE TUTOR

Martha Hansen dried her hair and wrapped her head with a towel, like a turban. Clutching her cotton robe around her body, she poured herself a cup of coffee and sat in a comfortable chair in the tiny livingroom. She picked up her College English Grammar book and settled down to do some serious studying.

Marty, as she was known by others, was tall with ash blond hair and hazel eyes. She regarded her figure as 'Midwestern farm-girl,' but co-eds on campus thought of her as svelte and willowy.

A knock on her door interrupted her reading. "Who on earth could that be? It's ten o'clock!" she said aloud. She went to the door, opened it as far as the chain guard would allow, and gazed upon a tall and young black man.

"Yes?" she asked.

"Martha Hansen?"

"Yes." She wondered who this fellow was.

"I'm Gilbert Lessiter."

Now she had it. He was a football hero already, making touchdown after touchdown in all the games they'd played so far this semester. Both men and women on campus had talked about him. He was a Boy Wonder and only a freshman. He had made a name for himself early on.

"And what is it you want, Mr. Lessiter?"

"Well, first of all, I'm Gil."

"Ah," she replied, "I'm Marty."

"Yes, ma'am. Well . . ." He hesitated, forgetting the speech he had made up before coming to her apartment.

"Yes?" She tried not to sound impatient.

"Well, you see, it's like this. I need help with some of my classes, and my friends told me about you, how smart you are, and how you're going to be a teacher--and they said you aren't tutoring anyone just now. Is that right?"

"That's correct. In what subjects do you need help?"

"'Rithmetic and English, mostly. The others I can manage. I like science, it's so interesting. But I gotta have math, so they tell me, to get through the science easy. Can you do that? Will you take me on?" He waited, holding his breath, hoping she'd say yes, hoping for all he was worth that she'd accept.

"Come on in, Gil, and have a seat. We'll work out something. Coffee?"

"No thank you, ma'am. Caffeine keeps me awake at night, and

I'm in training and have to get plenty of rest. He entered and let himself into a chair with the grace of a cat. She noticed that.

"Milk, then?"

"Oh, yes, ma'am. That'd be fine."

She poured his glass of milk in the cubby-hole kitchenette, just off the livingroom. After she handed him the milk, she sat in her usual chair, across from him. She looked him over, thinking, not bad looking, athletic type, big as a bear, agile as a deer, soulful brown eyes. She liked what she saw. But then, first impressions can be misleading.

During this first meeting between them, they discussed the cost of tutoring and the hours they could meet. She suggested Tuesday, Thursday, and Saturday afternoons.

"No can do Saturdays. That's game day."

"Sunday mornings I go to church," she said. He waited.

She nearly suggested Sunday afternoons but remembered that's her time to do catch-up from the previous week's studying and errands. What the heck, she thought, and said, "How about Sunday evenings?"

The schedule was set. They then discussed where to meet. They needed a table and chairs. The library was ruled out because of the regulation about silence. They decided to meet each time at the cafe across the street from the college's admin building.

* * *

Gil was a freshman and Marty was a sophomore. They attended Tracy College in Anders, Indiana. Gil was on an athletic scholarship. He still couldn't believe his good luck. He thought about the home he left behind.

Gil was the oldest of five children. His mother was raising the other four children virtually alone, maintaining two jobs. His father was an itinerant farmer, working his way across country as each section had crops ready for harvest. By the time he made it back to Recluse, Alabama, at the beginning of winter, he had enough money only to pay his way back north in the late spring. None was left for supporting his family. The mother didn't mind. Together they accepted the way things were, stoically and without complaint.

Marty, with no brothers nor sisters, had parents who were in academia. Her father was a professor at Chicago's Lewis Institute; her mother was a fifth-grade school teacher in mid-city. She took the "El" to go to work each school day. Marty was doing college on grant money. There was enough to live by herself in the tiny apartment. She loathed the idea of living in a dorm: all that trivial female chatter, the noise, the chance of having a disagreeable roommate. She loved her little apartment setup.

While Marty finished her coffee and Gil finished his milk, he said to her, "You know, you look great in a turban. If I was to put a jewel on your forehead, you'd look like a Rajah's wife."

"And that would make me a Rani, the Rajah's wife."

They smiled at each other.

"How d'you spell that? Ronnie."

She spelled Rani for him and said, "You're going to do just fine, Gil. You question what the tutor tells you. Keep it up!"

Later, Gil left the apartment, thinking that he needn't have dreaded the prospect of meeting her and asking her to be his tutor. It went quite well. In fact, already he was looking forward to their first session.

By the second week of tutoring, Marty had corrected Gil's use of "easy" to "easily" and explained the difference. She also explained the use of "if I was" versus "if I were." And, she corrected the way he had said forehead. She also helped him get rid of the "I gotta." She hoped she had not offended him, making the corrections. On the contrary, he was delighted to be set straight on things he never thought of, never knew.

In the third week, Marty said to Gil, "You really should be doing some reading for pleasure."

"Reading for pleasure! Are you kidding me? I have enough reading to do just for the courses!"

"Let's go to the drug store next door and pick out a paperback."

"Paperback? I can't do that!"

"Sure you can. Come on."

They entered the drug store, Marty with enthusiasm, Gil with anxiety. She led him to the paperback book section. He was overwhelmed at the selection, not knowing where to start. Not even wanting to start. She steered him toward a sports section. She selected a thin book and handed it to him.

"This is about football? Oh, sure I can read this!"

His trying to "read for pleasure" was a chore at first, but once he got into it, he could hardly leave it alone. The paperback resided in his back trousers pocket, ready to take out and read anywhere, anytime. He was hooked. Marty was pleased with his progress.

The next week, during the Tuesday session, Gil said to Marty, "You going to the game Saturday?"

"Good heavens! I never go to the games, not even during my

freshman year did I go to them."

"You gotta . . . I mean, you have to go to the game. Please. Cheer for us." No, he thought, cheer for me. "I want you to cheer for me, Marty."

She said, "I would love to go to the game and cheer for you, Gil. After all, you're the only member of the team that I know."

He said to himself, she said she would cheer for me. How does that make me feel? "Please say you'll go, Marty. Please."

"Very well. I'll get a ride with someone."

"That's my girl."

An awkward moment followed.

"I mean . . . "

"It's okay, Gil. I rather like the sound of that."

* * *

On Saturday night, Marty hitched a ride with three co-eds from her history class. One of them had a car. They followed the bus that carried the team to the stadium of a nearby town.

At the game, Gil was brilliant, scoring a touchdown in the last seconds of the game, bringing in the win. The Tracy College crowd went wild with joy.

Several Tracy fans, along with Marty and her three companions, waited at the bus for the team to shower, dress, and return to the bus. The fans wanted to reinforce their support to the team. Marty saw them approach, Gil among the first ones to appear. She ran to him, threw her arms around his neck, and said, "Congratulations, Gil! You were splendid! Your playing was dazzling!"

Gil was one of four black men on the team. He wondered if any of them, as well as the other team members, saw Marty's greeting. He was hugely pleased, as well as totally surprised.

She withdrew her arms from around his neck, wondering what on earth made her do that! Their faces were close. She effused further with, "I'm so proud of you, Gil."

"Gee, Marty. I don't know what to say. Except, thank you . . . a big bunch!"

The other three girls witnessed the rare scene, and they were appalled. In that moment, Marty became as a leper. The women did not speak to her once during the ride back to Anders.

The times were early sixties. Culturally, there was little or no fraternizing between blacks and whites. White women simply did not normally mingle with black men. It was unheard of.

They dropped Marty off at her apartment first. They gave her a more-than-frosty good night. Before the night was ended, those three co-eds spread the word "about Marty" throughout the women's dorm. The dorm was a-buzz for most of the rest of the night.

Marty didn't care what others thought about her. She felt good about what she did with Gil. Another thought came to her--he was like a kid brother.

When they dropped her off at her house, she opened the gate to the front yard, tripped up the steps to the porch, opened the door, and went upstairs. She saw him as she neared the top step. Gil was waiting for her.

She approached. He reached for her and wrapped his arms around her in a bear hug and squeezed, but not too tightly. Then he left abruptly, a huge smile on his face.

Marty noticed something different about Gil's behavior. Comparing him to other young men who had hugged her in the past, they always kissed her, too. Oh, well, she thought, can't fret about that now.

* * *

Their relationship had reached a new dimension. It was permanently altered. When Marty began explaining a point of grammar or a math formula, she put her hand on top of his and gave it a squeeze. Then he would turn his hand over and squeeze hers.

Gil had selected a second paperback. It was a spy-counterspy novel. He ate it up, not believing its veracity at all, but enjoying the narrative. One day he asked her, "Marty, what does this word mean?" He wrote down 'graciously.'

She said, "Let me use it in a sentence. 'He greeted her graciously.'"

"I still don't get it."

"He greeted her with warm and sincere courtesy."

"Like you greet me each time."

"If you say so."

"And I do."

* * *

A third paperback of Gil's choosing was a World War I story. He loved it, as much as the others. He was well into the book when he asked Marty at a Sunday evening session, "Okay, Teach, what's 'kest la- vi?'"

"What's what? Where did you hear that?"

"I didn't hear it. I read it in my book. He pulled the paperback from his back trouser pocket, and he pointed to the phrase he had read.

"Ah, yes. That's 'c'est la vie,' a French saying. It means 'that's life.'"

"French? I gotta . . . I mean, I have to learn French now?"

"No, no, not at all. But let me say this: it's good to pick up a French word or phrase now and then, as well as Latin, or German, or Spanish."

"I have to learn all those languages?"

"No, Gil. Just bits and pieces. You can throw them out in almost any group, and most people will understand each one. The world is becoming more and more cosmopolitan."

He gave her a baffled expression.

"I know," she said." 'Cosmopolitan' means worldly, so to speak."

"I'm so bewildered!"

"Good word, Gil, 'bewildered.' But don't be. You're doing just fine. You're going to have a solid foundation under you when you get out into the world. I guarantee it."

"Sure I will, with you as my tutor."

She smiled, and she felt as if she were glowing.

* * *

Beginning that evening, Gil began walking her home after the Sunday evening sessions. They talked some more about their families, their homes, how they missed all that at first but now they're content to be busy with the business of getting an education.

"Well, good night, Marty." They had reached the gate.

"Good night, Gil." He turned to leave. "Wait," she said. "Would you like to come up to the apartment?"

"Oh, Marty, I don't think so." He paused. "I don't trust myself."

"That's all right. I trust you."

"I better not . . ."

"I know, I know. It's late. And you're in training."

He gathered her into his arms and whispered into her hair, "Sometime, Honey. Sometime."

"Of course," she said. "And it's just as well. I'm not sure, after all, that I can trust *me*!"

* * *

The next day, he had an hour between his last class and football practice. He took a bus to the edge of town and went into the city's only "nice" restaurant. He asked for a menu to keep. He took it back to his dorm room and began reading it, vaguely recognizing certain words as being French words. Then he went to football practice.

Upon his return to the dorm, he picked up the menu again, along

144

with the French dictionary Marty had given him. He studied the French words on the menu, and other French words he wanted to know. He memorized them and vowed not to forget them before November.

Toward the end of October, at an afternoon session, Gil reached across the table, took her hands in his and said, "Marty, we should go out on a date."

"Whatever brought that on?

"You have a birthday coming up, and I'd like to take you out for dinner."

She smiled. "Here at the cafe?"

"Oh, no! At the Shadows, just inside our little city's city limits."

"Gil, that's an expensive place! You haven't funds to take me to dinner there!"

"Yes, I do. I have savings left from the summer job."

"But we have no car."

"You mind the bus?"

"Of course not."

"Then," he said with a smile, "it's a date. Right?"

He really would have liked to give Marty a topaz (because he had read somewhere, sometime that the birth stone for November is a topaz) for her birthday, but that was out of the question. He didn't have *that* kind of money. So he did the second-best thing he could think of: take her to dinner at the Shadows and . . .

* * *

They studied the menu, then Gil ordered for both of them, entirely in French!

Marty was amazed. "Gil, where in the world did you learn how to speak what sounded like almost impeccable French?"

He told her about borrowing the menu, studying the French words and the French dictionary, and practicing the sentences until he had them memorized.

"Gil, what a dear you are, to go to all that trouble."

"Nothing's too much trouble for you, Marty."

They returned by bus to the campus area and walked together to her apartment.

"Want to come up for awhile? Another cup of coffee?"

"I better not, Honey. It's already late, and I have to walk to the dorm from here."

"I know. You're in training, and you need your rest."

"True."

145

"Thank you, Dear one, for a perfectly lovely evening."

"My pleasure, Honey."

They were on the porch now. He put his arms around her, and he kissed her good night. Speaking softly into her hair, as they stood, embraced, he said, "Marty, Honey, I want you to marry me after we finish college and after I get a job, get established. Would you wait for me, Marty?"

"You know I would, Gil."

Later, in her bed, she had difficulty going to sleep. She reflected, indigestion? No. A first kiss from Gil? Yes! And don't forget the quasi proposal! She realized that no other boy-man had ever kissed her like she was kissed tonight. Somehow, she fell asleep, a smile on her face.

* * *

As the school year neared its end, Gil asked her a question that had been on his mind for several weeks. "Marty. What're you going to do this summer?"

"Go back to Chicago. My parents won't let me lolligag around the house, so I'll probably get a job there."

An alarm went off in his head. "Any chance of your getting a job here?"

"I suppose so. However, the job market in Chicago is far superior to the market here in Anders."

He looked askance.

"I'll check it out locally."

He brightened.

"So," she went on, "what are *you* going to do this summer?"

"I'm going home to visit Momma. Have to come back in a week, though, to start my job on campus, working in the Book Store. Summer students will be the only customers for books and supplies, until a week or so before the regular semester begins."

"You have a summer job on campus? How on earth did you arrange that?"

"It's part of the scholarship terms and expectations."

"That's great! I'm impressed!"

"With the job or the scholarship?"

"Neither. It's the word 'expectations' that got my attention. You didn't miss a beat when you said it. Your pronunciation is improving. Good work!"

"Pronunciation? Not pronounciation?"

"No, the verb is 'pronounce,' to be sure, but when it becomes a noun, it's 'pronunciation.'

"Thank God that doesn't happen with all verbs-to-nouns! Or does it?"

"I don't think so. None comes to mind, anyway." Then she said, "You're really sharp, Gil. A natural. That'll carry you far. Keep up the good work."

"Marty, I'm not worthy of all your praise."

"Oh, yes, you are, Gil. Worthy of every bit of it. Everything I've been teaching you, you retain it and apply it and use it. You really have a good head on that magnificent body."

"Marty! If I were a white man, I'd be blushing!"

She giggled. He grinned.

* * *

Marty had enough funds (thanks to the tutoring fees she had earned) to go to Chicago for a week's visit. She told Gil about that and thanked him for the pay she got from him.

"You know, Marty, what you give me is worth a whole lot more than what I'm paying you. I owe you big time!"

"No, Gil, I owe *you* big time."

"For what?" he asked, a bit skeptically.

"For your asking me to tutor you. I've grown intellectually, along with you. The challenges you bring to me give me invaluable experience in teaching. Yes, I owe *you* big time."

"Did you find a job in Anders?" He felt apprehensive, half afraid she'd have to stay in Chicago for her summer employment.

"Oh, yes, I forgot to tell you. I've been hired by the local newspaper to be proofreader for the summer while their regular one goes on a long vacation."

He breathed a large sigh. "I'm so glad."

* * *

Their week-long breaks, one in Chicago and the other in Alabama, ended too soon, for the families, but not soon enough for Marty and Gil. They were anxious to get back to campus and to get on with their busy lives. And, their seeing each other after a week-long break was something they both looked forward to, anxiously.

Traveling to Indianapolis by train and by bus to Anders, Marty arrived there in the early morning. Gil was to arrive by bus from Alabama in late afternoon of the same day.

Marty had enough time to unpack, put away some of her things, and launder the rest. She went to the supermarket to shop for items she'd need for a week. She was going to meet Gil at the bus station and bring him back to have supper with her.

Pork chops. Gil loved the pork chops his Momma made every week.

Marty met Gil at the bus station. He saw her as soon as he came down the first step. He tossed his duffle bag aside and let out a whoop, gathering her in his arms for one of his big bear hugs. Then he kissed her, lightly, at first. Then hungrily and longingly. She kissed him back, swept up with the pleasure of seeing him again.

Some people passing by smiled at them; other observers looked at them with visible disdain. Gil and Marty were oblivious to all of them.

The fact that this was their first kiss, in public, was not lost on her. She was breathless afterward, almost forgetting to invite him to her apartment for supper.

After the fine pork-chop supper, and after the dishes were washed and dried and put away, and after the floor was swept, Gil stretched out on the other chair in the livingroom. He was expansive with his compliments about the supper. "Momma couldn't have done better!"

"You jest!"

"No, I don't. I mean it!"

"And you do a commendable job at washing dishes."

"I'd better. I worked my way through high school washing dishes!"

"And you played football, too?"

"Yep. I mean, yes. Don't ask me how I did it. I just did it."

"Sheer grit, it seems to me, Gil."

He sighed. "I guess." He sat up straight in the chair and said, "Marty! I almost forgot to ask you. Can you tutor me through the summer? God, I hope so!"

"Of course. Working a job is less work than doing classes and studying and writing papers, etc."

"Oh, Marty, I'm so relieved. I missed our sessions that week we were away."

"So did I."

"In fact," he ventured, "I dreamed . . . dreamt?"

"Either one is correct. Your choice."

"I dreamed and dreamed and dreamt and dreamt about you every night for the week we were gone. It was like being with you every night. I hope I never stop dreaming about you, Honey."

"I hope you never stop, too, Dear."

He stretched like an awakening cat. "As much as I hate to leave, Marty . . . "

"I know. You're tired from the trip, and you're still in training--all your life, I'd venture to say, even though the season is over."

"Right. But football practice is just around the corner, beginning before the semester starts. I have to stay in shape, and so, you're right--I'm always in training."

He stood up, picked up his duffle bag, and went to the door. She stood beside him. Holding his duffle bag in one hand, he put his other arm around her, comfortably. He kissed her again, tightening his hold on her with his one arm. She responded. They parted.

"G'nite, Honey. And thanks a lot for the great dinner."

"G'nite, Dear one. You're welcome."

* * *

Gil was now reading his fifth novel, Pearl Buck's "The Good Earth." After the first chapter, he realized it was primarily about a woman in China. Why am I reading this stuff? he asked himself. Then he asked Marty.

She said, "Keep on reading, Gil. You'll find it captivating. Take my word for it."

"You read it?"

"Back in high school, an English assignment."

"Is that why you suggested it?"

She replied, "Yes and no."

"What's that supposed to mean?"

"Yes, because it's a classic for an English class. No, because, just as you pointed out, it's all about a woman. No shame in that, believe me. Just stick with it, Gil. For me."

And he did, and he did find it irresistible. He began to think differently about women in general, about Marty in particular. He began thinking about Marty a lot, in between their tutoring sessions, as well as every other waking moment.

Gil was so consumed with thoughts about Marty that one Saturday evening, after the game, he found himself knocking on her door. She opened it, and there she was, in her cotton robe and a towel-turban around her head.

"Gil!" she exclaimed. "What are you doing here? This is Saturday, not Sunday. And not only that, it's late in the evening."

"I know that. I just wanted to stop by to see you. And there you are, doing it again!"

"Doing what?"

"Wearing the turban. You really ought to have a jewel on your forehead," he said, pronouncing 'forehead' carefully, as Marty taught him to do, 'far-ed.' She noticed. He went on with "Maybe a red jewel, or no. How about your birth stone? A topaz?"

"Topaz, for November. That's correct."

He said, "Oh, yes, I know that. However, lately, I don't even know what month we're in. And, by the way, what decade are we in?"

She said, laughing, "Come on in and have a seat, Gil, and we'll get this Saturday/Sunday thing sorted out. Glass of milk?"

"Yes. Thanks." He sat in the chair opposite hers. "But you know, Marty, I really do know it's Saturday. We played a home game, for Pete's sake. I just wanted to see you and say 'hi' or something like that."

"Well, I'm glad you stopped by because I can tell you now, rather than tomorrow at tutoring time, how impressed I was with your playing today. Your were superb! As always. You never fail the team."

"Marty. Thanks for the accolades . . ."

"Excellent choice--accolades--I commend you for using it."

"Thanks . . . again. But I have to tell you, Marty, when I make all those touchdowns, time and time again, it isn't just my doing. Without my teammates running defense for me, I'd never be able to pull it off. And so, on behalf of my teammates, I accept your very generous tribute."

"My, my, what a pretty speech!"

"Thanks, Marty. You make some pretty nifty speeches yourself."

"Thank you, kind sir."

Changing the subject, Gil asked, "By the way, what does a topaz look like?"

"Tell you what. On Tuesday, before our session, we'll walk up to the jeweler's in the same block as the cafe and ask him to show us all the birth stones."

"You wouldn't!"

"Sure I would. For you, Gil. Call it a part of one's education."

The next day, Sunday, and after the evening's tutoring, Gil said to her, "May I walk you home, Marty?"

"I'd be honored, Gil."

He opened the gate for her. They walked up the front steps and onto the porch. He took her in his arms and kissed her. Again, she kissed him back.

He said, "That was what? the third time you kissed me back?"

"I know. I hope you liked it as much as I did."

"Honey, you'll never know how much I liked it. It goes off the scale!"

After that, Gil walked her home every Sunday evening.

Gil was now a sophomore and Marty a junior. She wondered if he were getting bored with the tutoring. No, she decided. She had noticed how enthusiastic he was, yet, with each new revelation in English or math.

The more she thought about that, the more she was convinced he was still eager to learn more and more. He was doing marvelously well. She was proud of him. She was fond of him. She thought, how did that slip in there? Like a kid brother? I don't think so!

With her conviction that Gil's tutoring sessions were not beginning to pall, she began to plan more activities to round out his general education. She suggested they take the bus some Sunday after church to visit a museum in Indianapolis.

He was eager to do that. It was only an hour's bus ride to get there. She had prepared a box lunch for them to eat while on the bus. They approached the somber-looking museum building. His initial interest began to wane . . .

Until they came to a Native American Indian display.

"Wow! Look at these models, Marty. They're so lifelike!"

"Must've had some very good professionals working on these. It's impressive."

They moved on to a geological display. Gil said, "I always wondered where all those little stones in the farmers' fields came from."

Then they encountered a gems display. "Look, Marty! There's a topaz! Your birth stone! Wow! It's a lot bigger than the one at the jeweler's!"

All in all, Marty was pleased with his reactions as they passed from one room to the next. It was not a wasted afternoon. They had supper in a restaurant near the bus station, her treat. Gil was reflective. "Honey, I wish I'd thought up a date like this for us. You had a great idea, coming here."

"It's okay, my dear. I don't care where we go. It's really a wonderful experience to be with you, anywhere, anytime."

He suddenly couldn't eat any more, he was so filled with the good feelings she generated for him. He grinned sheepishly.

"And that grin of yours is only one of your endearing charms." The grin grew larger.

"Marty, Honey, you're spoiling me rotten!"

Once the bus dropped them off in Anders, near the campus, they walked hand-in-hand to her apartment building.

Standing on the porch, he said, "Honey, thanks a whole lot for the great afternoon and evening. We may have missed our tutoring session, but the museum experience made up for it."

"That was part of the plan--to let the museum be an adjunct to the regular session."

"Ah. Clever!"

"Good night, Gil, dear one." This time *she* initiated the kiss. He was actually shocked. Marty had never before been the aggressive one. He liked it very much.

"Good night, Sweetheart," he said.

* * *

Another summer arrived. Again Marty went to Chicago for a week's visit, and Gil went to Alabama for his week's visit. This time, they both had jobs on campus. They ate lunch together every work day.

The sessions continued, all three days in the evening, after their jobs. Gil had virtually outgrown her math tutoring. Indeed, he had passed her in Math. She told him so, proudly, one day at lunch.

"Then can we still have the English tutoring sessions?"

"Of course we can. And I insist that we have them at my apartment!"

"'Sokay with me!"

* * *

Marty's senior year and Gil's junior year began with excitement for her, with dread for him. He realized it would be her last year on campus. That meant the tutoring would stop upon her graduation.

He tried not to become morose over that kind of immediate future. The sessions had been pure joy for him. He not only would miss the sessions, he would, for darn sure, miss Marty! Damn! he said under his breath.

Others on campus, knowing who Gil was and knowing him personally, as well, noticed soon enough the changes in Gil. He spoke properly, his grades were up, confidence was at an all-time high, and his friends and acquaintances observed that he had lost most of his southern accent.

* * *

When Marty graduated, her parents came down from Chicago. She introduced them to Gil. They tried not to look too surprised and greeted him cordially and politely.

After Marty's graduation, her parents took the bus to Indianapolis and then the train back to Chicago. The bus ride was quiet for them as they were both reflective about their daughter's choice for a beau. By the time the train ride to Chicago began, they both loosened up and discussed what they had been thinking about on the bus. The boy--no, the man--was a strapping thing, well spoken, seeming to be very bright. All pluses. So what's to worry about, they asked?

Before graduation, Marty had a job offer in Indianapolis for practice teaching eighth-grade English. Gil was both disturbed and relieved. At least, he thought, during my senior year, we can see each other on Sundays. One Sunday in Indianapolis and the next in Anders.

That was how they spent every Sunday. Sometimes Marty could manage to come to Anders on Saturdays, for the home games, and to be with him that evening and on Sunday as well.

Ostracization disappeared totally while Marty taught in Indianapolis. Although she had paid little or no heed to being left out by her campus "friends'" lives, it was a relief to be away from it. She thought, I'd better get used to it if we're really going to marry. Nobody here in Indianapolis has met Gil yet. . . that I know of.

* * *

Gil's graduation was a fulfilling and thrilling experience for him. A poor black boy from Alabama making it through college! Thanks to Marty, he murmured.

Marty came to the Tracy campus for his graduation day.

He sent for his mother to come up from Alabama for the ceremony. She farmed out the remaining four children with her sister and brother-in-law. She had never before made a bus trip so far away. And, she certainly had never before left her children in someone else's care. She was a little scared but put on a brave face and said goodby to the children (reminding them for the 100th time to behave themselves) and to her big sister Nelly who called out, "Be careful, Leta, chile, and come back safe!"

When Gil introduced Marty and his mother to each other, Leta, without missing a beat, proffered her hand and said a polite "Howdy-do?" Marty was enchanted with her down-home manners.

Leta thought to herself, while the small talk went on around her: My boy's done gone and got hisself a white woman! Bless his heart. A nice white woman, 'pon my soul. What in heaven's name is a tooter? Law-zee!

Gil's mother stayed for another day. The next day they took her to lunch, then to the bus station and said goodbye. She waved half forlornly to the pair, half resignedly. And in the back of it all, she was happy. Happy that her son was the first one in their families,

153

ever, to go to college. Not only did he go to college, he done went and finished college! I swan! She was going to miss him. Looked like they was going to get hitched. Well, she would be happy about that, too. Yessirree, she had made up her mind about that!

Marty spent the rest of the day with Gil. They went to the quad on campus where chairs were not yet folded up and taken away. They sat on two of the chairs. They held hands and looked distractedly into the space in front of them.

Marty said, "Another rite of passage--yours, Gil."

He nodded.

"So," she said, "what now?"

"Well, Honey, this is as good a time as any to tell you what's been going on here at the campus the past month."

She felt a constriction in her throat. She couldn't imagine why. A fear? Fear of what?

He continued. "I've been conferring with the headhunters who came on campus, looking for students looking for jobs. There's plenty opportunity out there. But not for a black man in a white man's world. Let's face it."

"Sad, but true."

"So, time before last when I visited you in Indianapolis, I went to the Marine Recruiting Office and made inquiries."

There, it came out--why she had the throat constriction, and why she felt a fear.

"And?"

"And, it's a great offer, a great opportunity. Now that I've graduated, I'd be eligible for the draft into the Army. But if I sign up in the Marines, I'll be sent to Officer Candidate School and graduate from that with a commission. I'd be an officer. Then, as a brand-new officer, I'd be sent to an officers' training school to learn the nuts and bolts of being a Marine officer, someone with authority. Then I could expect to get leave before being assigned to my first duty."

"Whew! That was a mouthful!"

"I'm not finished yet. When I get that leave, we'll be married!"

"And while you're in the two schools?"

"Some of the time," he said, "I could come to Indianapolis on a weekend pass. Honey, I promise you, I'll be there every weekend they give us!"

"Thank heaven for small favors!"

"Honey, I was afraid you'd be pis-. . . I mean put out when I said I was going to be a Marine. I most certainly will be assigned to duty

154

in Vietnam, sooner or later."

"Darling, I'm not put out, but I am seriously fearful for you. On the other hand, Gil, I'm definitely proud of you for volunteering to fight for your country."

"I'm going to be okay, Marty. I have to be so that when I return to you, we'll start a family."

"Yes, Honey, the one we've talked about so much: three children so that if there's a fourth, it'd be okay!"

"Right on, Marty!"

* * *

As it turned out, Gil did get his occasional weekend pass to come to Indianapolis from both OCS and OTS. They made the most of those precious times together, spending more time sitting on park benches, holding hands and talking than anything else.

Unfortunately for both of them, however, he did not get the anticipated leave before shipping out for Vietnam. They said a tearful goodbye on the telephone, each swearing loyalty and devotion to the other.

Gil boarded his military transport plane feeling incomplete and certainly worried about Marty's not being secured with the accouterments of marriage to a military man: no benefits and no privileges during his absence; and no benefits and no privileges if he should not make it back at all.

In her unawareness of the benefits and privileges of being a military wife, Marty set about to make herself busier than ever--so that she would have no time nor energy to think . . . and worry about Gil.

She made inquiries by letter and by telephone, she endured endless interviews by as many interviewers, she finished her contract at the school in Indianapolis, and she packed the allowed two suitcases and traveled to her training camp.

Marty was trained to survive under primitive conditions while teaching children English in a small village in Vietnam. All her mail, outgoing and incoming, had to go through a San Francisco address.

* * *

Two weeks after Marty arrived in Vietnam, she posted a letter to Gil, explaining all about her inquiries, her training, and her getting settled in the village.

The next day, after finishing teaching the children the English alphabet, she began teaching simple words: dog cat mother father brother sister. During the "sis" sound of "sister," there was a loud hissing noise, followed by an explosion.

The children on their benches under a tree, panicked, screaming and crying. Marty grabbed the nearest small child and picked her up and took the hand of her older brother. She thought desperately about what to do to protect them all.

Suddenly a booming male voice called out, "Take to the ditch! Everybody into the ditch!"

She shouted to the children in Vietnamese, "Follow me!" She threw herself and her two charges into the ditch, and the others followed her. Another explosion detonated near them. Marty felt a heavy weight land on her back. The little boy let go of her hand and put both his hands over his ears. The little girl in Marty's arms cried pathetically.

There were three more explosions, then silence, except for the whimpering children. The heavy weight on Marty removed itself, and she stood up, still holding the little girl.

Marty looked at the grubby fatigue uniform standing before her. She looked more closely and shouted, "Gil! Is that you, Gil?"

"Marty!" he roared as he took the little girl from her, the little boy already clutching his thigh. "What the devil are you doing *here*?"

A touchy moment followed. Then, he put down the little girl, and he wrapped his long arms around Marty. She was still shaken by the explosions and his explosive question. However, she stood comfortably in his arms and responded by hugging him back.

"I sent a letter to you just yesterday, telling you all about what I've been doing."

"Marty, Hon-ey! Never mind how and why you got here. We must get married . . . . . . today!"

"Are you serious? In the middle of all this chaos?"

"Of course I'm serious! We live with chaos. It's our middle name!" He took off in a big hurry, bent on two errands: getting permission to get married; and getting married.

Marty sorted the children into groups according to the direction in which they lived, and she and her assistant took them to their homes, what was left of them.

Gil went immediately to his CO's tent office, then to the chaplain's tent. He went back to Marty and helped her finish distributing the children to their homes. Together they went back to Gil's camp, near the village.

By that time, he had secured permission from his CO, the Major, to marry. Then they met with the chaplain. He said, "Are you both Catholic?"

"No, sir," Gil replied.

"Well," said the Catholic chaplain, "I can do Methodist, Presbyterian, or Baptist . . . in a pinch."

Gil turned to Marty and asked, "Baptist okay with you, Honey?"

"Oh, yes, Darling. Anything!"

* * *

The ceremony was short and very sweet. The Catholic Chaplain did a fine job. As it turned out, Gil had already purchased a wedding ring for Marty during a 3-day pass to Saigon. Plain. Simple. He had bought it to have for their future marriage. It was fortuitous. It rounded out the ceremony.

* * *

The Major had had a busy afternoon, twisting an arm here and there, pulling a string or two, and snipping yards and yards of the troublesome Red Tape--all to get permission for the Marine Lieutenant to marry a non-native, today!

After all that, he then began to feel like a hotelier. He summoned Lt. Lessiter to his tent office. The Lieutenant entered it, saying, "You sent for me, Major?"

"I did, Lieutenant. Congratulations on your marriage!"

"Thank you, Sir. Will that be all, Sir?"

"Indeed not! I ordered you to come here so I could tell you that your tent mate has been reassigned to another tent as a third member. Therefore, your tent will now be known as the 'Honeymoon Tent.'"

Gil, grinning broadly, said, "Thank you, Sir!"

"Don't thank me too soon, Lieutenant. You have a short honeymoon at best. Four hours from now, you have to be ready to move out. Have to take the next valley. Not going to be easy."

"Yes, Sir. Will do."

"Aren't you going to introduce me to your bride?"

"Oh, yes, Sir. Right away, Sir. She's just outside."

* * *

The honeymoon was spent on a blanket on the cloth tent floor which was hard and lumpy. Not that they noticed it--very much. It was pure bliss. Marty never believed in a million years that it could be this wonderful. Nobody, but nobody (not even her parents--especially not her parents) had told her what to expect, in all her growing-up years.

Gil took this moment to tell Marty that as soon as he left on his next mission, she must contact the chaplain who will explain all her benefits and privileges as a military wife.

Then he said to her, "Do not lose the marriage certificate, Honey! Keep it on your person, if necessary."

She promised to do that.

Then Gil reached into his backpack, located between him and the tent wall. He brought out a black velvet pouch and handed it to Marty. He turned on his flashlight so that she could see what it was.

Upon loosening the drawstring and shaking out its contents, she gasped at the sight of the thing: a good-sized topaz. Breathlessly, she said, "It's gorgeous! And bigger than the ones we saw at the jeweler's and at the museum! Where on earth did you get this topaz?"

"Here in Nam. Do you like it?"

"Like it? I love it!"

He said, "It was supposed to be your birthday present, but we may as well make it a wedding present. From me to you."

"There never was a more lovely wedding present, anywhere, anytime!" A pause. "Yes it *is* bigger than the one at the museum!"

He turned off the flashlight, smiling, and taking her again.

After they were satiated and resting, Marty said, "Darling, if I should get impregnated, and it's a boy, I want to name him after you."

"Good Lord!" he whooped. "We've been married for three hours and you're already naming the first baby? And we don't even know if there's one on the way?"

"And, if it's a girl, I want to name her 'Gilley.'"

* * *

Four months later, Marty was discharged from her new Vietnam job and sent to Great Lakes Training Center near Chicago. She appeared at the Navy hospital for examination, then rented a small apartment nearby.

Plenty of time to get settled in, she thought. And plenty of time to think about Gil and how he is passing her up. His Nam experiences are such that she will never have and will never know about, except second-handedly--perhaps.

Marty's mother came to stay with her during the final two weeks of her pregnancy.

* * *

One year after Marty's departure from Nam, Gil's tour was ended. He was flown to Point Mugu, California, bussed to Camp Pendleton, and given 30 days leave. He hitched a ride to Los Angeles International Airport for a flight to Chicago.

Emerging from the "tunnel" at O'Hare, he searched the sea of faces and found Marty waiting for him. He plowed his way through the passengers in front of him to get to her. They embraced tightly, hanging on for dear life. He gave her a passionate kiss, to which she eagerly responded.

Then he turned to the double stroller and picked up one of the babies. Not knowing which one he had, he looked to Marty for the information.

"That's Gilley," she said.

"My little girl! I have a little girl! Marty, she's beautiful!" He cooed into her ear. He kissed her on the top of her head.

He handed her to Marty and turned to the other baby in the stroller, picking him up gingerly.

"Come say 'hi' to your daddy, Gilbert Lessiter, the Second!" He cuddled his son and jostled him a bit. Looking at Marty, he said, "Honey, you delivered a double whammy package! I nearly fainted at the news of twins when I got the MARS message. Honey, you did a fantastic job!"

"Thank you, Hon." She smiled grandly. "We have our work cut out for us, haven't we? Raising two children at the same time."

"Can you tutor two at a time, Marty?"

"Of course!"

"I should have known. Once a tutor, always a tutor."

# # #

THE MISSIONARY

It was 1952. The French-Indo China Church Mission was attacked by rebels. At the Mission, all the men, both native and French, were massacred; the women were taken prisoner. They were three American women and five French women. The rebels tolerated none of them. They were all infidels, the white Europeans and white Americans alike.

Joanna Cutler, a widow and childless, with the other two American women and the five French women, were marched to a rebel outpost, an enormous structure that looked exactly like a medieval castle. They were herded into a room of stone, with bars at one wall. One small window, also with bars, high and not quite touching the ceiling, provided the only light coming into the room. The room provided a sink and a toilet, in the open. No privacy. Other than those amenities, the room was bare—no cots, no chairs, no benches. The structure was in the middle of the jungle-like environment.

On the third day of their imprisonment, the eight women missionaries were taken from the barred room and to the outside. They were instructed in broken English, Asian accent, to stand in a loose line on the parade ground. The spokesman had eight rebel soldiers clustered behind him. He addressed the women formally, as it were, with a short speech.

"Each of you will be selected by one of these men you see here." He made an all-inclusive gesture with his hand toward the soldiers who now formed a ragged line behind the speaker. "You will accompany the soldier who has chosen you, and you will be his personal slave, doing everything he demands of you. Cook, clean, wash uniforms, and anything else he may require. There will be no disobedience tolerated on the part of each woman.

"Do you understand me?" he asked forcefully.

Uneasily, the eight women nodded in compliance.

Joanna thought, "What choice is there?"

"Further, you must know that all these men have served our leader honorably and valiantly. Each of you is the reward for the bravery shown by each of these men."

The women exchanged glances, each asking herself, "I'm a reward? . . . ."

Joanna held her breath while she mentally reviewed her situation and recent past. She had been teaching 5-8-year-old native children how to speak English. She was a Christian woman, devout, staunch in her belief in God, trying her best to serve God at all times, in all things. She looked at the crew of eight men, most of them tight-faced, pseudo military. Their uniforms were rag-tag, indicating to Joanna that this was a loosely formed renegade military unit, or a unit half-forgotten by its headquarters.

Either way, she was filled with a tense fear.

The spokesman stepped aside and nodded to the eight rebel soldiers to begin their selections.

The other two American women were a blonde and a redhead. They were selected instantly by two of the honored soldiers. The five Frenchwomen, all brunettes, were selected next. Joanna, a chestnut brown head, stood alone, virtually shaking in her shoes. The one rebel soldier left was slight in build, but moved with animal-like fluidity. He would make a perfect jungle warrior.

That last one of the eight soldiers walked in a circle around Joanna. A pause followed. Then he touched her on the arm. She turned to face him. He began walking away. Hesitantly, she followed him. The spokesman frowned at her. Perhaps, she thought, she had not responded quickly enough.

She closed the space between her and the departing soldier. She followed him closely into a side entrance of the courtyard, where the parade ground was located.. They climbed a stairway, then another. They turned to the left into a corridor, then a right turn. She was becoming disoriented, not knowing where she was, where they were going.

Another flight of stairs, and at the top, there was a single door. The soldier opened the door and entered a large and airy room. Speaking in Chinese, he said something to her–totally incomprehensible to her. He motioned her to follow him. He showed her a bathroom, huge by anyone's standards, modern toilet, wash basin and a separate large room for showering. "So," she said to herself, half aloud, "this is a very modern-day castle. Nice."

Speaking in Chinese again, he led the way back into the spacious room that had a sofa, two easy chairs, each with an ottoman, some tables, a chest of drawers, a bookcase, a wardrobe, and a bed. A double bed, she noted. Still speaking Chinese, he led her to a nook that served as a kitchenette: it held a two-burner electric stove, a sink with a single spigot, a few utensils, and a small pantry.

He picked up a pot and placed it into the sink under the spigot. He took a small burlap sack out of the pantry and handed it to her. It was full of rice.

She said to him, "I guess you want me to cook some rice?"

He simply looked at her and . . . he smiled. He returned to the bedroom/sitting room. He opened the wardrobe and changed clothes in front of her, donning a silk robe. She turned to the rice-cooking chore.

He sat on an easy chair, feet on the ottoman, regarding her closely, saying nothing more. The rice was finished cooking. In the pantry, she found some bowls and removed two of them. Chopsticks. Where were the chopsticks? She looked at him, holding the two bowls and asked him, "Do we have chopsticks?"

He frowned slightly. She set down one bowl. She made a motion as if to eat the rice in the other bowl with her fingers. His face brightened, and he arose to produce the chopsticks. Water was boiling for the tea. She poured it into the metal teapot for the tea to steep. They sat at a table near the kitchenette. They ate. Joanna was glad she had mastered the tricky manipulation of chopsticks during her first week at the Mission.

When the tea was ready, they sipped the hot brew slowly. He moved back to his easy chair and ottoman, taking his tea with him. She sat companionably in the other chair with her tea. She pictured that this is how old married folks spend their evenings.

When they had emptied the teapot, she dumped the leaves, washed out the teapot, washed the rice pot, washed the bowls, rinsed off the chopsticks, and put everything on a drainboard to dry.

When she left the kitchenette and returned to the bedroom/sitting room, he had removed his robe and lay naked across the bed.

Joanna froze. The one thing she had dreaded, during the speech on the parade ground, was going to happen. Now she feared it, viscerally.

She wanted to flee out of the room. Walking to the door slowly but resolutely, she opened it and began to step into the small hallway, at the head of the stairs. A soldier on guard placed his rifle across the door, in front of her. Her leaving the room was nothing but a useless idea. Any attempt to escape would obviously be punishable.

Closing the door and turning to face the room again, she realized: of course, she was expected to perform.

Perform! A hated term!

He got up from the bed and walked up to her. He stood there, gazing at her for a long time. He took one of her hands and slowly led her to the bed.

When they stood beside the bed, he put his arms around her and held her quietly for a few moments. Then, he began to unbutton her dress, a shirtwaist dress with buttons down the front. He undid the belt, and continued unbuttoning the buttons below the waist-line. With deliberate movements, he undressed her, leaving the dress and underwear in a heap on the floor.

Joanna was trembling . . . .and praying. Aloud she prayed: "Lord, if I am to be saved from this act of fornication with a foreign devil– No, that's what *they* call *us*! Then take me now, Lord. Now!"

For whatever reason, she told herself, she is being spared death, or denied some other form of escape, and forced to lie with this enemy foreigner.

He pulled her down onto the bed with him, together. It was a flowing motion, as in a hazy dream. He could do that, she thought wildly. With careful strokes, he explored her body. She tensed at every touch. Then he took her to a place where she had never, ever been before.

* * *

When he had finished, she lay there beside him (he had covered them, after the act), breathing heavily. She was spent.

"Good Lord," she said aloud. "What has happened here?"

She touched his arm and spoke to him. "I know you cannot understand me, but I am going to tell you something I thought I'd never say in my life." She paused, squeezing his arm lightly. "You have given me a gift I never knew was possible for as long as I was married." She took a big breath. "It was never like this when I was married, I swear to you! My dead husband went to his grave never having given me this wondrous gift that you have."

"My darling," she said "My darling," she said again.

Suddenly the man sat up, startling her. "Did he understand what I said?" she asked herself aloud.

"Ling!" he almost shouted. "Ling!" He touched his chest with his hand.

"Ling?" she said.

"Ling! Ling!" he shouted, smiling, laughing, nodding, pointing to his chest over and over. Then, he sobered. Pointing to her chest, he said something in Chinese.

Finally, it came to her. Ling, out of 'darling,' was his name, and he's asking her what her name is. She sat upright, clutching the sheet to her chest.

Speaking slowly, and pointing back to her chest, she said, "Jo-anna."

He tried to say it. "Jo anna?"

"Yes!" she cried. "Joanna! And you are Ling!" This time, she poked her hand into his chest.

They threw their arms around each other, flung themselves back onto the bed, laughing joyously.

Ling and Joanna.

* * *

The next morning when Joanna awakened, she sensed that Ling was gone. A short inspection of the quarters confirmed that. She got dressed and went to the door. No guard was there. She went down the stairs. Ah, *there* was the guard. He looked at her sternly. She got the message and went back up the stairs, into the apartment and closed the door behind her.

Where was Ling? She looked out a window that faced the courtyard. A contingent of the rebel soldiers was drilling on the parade ground.

"Ah, that must be where he is."

Around noon Ling entered the apartment. He smiled at her as he came through the door and closed it behind him. Handing her a string bag, she accepted it and could see that it contained two papayas. It delighted her as much as she was delighted to see him again.

She asked him, "Do you want me to fix a meal?"

He took off his cap, flung it onto a table by the bed, unbuttoned his uniform jacket, and lay down onto the bed, otherwise fully dressed in uniform, and took a short nap.

She thought, But of course, he didn't understand me.

When Ling awoke, he used the bathroom. When he came back into the room, he buttoned his uniform jacket, put on his cap, grabbed her around the waist and hugged her tightly. She hugged back, not knowing why she was doing that.

Ling said a short speech in Chinese, then kissed her and left the apartment.

* * *

It must have been a goodbye kiss, of sorts, she thought, for he didn't show up again for another four days. Meanwhile, she wondered what he did for food that first morning and noontime. Perhaps he ate in a mess hall.

It was like a second honeymoon. On that fourth day after his departure, he came back to the apartment, late in the afternoon, ragged, dirty, smelly. He took a shower and put on his silk robe. He led her to the bed and had her for the second time since she became his personal slave. He murmured into her ear softly, all Chinese, of course. And fell sound asleep..

Joanna vowed she would begin teaching him some English. Should be easy. After all, she had been teaching the children at the Mission how to speak English. Should be the same method, with Ling, shouldn't it?

* * *

It was one week before Ling had to go on a mission again. She knew he would be leaving because he was dressed in full uniform, and he kissed her again, this time saying "Joanna. Good bye."

However, he took her with him out the door, down the stairs, a right turn, down a corridor, a left turn, two more flights of stairs, and onto the courtyard. He squeezed her hand before he got into formation on the parade ground. She stood watching him. He blended in with the unit, but she spotted him in the double line, third row from the front of the unit.

She watched them march out of the compound, the main gate closing behind them.

There was no guard on the route down to the courtyard, she now realized. To herself, she said, "And Ling left me here alone. Does that mean I am free to roam the place?"

A voice next to her said, "Mrs. Cutler, can you find your way back to your quarters?"

It was the spokesman who had addressed the eight women that day on the parade ground, explaining the "selection."

"Yes, I think so. But I'm curious. Why am I not guarded anymore?"

"You would be curious, of course. And I will explain: Your benefactor, shall we say? I speak of Ling Chow. He has declared you to be secure, I believe is the term."

"Secure? From what?"

"From being a runaway. He has sworn to his unit commander that if you try to escape and are successful at it, he will surrender his life to the commander. None of the other women has been declared in that way. Ling's woman, you, is the only secure one. I am at your disposal for whatever needs you may have. Just ask for Captain Yee. Good day, Mrs. Cutler."

* * *

Joanna returned to the apartment, reversing the path they had taken down the halls and stairs. She was thoughtful as well as grateful to Ling Chow. None of the other women has been declared in that way? Incredible! Then, at the top of the second flight of stairs, she paused to pray again, aloud.

"Dear Lord. You have answered my prayer in such a strange way. Now I know why I was not taken to be freed from what I feared to be an abominable act. I was spared to experience the fantastic coupling with Ling Chow. I thank you Lord, in His name. And, dear Lord, give me the capacity to be gracious to my benefactor, Ling Chow, at all times. Amen."

* * *

For three days, Joanna explored the castle. She tested her freedom and discovered that no one questioned wherever she went nor when. One thing she found in the castle was a catwalk over the main gate, on the second floor. She had a plan but had to seek out Captain Yee to ask him when was the latest mission expected to return.

"Ah, Mrs. Cutler, I cannot predict such an event, but I should learn by radio when the unit is on its way back to the castle. I will send you a note informing you of its return. Would that be satisfactory?"

* * *

The note arrived the next day at noon. The unit would pass through the gate around 1600 hours. She stationed herself at the catwalk, waiting and watching.

Soon, she heard the noises of a marching group. No voices. Just the clank of metal against metal. They came around a bend and up to the gate. She was watching carefully, trying to spot Ling. One head looked up at her and smiled at her. She recognized the smile, and she returned it.

She ran, not walked, to the apartment and waited for him. Eagerly.

Joanna had a towel, bath mat, washcloth and soap ready and waiting for him to come through the door. When it opened, her heart skipped a beat. Yegads! It was so good to see him again!

* * *

It became a ceremony. When Ling was on mission, and he returned with his unit, he marched around the bend and instantly looked up at the catwalk to find Joanna waiting and smiling and waving to him. Always. Without fail. It gave him great pleasure . . . and stature. The other soldiers were envious of his good fortune–to have an agreeable and obviously an obedient woman.

* * *

Joanna was provided, through Ling's persuasion to Captain Yee, some Chinese garments for her to wear, instead of the dowdy dress,

167

washed and dried, but never ironed.

She wondered from time to time why she had not seen any of the other seven women. Had she been able to communicate with Ling's fellow rebels, she would have learned that each of the other seven soldiers was having a terrible time with his disobedient and quarrelsome slave. With that kind of relationship with the soldiers, the seven enslaved women were allowed no privileges. Not like Joanna. Freedom to roam the castle was denied those seven women, as punishment.

Joanna did, however, request Captain Yee (through Ling Chow) to supply Chinese garments for the other seven women. The request was granted. The other women, when they were delivered the different clothing, wondered where in the world did these come from?

* * *

The rebels' missions became more frequent, and longer in duration. It was bound to happen, sooner or later, that one or more returning soldiers came back wounded. When Joanna began to notice that, she grew apprehensive for Ling. Every time she stood her "sentry" on the catwalk, she prayed that Ling would come back whole and unharmed.

Then one day the unit returned with one dead soldier whose body was to be disposed of in a military way.

Joanna's heart jumped up into her throat, fearing the dead soldier was Ling. But a few moments later, she saw him among the straggling unit. He was unhurt! She ran not straight to the apartment but to the parade ground where she could meet him sooner.

It was a momentous occasion–her first time to greet Ling on the parade ground. As soon as the unit was dismissed, she flew into his arms. Because he was dirty and smelly again, he was reluctant to respond. But she clung to him so possessively, he held her as tightly as he could, rifle and backpack's getting in the way.

As weary and spent as the other soldiers were, they were not that blind to what was going on between Ling Chow and his woman. The others were so jealous, it wracked them to the bottom of their souls. Each one was thinking how he had made such a bad choice among the women, remembering that Ling was the last one to have the pick of the last woman–no choice at all. And look at how it turned out! They were like lovers!

* * *

Joanna sensed, at the end of each mission that the fighting was not going well. More soldiers returned wounded and more returned dead.

Ling had two minor brushes with the French. But his surface wounds were patched up cleanly and professionally so that he was ready to leave on the next mission. Then the missions became more and more frequent, but now lasting shorter and shorter, with shorter and shorter rests in between.

Joanna expressed her concern.

"Ling, Darling, the fighting is getting worse every time you leave. More wounded. More dead. I am so thankful you are not among them."

Ling looked into her eyes searchingly. He understood some of what she said, but not all of it. "Joanna, ... dar-ling?" She nodded. "You right. Dead too much!"

"I pray for you, Ling, every time you have to leave me. I pray earnestly for you."

"Pray? Your American god?"

"Yes, and to any other god that may be around. Yours, if you have one."

He smiled. He thought she gave him a compliment but wasn't sure.

* * *

At some point, Joanna realized that the fighting was getting nearer and nearer the castle. It would be a real coup for the French to re-occupy the castle. It had long ago appeared to her that it was built by a European, not Chinese. The rebels had taken it over when the French deserted it, a few years back.

Her thoughts became a reality. The castle was under attack!

Ling, not bothering with buttoning his uniform coat, not putting on the uniform cap, grabbed Joanna by the waist, kissed her violently, and said, "Joanna wait here. Not go away! Joanna stay here! Please?"

"I will, Ling. I will. God be with you!"

He was gone

* * *

To start with, the rebels were low on ammunition. The French were seasoned veterans at jungle fighting, and attacking the castle was a sweet relief for them. This was *real* combat!

The castle fell into the hands of the French. When the French flag was raised, Joanna ventured down and into the courtyard. For the first time since their imprisonment, she saw the other women. They all hugged each other and cried for the victory.

As soon as Joanna could detach herself from the knot of the other women, she embarked on a search for Ling. First she went to the recently established morgue and searched carefully for Ling. Thank God he was not there. Then she went to the clinic. And she saw him instantly, badly wounded. She went directly to him, paying no attention to the medics as they tried to oust her from the clinic.

Joanna knelt beside the low cot where he lay. His head was bandaged. He had another bandage. When she looked at it, she realized his right leg was missing, below the knee!

She almost vomited.

Reaching for his hands, she said softly, "Ling, Darling. Can you hear me? It's Joanna. I've come for you, Darling. I will care for you from now on. Only me. Only you. Oh, my poor Darling."

Slowly he opened his eyes. He saw her. Weakly, he said, "Joanna. . . . . . You mine."

She put her arms around his shoulders, propping him up slightly. "Yes, Ling. I am yours. Only yours."

He died in her arms.

* * *

Although all eight women were freed from their imprisonment, the French took their time in arranging their return to that other civilization–their own countries. A week later, the women began their trek to the nearest road, a half-day's walk. A truck was waiting for them. They boarded it. It took them to a small port where a ship was due in a few days. A ship to take them home. The Church Mission had been devastated. It existed no more.

The three American women would be offloaded first, in San Francisco. The remaining five French women would be taken on the rest of the long voyage, to France.

They talked while they waited for the ship, sharing their experiences with each other, speaking of the rebel soldiers, the despised master/slave relationships. All but Joanna. One of the French women noticed that. She asked, in English, "Why you not tell us about your imprisonment, Joanna?"

Joanna gave her a baleful look. The others stopped talking, waiting for Joanna's answer.

Soberly, she answered, "Ling Chow was my benefactor, not my master. He died defending the castle against the French assault."

And, with a barely discernible smile, she added, " I'm pregnant with his child."

# # #

THE FAN

The great war between the states was declared. The Union Army called its men to arms, and they answered it. The new Confederate States of America was overrun with volunteers to form an army for the new republic.

Hilda Mae Culpepper of Wilmington, North Carolina, was just 17 years old and was swept up in the frenzied emotions of the times. Her brothers, Jed and Justin, ages 18 and 19, enlisted and were shipped out together to become members of the North Carolina 5th Infantry. Her father was awarded the rank of Colonel, and he too reported for duty as the head of a unit of the North Carolina 3rd Cavalry.

Hilda Mae's mother, Evelyn Culpepper, was left alone with her three young daughters. The slaves of the plantation were there for her, to help her with the chores of the fields and the house. Neighbors' menfolk all disappeared from their homes to fight the war against the hated Yankees.

Young Thomas John Whitfield came calling on Hilda Mae before he left to report to his unit in Richmond, Virginia.

"I declare, Thomas," said Hilda Mae. "You are without a doubt the handsomest Lieutenant in the whole Confederate Army . . . and the Union Army, to boot!"

"Miss Hilda Mae," he replied, "you flatter me beyond my worth! But thank you for such a grand compliment."

"You off to the War soon?"

"I'm on my way to Richmond at this very moment, after I say goodbye to you.."

"So soon?" Her question was heavy with pain. She liked this boy so much!

"Yes, Darlin'. I'm afraid so."

He took both her hands in his. "Hilda Mae, there's something I want you to do for me."

"Name it, Thomas. I am at your disposal for whatever you need."

Letting go of her hands, he produced from inside his tunic a ladies' fan. He extended it toward her.

"This fan belonged to my dead Mama when she was alive, bless her soul. I want you to have it, Hilda Mae. Take it for safekeeping, for me. And when I return, I will reclaim it . . . along with you."

"Thomas John! What are you saying?"

"I'm saying I want your promise to wait for me so that we can be wed when I return."

She was overcome with the sobering request. "Oh, Thomas, I will wait for you, as you ask, with a heart full of love for you. And I'll keep the fan for you. Write to me!"

"I will, Darlin' Hilda Mae."

They embraced. They indulged in a first kiss with each other. He mounted his horse. She waved to him as he left her. He gave her a salute with his riding crop touching the brim of his hat.

He was gone.

She stood there for many minutes, watching him disappear down the lane toward the road. Hilda Mae opened up the fan. Its pretty scene with a swan on a clear blue lake touched her soul.

* * *

The Civil War continued, ravaging the countryside relentlessly. Captain Thomas John Whitfield was wounded, ending up in a Union prison hospital at Andersonville. The Confederacy awarded him a medal for his bravery, in absentia.

The Culpepper brothers were both killed at Gettysburg. After the cessation of hostilities, their father returned a broken man. Broken in spirit, broken in body having sustained a significant wound. The loss of his only two sons was more than he could bear.

* * *

Hilda Mae's mother stood on the porch of the plantation house, watching still another soldier limping up the lane, probably looking for food and water and a place to sleep for the night. That was all right. She had a big heart for those wounded souls straggling in from the North. They had served the Confederacy and deserved the best treatment she could supply.

The young (?) man–she wasn't sure, they all appeared older and wiser to her as they approached her.

"Sakes alive!" she shouted. "Thomas John?"

"Yes, ma'am."

"Come on up to the house, my boy, and rest. And I'll get you something to eat!"

"Oh, no, ma'am, I'm too soiled to come near your house. I've come to see Hilda Mae! Is she here?"

"Hilda Mae?" Evelyn asked, with caution.

"Yes, ma'am! Did she tell you about her promise to wait for me? So that we could be married after the War?"

"Oh, my poor boy. Yes, of course she told us!" She looked at this young man, appearing to be older than she knew him to be. "But, didn't you get my letter?"

"A letter? From you, ma'am? You wrote to me? But I heard nothing the last three months. I've been in a Yankee prison for a year."

"Lord have mercy! Then you don't know about Hilda Mae?"

"Well, no, ma'am. What is it?" A feeling of dread overtook him.

"Hilda Mae, poor soul, died of pneumonia. Her body rests in the family grave site."

* * *

Thomas could not believe what he heard. "Hilda Mae? Dead?"

"Yes, Thomas. About four months ago."

He tried to steady himself by leaning against one of the great pillars at the front of the house. Then, Evelyn assisted him to sit on the top step of the porch.

"I can't believe my own Hilda Mae is gone. Tell me, Miz Culpepper, that it's not true!"

"No, son. It is true. My poor boy, I'm so sorry."

"It's me that needs to comfort you, Miz Culpepper. Hilda Mae was your firstborn girl."

"Yes, and thanks be to God, I still have my other two girls and my husband."

"Your sons? What about your sons?"

She lowered her head. "I've lost them as well."

"Oh, Miz Culpepper, your losses have been far greater than mine. I'm so sorry. So sorry."

"Thank you kindly, Thomas John."

Thomas tried to gather his thoughts, in the midst of all his pain, all her pain. He asked, "Miz Culpepper, did Hilda Mae ever show you the fan I gave her before I departed for the War?"

"Why, yes, she did. Many times. She was so taken with it, it coming from you. She was mighty smitten with you, Thomas. She saved every letter you wrote to her. She cherished the fan with all her heart and soul."

"Is the fan somewhere you can retrieve it for me? It was my mother's. I'd be much obliged to have it back."

"'Pon my soul, dear boy. The fan was buried with her. Clasped with both hands."

* * *

Thomas approached Hilda Mae's grave slowly and deliberately. He knelt before it. He vowed that when flowers bloomed again in the South, he would bring them to her every month, on the anniversary of her passing.

Suddenly, he was overcome with a grief almost too great to bear.

"Hilda Mae, I've come to claim you, as I vowed I'd do at the end of the War. Darlin' Hilda Mae, I'll never be able to touch you again. I grieve your loss of life. I'll never forget you.

"Take care of the fan, Darlin'. And wait for me to join you in the hereafter. I don't know how I can go through the rest of my life without you. "

He wept tears that came from the depth of his being.

* * *

The Culpepper family took the forlorn Confederate Captain into their home. His own family was scattered, their house in ruins.

The young Captain Thomas John Whitfield was never quite the same afterwards. He visited Hilda Mae's grave daily

"I can't wait to see you again, Darlin'," he said tenderly. "Don't lose the fan!" he commanded.

* * *

A lone figure stood on the hill near the family graveyard, watching Captain Whitfield. She was in tears–tears for her sister's dying so young. And tears for the broken-hearted Thomas. She hoped he would be mended, soon. She hoped she could be the instrument to bring that about.

She hoped.

# # #

THE COMING TOGETHER

Most of the fourth graders in an elementary school in Flint, Michigan, had known each other since kindergarten. Rhoda Mae Bertram was a flaming redhead with green eyes; spindly but quick. Her best friend was Bonnie Lee Grimes, not only the tallest girl in the room, but the tallest one. She had blue-green eyes, framed with plain brown hair, and, like Rhoda Mae, was fast on her feet. Mack Raessler, also with plain brown hair and hazel eyes, was a solid boy, stocky for a nine-year-old. A new boy came to the school in fourth grade. He was Unsell Hand. He, like Mack and Bonnie, had plain brown hair, brown eyes. He was as lanky as Mack was stocky, and he was as tall as Bonnie. She was thrilled about that!

By sixth grade in 1934, the pair of girls and the pair of boys were in competition with each other, one team against the other. All four of the two doubles were fast runners. The girls really liked the guys who tried to outrun them at every chance during their gym-class races and games. Those two girls thought that those two boys liked them because they were so competitive with them. It was a girl's intuition thing. The competition was sharp, very well honed.

One day during a free break in Home Room, Rhoda Mae and Bonnie sat at their double desks, each writing a note to each of those two boys.

Rhoda Mae wrote to Unsell, "Bonnie likes you a lot. Do you like her?"

Bonnie wrote to Mack, "Rhoda Mae likes you a lot. Do you like her?"

Together, the girls dropped their notes in front of the addressees. Then they raced back to their desks to watch and see what would happen next.

The boys opened their notes and read them. They compared messages. They conferred in whispers. Then they looked past the empty desks in front of them, zeroing in on Rhoda Mae and Bonnie and sang together, "Yes, yes. A thousand times yes!"

It was a parody on a popular song of the times, "No, no. A thousand times no."

The girls ducked their heads and giggled together, immensely pleased with the results of their girlish inquiries. The boys were grinning from ear-to-ear, indicating their own pleasure.

* * *

The end of sixth grade signaled the rites of passage into seventh grade: junior high school. During the summer of that year, Unsell Hand's family moved to Saginaw, a city 26 miles north of Flint. He was not among the new seventh graders when the first semester began.

Bonnie was devastated. Rhoda Mae was glad that such an event had not happened to Mack!

At the end of ninth grade, Rhoda Mae's family moved to Akron, Ohio. Bonnie's family moved outside the city limits of Flint. She finished high school studies at an agricultural school outside Flint.

Rhoda Mae and Bonnie lost touch, after writing a few far-spaced letters.

After high-school graduation, Mack went on to earn a degree from the General Motors Technical Institute in Flint.

As was later determined, Unsell went on to a Midwestern college, becoming a civil engineer.

* * *

World War II was in full swing. Mack had a deferred Draft Board standing while he was at the Institute. Then he was deferred further upon being hired by the Chevrolet Division of General Motors. He had a defense-sensitive job.

Unsell was also deferred while in college. But he was drafted upon graduation. He served his Army time only in the U.S.

Rhoda Mae attended a junior college in Ohio. After that, she moved back to Flint and got a job in an office of the AC Spark Plug Company, a division of General Motors.

In 1944 Bonnie enlisted in the Navy. She had had one year of junior college and two years business experience. While she was on leave after boot camp and yeoman's school, she took the train back to Flint for a visit with her family.

Because Bonnie had no automobile in those days, and because of gas rationing, she took the bus and trolley everywhere she needed to go in Flint. She was waiting for a bus downtown to go home one afternoon while on leave and miraculously spotted Rhoda Mae walking up the sidewalk toward her. They had a happy reunion, going to a restaurant for dinner. Bonnie phoned her mother to tell her she would not be home for supper and explained the encounter with Rhoda Mae. Mrs. Grimes remembered Rhoda Mae and expressed her happiness that they had met once more.

"Good grief, Rhoda Mae! You are a sight for sore eyes!"

"Well, so are you, Bonnie!"

"I see you still have the flaming red hair," Bonnie remarked.

"Yes. And I still get called 'Carrot Top'!"

They laughed together.

"So," Bonnie asked, "what's going on in your life since we were in school together?"

"Just keeping busy at my job at AC Spark Plug. It's only office work."

"Doesn't matter," said Bonnie. "It's still a contribution toward the War effort."

"But nothing like *your* contribution."

Bonnie smiled at the compliment. It had been true that she felt no feelings of patriotism the day she signed up. But three weeks into Boot Camp, when she and her bunkmates put on their uniforms for the first time to be worn every day during the War, and for some time afterwards, the feeling of patriotism washed over her like a waterfall. She felt really good about it.

"So," Bonnie said to Rhoda Mae, "you ever see Mack Raessler?"

"Funny you should ask. I called him up just yesterday, after I talked to his mother on the phone and found out all about Mack. He has a job in Flint! . . . . We have a date for Saturday night."

"Fast move, Rhoda Mae!"

Rhoda Mae's fair skinned turned beet red. "I was kindof forward, wasn't I?"

"Well, maybe just a little bit. But I hope it turns out well for both of you!"

* * *

It did turn out well for them. Rhoda Mae quit her job and married Mack. They moved into an apartment, difficult to find in a wartime industrial city. Eventually Mack was transferred to another General Motors office near Detroit. They moved to a suburb. They began their family, five boys that included a pair of twins.

Unsell was discharged from the Army, and he took his engineering degree to Chicago where he was hired 'on the spot' by a worldwide construction company. His duties took him to faraway places on the globe. He married, and his wife died of cancer. He remarried, and later he got a divorce. At retirement time, he moved to Maryland to live with one of his sons.

Bonnie married while in the Navy, and she was a Navy wife during the last 18 years that her husband had served for a total of 23 years. Ten years later, she left him and struck out on her own with a job as a technical writer and editor. She began to travel on land tours and cruises to places she had always wished she could see.

Even to some places she had never heard of. It was all a thrilling experience, full of people, new friendships. She lived in Southern California.

* * *

Bonnie and Rhoda Mae corresponded with each other only at Christmastime, an exchange of cards with a note or letter to bring each other up to date.

When they reached the age of 75, Rhoda Mae and Mack invited Bonnie to come to their house near Detroit for a short visit. A long weekend was agreed upon, and Mack and Rhoda Mae met her at the Detroit airport.

While they waited for Bonnie's aircraft arrival, Rhoda Mae said, "Honey, I wonder if Bonnie and I should have exchanged snapshots of each other. I know I've changed–big time!"

"Yeah, that would've been a great idea."

"Well, anyway," Rhoda Mae said after thinking about it, "she did tell me on the phone that she'd be wearing a mousey-gray raincoat."

"That should help."

Bonnie's flight arrived. They were on the lookout for the gray raincoat and spotted it. It was being worn by a medium-height, white-haired woman. She stopped in front of Rhoda Mae and Mack.

"Rhoda Mae?"

"Bonnie?"

* * *

After arriving at the Raesslers' house, Bonnie pled tiredness and was shown the guest room. After she took a shower, she returned to her room and crashed.

The next morning, Rhoda Mae made breakfast for the three of them. They talked about the activities they would do that day: a visit to Mack's office; meet some of his co-workers; a drive to the park to have lunch from the basket that Rhoda Mae had prepared ; a tour of the town, viewing the city hall, the fire station, the police station, and the modest college campus. It was a small suburb so that they returned to the Raessler house early. Rhoda Mae disappeared into the kitchen to begin preparing dinner.

"Rhoda Mae. Can I help you out there in the kitchen?"

"Oh, no, Bonnie. Thanks. I'm fine. You and Mack have a little talk."

"Please, no fussing about dinner for me! That lunch you made was more than substantial."

"Not to worry, Bonnie. I prepared almost everything two days go.

Just have to pop it into the oven."

"Well. Okay."

Mack and Bonnie sat in the living room, chatting. Rhoda Mae came to the door leading to the dining area, next to the living room and said, "Mack, Honey. Can you come out to the kitchen and help me with something? It's too heavy for me to lift."

"Sure thing, Rhoda Mae."

Mack excused himself and said he'd be back in a jiffy.

While Bonnie waited, she got up from the chair where she had been sitting and walked to in front of the fireplace mantel. She looked at the trophies, the photos, the ivy plant, traveling in two directions all across the mantel and down its sides. Nice touch, she thought. A mirror was affixed to the wall immediately above the mantel.

She saw, reflected in the mirror the lower body of a man walking down the stairs. It was an elderly gentleman, sparse head of hair, tall, and lean.

She turned to face him. What should she say to this stranger? And who in the world was he? Neither Rhoda Mae nor Mack had said anything about a second visitor–and already in the house?

She extended her hand toward him and said, "I'm Bonnie Manford. And you are?"

He took her hand and smiled broadly.

She disengaged her hand from his and said, "Am I supposed to know you?"

The smile became even more pronounced.

"Wait a minute," she said half to herself and half to the stranger. She turned to face the mirror over the mantel. "If I were Rhoda Mae and Mack, and I wanted to surprise me . . . ." She looked at his reflection in the mirror. Then, turning to face him again, "You're Unsell Hand, aren't you?"

He took her into his long arms and hugged her warmly.

"Unsell," she breathed.

"Bonnie. At long last."

* * *

Rhoda Mae and Mack stood in the doorway, holding hands and smiling. They looked at each other and nodded. Their plan: It had worked. Thanks to the Internet and its White Pages.

# # #

179

THE DOG

Marine Corporal Luke Morrow had served in Vietnam for five months when one night on guard duty, it began to rain—a pelting rain. The monsoon season had begun. Hastily, he retrieved his rain poncho and hat and returned to his post.

He was assaulted by the rains coming down in great sheets, and through it all, he heard, faintly, what sounded like a whimpering. He looked down at his feet, and there stood a small dog with a puppy in her mouth.

Luke picked up the puppy, soaking wet, and put it under his poncho, anchoring it inside his shirt where his body heat could warm the puppy. The rain-soaked bitch trotted away from Luke, stopping once to see if he were following. He then followed her. And she led him to a washed-out hole near the top of a bunker. Three other puppies lay in the muddy water of the hole, drowned.

He gathered them up and put them down on the wet ground. With his hands he scooped out a shallow grave in the mud for the dead puppies. The mother dog whined and whimpered throughout the process.

"Sorry, little friend," he said to the dog, "this is something we gotta do."

After he returned to his post, the dog following him, he picked her up and put her inside his shirt, along with the surviving puppy. She shivered from the shock of whelping and from losing three-fourths of her litter. The puppy began to nurse.

At the end of the watch, Luke made his way back to his bunker with the dog and her puppy. He removed them from inside his shirt, toweled them dry, and put them together at the foot of his cot, a blanket over them.

The Sergeant then undressed, dried off, put on fresh underwear, and crawled under the blanket at the opposite end of his new bed mates. He curled up in such a way that he did not disturb the dog and pup. They all slept soundly, dry and warm again.

* * *

In the days and weeks that followed, Luke fed the dog and gave her water. And when the puppy was weaned from its mother, another Marine in Luke's unit adopted the now frisky puppy. He was carried away and into a tent, making his home with his new caretaker.

On a following night patrol that Luke was assigned to, he decided to take his dog with him. They walked through deep jungle, treading carefully and quietly. Suddenly, the dog lowered her body so that her belly touched the jungle floor. Luke barely noticed that until he heard a sound coming from her. It was a quiet but intense growl. It seemed to come from some place other than her throat. It was from a place much deeper than that.

Luke was alarmed and consequently was alerted. He stopped in mid-step, signaling the others behind him to do the same.

Then, they watched a Cong jungle patrol march across their path. They were unaware of the U.S. Marine presence. Had Luke and his patrol continued their march, they would have tangled with the Cong, resulting in a bloody encounter.

Later that night, back at the encampment, Luke realized that the dog had saved his life and the lives of the others in the patrol unit. It was a defining moment. He felt a closeness to the little mutt that prompted him to let the dog sleep with him *in* his cot, from that day forward.

The same thing happened on every patrol. The dog, accompanying Luke, would give the alarm, crouching onto the jungle floor, and emitting the nether-world sound from her depths. In every instance, she saved lives–Luke and his fellow warriors.

* * *

On a day that was devoted to shaving, bathing, doing laundry, cleaning the mud off boots, and cleaning their weapons–always cleaning their weapons–Luke heard the dog make a little yelp. He looked in her direction and saw that she was moving to another place.

Then, another Marine who lay half on the ground and half against a tree, picked up a second rock and threw it at the dog, hitting it. Again, the dog yelped, got up and moved away. Luke was appalled and said to the Marine, "Don't do that anymore!"

The other Marine looked at him insolently, picked up another rock and threw it at the dog, hitting her again. She yelped and once more got up and moved away.

The action was so fast, no one remembered exactly how it came about. Luke, enraged at the mistreatment of *his dog*, grabbed his bayonet, threw himself onto the inclined Marine, put the point of the bayonet at the throat of the Marine, hissing at him, "You throw one more rock at my dog, and I'll *kill* you!"

Others witnessed the dramatic scene. Time seemed to stand still. Finally, Luke got up suddenly, bayonet still threatening, and the other Marine got up from where he lay and left the area in double-quick time.

That night, the dog was ensconced in Luke's bed, curled up against his chest. Luke thought about the awful scene that left him drained of all energy. Left him wondering whatever made him react that way–threatening the life of another Marine? He must have been out of his mind.

Luke realized that he and the dog had not only a partnership. It was a bond–the dog alerts Luke, and Luke answers to it–but Luke feeds the dog, gives her water, washes the mud off her feet before going to bed, and pets her . . . a lot. Yes, they have a partnership and . . . what else? he asked himself. He lay there with the dog at his chest, thinking about the dog and himself. It came to him. They have love–pure love.

He thought: Yes, he took drastic measures to shield her from the rock-throwing. But it got the desired result, and that is what matters.

He began to sweat, anyway. He asked himself, "Would I have really killed the bastard? What have I become?"

* * *

The end of Luke's tour was one week away. He was troubled: what to do about the dog? No one was willing to take her in and give her the care that he himself had done for her. He hated the idea of abandoning her in the jungle, or to take her to some village where, eventually, she would be killed and eaten. And Navy Regulations would *never* permit her to accompany him on a ship nor in an aircraft!

In the end, the unit Sergeant agreed to let her be the camp mascot. He would see that someone fed her and gave her water. Maybe some new and raw recruit would come into the unit and adopt her to keep from feeling homesick. Maybe.

That seemed to be the best thing to do for the loyal little mutt.

It tore Luke's heart into a million pieces, picking her up for the last time, before he got onto the truck, stroking her back, scratching her ears, clucking with his tongue against the roof of his mouth.

"Goodbye, little buddy. You trusted me with your puppy, and then you became my lifesaver."

He set her down onto the ground. He threw his barracks bag onto the back of the truck. Then he swung himself onto it. He sat on the bench where he could look down at the dog. She seemed to sense what was about to happen. She looked up at him. She twisted her head, just a notch.

"Goodbye, faithful friend," said the Corporal.

Two other Marines were already on board. They had watched Luke handle the mutt. Then, as they saw the Corporal's eyes fill with tears, they turned away, leaving him to his private grief.

# # #

THE NEWSPAPER

Concord Tribune

April 25, 1962. Concord, Calif. BIRTH ANNOUNCEMENTS. Daniel F. Smithson, born at Rutledge Hospital. Parents, Mr. And Mrs. Willard F. Smithson of 2343 Hickory Place, Concord.

July 20, 1963. Concord, Calif. Most Beautiful Baby Contest was held by the Ladies' Club at the Presbyterian Church yesterday. It was open to all babies in the city between the ages of 1 year and 2 years. Little Daniel Smithson, age 15 months, was the winner—curly light brown hair, big brown eyes, and a beguiling smile. Congratulations to the parents, Mr. And Mrs. Willard Smithson. And, of course, congratulations to the little guy.

"What is this monstrous nonsense?!" croaked Willard to his wife. "Our Danny won a beauty contest? He's a boy, for Pete's sake!"

"Doesn't matter, Honey. Face it; Danny looks like an angel and has the personality of a real-live doll."

"How dare you compare my son to a doll!"

"Hon-ney! Calm down. It's only a contest." Then she added, "And for the record, Will, he's *my* son, too . . . ."

"Well," he said reluctantly, "I have to admit he is cute as a button." His smile faded. "What the hell am I saying? A beauty contest?!"

May 20, 1968. Concord, Calif. Kindergartners of the Concord Elementary School presented a spring program of music and poetry. Among the singers, a mellifluous voice arose to dominate the youngsters' chorus: Daniel Smithson. Another group from the kindergarten class recited two poems about nature and love.

"A mellifluous voice?" Willard stormed. "How in tarnation can you describe a five-year-old voice like *that*? Sounds like a girl!"

"Oh, Honey, don't be so critical . . . and grumpy!" said his wife, Eileen. "Some aspiring writer on the 'Tribune' is trying for a promotion, no doubt."

"Hmph!"

October 15, 1975. Concord, Calif. Daniel Smithson wins the annual spelling bee at Emerson Junior High School. It was touch and go with runner-up Christine Baker--each one trying to outspell the other. Baker went down on "banana" with Smithson spelling it correctly. Four words later, Smithson went down on "shining."

"Will! Aren't you proud of our boy? He won the spelling contest, an 8th grader against 7th and 9th graders!"

"'Bout time he got credit for doing something not looking or sounding like a girl!"

"Will. . . . Really!"

April 16, 1977. Concord, Calif. The Boy Scout medal for Eagle was awarded to Daniel Smithson in a ceremony at the Presbyterian Church Fellowship Hall. The ceremony followed a potluck dinner. Boy Scout Smithson worked diligently for his new status. His parents, Mr. And Mrs. Willard Smithson, stood with him when the award was presented. Photo above.

"I'm proud of you, son," Willard said to Danny. "You worked hard for the Eagle. I was watching."

"Yes, Dad. But you know, you helped me a lot. Thanks a bunch, Dad." Turning to his mother, he said, "You, too, Mom."

June 1, 1979. Concord, Calif. Drivers' Licenses Issued: Lori Seeley, 159 Oriole Dr.; Harold Sheldon, 2940 Fir St.; and Daniel Smithson, 2343 Hickory Pl., all of Concord.

"Dad, could I have the car tonight?"

"What for, Danny? A game somewhere?"

"No, Dad. And could you start calling me Dan? Please?"

"Well, then." A pause. "What do you want the car for?"

"A date."

Willard sputtered, "You want the car for--what-did-you-say? A date?!"

"Sure, Dad. I'm 17 now, and I have my driver's license. I'd like to borrow the car for a date tonight."

Dan's mom, Eileen, walked in at the part of 'a date' in Dan's request.

She said, "You're going on a date, Danny?. . . .I mean Dan. Honey, that's great! Who's the girl? What's she like? What's she look like?"

Dan realized an ally when he saw one . . . and heard one. "Oh, Mom, she's really nice. Long blond hair, blue eyes. Perfect!"

"She have a name? And where did you meet her"

"Lucy. We've known each other since kindergarten."

"How sweet! Well, have a good time. But be careful! . . . . You know what I mean, don't you?"

"Yes, *Ma'am!*"

"Now just a darn minute, here," Willard interjected. "I haven't given the boy permission to take the car!"

"Well, Honey, what're you waiting for?"

Dan could have hugged his mom on the spot.

Fishing the keys from his pocket, Willard grumbled, "Can't get anywhere with the two of you ganging up on me." He tossed the keys to Dan, who caught them in the air, easily. "Fill it up with gas before you come home! You hear?"

June 12, 1980. Concord, Calif. Edison High School's graduation exercises were held in the auditorium of the school. Valedictorian honors went to Elizabeth B. Leonard, and Daniel F. Smithson was designated Salutatorian. The graduating class will be leaving next week on two school buses for a trip to San Francisco. See photos above.

"Dan!" Eileen cried out. "I'm so glad you're home again and safe and sound! Did you have a good time in San Francisco, Honey?"

"Oh, sure, Mom. It was great. . . . I guess."

"What do you mean, you guess it was great?"

"I don't know for sure, Mom. We walked down the streets of San Francisco, and I had this creepy feeling about–I don't know what. It was weird."

Eileen zeroed in on his unease immediately. San Francisco was notorious for its gay population, overtaking the streets, as it were. She made no further comment.

Dan went on. "But the sights were great. Man, that Golden Gate Bridge is awesome!"

June 10, 1983. Chico, Calif. University of California, Chico, held its graduation ceremony outdoors, next to the stadium on Saturday. Among those graduating was Daniel F. Smithson, of Concord. He earned a Bachelor of Science degree with two majors–Geography and Geology.

Willard and Eileen Smithson waited near the speaker's podium, an agreed-upon site to meet Daniel after the graduation ceremony was ended.

Willard said, "Son, I'm proud of you today! You already passed me up! I'm so proud."

"Oh, Danny. . . . . Dan. You did so well in college, I'm bursting with pride!"

"Aw, Mom, Dad. It isn't that big a deal. But thanks for all your support. Your checks came in handy when my part-time job pay and Grant money didn't quite make the grade for all the expenses. So, I'm just one of a lot of people who did the same thing I did. Really." There was a significant pause. He continued. "What's ahead of me is what's important. I'm just a statistic, poised to pound the streets, looking for a job."

August 4, 1983. Concord, Calif. MOTOR CYCLE ACCIDENT INJURES 1. Mr. James T. Jones, 18, riding his motorcycle yesterday in the 1200 block of Grand Blvd., had an accident that ended in his motorcycle's falling on top of his left leg. Jones was unconscious for a few moments, witnesses said. A Mr. Daniel F. Smithson, seeing the accident happen, stopped his car, ran to the site, lifted the motorcycle off Jones and relieved him of some of the excruciating pain. Smithson then called to a bystander to get to a phone and request an ambulance. Smithson stayed with Jones until the ambulance arrived. Smithson followed the ambulance to the hospital and remained in the waiting room for five hours, until Jones's surgery was finished. Smithson then departed from the hospital.

"Honey! Dan! This article is about you?"

"What article, Mom?"

"This one in the paper, about the motorcycle accident. It tells all the things you did for the victim! You did all that?"

"That's in the paper? Today?"

"Yes! See for yourself." She handed him the paper.

Daniel read it through to the end. He looked at his mother. "It was no biggie, Mom. I just did what had to be done."

"Will the Jones boy be all right?"

"The doctors seem to think the leg will take a long time to heal, but he should be able to walk, eventually, and maybe with a slight limp."

"Thanks be to God!"

August 7, 1983. Concord, Calif. HERO RECEIVES ACCOLADES. County lauds heroism of Mr. Daniel F. Smithson, resident of Concord, for his assistance on Aug. 4 to the motorcycle accident victim, Mr. James Jones. The rest of the story was revealed by Mr. Charles Wicket, Human Resources Department Head at the County Government Center. Wicket reported that Smithson had an interview appointment with Wicket that day and that Smithson missed the appointment altogether. When Wicket read the article the next day, he realized why Smithson had missed the interview. Today, Smithson kept a new appointment, was interviewed, and was hired by the County to be a county assessor. See photo at right.

November 10, 1985. Concord, Calif. ENGAGEMENT AN-NOUNCEMENTS. Miss Lucy G. Hendricks and Mr. Daniel F. Smithson announced their engagement at a gathering in the home of the bride-to-be. Mr. And Mrs. John Hendricks hosted the festive party at 3345 Hickory Place, Concord. Refreshments were served, and Miss Hendricks rendered a violin number, "Humoresque," with Miss Jane Baylor accompanying her on the piano. Both Miss Hendricks and Miss Baylor are members of the Concord Symphonette Orchestra.

Eileen said, "Oh, Mrs. Hendricks, it was a lovely engagement party. Thank you very much."

"No, no, Eileen. Thank *you* for all your assistance. I really appreciated it. And, please . . . . .Call me Hester."

"Thank you, Hester."

"Very nice party, Mrs. Hendricks." Daniel didn't know whether to shake her hand. She always seemed to be a nice enough person—and should be, to be Lucy's mother. Still, he just didn't know her that well. "Thank you," he said.

Hester smiled at him, thinking, Well, he seemed nice enough since the first time Lucy brought him home to introduce him to us. Yes, a nice enough person, thank God!

November 20, 1986. Concord, Calif. WEDDING ANNOUNCE-MENTS. Miss Lucy G. Hendricks and Mr Daniel F. Smithson were joined in wedlock Saturday at the Presbyterian Church. Miss Hendricks' younger sister, Chloe, 8, was flower girl. Her older sister, Eleanor Hendricks Newman was matron of honor. Mr. Smithson's father, Mr. Willard Smithson, was his best man. The newlywed couple left for a honeymoon in Palm Desert. Upon their return, they will reside at the Prescott Towers in Concord.

"It was a beautiful wedding, a beautiful bride. I'm so happy for them, Willard."

"Yes, it was nice, 'Leen. All of it. I just hope they don't have a rocky road ahead of them."

"And why should they? I declare, Willard, you do look on the down side of just about everything!"

"Hmph!"

December 14, 1989. Concord, Calif. BIRTH ANNOUNCE-MENTS. Gina May Smithson was born on December 12, 1989, at the Rutledge Hospital to parents Mr. and Mrs. Daniel F. Smithson of Concord.

February 7, 1991. Concord, Calif. BIRTH ANNOUNCEMENTS. Daniel F. Smithson II was born on February 5, 1991, at the Rutledge Hospital to parents Mr. And Mrs. Daniel F. Smithson I of Concord.

November 3, 1993. Concord, Calif. The elections yesterday produced an upset in countywide offices. The surprising victory was won by Daniel F. Smithson, who is now the new County Assessor. He was a long-time employee of that office. His hard-working, hard-hitting campaign led to his election. The outgoing County Assessor has announced his early retirement.

"Dan! It's wonderful! I'm so proud of my husband!"

"Lucy, I couldn't have made it without your help. You were stumping for me as hard as I was stumping for me!"

"And loving every minute of it, Darling."

"And I love you, Lucy, big time . . . as much as I did when we were in school."

"Just how far back did that go, Dan?"

He heaved a heavy sigh. "Well, let me see. I remember the first time I saw you on the first day of kindergarten. The blonde hair, the blue eyes. Perfect. Yes, it goes back to the first time I set eyes on you. You were so darned cute! . . . . Still are." He looked at her. And you? When did you *know* I was out-of-my-mind crazy about you?"

"That's easy. It was when you began tripping me on the playground, in second grade."

They laughed together.

January 5, 2000, Sacramento, Calif. The County Assessor Daniel F. Smithson has moved to his newly elected job as Director of the

State Equalization Board after a stunningly won election last November. Director Smithson is a native of Concord, Calif.

"Hmph!" groused Willard. "Must be the same reporter on the Tribune, bucking for a promotion."

"Why is that, Hon?"

"It says here, 'a stunningly won election.' Give me a break!"

"Well, my dear, it *was* a stunningly won election."

"HMPH!"

November 5, 2003. Sacramento, Calif. NEW GOVERNOR WINS BY HISTORIC LANDSLIDE. Daniel F. Smithson, won the governor's seat yesterday in an unprecedented landslide. Every county in the state turned in a wide-margin win for the popular candidate, without exception. The Governor-Elect promises to lower taxes and still be able to support schools, repair and build new highways, improve benefits for state government employees, and to protect our State Parks along with the National Forests. When asked if he were going to raise the state's minimum wage, he replied, "If we raise the minimum wage, we, in effect, raise prices on every commodity and service in this great state of ours." Smithson, age 41, will be the youngest Governor in the state's history.

"Lucy! We did it! We did it!"

"No, Dan. *You* did it."

"Honey, you know your teas and speeches in schools and women's clubs and Party meetings, and the rallies, and . . . I don't know what else . . . did the trick. For sure!"

She smiled. It was true that the newspapers had talked her up, big time, and she enjoyed every moment of the attention she got. "So, now I get to settle in to being the governor's wife. *Surely* my job is done?!"

"Not a chance, Lucy. You're going to be almost as busy as the governor's wife as you were with the campaign. I can almost guarantee it. Before I even take office, we have all those elections parties to attend, we have to get oriented for the Governor's Mansion and how it all works, we have to get used to new kinds of schedules and responsibilities, we have to get accustomed to riding in a limousine . . . I think."

"A limousine? No way! I want to do my own driving!"

"It might not be an option, Dear."

"Is this going to be our first argument during the governorship?"

He laughed. Heartily. "I don't think it'll count, right now. I'm not the governor yet, officially."

"Spoil sport!"

During the next year, Lucy, between all her commitments as the Governor's wife, kept an album of every newspaper article she saw in local papers and in the San Francisco and Los Angeles papers that addressed her husband's new career. In no time at all, she had to purchase another album to hold the newspaper articles she collected. It, too, was almost filled.

She said to Dan, "I'm going to have to buy another one. No, wait," she said. "I forgot. There's a Governor's wife's assistant who can take care of this little detail. Can't she?"

"Of course, Lucy. You barely make it feasible to keep her on staff. By all means, give the chore to her!" Shifting gears, Dan asked, "How are the children doing in school now?"

"Well, as you know, they were both unhappy to leave Concord and all their friends. But once they got into the swing of things in Sacramento, and saw how they were deferred to every which way they turned, because they are the Governor's kids, they've come around and are liking it here very much."

"Thank goodness for that!" he said. "And thank goodness for you, Lucy. You're my rock. I swear."

"Hon-ey, you don't have to swear . . . ."

"I know."

March 20, 2004. Sacramento, Calif. OBITUARIES. Governor Daniel F. Smithson died yesterday in an airplane crash. He had departed San Francisco for St. Louis, Mo., to attend a national governor's conference. The United aircraft crashed one-half mile from the runway in St. Louis. Three houses were damaged. Two were injured in one house. There were no survivors in the aircraft. Funeral services for the Governor will take place on March 27. He will lie in state at the capitol building upon the return of his body to Sacramento. He is survived by his wife, Lucy Hendricks Smithson, his daughter Gina May Smithson, his son Daniel F. Smithson II, and the Governor's parents, Mr. And Mrs. Willard Smithson of Concord.

"Don't cry, Mom. It's going to be okay." Gina tried to console her mother.

Danny was mute, unable to utter a sound . . . until he went to bed that night. Then it began. The sobs, the tears, the emptiness . . . and the fear. Fear of the unknown was the scary part. He had just turned 13 years old. He had to get a hold of himself. Now he was the man of the house. Wasn't he?

He got up from his bed, wiped the tears off his face, and tiptoed to his mother's room. Her light was on. He knocked lightly.

"Who is it?."

"It's me, Mom. Danny."

"Ah, come on in, son. I'm just finishing up this one little chore, and then we can talk, After that, we can go back to bed."

Danny walked to stand beside her, at her desk. She was clipping some newspaper articles and mounting them in an album.

She finished clipping and finished putting them into the album.

"There," she said, closing the album. "That's the last article of the last album." She stroked his arm. "I don't think I'll ever clip another newspaper article again." She smiled at Danny. "I haven't the heart for it."

He put his arms around his Mom. He realized that in spite of her smile, she was hurting as much as he was.

October 5, 2004. Concord, Calif. Emerson Junior High School was renamed at a ceremony yesterday on the front steps of the school. The new name is the Daniel F. Smithson Junior High School, named for the late Governor of the state of California. The deceased Governor Smithson had attended Emerson during his junior high school years. His widow, Mrs. Lucy Hendricks Smithson was accompanied by her daughter Gina May, and son Daniel F. Smithson II for the ceremony. It was a tribute to the former Governor for his attention to the public schools in California, seeing that they were fully funded, well staffed, and professionally managed. There is further tribute made by the newly installed Governor, who has kept all laws providing educational facilities at the same level as Governor Smithson had mandated.

Danny, holding a newspaper, went with Gina to their mother's room. Danny knocked.

"Who is it?"

"It's me, Mom. And Gina."

"Come on in, children."

"Mom," Danny said, holding the newspaper toward her, "there's just one more newspaper article to put into the album."

Gina said, "It's the one about re-naming Emerson School, Mom.

It's a nice tribute to Dad."

"Yes, I know. Thank you. Thank you both. So very, very much."
She pointed to the album from her desk. "I already brought this out
from the closet. And I was waiting for you."

She took the newspaper from Danny. The son and daughter
watched their mother clip the article and put it into the album.

The wounded newspaper was then dropped into the trash basket.

# # #

THE GRYMWADE COLLECTION

OF

NOVELLAS

THE HALF-BREED

The town was small and dusty, a bump on the Wyoming landscape. The country back East was recovering from a civil war with difficulty. The war barely touched this town.

A blacksmith, a general store, a bank, a barber shop, a hotel for the occasional transient ranch hands and cattle herders, a café, and three saloons pretty much described the whole town, Spider Leg. The homes of Spider Leg belonged to the townspeople who maintained their businesses there. At the farthest western edge of the town stood a small but proud church building. The parsonage, also small but adequate, stood nearby.

Besides the itinerant ranch hands and cattle herders, ranch owners and their families were the only other customers coming into town. The ranchers' and businessmen's wives and children were the only parishioners to attend the weekly church service. In good weather, dinner was spread on the grounds of the church building. When that happened, the otherwise non-practicing Christian businessmen and ranchers showed up for the bountiful spread. On those occasions, services became an all-day event. Gossip was often the main topic, in spite of warnings against it from the Reverend Smith in some of his most fiery sermons.

Reverend Smith was a visionary. He came to Spider Leg with high hopes and a wagon full of school books and supplies, along with his collection of Bibles. Knowing that schools often took a back seat in the small pioneer towns, he came prepared to teach the three Rs to the children living in the community. A fifth-grade level was as high as he could go, however, wagon space being as limited as it was. As children reached their teens, Reverend Smith kept as many of those in his school as possible in an attempt to teach them something more than basics. Teaching, as it turned out, was his secondary mission; the church was his first. His make-do classes took place in the church house. It was a house of God and a house of learning.

* * *

Mary Lou Dinsmore lived with her aunt and uncle in Spider Leg. Her rancher parents had been attacked in an Indian raid, losing their lives and their scalps. Thankfully, Mary Lou had no memory of the tragedy because she was merely an infant of six months. By chance, her uncle Fred Hopkins came to the ranch to see his brother-in-law and sister and found the remains outside, in front of the house. The baby was still inside the house and unharmed. She had awakened and was crying piteously.

Fred went home, carrying the baby in his arms, grasping the rein with one hand. His wife Myrtle came running out from the house, sensing something dreadful had happened. She nearly fainted at the terrible news.

Fred proceeded to call on the town barber and then to the parsonage to arrange for the bodies to be collected and prepared for burial.

* * *

Fred was the owner and operator of the general store. Myrtle assisted him on busy days–when ranchers and their ranch hands came into town on Saturdays to shop and to while away some time in a saloon.

Now that Mary Lou was almost 17 years of age, she helped out her aunt and uncle in the store every day, thanks to the efforts of the Reverend Smith. He had taught all the children how to read and write and how to do ciphers. Her Uncle Fred taught her to keep books. It was gainful employment for a young woman, unwed, owing her aunt and uncle for caring for her while she grew up. She had room and board, sturdy clothes to wear, and had a sense of accomplishment in their small world.

Mary Lou got Sundays and Thursdays off. Since they went to church on Sundays, she used the Thursdays off to wash her hair. It was long and a luxurious light brown. It took hours (it seemed) to wash and rinse it with pump water, spewing out the spout, in a less-than-strong stream. And cold.

Shampooing her hair was simplified considerably, in warm weather, by doing it in a stream about a mile and-a-half south of town. The stream was fed by a nearby bubbling hot spring.

A butte faced the stream, barely a quarter-of-a-mile farther to the south. She had just finished rinsing her hair and was toweling it and brushing it dry. Her tethered horse stood nearby. She was facing the butte to the south.

She saw something that made her "freeze."

A man–or boy–stood at the foot of the butte, his pony not far away. A mountain lion stood at the top of the butte, poised to leap downward upon the man. She removed her rifle, from its leather sheath at the side of her horse, took careful aim, waited, and in the moment before the animal began its downward plunge, she pulled the trigger.

The man/boy heard the shot, fell to the ground and rolled to one side. The puma lay dead, not more than one foot away from him. His horse whinnied, reared upward, and pawed the air. When his forefeet came back down, he tore across the countryside, disappearing altogether.

Mary Lou dropped the rifle and fainted, falling into a heap. The young man realized where the shot had come from. He ran toward the long-haired figure, now a lump on the grassy water's edge.

* * *

Mary Lou opened her eyes, feeling a warm damp cloth on her forehead. She looked into the dark brown eyes of a young man, a stranger, with rich black hair. Indian? she wondered. She tried to scramble to her feet. He restrained her.

"Don't be afraid, Miss. I think you just fainted. Rest awhile before you try to get up again."

She melted inside. That voice was mesmerizing. She said, "I don't remember anything after I took a shot at the puma."

"Apparently you fainted right after that," he said.

His gaze took in her smallish frame, her blue-green eyes. Up close, the long light-brown hair was like spun silk. Or, what he imagined spun silk to look like. She was worthy of his appreciating all her charms.

"You saved my life, you know."

"Did I actually hit the puma?"

"Exactly where it counted most. The big cat is dead. I am indebted to you for as long as it takes me to repay the debt."

Now she sat up. "What do you mean, 'as long as it takes you to repay the debt?' You owe me nothing. Nothing at all!"

"Yes, I do. I'm a half-breed, and the blood of the Shoshone runs through my veins. It is their law. It is their way."

"You're 'breed?"

"Yes. From my mother's side. My father is a Scotsman. My Shoshone grandparents live with him in his mountain cabin."

"And your mother?"

"She died in childbirth. Her second baby, when I was just three years old. I have no clear memory of my mother. Only shadows."

"Oh, I'm so sorry."

"My grandparents, along with my father, raised me. I was not alone."

She was ready to stand up. He assisted her.

She said, "And now? Are you still . . . . . not alone?"

"I live in two worlds, actually. Sometimes I am with my mother's tribe; sometimes I am with my father and grandparents; and in between, I am alone. I have been alone for a few weeks until this moment. Now *you* are with me."

The words were left in the air. She didn't know what to do; what to say.

Ducking her head, she tried to step around him. He did not move out of her way. He asked, "Where do you go now?"

"Home. I live with my aunt and uncle in town."

"In Spider Leg?"

"What else is there in this god-forsaken countryside?"

"Interesting question. So," he said, pointing to her horse, "you came on your own mount?"

"Yes. What about *your* mount? I saw a pony before I spotted the puma."

"He was frightened away."

"But how will you return to . . . wherever you were headed? It's a very long walk to anywhere but to Spider Leg."

"The pony will find me. I need only to wait for him. I owe you every favor I can fathom until my debt to you is paid off."

"Really?! But I cannot expect you to do such a thing!" . . . she thought a moment. "What is your name?"

"White Elk. And yours?"

"I'm Mary Lou. Mary Lou Dinsmore."

He smiled. "A beautiful name, Mary Lou." He paused. "Miss Dinsmore."

"And 'White Elk' is a noble name. How did you come by it?"

"My Christian name is Jeremy MacGregor. When I was 15, I bagged my first wild animal, which was used for the hide and the meat and the bones: a huge white elk. The tribe presented me with the hide. It is my trophy to prove my new name, 'White Elk.'"

"What a lovely custom." She considered a bit what she wanted to ask him. Then, "Tell me something, White Elk. How come you speak so well? You remind me of the Reverend Smith who was educated back East. His speech is eloquent."

"And where did you learn the word 'eloquent'?"

"The Reverend Smith brought books to our town when he arrived several years ago. The first time he lent me one to read, I had to ask him what 'eloquent' means. And you? You have books to read?"

"Yes. And my father taught me to read and write. To this day, when I visit him and my grandparents, the lessons continue. It appears I will never finish my education . . . from my father."

"And that is just as it should be. I am so lucky to have the Reverend Smith to teach all us children in Spider Leg."

"You say you live with your aunt and uncle. Where are your parents?"

She told him the gruesome story. He was shocked. He took both her hands in his and said, "I am very sorry." He considered a question. "Were they Shoshone?"

"We're not sure."

Again, he said, "I am very sorry."

They shared a quiet moment, wondering what to say next.

White Elk looked up suddenly, hearing something. Mary Lou watched him. She followed his gaze. On the horizon was White Elk's pony, heading straight for White Elk.

* * *

"Consarn it, Mary Lou! What kind of nonsense story are you telling us? You killed a big cat, saved somebody's life, a 'breed, no less, and now he says he's gonna pay back the debt?"

"Uncle Fred, don't say 'Breed'! He's a very nice gentleman, nicer than any of the rough cowboys who come into town, shooting, cussing, and drinking whiskey!"

"And how would you know that?"

Fred Hopkins was 40 years old and just barely showing some gray hair. Tall but not muscular, mostly because of his light duties as a general-store owner. Lifting a sack of flour was his biggest physical challenge.

Ignoring his question, she said, "Like I told you, Uncle Fred. I shot the mountain lion, saved White Elk's life, probably, and now he feels he owes me a debt."

"All right, then. He accompanied you home, big dead cat across his horse. The debt is paid! I forbid you to see him again for the rest of your life, and that's that!"

"You can't mean it!"

"Good Honk, girl! Have you forgotten already that yore pore mamma and daddy were killed by Indians?"

"Uncle Fred! That's not fair!" She stomped into her small bedroom at the back of the house, half pouting, half enraged.

She thought about her rage and believed more than ever that her uncle was being unfair about White Elk.

Myrtle was noncommittal, like a good pioneer wife–strong enough to help pull a wagon out of a mud hole, but unwilling to argue with a hard-headed husband. She was nearing 40 and had a stringy figure, tall and lean, with hair that was grayer, much grayer, than Fred's, her husband.

Still, Myrtle had a tendency to agree with Fred's anger, just this once. *Mary Lou ridin' through town with a 'breed in tow? By the Saints above!*

* * *

White Elk had begun his day with no particular place in mind to go to, no particular chore to tend to. But after his encounter with the Mary Lou person, and after riding next to her on her way home, he went straight to his father's mountain cabin.

"Father," he said, addressing Sean MacGregor, always formally, as his father had taught him. "I have had a harrowing experience."

He then related the entire puma and Mary Lou episode, ending with, "I now owe the Mary Lou young lady a life's debt. I will follow her wherever she goes, keep her from harm, protect her from unwanted trouble–until I've paid the debt."

MacGregor said, "I understand your Shoshone custom, Jeremy, but you're only half Shoshone. Surely the tribe would not hold you to this practice?"

"It is not a matter, Father, of whether the tribe expects me to do this for Mary Lou Dinsmore. It is my personal decision, my personal desire." He looked down at his feet. "I like her, Father. Very, very much." Lifting his head again, he said, " I want to shield her from the ugliness of this world–for the rest of my life–for the rest of her life, if need be."

His father sighed, deeply. The boy was 19 years old. He was a man and as a man, he was free to make these kinds of life decisions. Sean sighed again, nodding to the boy . . . no, the man . . . his consent.

* * *

Mary Lou was a-twitter about the barn dance to be held at the ranch nearest to Spider Leg. Aunt Myrtle fussed over the dress she had made for Mary Lou, even though she had put her through two fittings already. It was the nicest dress Mary Lou had ever owned. She was so proud!

At last both the women were ready, Fred waiting in the wagon. Myrtle climbed aboard to sit with him in the wide seat at the front of the wagon; Mary Lou sat on a rug in the back, riding backwards, legs dangling from the edge. She tried not to muss up her fine new dress. Nearby were a cake and two pies–Aunt Myrtle's contribution of food for the barn dance. Fred had already put them into the wagon, while he waited for the women.

It did not take long to get to the Richards' ranch. Both the front yard and the barnyard were crowded with wagons and a few carriages. The fiddlers' music filled the air. Dancing had already begun. Ladies put out their food for the party.

As soon as Fred tied up the team at a tree branch, he helped the ladies down from the wagon and helped carry in the food.

The Richards boy, Earl, had been watching to see when Mary Lou was going to arrive. He was slight of build, light brown hair and watery blue eyes. He spotted their team, recognizing the horses, and ran outside to greet Mary Lou and her aunt and uncle.

"Howdy, Mr. Hopkins, Miz Hopkins." Looking at Mary Lou with wonder he stammered, "'Evenin' Mary Lou."

"Good evening, Earl." Fred and Myrtle nodded their greetings and hurried on into the barn. Mary Lou began to follow them. Earl put out a restraining hand on her arm.

"Don't go in yet, Mary Lou. I wanna ask you somethin'."

"And what would that be, Earl?"

"Mary Lou, I'd be much obliged if you'd save every dance for me." He turned several shades of red, asking himself, how could he be so forward?

"Well, Earl. We'll see." She marched into the barn, anxious to meet up with girl friends from the neighboring ranches. See what they were wearing. Wanting to show off her own new gown.

Earl tagged along behind her like a puppy.

* * *

Since the barn dance was being held in the Richards' barn, Earl felt he had first choice on asking Mary Lou to dance, as soon as she entered. She danced with him once. Then, for the rest of the evening, other young gentlemen cut in on each of her partners. This happened throughout the entire evening. Earl was steaming.

Somehow, Earl managed to work his way to Mary Lou's presence again. Instead of dancing with her, he said, "Mary Lou, you must be sorely tired, dancin' all evenin'. Let's go outside for a breath of fresh air."

"Of course, Earl. That would be nice. I *am* getting a little tired. I think my dancing shoes are too tight!" She said, "Dancing shoes? What a joke! These are my *only* shoes. I'm such a hypocrite!"

They giggled as they left the barn and walked toward a tree just behind the parked wagons and carriages. He stopped and took her by the hand to stop her as well. He tried to steal a kiss.

Mary Lou was outraged! She shoved him away from her. He lunged for her, but missed because something....no, someone....dropped from an overhead tree branch, knocked Earl silly, sent him on his way, howling that he had been attacked! But he stopped in his tracks, suddenly realizing it was not very manly to admit to an incident such as this. Without a backward glance, he proceeded to walk slowly to the barn.

Now Mary Lou was shocked. The attacker was none other than White Elk!

"What on earth are you doing here?" she demanded.

"Watching over you, Mary Lou. I am indebted to you for my life. Remember?"

"Well, this incident was not life-threatening, White Elk!"

"The way I see it, Mary Lou, the young whelp was up to no good. If not to take your life from you, he could easily have *ruined* your life. Almost the same thing."

She thought about what White Elk had said. Carefully. She ventured to say, "You're probably right. I feel I owe *you*, White Elk!"

He smiled grandly. She could see his teeth in the darkness. They were the most beautiful teeth she had ever seen . . . in the dark.

* * *

Finally, the fiddlers put away their instruments; the food table was cleared, practically no food was leftover; and the party began to break up. The barn dance was over and friends and neighbors began to depart, some in wagons, some in carriages. Fred and Myrtle and Mary Lou made their way back to town and into the shed. The two women barely made it into the house when an unusual rain storm came down onto the town of Spider Leg. Fred unhitched the horses and put them into their stalls. He ran from the shed toward the house through the pelting rain. He stomped into the kitchen, drenched to the skin.

When the three of them finally got settled in for the night, Mary Lou lay in her bed in her tiny bedroom. The rain was lighter now. She was wide awake. The Earl/White Elk scene ran through her head over and over.

Suddenly, she sat up. It was still raining, but softly by now. Mary Lou had a sobering thought, and she acted on it immediately. She put on her robe, slipped into her only pair of shoes, and went to the kitchen anteroom where the rain gear was kept. She put on a slicker and rubber boots. Then she threw a shawl onto her head and around her neck.

Easing herself out the back kitchen door carefully, she quickly walked the four steps across the back porch, down two steps and out under the sycamore tree. Looking upward, she said, "White Elk! White Elk! Are you up there? In another tree?"

"Yes, Mary Lou. What is it? Are you all right?"

"Never mind me! Are *you* all right? Aren't you getting wet?"

"Of course not. I'm all right. I am Indian. I know how to sleep in a tree and not get wet."

"I insist you come down from there this instant!" she almost shouted, not wanting to wake up her aunt and uncle.

"Mary Lou, I'm all right, I tell you."

"Stop arguing with me and come down. At least sleep on the porch. It has a better protection than the tree, for heaven's sake."

He thought about that, but for only a moment. "All right. Stand aside. I'm jumping down."

She ran up the steps and onto the porch, White Elk behind her.

"Here," she said, removing her slicker and shawl. "Use the shawl for a pillow and cover yourself with the slicker. I hope you'll be warm."

"Do not fuss over me, Mary Lou. I am Indian. I can stand all kinds of hardships!"

She removed the boots. She took a step toward the back door, but turned back to him and said, "Well, are you waiting for me to tuck you in?"

"Tuck me in? That sounds so very nice!"

She fled into the kitchen and back to her bed.

* * *

The next morning, White Elk was gone. Mary Lou wondered about that. She was prepared to give him breakfast. As long as he was keeping watch over her, the least she could do was to give him a meal as well as a dry place to sleep.

Neither Uncle Fred nor Aunt Myrtle knew about the visitor on their back porch, for Mary Lou had brought in her boots, disposed of the slicker and shawl. White Elk had left both of the last two items neatly folded and placed over the bannister.

* * *

Two days later, on Monday, Mary Lou went on an errand to the bank. She had to pass one of the saloons. Sam, the town drunk, came reeling through the double swinging doors and almost collided with her. Pretending to keep her from stumbling, he grabbed her crazily around the waist.

But that was as far as the drunken oaf got. Suddenly he was pulled away from Mary Lou by a mighty force, and next, he found himself rolling in the dirt in the street. The hollering by the drunk and a scream from Mary Lou brought several saloon customers outside to see what the commotion was all about.

"It's the 'breed!" one man shouted.

"Gittim!" yelled another.

The bar tender hollered, "Somebody git the Sheriff!"

At that, Mary Lou came to her senses and recovered her dignity. The men from the saloon were right. She now saw that it was White Elk who had intervened and saved her from further embarrassment with the town drunk. "Forget the Sheriff!" she called out for all to hear. "This young man prevented old Sam here from making a fool of himself by trying to assault me!"

Ump, the bartender, said to her, "Miss Mary Lou, you takin' up for the 'breed?"

"Of course I am! White Elk, here . . ."

"White Elk? Who the hell is that?" asked a customer.

"The young gentleman here who came to my assistance just now,." she said.

"What? The 'breed?"

"Do *not* call him that! Not in my presence!"

"Then what do we call him, eh?"

"White Elk."

The gathered crowd began to laugh and jeer. Some women passing by gave Mary Lou a withering look, having heard her defend the 'breed. Very unladylike, in their estimation.

The laughing crowd diffused the moment of anger toward anyone. They were no longer angry at Sam nor Mary Lou, and strangely, they were not angry at the half-breed.

When the furious moment was passed and all had gone back to their separate activities for the morning, Sam was hauled to his rooming house in a wheelbarrow and dumped onto the front porch. Mary Lou continued on her way to the bank, shaking her head and wondering, "Where in heaven's name did White Elk go?"

He had disappeared—as mysteriously as he had appeared.

"Damn Indian," Ump muttered under his breath, as he re-entered the saloon.

* * *

Some weeks later, Mary Lou went out the back porch with the

dishpan to heave the dishwater onto the ground. Turning toward the back door, she noticed something resting across the back-porch bannister. It was in the same spot where White Elk had left the slicker and shawl, after that very rainy night.

She approached the object, set down the dishpan, and rubbed her hand over the item. It was furry. "What on earth?" she asked no one in particular. Then she picked it up and unfolded it.

"Glory Be!" she exclaimed. Running back into the house, she showed Aunt Myrtle and Uncle Fred what she had found. "It has to be the puma hide!" she announced with excitement.

Fred Hopkins, curious, and suspicious besides, took the hide from Mary Lou. "By Jingo. I believe it *is* a cat hide! What a beauty!" He looked at her and asked, "You think it's from the 'breed?"

"I *know* it's from White Elk! It's a Shoshone custom to award the hide of a big kill to the one who brought it down."

"Well, I'll be danged!" For a tiny moment, Uncle Fred was proud of his niece's ability with the rifle.

* * *

Mary Lou covered herself in bed with the puma hide every cold night of the beastly Wyoming winters. It warmed her body; it warmed her heart.

* * *

Fred Hopkins looked at his niece, her head bent over the store's books. She was 17 now, and Fred remembered how his sister, Mary Lou's mother, had often said, after Mary Lou was born, that she wanted the baby to grow up and "get educated real nice."

Fred wasn't bound by a death-bed promise, for sure. But he felt a duty to his sister by considering sending Mary Lou to a ladies' finishing school in Denver. Might be a good hunting ground for a husband, was his secondary thought.

The general store had done well (with no competition in sight), and money was not a problem. Fred knew in his heart and in his bank book that he could afford to enroll Mary Lou in the finishing school.

His next thought went back to the not too-distant past's news from certain townspeople coming to shop in the store. They said that one day, Mary Lou had intervened on behalf of the 'breed in front of the Cow Town Saloon, preventing his getting arrested by the Sheriff.

Fred thought about that a lot. Funny that when he thought about that, he then began thinking about the finishing school. Could be a sensible solution to the impending problem. Just send Mary Lou to Denver for a couple of years until all this blows over.

* * *

A letter from Fred to the mayor of Denver, asking for the name and address of the finishing school for young ladies, produced a reply from the mayor within the month. In the next month, there was a reply from Miss Minnie May Lovelace, superintendent of the finishing school. Did Mr. Hopkins wish to enrol his niece for the next semester, beginning the following September?

Indeed he did. And the arrangements went forward without a hitch.

Mary Lou had mixed feelings about going away so far to go to a school. She would miss her friends in Spider Leg. But she'd make new ones in Denver. She'd miss Uncle Fred and Aunt Myrtle, who had so faithfully cared for her since her infancy as if she were their own. But she'd be back.

It struck her moments later: she would lose the White Elk protection, his showing up in the most unexpected places at the most surprising times. "Oh, well," she said to herself, "the Shoshone law as it applied to White Elk, regarding her safety, would have to be set aside. It can't last forever, anyway. Just a superstition, probably."

Still. She wondered. She would have given her right arm for the opportunity to say goodbye to White Elk. She dismissed it fatalistically, saying to herself softly, "What can't be, can't be. What is, is."

* * *

To go by stage from Spider Leg to Denver, stopping at night for resting and sleeping, it would take the best part of two weeks or more to complete the journey. Fred and Myrtle Hopkins put Mary Lou on the stage early one morning, saying goodbye. Myrtle dabbed her eyes. She would miss the girl, just as she would her own child. Fred swallowed hard, trying to get rid of a big lump in his throat.

Mary Lou noticed what was happening with both her aunt and uncle. She smiled at them and said, "Goodbye and thank you, Aunt Myrtle, Uncle Fred. I'll see you in two years. You take care of yourselves."

"G'bye, Honey."

"So long, Chile."

* * *

By the middle of the second week of traveling, the stage had made many stops. People getting off, other people getting picked up, all along the way. They had passed into Colorado and on that day, Mary Lou found herself alone in the coach. She was getting tired of the dusty miles, the unchanging scenery, except for the nearby Rockies off to the west. She nodded off, half sprawling across the empty seat. That was an unexpected luxury, having the coach to herself.

She sat up, suddenly awake. What wakened her? Rifle shots? She looked out the coach's window. "God help us!" she shouted to no one. "We're being attacked by Indians!" She hunkered down onto the seat while an occasional arrow flew into the coach. From both sides! She was petrified. But it must have been a short-lived battle. The coach came to a stop. She sat up. The door was opened by an Indian. Mary Lou was even more scared than before. Until . . . She looked at the Indian carefully.

"White Elk! What is going on here?"

He climbed in and sat beside her. "Are you unhurt, Mary Lou?"

"Yes. I'm all right. Shaken, but all right."

"I thank the gods . . . I mean, I thank God for that!"

"White Elk. I don't understand. You are in the attacking party? This is insane! How did you know I was on this coach? I don't understand anything any more!"

"It's going to be all right, Mary Lou. Don't worry."

"What do you mean, 'Don't worry'?"

"I've been following you on my horse from a distance, since you left Spider Leg. Then I saw the attack. They're Hopis. They have captured you . . . . . . and me."

* * *

By late afternoon, the coach was pulled into the Hopi camp. Mary Lou and White Elk were forced to get out of the coach and were pushed into an outdoor holding area. Both coach drivers had been forced off the coach during the chase and were subsequently trampled to death by the hooves of the Hopi horses.

Mary Lou watched as the Hopi women went through her valise, trunk, and a suitcase. They went through everything she owned in the way of clothing and personal treasures, namely a portrait of her mother. They tried on the dresses (including her best dress, the one she had worn to the barn dance), and jackets; put shawls around their shoulders, and examined the foreign-looking underwear with awe and a childlike delight. They had no idea what to do with it. But it was white, like the pale face. They were interested in the white bloomers and camisoles and petticoats, still wondering what to do with them. Never mind. They would figure out something.

The braves who crowded around the coach spotted the drivers' valises and went through them, trying on shirts and jackets, holding the pants next to their bodies to determine if they might fit them.

White Elk was taken into the Hopi Chief's tent where the chief examined the complicated prisoner status. The Hopi recognized White Elk as another Indian, who had shown up in battle to help the pale-faced passenger. Although White Elk's language was different from the Hopi, he could understand most of what was said to him and could make himself understood by the Hopis.

White Elk told the story to the speaker for the Chief, and the speaker relayed it to the Chief. The Chief spent some minutes conjuring up a solution–other than executing them both, a pale face and a half-pale face–he pronounced his decision, through the Hopi speaking for him. White Elk was allowed to return to the holding area and inform the pale face what was to become of them both.

"Mary Lou," he began. "Make a serene face, for the Hopi to see. No, no, do not frown. I will explain. This is the story I have told for the Chief.

"I am a half-breed, I told him, and you are a pale face. We wanted to mate, but your people would not allow it, and neither would my people approve of it. You were on your way to meet me in another state where we could be married. I was following, at a distance, to join you later at our agreed-on meeting place.

"The Hopi raiding party has interfered with our secret plan. And, I said to the Chief, 'We are at your disposal, Great Hopi Chief. Do with us what you will. But do not separate us and keep us from our destiny to be joined.'"

"You said what?"

"Be careful, Mary Lou. Remember to smile at all times. We are being watched. And now I will tell you what happens next. It is the Chief's decision. You will be prepared tonight by Hopi women, in a tent set aside for you. I will sleep in the holding area. Tomorrow we will be joined in a Hopi ceremony. All very proper. The Chief is a romantic, at heart, so it seems."

Mary Lou was astonished beyond comprehension. She almost burst out a protest, but White Elk, putting a strong hand onto her arm, reminding her again, said, "Mary Lou. Smile. Smile ever so grandly, to show the Hopi that you are overjoyed to know that tomorrow we will be joined."

"I cannot find words to describe my utter disbelief! We are going to be what? . . . . . Joined?" Still smiling, she said, again, "Joined?"

White Elk could imagine what fears the word 'joined' was meaning to her. He tried to explain. "My dear. It is only a ceremony, and meaningful only to the Hopi. We are not to be married in a Christian sense. I do not know for certain what the 'joining' ceremony entails in the Hopi camp. We must wait until tomorrow and do what they say. Please do not be dismayed. We will be on our way shortly afterwards. If we're lucky, the Chief may even let us have a horse. Perhaps a horse from the stagecoach team! He still ends up with five extra horses to add to his pack."

"What happened to your own pony, White Elk?"

"He was lost, I think. At any rate, I haven't been able to spot him in the camp's horse corral."

"Oh, White Elk. I'm so sorry. I know that you were very much attached to your pony."

"Thank you, Mary Lou. I have no idea what happened to him."

She decided to change the subject. "You talk of a horse gift, a joining, a ceremony as if it is something that happens every day!"

"Mary Lou. I am trying to help you to realize the gravity of our situation. Understand the need to go along with what the Chief at this moment is arranging."

"I swan, I don't know *what* to think!"

He smiled at her to give her courage, which she was going to need through this night, the morrow, and perhaps . . . . tomorrow night, as well.

She regarded that beautiful smile. It was even more beautiful in the daylight, she noticed. She sighed. She tried on her own smile. Something inside her told her to . . . . what? . . . enjoy what is to come?

* * *

Dressed in a soft-leather Hopi garment, Mary Lou Dinsmore walked under a "tunnel" of sagebrush boughs being held over her head by the Hopi women, both young and old. At the same moment, White Elk, dressed in his same Indian clothing, walked under a similar "tunnel" of battle axes being held over his head by the Hopi warriors.

Listening to the pronouncements of the Shaman, they meant absolutely nothing to Mary Lou. They had deep meaning for White Elk. He was moved by the solemnity shown by all who were present.

Then, the ceremonial mixing of blood began. A tiny nick by the knife of a warrior in the pad of Mary Lou's left thumb (which frightened her out of her wits), and another small cut made in the pad of White Elk's right thumb prepared them for the "mixing." White Elk understood the custom: he placed his cut thumb against hers, rubbing it in a circle, slowly and gently. And they were joined.

* * *

After the joining ceremony and after a meal for everyone–deer meat stewed with cornmeal–and after the ceremonial dances were finished, it was just past dusk. The Chief signaled the end of the feasting and dancing. The two joined ones were escorted to their tent–arranged by the Chief's aides.

The flap was held open. White Elk entered first, and Mary Lou was obliged to follow him. The tent flap fell closed. They were alone. On the dirt floor of the tent, in the center, hot embers glowed. A bearskin and a deerskin were placed to one side of the embers.

"What now?" she whispered.

He answered, not whispering, "We rest." He spread the bearskin onto the dirt floor, the deerskin folded at the foot. "Come. Sit," he said. "Beside me."

Mary Lou waited, thinking. Then she moved around the embers and sat onto the bearskin, next to him. She shivered.

"Are you cold?"

"No. Just scared."

"No need to be. We are safe. And tomorrow we leave this camp and make our way back to Spider Leg."

"And how long will that take?"

"It depends. If the Chief is magnanimous, he will give us a horse and some supplies for the journey."

"I'm still scared. I don't know what to expect." She began to weep, quietly.

He put his arm around her shoulders, and said to her softly, "We will sleep together, you and I."

She jumped involuntarily, tears forgotten. "We will what?"

"Just sleep, Mary Lou. I will not touch you in the husband way. But we must lie abed together because the Watchers can see our shadows cast against the tent wall by the light from the embers."

"The watchers? What does that mean?"

"Since we were captured, the Shoshone's not knowing if we are enemies or just hapless travelers, will be watching us to determine if we are truly mated."

"That's impossible!"

"I know that, Mary Lou. You and I cannot be mates without a

proper Christian ceremony." He reflected on what he should say next. "But we have to *look* like we are mated."

Gently, he eased her onto her back. She did not resist. He was totally non-threatening. However, she was rigid with fear again. He spoke as gently as he had touched her. "Do not be afraid, Mary Lou. Trust me. Please."

She closed her eyes and swallowed hard. She began weeping again.

"Sh-h-h-h," he whispered softly. "It's going to be all right, Mary Lou. Try to sleep now." He stroked her hair, that gorgeous, silky light brown hair. He stroked her shoulders, slowly, with extreme care and gentleness. He picked up her hand, the one that had the thumb prick. Putting her thumb into his mouth, he cleansed it with his tongue. Then, removing her thumb from his mouth, he pressed his lips lightly against the wound, lightly kissing her thumb.

She stopped weeping. "And what is the meaning of this?" she asked.

"A personal token of my concern for you, for your safety, and a mate's act of cleansing."

She took a few deep breaths. She felt safe. She felt . . . . loved. Soon she was asleep.

White Elk sensed that she had drifted off. He rested his head next to hers, one hand on her shoulder. He was deeply affected by the ceremony, the blending of blood. And the "cleansing" by mouth that he did for her. Soon, he, too, was asleep, a smile on his lips

* * *

As White Elk expected—and predicted—the Chief, still performing the role of the romantic, gave the two newly joined couple a horse and provisions for their journey home. The horse was indeed from the stagecoach team. After profuse thanks to the Chief and all his tribe, White Elk mounted the horse. Mary Lou wore her traveling clothes again. As White Elk had instructed her earlier that morning, she took her place alongside the horse and White Elk, and they left the Hopi camp. A fitting farewell—The Warrior astride his mount, his woman walking.

* * *

When they were well out of sight from the Hopi camp, White Elk dismounted and walked with Mary Lou.

For the first day of their journey home, they ate pemmican during a short respite, and this was to be repeated each day as long as the pemmican lasted. During the afternoon part of the first day's trek, White Elk bagged a squirrel with bow and arrow (a part of their provisions). At dusk, they made their first night's camp in the edge of a small birch forest. He skinned the squirrel and eviscerated it, saving some of the innards for a stew. The squirrel was cooked over the campfire, and Mary Lou had never before tasted anything so delicious in her life! The squirrel bones were added to the "stew," which was cooked in a hollowed-out stone, over the all-night fire. Except for the bones and some of the innards, they would eat the stew for breakfast the next morning. The bowl-shaped stone was also a part of the equipment provided by the Hopi.

After their first evening meal, Mary Lou saw that White Elk was preparing a bed of one blanket on the ground and one blanket for cover. She asked, "Why are you fixing a bed like that?"

"It is for the benefit of the Watchers," he replied.

"The Watchers? Here?"

"There are at least two braves following us from the Hopi camp. To ensure, for the Chief, that we are living as mated man and woman."

Out here? Surely we are not being watched!"

"Oh, but we are."

"How in heaven's name do you know that, White Elk?"

"I am Indian. I know they are somewhere near, in this little forest. Watching us. Making sure we are still joined."

"That's ridiculous!"

"Do you want me to summon them, confront them, and send them back to the Hopi Chief to report that we are 'faking' our union?"

"Do you mean to tell me that we have to sleep together . . . again?!"

"Exactly, my dear."

"Don't you 'my dear' me!" She had second thoughts about what she just said. In truth, she liked being called 'my dear' . . . by White Elk. "I mean. I didn't mean to say that, White Elk. You have been honest with me throughout this whole ordeal. Who am I to speak so sharply to you?"

"I understand your feelings, Mary Lou. This is a difficult time."

"I'm sorry, White Elk. I feel like a child who's had a temper tantrum."

"After all's said and done, though, we still have to 'pretend' to be mated. Until the Watchers are gone."

"And that will be?"

"A few days more, perhaps. We shall see. Come, Mary Lou. We must bed again."

This time, it looked so inviting. He lay there with his right arm extended. She was exhausted. She lay down beside him, her head resting on his arm. He pulled the top blanket up and over them. He was breathing into her ear, slowly, evenly. She felt safe. Let the Watchers watch. She did not care.

* * *

On the morning of the eighth day of travel, White Elk said to Mary Lou, "They have gone."

"They?" she asked. Then, "The Watchers?"

"Yes."

"How on earth can you tell? I am mystified!"

"I can just tell. They are gone. In the night. I sensed it, even as we slept."

"You are an amazing man, White Elk. I am happy to be joined with . . . What am I saying?"

White Elk smiled, the one she learned quickly to admire. "I hear you saying that you are happy to be . . ."

"I know what I said. I just can't *believe* what I said!"

That morning, after their breakfast, White Elk had Mary Lou ride the horse while he walked beside her. Now that the Watchers were gone.

When their supper was over that evening, the utensils were cleaned, and the fire was banked, White Elk prepared the two blankets separately: one for Mary Lou, and one for him.

"White Elk."

"Yes, Mary Lou?"

There was a catch in her breathing. Finally, she said, "Please, prepare the blankets as we have in the past. One beneath us; one over us."

He stared at her for long moments. Then he re-arranged the blankets, as they had been arranged during the first part of the journey home. "Like this?" he asked.

"Exactly like this. Let us abed." She lay down first.

White Elk looked at her with new eyes. He lay down beside her. She nestled comfortably next to him. She reached across his chest and put her hand on his opposite shoulder. Their heads were touching.

White Elk's heart was filled with immeasurable joy.

* * *

When the morning sun awakened him, White Elk arose and said, excitedly, "Mary Lou! Mary Lou! Wake up!"

"What? What is it, White Elk?" She sensed an urgency in his voice. She got up from the blankets and looked around. Then she saw it. . . . . the reason for his calling her.

"White Elk," she said softly. "It's your pony, isn't it?"

"Yes, Mary Lou. He found his way to us. There's no telling how long he's been following us, waiting for the watchers to disappear."

"Yes, of course, my dear. He is an amazing animal–almost human."

"No truer statement was ever spoken!" he said with deep feelings for the faithful pony. He walked quickly to the pony to stroke its neck and back, to let it know that he appreciated his animal intelligence. . . . almost human.

* * *

On the next night, Mary Lou herself prepared the blankets, exactly as they had been before. She lay down on the lower blanket, facing outward, her back toward the center of the blanket. White Elk lay down beside her and put his arm around her waist.

Mary Lou turned over to face him. White Elk held her head in place, with his two hands. Leaning over her, he rubbed his nose against hers, side-to-side. "What is this?" she asked.

"It is the Shoshone kiss."

Then he placed his lips upon hers and kissed her. "And this," he said, "is the white man's kiss."

Her heart began pounding like a sledge hammer, but she managed to ask, "And where and how did you learn *that*?"

"As in everything else I've learned, I learned the white man's kiss from my father. He explained it to me, thoroughly. He kissed the back of my hand to demonstrate." White Elk looked up at the stars. "In fact, it is the only real but faint memory I have of my mother: she and my father were kissing each other."

"What a beautiful thought. And, my dear White Elk, it was a beautiful experience to be kissed by you, so sweetly, so gently, so . . . The white man's way, that is."

She then placed her lips upon his and kissed him more soundly, more intensely. "And that," she said, "is the white *woman's* kiss." He had responded in like manner. They were both profoundly affected.

Mary Lou felt a stirring inside her body, deeply inside her body. She moaned. White Elk lay back down, pushing away his elemental instincts.

White Elk said, "We must not do this, Mary Lou. It is not the Christian way."

"I know."

He held her closely, carefully keeping in check where his hands were wanting to wander, wanting to explore.

She remained quiet for many long minutes, not daring to breathe nor to speak. It was so comforting, lying in his arms. She felt at peace. She slept. And then he slept.

* * *

"Today," White Elk announced, "we enter Spider Leg. I will take you to your home. We will tell your aunt and uncle everything."

"Everything?"

"Not to leave out anything. It is the only way to assure them that all is well--after they see us enter the town, me on my pony; you on the Shoshone horse gift."

"If I know my Uncle Fred and Aunt Myrtle, they will find little or no comfort in whatever we tell them. Uncle Fred will be fightin' mad . . . even when I tell him and Aunt Myrtle that you saved my life, or saved me from a life of slavery in the Hopi camp.

"Then . . . . . when we tell them about the joining . . . . I dread to think of what their reactions will be!"

"There might be one way to assuage their horror: we can, at first, request your Reverend Smith to join us in a Christian ceremony."

"You'd do that with me, White Elk?"

"Of course! It is something I desire, Mary Lou. I desire you, desperately. Please say you will stand with me while I ask the Reverend Smith."

"Of course. Oh, White Elk, what is to become of us if the Reverend refuses?"

"Then we will travel to the ends of earth to find someone who will marry us."

* * *

Mary Lou was not in error by describing her aunt and uncle's reactions. They were livid! They were appalled! And they were dead-set against the girl's marrying a 'breed! A Hopi ceremony meant nothing to Fred and Myrtle. Intolerable! To Mary Lou, on the other hand, the Hopi joining was beginning to have more and more significance for her. She longed for White Elk's tenderness, the peace she felt when she was with him.

At any rate, the Reverend Smith was just as adamant as Fred and Myrtle in his being opposed to Mary Lou's marrying the 'breed.

White Elk said goodbye to Mary Lou; he had to report to his father all that happened since his leaving for Denver, to protect her. It was an emotional moment, their goodbye.

"When will I see you again, White Elk?"

"As soon as I visit my father and grandparents, and as soon as I can find a solution to our dilemma. I truly want to marry you, Mary Lou."

"And I want to marry you, White Elk. In the worst way!"

* * *

Mary Lou had no means whatsoever for contacting White Elk. She did not know where he lived at this moment—with the Shoshones or with his father. She had no idea where his father lived, other than in a cabin in the mountains. Or was White Elk by himself, somewhere in the territory? She was beside herself.

Fred and Myrtle, however, were, after all, relieved that she had survived the Hopi attack on the stagecoach she was traveling in. Fred sent a letter to the young ladies' school in Denver, explaining why she did not show up at the expected and intended time. And more time is what they, in Spider Leg, needed to sort out the mess.

* * *

Months later, in the middle of spring, it happened unexpectedly, almost wordlessly. As Mary Lou walked through the town, from her uncle's house to the general store to go to work, someone stepped from around the corner of the barber shop, facing her, and said to her almost inaudibly, "Meet me at the stream on Thursday." He kept on going and soon disappeared between the next two buildings.

It was not a difficult thing for Mary Lou to do. After all, Thursday was her day off, and she was overdue to accomplish a shampoo in the warm waters of the stream, now that the winter was ended. When she arrived at the stream, she began the chore of shampooing, trying to keep an eye for the approaching White Elk. She was nearly finished drying her hair when a pair of hands on her shoulders, turned her around.

It was White Elk. She was overjoyed, it had been so long since they had parted. They hugged each other intensely and kissed each other passionately. They held each other for a long time, savoring the feel of each other, enjoying the moment to the fullest.

He took a blanket from his pony and put it on the new green grass. They sat upon it. He took her hands in his and said, "Mary Lou, I have longed to be with you so much that I ache for you."

"It's the same for me, White Elk. I could hardly wait for today to come, the day that you would try to be with me."

"I have news for you, my dear. It's going to take a long time to tell it all to you."

"I'm listening."

"To begin with, as soon as I left you at your aunt and uncle's house, upon our return to Spider Leg, I went straight to my father's cabin and told him absolutely everything that has happened. I told him of the Hopi attack, the capture, the Hopi joining, the blanket sleeping, the wish to be married to you in the Christian way, the Reverend Smith's refusal.

"My father had no room in his heart to deny us that wish, for, to begin with, he himself had married a tribes woman, against her family's wishes. She was shunned at first, but when my father brought her back to the tribe, and he lived among them, he gained great stature there, behaving like a warrior, helping the Shoshones in their skirmishes. In short, he won them over, especially when he and my mother had a child–me."

Mary Lou hung onto every word he spoke, wondering where all this was leading to.

He continued. "So, with that history in mind, my father could not in good faith deny me my wish to marry a pale face. My own mother married a pale face, him. He gave me–and us–his blessing."

"How wonderful for you, White Elk! I am happy to know that. But how is that going to help Aunt Myrtle and Uncle Fred overcome their obstinance about my marrying you?"

"My father helps me in this matter. He said that for some time now, he has wanted to send me to Denver for added schooling. A law school."

"Law school? Why a law school?"

"My father has listened to me throughout the years, agonizing over the conditions of the Indian population at large, in Western America. He felt that, with the education he gave me from his home since I was old enough to talk, I could handle university material, learn the law, work with the U.S. government toward helping the American Indian."

"That's a very big burden! And what do I do back in Spider Leg? Pining over your absence, day in and day out?"

"I'm getting to that part. Again, my father, considering all angles, suggested that your Uncle Fred write another letter to the finishing school to re-enrol you, beginning next September. You will once more take the stagecoach to Denver to do that. I will, once more, follow you to make sure the same thing does not happen again–with the Hopi or any other tribe."

She shuddered. "I pray to the heavens it does not happen again!"

He smiled. "Does that mean you go along with the plan so far?"

"Oh, my darling White Elk. I'd go along with *anything* just to be with you again. So what happens after we get to Denver, providing Uncle Fred does his part, and providing you get accepted by university?"

"Here we get to the uncertain part." He took a deep breath. "Once more, my father has come to the fore in that he has given me the name and address of an old preacher, a fire-branding, Bible-thumping fundamentalist who will marry us."

"And how does he know that?"

"Because, when the preacher was on his circuit one year, he wandered into Spider Leg, while my mother and father were shopping for supplies in town, and the preacher married them, all legal and proper!"

Mary Lou was fascinated. "Well, I swan!"

* * *

It all came to pass, exactly as Sean MacGregor had laid it out. Fred wrote the letter to the finishing school in Denver. MacGregor enroled his son Jeremy at the university's law school. Mary Lou took the stagecoach again. And again, White Elk followed discreetly behind the stagecoach. They arrived in Denver. They changed their clothing from traveling clothes and into "city" clothes. They contacted the preacher, Brother Skaggs.

And they were married. The white-bearded preacher never knew that Jeremy MacGregor was a half-breed. Didn't matter. He had already conducted marriage services for several Indian/pale face unions. Only man in the territory who would!

At the close of the Christian ceremony, Mary Lou and White Elk hugged each other as tightly as they could—for long seconds. Then they kissed one another. And back to the hugging. Preacher Skaggs feigned a cough. He was almost embarrassed. But pleased to see the happy couple, newly wed, showing real affection for one another.

* * *

Dear Aunt Myrtle and Uncle Fred,

I begin this letter to tell you first off that I want to thank you both from the bottom of my heart for not only rescuing me from the empty house when I was a baby, but for fulfilling all my needs, physical and spiritual, as I grew up under your watchful care.

What I am going to tell you now will not please you, but I beg your forbearance in this matter because of the seriousness of it all. White Elk and I are wed, by the preacher, Brother Skaggs of Denver, in a true Christian way.

White Elk, or Jeremy MacGregor, his Christian name, is attending a law school in Denver and living in a big house with fellow students. And I am attending Miss Lovelace's Finishing School for Ladies. I live at the finishing school dormitory. White Elk and I are joined, but we are not living together as man and wife. We will postpone that day until we both finish our two-year courses.

White Elk has already received notice that upon graduation, he will be assigned to a post in Spider Leg as a representative from the Bureau of Indian Affairs, of the Department of the Interior. It is an honor to receive such a posting, especially in advance of graduation. Before he goes back to Spider Leg, however, he must report to the Interior Department in Washington, D.C., for training. I am fortunate to be able to accompany him there. They say that a visit to our nation's capital is like a history lesson. I look forward to that.

I also look forward to the day we come back to Spider Leg. That is where White Elk's office will be. His ambition is to help all Indians everywhere, in their day-to-day struggles to live in and near white man's civilization. I feel it in my bones that he will do well.

It will give us much pleasure when we, together, return to Spider Leg and begin our new life there. We may even have an infant to bring home for you to see and, I hope, to love as much as you have loved me.

And, I hope, with all my soul, Aunt Myrtle and Uncle Fred, that you can find it in your hearts to accept White Elk, or Jeremy MacGregor, as my husband, my life-long mate for whom I am consumed with perfect and enduring love.

Your devoted niece, Mary Lou Dinsmore MacGregor

* * *

Upon the graduations of both Mary Lou and White Elk, they celebrated by going to dinner at the hotel where they had registered as Mr. And Mrs. Jeremy MacGregor.

After dinner, they retired to their room. It was momentous, for they had remained chaste throughout the first two years of their marriage. It was their plan not to start a family until the schooling for the two of them was over. In those times, celibacy was the only way. Now that could be put behind them. They had been joined, twice: once by the Hopi and later by the Brother Skaggs.

They entered their new life together, as one. The full expression of passion and love was a moment of beauty, of intense pleasure. It was a moment of fulfilled yearning for one another. Never again would they be separated by man's cultural concepts. They had satisfied every rule.

They had satisfied their infinite desire for each other: the pale face and the half-breed.

# # #

LEESVILLE

PROLOGUE

In 1849 Rhee and Lu Lee arrived in San Francisco from China by schooner. They were newlyweds embarking on what they perceived to be a great adventure. News had reached them in China of the great gold rush in California.

Upon their arrival in San Francisco, Lu had determined that she was about three months pregnant. Six months later their first child, a girl whom they named Ah Ming, was born. The following year came their first son, Hue; then another son, Ho; another daughter, Bahn; and finally the third son, Tao.

Rhee never intended to mine for the pure gold to be found, but he wanted to cash in on the push toward gold fields. He and his wife opened a small store near a prospectively large gold field. Enough gold to go around for everyone. Little by little, as they outfitted the hordes of men, individually and in pairs and in larger groups (such as families), the Lees were close to paying off their loans.

Although the five children were born in America, their parents taught them the Chinese language and way of life. There was little opportunity for the children to mingle with the pale round-eyes. There was no school in the community, which was yet to be developed. It was a community that began with the Lees' general store.

When Hue was 15 years old, he left the family and their store and signed up for working on the Intercontinental Railroad. On May 10, 1869, the last spike, a golden one, was driven at Ogden, Utah.

Picking up some "bad" and incorrect English from the American railroad crew bosses, it was enough for Hue to be able to apply for a homestead in Eastern California and to be granted one. The homestead was located between the Cascades and the Rocky Mountain Range.

After enduring the painful experience of applying for the homestead, Hue vowed strongly to learn better English, in earnest. At the bottom of his knapsack lay an English grammar book and a dictionary.

Hue had developed a sturdy and muscular body, as a result of his railroad work. Alone, at age 21, he built his log cabin, drilling first for a water supply and for installing a hand pump in the cabin. Alone, he planted a sizeable vegetable garden. And alone, he planted some fruit trees. He acquired two horses, a wagon and a carriage, and he built a sketchy stable with storage space for the carriage. The wagon was relegated to the outdoors.

In 1875, Hue sent for his two sisters and two brothers to assist him in working the ranch. He was 25, Ah Ming was 26, Ho was 20, Bahn was 19, and Tao was 18.

The parents carried on with their business, enlarging it along with a village's growing around their store. They worked together, each happy for their children who struck out to help their eldest brother with his farming endeavor.

Chapter One

Upon the arrival, of his brothers and sisters, Hue put them all to work: the brothers tended the gardens and orchards; the sisters kept the log cabin clean and orderly (while Hue and his brothers built the additions to it), did all laundry, and cooked for all of them. In due time, they established a laundry service for the nearby town of Stoney Ridge. The residents of that town were eager to take advantage of the laundry service since most of the pioneer resident women had come from fine homes in St. Louis, Philadelphia, and Chicago. There they had servants. A far cry from Stoney Ridge inconveniences, to be sure.

To spread the word about the new laundry service among the households of Stoney Ridge, Hue Lee went to the local newspaper office where a weekly was published. The editor, owner, printer, and all-round operator was Rupert Johnson, a transplant from Kansas City. He was tall and lanky with graying brown hair. His countenance was solid, and sometimes stolid, a Midwesterner. He had itchy feet, at age 45, and went West to find a new life.

Johnson was now almost 50 and had the ruddy complexion of a rancher, but that was not his life. He was naturally red-faced. as though he were eternally embarrassed.

He tried not to believe that the loss of his wife was the real impetus for his leaving Kansas City. After all, he still had his daughter, Emily, now age 18, to take care of. He also thought now and then about his duty to find a suitable husband for her. She was not getting any younger. Rupert sometimes asked himself why on earth had he brought Emily here, one of the farthest outposts of the West. However, he mused one day, they may be at a farthest outpost, but just over the mountain range is the glitter of San Francisco.

Hue Lee, upon entering the newspaper office, removed the cap from his head, and revealed his straight, blue-black hair. He was a bit taller than an average Chinese man but still had to look up to Rupert Johnson.

"Good morning, Mistuh Johnson," Hue greeted him. "I Hue Lee." He pronounced his first name as though it were spelled "Whay."

"Good morning, Mr. Lee," Rupert responded. "What can I do for you?"

Hue was a bit surprised at the friendly way Mr. Johnson had spoken to him. His American experience told him that all western peoples looked down at the Chinese with contempt and disrespect.

He went on. "Mistuh Johnson, I wish to buy advertisement?" He wasn't sure he was pronouncing it correctly, but . . .

"An advertisement, Sir? What kind of advertisement?" Johnson used the word twice so that the Chinese man would be assured he had said it right.

"Ah, forgive my poor printing, but here," he withdrew a folded piece of paper, "is my advertisement. I bring it to you to make prints of it, many prints, so that I may tell missy housewives about new business."

"New business, eh? Well, I see here you have drawn a wash board and a wash tub and a clothesline with clothes on it. Very artistic."

"No, not my doing. My sister. I do the poor printing."

"Tut, tut, Mr. Lee. Not poor printing at all. Also very artistic."

Hue bowed, smiled, and said, "A thousand thank yous, Mistuh Johnson."

They decided on an acceptable price, and Hue Lee turned to leave.

At the moment he turned, Emily Johnson entered the newspaper office. Lee caught his breath. This was the most beautiful woman he had ever laid eyes on. Friendly hazel eyes, long and wavy chestnut brown hair, standing before him, as tall as he. Quickly he averted his eyes. He started to leave.

"Wait up, Mr. Lee," Rupert called to him. "You might as well meet my daughter Emily, who helps me with the newspaper. Emily," he looked at the name on the paper Hue had left with him. "This is Mr. Hue Lee. Mr. Lee, Emily Johnson." Rupert wondered how you could get "Whay" out of "Hue." He shrugged.

Hue drew himself upright, as tall as he could make himself to be, gathered up his meager knowledge of western etiquette, then bowed slightly, saying, "Ah, Missy Emily, how do you do?"

Emily, eyeing him carefully, and noting a definite twinkle in his eye, replied, "I do very well today, thank you." Looking him over again, she added, "Very well, indeed, Mr. Lee."

Hue wanted to stay longer, but a primitive instinct told him it was proper to leave now. Bowing once more to Emily and another to Rupert, he left the office.

Emily said to her father, "Is that the Chinese man who's homesteading just west of town?"

"Probably," he answered. "But only because he's the only Chinese we've seen 'round these parts since the railroad came through."

"No, wait," she said. "I saw a Chinese woman last week. At the general store, buying tubs, washboards, clotheslines."

Johnson raised his eyebrows. "Probably Lee's wife," forgetting about the reference to the sister. "They're starting a laundry business. Mr. Lee just ordered some ads."

Emily's heart made an extra beat. Wife? she asked herself. Further, she wondered, and why does that make any difference to me? Silly girl!

* * *

Nonetheless, as soon as her father came home with one of the ads, as ordered by Hue Lee, Emily made a sudden decision. But what would she use as an excuse? She already had a sometime laundress, an Indian woman from a tribe to the south.

That was it! A regular laundry service is better than a sometime laundress. Isn't it?

Emily's oval face with creamy skin had not grown weathered from the sun and wind in the short time she had lived in Stoney Ridge. Her lips were pink and inviting, a man might say, assessing her thoroughly. Her average height was something she inherited from her mother's side of the family.

"So what do you think, Emily?" her father asked. "Should we use the Lee Laundry Service? I can work a deal, I think. I'll give him a weekly newspaper for reduced rates on the laundry service."

"But Father," Emily said, "does he read English? I mean, a lot?"

"He knew and used the word 'advertisement'. Must mean something."

"And what'll I do about the Indian woman, Running Deer? What'll I tell her?"

Her father said, "Been meaning to engage a clean-up man at the paper. Reckon she'd want to do that? Say, once a week?"

"Very likely. I'll ask her when I tell her not to do our laundry anymore." Another thought occurred to her. She asked, "And . . . maybe we could engage her to do cleaning here at the house?

"Why not?" Rupert answered, thinking that Emily would be free to spend more time helping him with the newspaper.

* * *

With flashing black eyes, Hue Lee told his sisters the good fortune they were about to acquire. Ah Ming, the elder, took the news stolidly. The younger sister, Bahn, was more elated, more excited. Could she make the deliveries and pickups with him? She had a plan and a hope. To her request, Hue said no and that she must stay with Ah Ming and help her with any other duties the laundry service and the house needed done.

"But my Brother," Bahn implored, "I need to be shown in the town, by you, of course, to find a husband!"

"Rubbish! As head of this household, it is *my* task to find you a husband, not yours. And he shall *not* be a pale-skinned round-eye!"

"But, honorable Brother . . ."

"Enough! At the right time, I will send an advertisement to China to seek a suitable husband for you, to come here to this land to make you his bride."

Sufficiently chastised by her older brother, Bahn accepted his pronouncement with a measure of disappointment. Although, she thought, it would be better to have Chinese husband than a roughly hewn pale skin!

Ah Ming listened to this exchange between Hue and Bahn with mild interest. At the end of it, she wondered what Hue might have in store for her. Permanent housekeeper for all of them? Hah! Sensing that husband-talk might not be appropriate just now, considering the dialogue about a husband for Bahn, Ah Ming dumped the rice into the pot of boiling water. And said nothing. Nothing at all. In a real pinch, she would marry a pale-skinned round-eye herself!

Later that evening, when all chores were done, and the five Lee family members sat in the main room of the log house, Lee contemplated the words he and Bahn had said to each other. A plan began to form. He could, he thought, advertise for two brothers to come to America and marry his two sisters. That should work!

Ho and Tao, the two younger brothers, entertained themselves with a game their parents had brought from China. Ah Ming and Bahn darned socks and sewed on buttons that had come off the American shirts. Hue picked up his monthly San Francisco paper and began to read. It was painfully slow, mostly because he had to use his dictionary so often. But little by little, he gained speed in reading and could, upon occasion, read an entire simple sentence without having to stop for referencing something in the dictionary.

His thoughts wandered. Tomorrow he would return to Stoney Ridge, call on each house where he had left his ad, and pick up the first set of orders.

He wondered if he would see the Emily person. It would give him great pleasure to do the laundry for her and her father. It would give him great pleasure to deliver fresh laundry and pick up soiled laundry every week. It would give him great pleasure just to see her again, to speak to her, to . . .

He couldn't go on thinking this way. It was interfering with his English reading!

* * *

A serious announcement came from Hue the next morning. It had occurred to him during his practice English reading the evening before.

"Beginning today, we will all learn to speak English. Later, we will all learn to read English. We will never go to China. We are American citizens. All of us. And first, we must all learn English to speak well and to read intelligently"

Ho and Tao were inclined to argue with Hue, but they respected their older brother immensely, in the absence of their father who had long ago emphatically declared he would never leave his home and store in his part of California.

Ah Ming accepted the announcement as stoically as she had listened to the "husband" talk with Bahn. Bahn, on the other hand, being the spirited one among Hue's four siblings, balked.

"Honorable Brother takes great pride in his importantness!"

"I am sure," Hue retorted, "that the word is 'importance.'"

"Pah!" said the younger sister, with undisguised loathing.

Hue shrugged his shoulders. He thought, what am I to do with the girl? Serve her right to marry her off to a pale round-eye--one who would put her in her place for an eternity.

* * *

In due time, the brothers Ho and Tao and the sisters Ah Ming and Bahn managed to speak a pidgin English, even though they had not had the exposure to English that Hue had on the railroad. But that was not good enough for Hue. He was a virtual slave driver, insisting that they all, himself included, get rid of the chopped-up way of speaking English. He demanded that they speak a very proper English. It was not easy. Old habits are difficult to shed.

Meanwhile, Hue had "graduated" in English from using the "Missy" to using the proper "Miss Emily." He looked forward to each Friday morning, laundry pickup and delivery day. Early in the second month of doing laundry for the townspeople (those who had ordered it), Emily greeted him one Friday morning with, "Good morning, Hue. I hope you are well?"

"Ah yes, Miss Emily. I am extremely well."

She had previously made up her mind to ask him a certain question. "And how is your wife?"

Hue blinked once or twice and answered, "Ah, Miss Emily, it would be my greatest desire to have a wife. But perhaps you refer to one of my sisters?"

"Your sisters!" A brief sigh of relief almost left her body. But she gained control quickly. "I did not know you had sisters. How many?"

"Only two. They came from my parents' home in other part of California with my two youngest brothers to live and labor with me here, near Stoney Ridge."

"That's nice. Having family with you in a strange place must be comforting."

"Excuse, please, Miss Emily. What is com-for-ting?"

"Well," she hesitated about how to do this. "Do you know the word comfortable?"

"Yes!"

"Then, comforting comes from comfortable. Family members are comforting and consoling, making life comfortable."

"Ah-h-h. A thousand thank yous for the lesson in English, Miss Emily." He made a mental note to look up "consoling" as well.

"I just hope it was truly helpful."

"Ah Miss Emily. It was most helpful."

She smiled her prettiest at him. He tucked his head downward. That smile was too dazzling for him to bear.

"Good bye, Miss Emily." He picked up the bag of soiled laundry.

"Good bye, Hue. Wait. If I call you Hue, no title, then you must call me Emily, without the Miss. It would please me if you did that."

"Indeed, Mi . . . Emily!" He almost shouted her name without the title. He went away a very happy man.

* * *

That evening, at the supper table, Emily told her father about the conversation she had with Hue.

Rupert said, "Do you think that a wise thing to do, Em? Telling him not to call you 'Miss?'"

"Of course it was! He's almost like a member of the family, washing and hanging up our clothes to dry and then ironing all of them!"

"I seriously doubt Hue does all that. What about the wife?"

"Oh, yes. I asked him about his wife today--how was she--and he said he had no wife and that I must be referring to his sisters."

"His sisters!"

"Yes. Two sisters." She paused before saying, "I like Hue, Daddy. A lot."

"I can't believe I heard what I just heard. Are you out of your mind?"

"But Daddy, you've always been open and understanding about

232

foreign people."

"There's a limit, my dear."

"Well, you needn't worry, Daddy, because Hue is so tied up with his gardens and orchards and the laundry business, I don't think he has time for . . . ."

"For what?" he asked.

She suddenly became mute. Then, "I--I don't really know what."

* * *

Hue tired of reading only the San Francisco paper and the local paper that Mr. Johnson gave him each week. He longed for something else to read. A book, perhaps. He saw one reviewed in the San Francisco paper. He wrote to the newspaper and inquired about buying a book, to be delivered by regular mail.

Six weeks later, the book arrived. Hue devoured it. Upon finishing it, he demanded that Ho, Tao, Ah Ming and Bahn read it, too, each one taking his or her turn. When all of them had finished reading it, a novel, they held long discussions about it.

Hue was indefatigable in his search for another book--any book. He saw one laying on Emily's kitchen table, opened. He asked her about it. She lent it to him. He was grateful beyond words, initially. But when he returned it, he waxed eloquently about it, naming its charms and allure. He and Emily talked about it, together. She had invited him to be seated on a chair at the table. She poured him a cup of coffee. Then, she remembered something.

"Oh, Hue, you must surely prefer tea?"

"No, Emily. I smell the coffee in every household where I make deliveries and pickups of laundry. It always smells so inviting. Please, I will try your coffee."

After their talking about the book, and after he finished the cup of coffee, he asked, "And where, Emily, can I find this coffee to buy?"

"The General Store carries it in a big barrel. You just ask for a sack of it. Should I show you how to make it? You'll also need to buy a coffee pot at the General Store."

Chapter Two

The Lee Laundry Service became well established upon Hue's first round of visits to households in Stoney Ridge. The ad had been very successful toward beginning his new business. Eager housewives jumped at the chance to rid themselves of one weekly chore that took up two entire days: one for the washing and hanging out to dry; and one for the ironing. The housewives were pleased to learn that the ironing was included. Another full day of work saved. Bonanza!

Hue's sisters did the work. He made the deliveries and pickups. On his first contact at each house, he had left a laundry bag for each family to use. Mr. Johnson had received his first laundry bag, and Hue had been disappointed that it was not Emily to do that.

The next week, Hue grew anxious as he approached the Johnson residence, which was in the middle of his newly established route. He wanted to be early enough to see Emily Johnson again, before her leaving for the newspaper office.

Timing was perfect. Emily answered the knocking at the back door moments before she left the house. She was ready for Hue's arrival; her clothes and her father's clothes and the linens were ready and inside the laundry bag.

"Ah, good morning, Emily," Hue greeted her in his best English pronunciation and enunciation.

"And a good morning to you, also, Hue. Here is our laundry bag. Each week, I will wait until you come to our house with the fresh laundry, before I leave to go to the newspaper."

"A thousand thank yous, Emily! I will be honored."

"As will I, Hue."

"Good day, Emily."

"A good day to you, Hue. I look forward to next week."

Hue turned to leave before she could see he was turning a peculiar yellow-red. He was certain he was blushing, for his face tingled, along with his entire body. He thought, no Chinese woman ever made this happen to him before.

* * *

The weeks passed; the laundry business thrived; the newspaper plodded along. Hue made his rounds with fresh laundry and picked up used laundry. And each Friday, he approached the Johnson house with eagerness. He would see Emily again. She was always there.

Hue strode up the back steps and onto the back porch. He knocked on the back door. There was no response. He knocked once more.

"Hue! Is that you, Hue?"

He could hear her voice faintly. He called out, "Emily? Where are you?"

"Open the door, Hue. It's not locked."

Cautiously he opened the door. Emily was a lump on the floor, in front of the kitchen range. He rushed toward her. "Emily! What happened?"

She tried to look up at him, but she was obviously in pain. "I twisted my ankle and fell. I can't get up. Help me, Hue, please?"

Although they were the same height, Hue was well muscled and strong from his railroad work, and his ranching work. Picking her up was not at all difficult for him. "Do you think you can walk?" he asked.

"I'm not sure. It's painful all the time."

"Then," he said, "where is your room? I will place you upon your bed."

"Upstairs."

He maneuvered the stairway deftly. She said, "All the way to the front, last door on the right."

He placed her upon her bed, their heads almost touching, they were so close. He caught his breath. She smelled so clean, so fresh.

"Let me remove your shoes, Emily."

"Yes. That would be a good idea."

There was a quilt folded across the foot of the bed. He unfolded it and placed it over her body. The nearness to her, the intimacy of carrying her upstairs, and the indulging act of covering her with the quilt--all of it--unnerved him in a most peculiar way.

"And," he added, "let me put a pillow under your ankle." She nodded in assent.

"Ah-h-h," she breathed. She felt better already.

"Would you like a cup of tea?" he asked. "Or coffee? I have known how to make tea for long time; and you taught me to make coffee."

"I don't think so, Hue. But, thank you very, very much for your help, for bringing me up here."

"I am so sorry you are in pain."

"It's better lying down."

"That is good."

A moment of awkwardness followed.

He said, "I see your laundry bag is waiting in the kitchen. I will go now and then go straight to the newspaper to tell your father what has happened."

"Thank you again, Hue. For everything. Tell my Daddy that I'll be all right until he gets home at noon. Please."

"Of course. And, Emily, you are welcome." His head was still spinning, from the familiarity of the last few minutes. On his way out of the kitchen, he almost forgot to pick up the bag of soiled laundry. He nearly stumbled over the basket of fresh laundry. He took a deep breath, collected his wits and dangerous thoughts, and left the house.

* * *

Rupert was alarmed at Hue Lee's information about Emily. "I'll go home right away and look in on her. But damn!"

Hue had heard that word many times among the American bosses supervising the Chinese railroad laborers. "What is it?" he asked.

Rupert said, "I have an interview with the church pastor this morning. I can't look in on Emily until after dinner. The interview includes dinner at the pastor's house."

"Not to worry about Emily, Mr. Johnson. I look in on her."

Rupert was too distracted to wonder about the implications, the situation. He nodded his agreement.

Hue finished his laundry route, then guiding his horse and wagon back to the Johnson residence, he entered by the back door, raced up the steps, and called out to Emily.

She said, "Is that you, Hue? Where's my Daddy?"

He explained why Mr. Johnson was occupied with the pastor and wouldn't be back until after dinnertime. "I've come back to fix you something to eat."

"Dear, dear Hue. You needn't have done that. For sure!"

He heard the 'dears' and smiled inwardly. He knew what 'dear' meant. He had, in the past, worked hard on separating dear from deer.

"My pleasure, my dear," he replied.

She closed her eyes, smiling.

He went to the kitchen to cook something for both of them.

* * *

"You wretch!" (this in Chinese) yelled Bahn at her big brother. "What do you mean by coming back from town so late! Ah Ming and I do not have enough time to wash clothes and get them hung out and get them dried before nightfall!" The fury continued. "What in the name of our ancestors were you doing all afternoon? Inconsiderate idiot!"

Hue Lee was not surprised. Bahn had every right to be outraged and rude for good measure. As usual, Ah Ming took it all in stride and began separating lightweight clothing from heavyweight clothing, deciding that she and Bahn could at least wash out the lightweight clothing and get that much dried by nightfall.

Hue let Bahn have her rein. He made no explanation. No excuse. Bahn's wrath was unending! He thought an explanation would be putting himself in a difficult position with the family--if they were to determine that he was even remotely interested in Emily Johnson. He kept his silence with Bahn.

As it turned out, that was even more infuriating to Bahn. The silence. Such a brute, she thought! But with the need for her to assist Ah Ming, she simmered down to her usual sunny self. Her ire was, Hue thought, gratefully, short-lived.

Another plus in this fiery exchange: after Bahn's rage subsided, she lapsed into English, and once more Hue was grateful--for that!

* * *

Hue Lee, a normally patient man, overall, found himself wishing he had an excuse to visit the Johnson household--before the next Friday came around. He wanted desperately to know if Emily's ankle were getting better. No excuse was forthcoming. He was on pins and needles, waiting for Friday.

Ah Ming and Bahn noticed his fidgeting about the laundry baskets of fresh laundry and the number of clean laundry bags to leave at each house for their following week's pickup. Even Ah Ming made comment, after Hue departed on his laundry rounds, that he was a virtual bear this morning! Bahn sided with her sister, jumping to the conclusion that something was amiss in their big brother's demeanor. He was anxious, he was cranky, he was downright grouchy. Not his usual otherwise pleasant self.

Hue drove his horse and wagon at top speed, or as much speed as he could get out of the nag. He asked himself, why didn't I harness up my own favorite horse; we would have made it into town much sooner than this!

He reined in his nag, upon entering Stoney Ridge. He argued with himself: should I go straight to Emily? Or should I do the route as usual, getting to her the usual time? Damn! He was astonished that he had borrowed the term from the Americans! But it was so appropriate.

Hue chose restraint, against his dearest wishes. He did the usual route, arriving at the Johnsons the usual time, in the middle of the route. With shaky hands, he hauled down the Johnson laundry basket. He purposefully strode up the back steps, onto the porch, and knocked on the door.

"Is that you, Hue?"

His heart skipped a beat. That was surely Emily's voice. "Yes, it is, Emily. Should I come on in?"

"Oh, yes, my dear. Come straight in."

Now his heart was pounding thunderously as he entered the kitchen and found Emily seated in a rocking chair, near the hand pump, and near the table, and not too far from the pantry (where he had found food items the previous week, making something for her to eat).

"My Daddy fixes me up like this every morning, Hue, so that I can at least get a drink of water and fix a cold dinner at noon for both of us. It's so good to see you, Hue. I've missed you. You were so nice and comforting--ah, I used that word again."

"Yes, Emily. I remember it. I am pleased that you seem comfortable today. I was wishing all week that I could come to see you and find out how you are doing. But . . ."

"Oh, I wish you could have come, too, Hue. Really. I've missed you. I wish you could come calling anytime."

Something rang a bell in Hue's mind. He was remembering a phrase used in one of the books he had read: "come calling," it was. And then he remembered that it was used to convey a swain's wooing a maiden. 'Swain' he had to look up, and now he was recollecting the meaning: a sweetheart, a true love.

Then it struck him that Emily had just invited him to be her sweetheart, her true love? Did I misunderstand? he asked himself. Lord, he said silently, I hope not!

"My dear Hue. Why don't you come for dinner this Sunday? I probably won't make it to church, but a neighbor lady said she'd bring our dinner over here after services. Won't you do that, Hue? It'd make me so happy to entertain you properly."

He was totally astonished. His thoughts ran wildly. This lovely American young lady is inviting me here to dinner on Sunday afternoon? Incredible! he thought. He was almost tongue-tied. He did manage to say something.

"I don't know what to say, Emily. Do I understand you right? You are inviting me to take Sunday dinner with you and Mr. Johnson?"

"Exactly! You will come, won't you? I'd be sorely disappointed if you didn't. Please?"

"Of course, my --" He hesitated. What endearment should he use at this point? He decided to play it safely with, "Of course, my dear."

* * *

That evening, when Emily told Rupert that she had invited Hue to come to dinner on Sunday after church services, Rupert exploded. "You what?"

"I said . . . ."

"I heard what you said! I just don't believe it!"

"Daddy, don't tell me you're objecting to having a "Chink" at our dinner table!"

"Mind your tone, Emily. This is profound territory. And no, I'm not going to call him a Chink!"

"Then what," she asked, "are you objecting to?"

"Good Lord, girl, he must be courting you! That's what I'm objecting to."

"Well, certainly, Daddy. I asked him to come calling sometime. Then I invited him to come to Sunday dinner. What's the harm in that?"

"I don't understand you, my own daughter! You want a Chinese man to woo you, in broad daylight?"

"Would you prefer he do it in the dark of night?"

* * *

In the end, Rupert Johnson threw up his hands in a hopeless state of uncertainty. In the past, he had sworn to himself that he'd never let a woman get the best of him. That's for a wife. A daughter is different. So different!

Emily's ankle was a bit better by Sunday, but she could walk only with assistance: a cane, a chairback, a strong arm.

The neighbor's dinner was a success. Emily was so obligated. There'd be a time in the future when she could do something for her kind neighbor, she told herself.

The main thing, for Emily, is, did Hue like the American food? He seemed to. His manners were nearly stilted, his not knowing what to do next. But he watched Rupert for clues on what to do next. He watched Emily the rest of the time, not getting enough of looking at her. He was clearly affected.

After dinner, with Hue's assistance, Emily walked from the house's front porch to the horse and carriage. He helped her into the carriage by picking her up and placing her onto the carriage seat. They went for a ride in the country. They neared his spread but did not go onto it. Another time, Hue thought.

240

A cottonwood tree growing next to a creek was where they stopped.

"I'll help you off the carriage. It's grassy around the tree. We could sit there."

She agreed. He lifted her out of the carriage and carried her to the grass under the tree. He sat beside her.

"Hue, I like you very much. Did you know that?"

"I am at a loss for words, Emily. But, yes, I did know that, and no, I wasn't too sure of it, after all."

"I'm telling you, Hue. Be sure of it!"

He leaned toward her. He touched his lips against her cheek. She turned her head so that their lips touched each other. He put his arms around her waist. She put her arms around his neck. They shared a pristine kiss.

* * *

It was Emily's first kiss, and truth be known, it was Hue's first as well.

She took the sweet memory of it all the way home, into her room, and into bed. She savored the experience with excitement until she fell asleep.

Hue was not that fortunate. He also savored the experience, taking it all the way to his spread, into the cabin, and into his bed. But he was too deliriously happy, to the point that he could not sleep until just before dawn.

The rooster's crowing awakened him, but he wanted to go back to sleep and continue the delicious dream he was having about Emily. Emily. What to do about Emily?

There was work to do! He caught himself sharply to keep from going back to sleep. Never mind. He could think about Emily endlessly, work or no work. Thinking about her made the work be done more quickly.

* * *

Hue's first crop of peaches was ripe and ready for picking. Another opportunity to see Emily, he suddenly remembered. This very afternoon, he would take the harvested peaches into Stoney Ridge and sell them door-to-door. Emily's door included. And first!

"Hue!" she shouted, when she opened the back door. She was beginning to walk without assistance, albeit with a slight limp. "What are you doing here so soon? Not that I'm not delighted to see you again so soon. This is wonderful!"

"I brought you some peaches, Emily. I hope you and your father like peaches."

"Like them? We love them! Oh, Hue, these are so many! I'll have to make a peach pie to keep the last of them from spoiling. Do you like peach pie?"

"I confess, my dear, I've never tasted peach pie. Don't even know what it is!"

"Well, we'll fix that. Can you come here tomorrow evening after supper and have a piece of peach pie with us? That'd make me so happy, just to see you and be with you again, Hue."

He accepted, and the evening of the next day he rode his favorite horse into town to have a piece of peach pie with Emily and Mr. Johnson.

Not knowing what a piece of pie would look like, he sat in the kitchen with some misgivings, hoping he did not embarrass himself . . . nor Emily, as well, for that matter. No need to worry, he realized later. The pie was a wedge of pastry filled with the sweetest, best tasting peach filling he could imagine. He told her how delicious it was. She reddened at the compliment, for it was her first time to make a peach pie. She had her mother's recipe. She offered up a prayer to her deceased mother and for her now famous recipe. Made famous by having a Chinese man pass judgment on it

Hue spoke ruefully, "Emily, dear." Rupert looked at Hue sharply. Hue ignored it. "I must be heading back to my spread before it gets too late. It's already dark."

"Of course, dear." Rupert noticed that, too. "I'll walk you to your horse."

"I'm so glad," he said, "that your ankle is much better."

"And so am I." They reached the horse, standing under a maple tree, and tied to a lower branch. Their being the same height, she leaned toward him and gave him a kiss. He responded and put his arms around her, drawing her closer to him. She did not hold back but leaned her entire body against him.

He was electrified. The closeness nearly made him dizzy. They ended the kiss. He released her, reluctantly. She said, "Good night, my darling."

'Darling?' he said to himself. Another endearment, no doubt? Yes, he thought, he had read that word, too, in a book . He tried out another word from his recent past readings.

"And a good night to you, Sweetheart."

In the darkness, he could discern her wide smile.

* * *

The next day, first thing in the morning, Emily saw the large basket of fresh peaches. She made a decision. She prepared another peach pie and took it to her neighbor, the one who had prepared for them a Sunday dinner.

Chapter Three

Rupert Johnson threw a first-class fit when Emily told him of the progress of her romance. She shared with him the fact that she and Hue had discussed marriage. Later, Hue made his intentions clear to Rupert and now was waiting to seek his blessing. It was not forthcoming. Hue decided that he needed to be a more successful rancher and businessman. That should work wonders with Mr. Johnson, he thought. Johnson had never treated Hue in any manner other than polite and friendly.

But Rupert Johnson drew a line between Emily and Hue. It was not negotiable. Then Rupert had the suspicion that they might elope, and that would be worse! So he took measures.

Rupert wrote a letter to his sister in Philadelphia and asked her for a badly needed favor. Using the new telegraph system she informed him that she would do it. And so it was arranged that Emily would take the train to Philadelphia and stay with her Aunt Hilda for two years. Emily was to attend a school for young ladies. And that was that.

Emily balked. She was NOT going to leave Stoney Ridge, her Daddy and Hue.

The fatherly command took precedence over whatever Emily felt and wanted. She was given one month to prepare for the long train journey.

"But Daddy, I don't have the proper clothing for living in and going to school in Philadelphia!"

"Not a concern of yours nor mine. Your Aunt Hilda will arrange everything after you arrive at her home--clothes, matriculation, everything."

That was another scorching indignation that Emily was suffering: after her mother died, Emily enjoyed the liberty of choosing her own clothes, she was free to make her own decisions (with her father's blessing) (and except where Hue was concerned), and she could run the household with little or no interference from her father. Even the weekly laundry arrangement was acceptable to both Rupert and Emily.

Doggedly, Emily packed a trunk and two suitcases. Her mother's portrait was carefully placed between voluminous dresses and petticoats.

* * *

"Hue," she cried, "what are we going to do?"

"Do not worry, Emily. Of course, I will miss you. I will write to you every month."

"And I'll do the same for you, Hue. I cannot understand my Daddy's interfering with our loving connection. I cannot understand why he is shipping me off to go back East."

"He means well, Emily. I'm sure he is trying to protect you and your best interests. But that will not keep us from marrying when you return to Stoney Ridge. I promise you, my dear, I will wait for you. It's only two years, Emily."

"It'll seem like two centuries!"

"It will give me time to become more prosperous." He paused for a moment, then said, "Make unworthy Chinee-man more worthy."

She said, "Hue! You slipped back into pidgin English! How come?"

"This way more emphatic." A large grin spread across his face. Emily could not help herself; she grinned with him.

* * *

The fateful day arrived. Rupert hired a horse and wagon from the livery stable to haul Emily's baggage to the train station, such as it was--Stoney Ridge was barely a whistle stop. Emily and Rupert rode in a carriage–also from the livery stable. Rupert saw to the trunk's being unloaded from the wagon. He dismissed the livery stable man, horse and wagon.

Through all this, Hue Lee stood aside and apart from the father and daughter. Johnson saw him watching; Emily looked to him longingly. The East-bound train stopped. Emily gave her father a daughterly kiss and hug. She resolutely marched up to Hue and hugged him firmly. She did not dare kiss him, not in front of her father, who stood at a distance, watching.

Hue Lee whispered into her hair, "Good journey, my darling. Make the best of it all. That is what you can do for your father . . . and for me. Goodbye, my dearest sweetheart."

Her throat constricted, tears filled her eyes. She said, bleakly, "Dear, dear Hue. I can't bear to leave you. Two years! A lifetime!" She swallowed with difficulty. "Goodbye, my beloved. Do not forget me!"

"I won't, Emily. Rest assured."

They parted. Rupert saw that her trunk was loaded into the baggage car. She walked rapidly toward the train's stairs, hastily climbing up onto the vestibule. The train began to pull out. She waved first to her Daddy. Then, turning so she faced Hue, waved to him and continued to do so until he was no longer visible.

Emily stepped into the parlor car, next to the sleeper car. She sat in an empty seat and holding her hands up to her face, began to weep.

* * *

Aunt Hilda was moneyed, even by such standards as were set in wealthy Philadelphia. She did not, however, have the kind of money to purchase Emily's transportation in a private car. But Emily was impressed with the parlor car/sleeper car. A far cry from the wagon train she and her father traveled with from Kansas City to Stoney Ridge.

When Emily arrived in Philadelphia, she was met by Aunt Hilda's butler, a black man from Alabama. Hilda Franks had helped him escape on the Underground Railroad. His name was Jeremiah. He had no surname.

Jeremiah delivered Emily to the Franks mansion, bag and baggage. The carriage driver was another black man, Jeremiah's younger brother, Elijah, also an escapee from the South.

At the house, Emily was escorted by Jeremiah to her room, where her bags and trunk were placed in due time. Emily began to wonder where Aunt Hilda was. She just did barely remember her, having seen her last in Kansas City when Emily was seven.

Jeremiah knocked softly on her closed bedroom door. "Miss Emily. Y'all come on down to de kitchen to meet Miss Katie."

Miss Katie, as Emily soon found out, was a middle-aged Irishwoman who served the Franks family as the cook. She had a helper, Maggie, her niece. They shared a room on the third floor.

Emily began to be concerned about Aunt Hilda and asked where she was.

"Faith 'n' begorrah, Dearie," said Miss Katie, "Mrs. Franks be attendin' a big charity ball. She'll be home later. Much later, if truth be known."

And that was Emily's greeting into Philadelphia society: a quiet dinner in an enormous dining room, alone. Jeremiah did the serving; Maggie did the take-aways.

* * *

The whirlwind began the next morning. Aunt Hilda, up bright and early, in spite of her late-night partying, woke up Emily and greeted her with a hug and a brush-kiss against the cheek.

"Up, my dear. Get up! We've a million things to do. You start at Mademoiselle Dubay's school next Monday. Let's have a look at your wardrobe. Tsk, tsk, tsk. These will never do! Come, girl, break-

247

fast is waiting! I'll see you in five minutes!"

Out of the room she swept, skirts and petticoats in a flutter. The rest of the day was marked by the same frenzy, a pace set by Aunt Hilda. The shopping was exhaustive, trying on this, its being dismissed; trying on something else, its also being dismissed; and so forth. Picking out shoes--Aunt Hilda doing the selecting. A fast lunch between shops. Choosing tea-dance dresses, Sunday services dresses, and ball gowns. Acquiring a shawl or two or three for cool nights and days. Looking at fur coats for the winters (to be purchased later). Ordering school uniforms.

It was a heady ordeal for Emily, all that shopping, everything going onto Aunt Hilda's account. Emily felt a tad guilty, accepting all the luxurious clothing at Aunt Hilda's expense. Would her father have to reimburse her for all this? Where in heaven's name would he find *that* kind of money?

Money! Suddenly, she thought of Hue. How could she, she wondered, forget Hue during all that exhaustive trying on clothes and seemingly buying everything in sight? She must write to him this very night, telling him of her train journey, the servants, the house, her room, Aunt Hilda. But not the clothes. Somehow, she felt ashamed to tell him about the clothes.

The next morning, she asked Aunt Hilda how and where she could post her envelope.

"Oh, my dear, give it to me, and I'll have Jeremiah post it for you. It's just down the street from here."

"Thank you, Aunt Hilda." She felt she must add, "And thank you for all the beautiful clothes you selected yesterday. Everything is lovely. I shall be honored to wear them."

"Hmph! Wait til you see the uniforms. Ugh!"

"Yes, ma'am."

* * *

The days went by quickly, each one defining its own controlled hysteria. That was the only way to describe Aunt Hilda and her hectic pace. It should have been invigorating for Emily, but frankly, she found it to be tiring. The tea dances, the charity balls, the debutante festivities, the tennis matches, the croquet games, the whatever-excuse-Philadelphia-society could dream up for another useless activity.

Emily attended the debutante balls only as a guest, not as an honoree because she would have had to be presented by her father, or an uncle. But Aunt Hilda was widowed.

Looking for a letter from Hue every day was beginning to tire her, also. It was now two months since she came to Philadelphia. There was no letter from him. She wrote him in the second month, anyway, hoping against hope to hear from him.

Another charity ball was on society's calendar--something for the benefit of children from a deprived neighborhood. Aunt Hilda chose the ball gown that Emily absolutely must wear.

"You must get rid of that ugly Navy blue taffeta ribbon bow back at the base of your neck, my dear. That's only for your uniform. For tonight I want you to wear your hair loosely around your shoulders--a pretty frame for your pretty face." Aunt Hilda rattled on and on about what Emily should wear and how to fix her hair, what pumps to wear. And, Aunt Hilda lent her a handsome, medium length strand of pearls. Then there was a beaded evening bag, matching the pearls. Emily felt like a show horse!

She looked at the reflection of the finished product in her full-length mirror. She was alone by now. She said to herself, "If only Hue could see me now. Probably wouldn't recognize me at all!"

* * *

The dancing was in full swing. Seemingly, everyone had a partner. A few sideline elders watching the young ones, and making the odd comment now and then. Even Aunt Hilda was dancing with a courtly looking gentleman.

Emily had just been introduced to the fifth young man at the ball. He was Bradford Hillmont III, a bit older than the other young men at the ball. His father and Aunt Hilda's deceased husband, Herbert Franks, had been co-owners of an eastern railroad company. Aunt Hilda, in name, owned Herbert's interests in the company, but she had only the voice of Herbert's attorney. For the most part, he controlled her money. But he was a generous manager. She did not have to beg.

Brad, as he asked Emily to call him, was tall, thin--almost spindly--with a shock of dark brown hair. She looked into his eyes, brown, and red-rimmed. What does that mean? she wondered.

He said, "Miss Emily, you dance like a sprite!"

"Thank you kindly, sir."

He laughed loudly. Too loudly, she thought.

He said, "'Thank you kindly, sir?' Mrs. Franks was right. You are straight from the wild west! How quaint!"

Somehow, she felt as though she had been mocked, then insulted. and finally, disparaged. She had to respond, for some reason. "I'm happy to see you are appropriately amused."

"Amused?" he asked. "You are a jewel!"

Will he make up his mind? she asked herself.

Somehow she finished the dance with him and hoped he would not ask her again. Something about him made her skin crawl.

* * *

The following weeks and months, Bradford Hillmont III courted Emily relentlessly. She found him somewhat of a nuisance and said so to Aunt Hilda. Aunt Hilda was appalled.

"You must be polite to the Hillmont boy, Emily, dear. His family and I have a very strong connection: business, and they are personal friends. You would make me most happy if you would at least be polite to him."

"Oh, I *am* polite, Aunt Hilda. But when he makes fun of me, I feel very uncomfortable."

"Pshaw! A little teasing never hurt anyone!"

When Emily went to bed that night, she wrote her sixth letter to Hue in spite of the fact that he had not written a single note since she left Stoney Ridge. She thought about his promise to write. What could be wrong? I hope Daddy hasn't been working on him, discouraging him, or whatever it is disapproving fathers do to the suitor.

* * *

The first year was finished. Emily faithfully wrote to Hue every month, never receiving a single letter from him. Although she became discouraged, she never faltered in her monthly letter to him. The thought that he was giving his attentions to someone else was troublesome. She told herself to stop thinking like that! There must be some explanation. Perhaps it will come later.

The Pest (as Emily referred to Brad, privately) was persistent. He took her to church services every Sunday morning. They went to the tea dance every Wednesday afternoon. He took her to the opera, to the symphony, and to dramatic plays from New York. And to the parties--always there were parties to fill their otherwise empty lives.

She missed Hue terribly. Every time Brad took her in his arms, she imagined it was Hue. Whenever Brad stole a kiss, she wished it were Hue. She was driving herself crazy, thinking about Hue and having no response to her letters.

But she never hesitated in her letter-writing. After a long time, she began to wonder if Jeremiah were really posting her letters. She had no reason to believe that. She dismissed such a possibility, chastising herself for thinking ill of Jeremiah--faithful to the family and steady as a rock. She dared not ask her father about Hue. He would not take kindly to such an inquiry. That source of information was closed to her, she realized.

* * *

Bradford wooed Emily persistently. He asked her to marry him . . . frequently. She remained detached and adamant in her repeated refusals. It was unthinkable!

Brad was confident that he could convince her to give her heart over to him. But he was sorely unsuccessful. She always refused his offers of marriage.

She thought: If only he knew about Hue. And how she felt about Hue.

Chapter Four

Blessedly, the two years in Philadelphia came to an end. When Emily began to pack, she discreetly left all the uniforms, all the tea dresses, all the ball gowns hanging in the wardrobe. And she left the luxurious fur coat. She wanted no part of any such clothing in Stoney Ridge. Aunt Hilda, with her boundless energy and resources, could find someone to give the clothing to.

Emily was twenty years old--refined by Mademoiselle Dubay's School for Young Ladies--and unmarried. That did not trouble her at all. She, guardedly, was looking forward to seeing Hue again. But she did not know how to approach him when she got home again. Let nature take its course, she decided.

Rupert Johnson was waiting for her at the Stoney Ridge train platform. He greeted her with a big smile, a big hug, and a big welcome-home party. Hue was nowhere in sight. She felt disappointed, dejected; at the same time, however, she realized that Hue had no way in the world to know that she had returned. Especially if he had lost track of the end of her two years back East. Even though she had written him that she was coming home soon, she had no knowledge of the train schedule to alert him to her arrival from Philadelphia.

But she put on a big front for her Daddy and his big party, which was held at the newspaper office. Neighbors came by to greet her on her return. New businesses had sprung up in Stoney Ridge, and those new owners and their wives also came by to meet the editor's daughter. Still, Hue was not among any of the guests.

Now she was convinced that something terrible was amiss. She began to worry. Was Hue injured in some way? Was he dead? What! She couldn't bear to think anymore about what might have happened to him.

The next day, for nostalgia's sake, Emily rented a carriage with horse from the livery stable and trotted out to a road that led up the side of a mountain that was a part of Hue's property. She guided the horse and buggy a short distance up the mountainside. She stopped the horse, alighted from the carriage, and tied the reins to a low-hanging tree branch. She stepped in front of the horse and spent long moments looking at Hue's spread. His house looked larger. Then she noticed a second house nearby. A grand house, built with boards instead of logs. It gave her a tug. Has he married someone else?

Realizing the thought was tearing her apart, she almost sobbed aloud. But a noise to her right stopped her. She looked toward where she thought she heard the noise. It was like a cowbell. It came closer and closer, until it came in sight from around the mountainside.

It was a mule being led by a man who was medium height, dark hair with a headband around his head, tied in the back, and dressed in well-worn laborer's clothing. The mule was loaded down with bags on both its sides, the cow bell attached to the rope for leading the mule. A pick axe and spade were attached to the bags. She looked carefully at the man, wondering fleetingly if she were in some kind of danger. Taking the horse's bridle by her hand, she looked at the man again, carefully.

"Hue?" she questioned the man. "Is that you, Hue? Really you?" she asked, disbelievingly.

"Emily!"

She took a step toward him, and he took a step toward her, then they both stopped.

She demanded, "Why didn't you write me? You promised!"

"But I *did* write you, Emily. I might ask you the same question!"

"And I wrote to you, faithfully, every month, without fail! What do you mean, 'why didn't I write to you?'"

Hue pondered this a short moment. "Something is wrong--terribly wrong. You wrote to me, but I got no letter from you; I wrote to you, and you got not one letter from me?"

She began to protest further when something occurred to her. "Oh, no. No, no, no!" she wailed. "I can't believe this!"

"Can't believe what, Emily? What is it?"

She drew herself up deliberately. It all fell into place. She remembered: Aunt Hilda always insisted that Jeremiah post the mail for Emily. And Jeremiah always gave the mail delivered to the house directly to Aunt Hilda. Then she would hand Emily her mail, an occasional letter from Rupert. Emily explained to Hue what must have occurred.

"Hue, dear one. I believe my Aunt Hilda has prevented my letters to you from ever leaving Philadelphia, and she has prevented all your letters to me ever getting into my hands. She either destroyed them or, heaven forbid, read them and kept them?"

She released the bridle; Hue dropped the rope that he led the mule with. Each one took another hesitating step toward the other. Then, breaking into a run, they raced into each other's arms. Kissing the eyes, the cheeks, the lips, all cares falling away so suddenly.

At last they broke apart and looked at each other. They held each other once more, not getting enough touching one another, loving each other more and more tenderly than they could ever imagine possible. All worries about each other, all questions about each other fell away into a void.

Suddenly, Hue stepped back and away from her. "A thousand pardons, dear Emily. I am not clean, my clothes are not clean. I do not want to soil you in any way."

"But Hue, I never noticed! However, now that you point it out, have you been farming--on the mountainside? Doesn't seem possible nor practical."

"You're quite right, dear one." He hesitated. Then continued. "I am going to tell you something that no one else knows--except for the assayer in the next county."

"Assayer? For what, for heaven's sake?"

Again he hesitated. He took a deep breath. "Emily, know this: I have found gold on this side of the mountain. I take it to an assayer in the next county to prevent such knowledge from spreading to the people of Stoney Ridge. Most everyone is trustworthy and sincere. But among them are those who are fraudulent and outright thieves!

"If this discovery were known, I would be plagued with poachers. Perhaps be dead by now. There's no accounting for the thugs in this part of the world. The greed destroys all sense of decency, I'm afraid.

"I can tell you about the gold because you can now become my wife, and I want there to be no secrets between us. The only other person I must make aware of my new situation is your father. He must be informed that the unworthy Chinese man is now worthy of marrying his daughter."

"Hue, this is an unbelievable development for you. How long have you been mining?"

"Since the week you left for Philadelphia. I was so despondent that I took a walk up the mountainside to look for comfort of some kind, any kind, and spotted a yellow glint in the sunlight. It was gold, as I discovered the next day when I returned with tools. I have been mining ever since.

"Emily, my dearest one, today I am an extremely wealthy man."

She was so stunned at this turn of events that she could only whisper, "Incredible!"

* * *

255

Emily invited Hue to come to her father's house for supper that same evening. He continued on his way back to his main house, the log house. The new house, the one he had built for Emily and him had not yet been occupied. He had waited for Emily's return.

He had an extensive bath and dressed in his best western clothing, including a white shirt and black string tie, he mounted his saddled horse and rode into town.

Various laundry customers did not recognize him--only his horse --and wondered who is the stranger riding into town on Hue Lee's horse? It was someone very finely dressed. When Hue smiled at the neighbors he was passing on the street, he smiled grandly at them. Then and only then did the townspeople recognize him. It was that smile they had seen every week.

"Good evening, Mrs. Burt. Good evening, Miss Coralee."

The mother and daughter stared with incomprehension. He did cut a fine figure, riding so smartly on his horse! Others took note and thought pretty much the same as Mrs. Burt and her daughter.

It did not take long for the bulk of Stoney Ridge's population to realize Hue Lee had come to town to visit Rupert Johnson. And they remembered that Emily was home again. Tongues wagged vigorously.

Hue came down from his horse and tied the reins to a new fence post. He walked up to the front porch steps and climbed them. He strode across the porch, then knocked on the door. Emily answered instantly. She hugged him, then invited him into the house.

Rupert Johnson came down the inside steps and greeted Hue warmly.

Hue thought, a good sign. Very good sign.

At the supper table, Emily said to Hue, "I've told my Daddy that you have some wonderful news to tell him. Go ahead, Hue, tell him what you told me this afternoon."

And so Hue unveiled the story, leaving Rupert speechless.

"I don't know what to say," he said.

Hue answered with, "What you can say, Mr. Johnson, is that with a fortune sitting in my bank, surely you can approve of Emily's marrying me. I ask you once more, Mr. Johnson. Will you consent to our marriage?"

Rupert knew when he was in a corner, but he had other plans afoot, which he did not share with Emily nor Hue. But he said, "Surely I *can* approve and consent. And tell me, when are the nuptials to take place?"

"About two months, sir. It will take that long for the furnishings for the new house to be ordered from San Francisco and for them to arrive by train."

"Ah," was all Rupert said.

Supper was concluded, the table cleared, and Hue begged to be excused to go home. Emily accompanied him to his horse, tied at the fence post.

She hugged him and kissed in parting. Hue was amazed that she would do that in public. He had the feeling that many eyes, behind curtained windows, were watching them furtively. With a mental shrug, he hugged her back and kissed her passionately.

When Hue returned to his log house, he went to his room and, without changing into oriental clothing, sat at his desk and removed a catalog. He filled out the order blank, using a plain extra sheet for completing the full order. And mailed it on the westbound train the next week. That was the next step in his and Emily's plan to marry. He wondered if she were going to insist on having a Christian wedding in a Christian church building. Didn't matter to him--he was ready to embrace her spiritual life himself!

That would be another surprise for Emily. One that Hue cherished. He had spent two years reading the Bible and studying with the pastor. He was convinced that he wanted to be a Christian.

* * *

One month later, the westbound train from Philadelphia stopped in Stoney Ridge. The whole town turned out to see the private car that was attached to the rest of the cars. It belonged to Brad Hillmont. He had traveled in the family's personal railroad car. He called on Rupert and Emily.

Rupert knew why he was here--he had initiated the plan (in an urgent telegraphed wire to his sister Hilda) to force Emily to marry Bradford Hillmont III and to have him spirit her away on the train going to San Francisco. Once there, they were to board a ship, owned by the Hillmonts, as soon as it was provisioned and had taken on cargo. Then the ship was to go around the Horn and up to New York, docking there. The honeymooning couple would take a train to Philadelphia to make their home.

Brad revealed his reason for coming to Stoney Ridge, to ask Rupert Johnson for the hand of Emily in marriage.

"Daddy!" Emily exclaimed with alarm. "What kind of madness is this?"

"There's not time to argue, daughter. Do as you're expected to do. Put on your prettiest dress, and the pastor will marry you and Mr.

Hillmont before you get on the train ."

"You must be joking! I am not going to do any such thing!"

"I'll leave you two alone while he urges you to go along with the plan."

"Daddy! You can't be serious!"

* * *

Brad came bearing an enormous bouquet of roses. "Roses?" she asked him. "Where, in the vast and dry west did you find roses?" At least she was impressed with that much.

"I brought the rose bushes in pots on the train. These were clipped just this morning."

"You know it's impossible for me to do what my father says I must do." She spoke as calmly as she could muster although her insides felt like jelly.

"No, I do not know that it's impossible. Let me explain a few things to you, Emily. If you refuse to marry me today, I will, with my father's influence and power, force your precious Hue Lee to leave America and emigrate to China, the homeland of his parents.."

"You'll never make him go there."

"We will if we revoke his citizenship, confiscate his land, and deport him to China."

"You wouldn't!"

"Oh, yes, we would. And good riddance of one more slant-eye!"

"Hue will never leave me and go to China."

"Yes, he will. You'll see. And if you refuse to see that's happening, listen to this. If you insist upon marrying the Chink, I will personally see to it that your father's pitiful little newspaper is hit with hard times, and he will lose it. Probably lose this house, too.

"Come, my dear."

"Do not call me that!" She was ready to spit fire!

"Come, then, Emily. Wear what you have. The pastor is waiting outside. We can have the ceremony right here in your parlor."

"I can't do this!" she cried.

"Then think of what will happen to your beloved--not to mention your own father!"

* * *

She spent so much time protesting that she hadn't the time to change into a "prettiest dress," as her father put it. And now the pressure was too great. She would lose Hue and her father would lose everything--all because she refused to marry Brad. Ah, she thought, the pest has arrived to badger me again!

Emily was breathless from hearing the threats coming from Bradford Hillmont. She was beaten. She was cowed. She had to obey. But it's the wrong man. All of it was so wrong and so unfair. These thoughts she harbored while the pastor intoned the shortened ceremony in her father's parlor. Even if she had the opportunity to say goodbye to Hue, she would never have the nerve to do so. Not like this! A married woman--to someone else! What had she done to deserve this dilemma?

* * *

Rupert waved to Emily from the platform. Emily forlornly and half-heartedly waved in return. She dreaded to think what was ahead of her. The events of the past half-hour had been so devastating. She could not think straight. She could not think!

As soon as the train pulled out of Stoney Ridge, Brad fixed himself a drink. "Drink?" he asked Emily. She declined.

"Not even to celebrate our marriage?"

"Never!"

A knock on the door prevented the exchange to continue.

"Come!" said Brad.

The door opened and a burly-looking gentleman entered, dressed almost like Brad, a bit taller, very muscular, with well-combed medium brown hair, brown eyes, and a ruddy complexion.

Brad said to him, "Come on in, Frank. Have a celebratory drink."

"No thank you, Mr. Hillmont." Turning to Emily, he said, "I'm Frank Owens, secretary and bodyguard for Mr. Hillmont."

She noticed that Brad had not introduced them and that Owens introduced himself. Noteworthy, indeed. "How do you do, Mr. Owens. Secretary and bodyguard?"

"Yes, ma'am."

Brad finished his drink and poured another.

Owens and Emily stared at one another.

Brad went into the privy, at one end of the private car.

Emily addressed Owens again, "Mr. Owens, you look like a bodyguard, all right, but what on earth do you do as a secretary?"

"Mr. Hillmont took me off the streets in Philadelphia when I was 19, sent me to schools where I received a general education, learned a bit of law and the customs and etiquette of a gentleman. And while I was occupied with the years of learning, he supported my mother in her neighborhood, and still does. I then became his serf, so to speak."

"His serf!"

"Well, slave, if you like."

Brad returned to the main part of the car, joining Emily and Frank.

He finished his second drink in two gulps, then poured himself a third drink. It did not go unnoticed by Emily. She was appalled at the drinking. Owens was unaffected.

"Come on, Frank. Join me with a drink!"

"No thank you, sir. You know I don't drink."

"Oh, I thought you might let down your hair and help me celebrate. My bride won't do it."

"No, sir. And no, sir."

Brad blew out his breath. "Agh! I think I'll go out on the observation platform at the rear and get some fresh air."

Again, Emily and Owens stared at each other.

At last, picking up where they had left off, she said, "Serf? Slave? Whatever are you talking about?"

It's very simple, ma'am. For my services, I get room and board, clothes befitting my position, and a pittance of pocket money, plus continued support of my mother. Slavery or serfdom, if you please."

"It appears that you are paying back for everything he's done for you."

"Exactly. Until it's all paid back."

"But that's monstrous!"

"Call it what you like, Mrs. Hillmont. But it's that and more. Perhaps worse, as well."

She finally spoke again, "So, then, how long will it take to pay back what you owe?"

"I have no idea. Maybe the rest of my life. My mother needs looking after, when all is said and done."

"I cannot believe this!"

"I appreciate your concern, Mrs. Hillmont, but there's nothing more to do about it. Except ride it out. Thank you, Mrs. Hillmont."

"Mrs. Hillmont this. Mrs. Hillmont that. Isn't it tiresome? Try 'Emily.'"

"I'd be glad to do that, Mrs. Hillmont, but it would be unseemly upon a short acquaintanceship. And, after all, you're my boss's wife."

"Phooh! It means nothing to me.!"

"I know."

She looked at him with curiosity. "You know?"

"Yes." He looked away, then at her again. "I'm sorry."

She was thoughtful for a moment before saying, "Are we both in much the same predicament?"

"Pretty much, I'd say."

"Well!"

He had been standing all this time. Then he bowed slightly to her and said, "I will return to the next car, now. It was a pleasure meeting you, Mrs. Hillmont."

"I don't think I'll ever be the same. I know I won't."

"No, ma'am. Do not let an impossible situation ruin your life. Try to stay the same person. Please."

He left, closing the door to the private car.

*　*　*

Emily sat, thinking about their conversation. Brad re-entered, empty glass in hand. He poured another drink. Emily was losing count. Did it matter? she asked herself. Apparently it did not matter. Brad was so drunk, he stumbled, spilled the contents of the glass, dropped the glass, and landed in a heap on the floor.

A soft knock on the door, which she could hear in spite of the railroad noises, distracted her from the sight of a drunken husband on the floor. "Come in," she said, not caring who saw Brad sprawled and ungainly and ugly, were her words for the over-all situation.

An older Chinese man entered and asked if they were ready for dinner to be served. She replied, "I am, sir, but it seems my husband is incapable of feeding himself. Please continue."

The servant bowed low and backed out of the private car. It made her feel like some kind of royalty, but one glance at the heap of husband on the floor erased such a feeling.

Another knock on the door, this time more insistent. "Come in," she said.

Frank appeared, nodded toward her, then went straight to the unconscious Brad. He picked him up like a bale of hay and put him into the double-bed compartment. Emily watched the ritual. It was obvious that this truly was a ritual, one of Frank Owens' duties as a secretary/bodyguard.

When Frank came out of the larger sleeping compartment, Emily acted on a sudden impulse. She said to him, "Mr. Owens, who is the Chinese servant?"

"Choy, the cook. New man on the payroll. Your husband fired the former cook, an Italian immigrant, unceremoniously, just before we left Philadelphia, and hired Choy in his place."

"Why am I not surprised at that?"

Owens made no attempt to answer, thinking it was a rhetorical question, anyway.

She went on with, "Frank! Take supper with me."

He gave her a startled look.

"Don't be surprised. I'm a newlywed, my husband has passed out, and I'm already lonely. Please join me for supper." As an afterthought, she said, "We'll leave every door in the car open, if that will make you more comfortable."

He smiled, and, knowing that Brad Hillmont, his boss, will be out of it until late the next morning, he decided to take her up on her invitation. "Of course."

* * *

On her wedding night, Emily slept alone in the single-bed compartment. She had fallen asleep, finally, with dreams about Hue. Impossible dreams. In the morning, she awakened, dressed, and had breakfast. Frank knocked on the door just as she was finishing. Again, she said "Come in."

He said, "I hope you slept well, Mrs. Hillmont. You have traveled by train across country before, is that not so?"

"You know everything, don't you? Coffee?"

"Not everything. Yes on the coffee. And thank you."

He sat across from her at the small round table, companionably. They chatted. He looked in on Brad who was still dressed from the day before and still asleep. "In another hour or so, he should be waking up. He'll be a bear–if you'll forgive my saying so."

"And I thank you for the warning. I guess it is a warning?"

"Exactly. He won't be in a good mood at all, not until this evening."

"So that's what I have to look forward to."

"Your situation may improve once we arrive in San Francisco and transfer to a hotel. It'll give you time to get ready for the voyage."

"I understand there'll be a lot of shopping going on for me–for the voyage."

"There will be."

It seemed to her that there was nothing more to say. She hardly knew this man. He filled in the silence with, "I must return to the other car now. I have paper work to attend to. Mr. Hillmont should be awake in time for lunch, I'm sure."

"Thanks again, Frank."

It gave him a tug, hearing her call him 'Frank,' familiarly. He thought, I don't deserve the company of this young woman. She's so pretty, so bright. She's so unavailable. . .

A few minutes after Frank left the private car, Brad woke up. Stumbling out of the double-bed compartment, he moaned about his splitting headache. He poured himself a drink to settle his stomach.

Didn't he know that makes it only worse? she asked herself. She vowed not to say anything to him unless and until he spoke to her first. She did not expect any trace of civility from him. And, indeed, it was not forthcoming.

"Where's my breakfast? I need food! Can't you do anything but stare at me? I want something to eat!"

Emily arose from the chair, walked to the front of the private car, and went into the next car. The first thing she saw was a compartment containing a desk and chair. Frank was seated but stood up as soon as she came in.

"Yes, Mrs. Hillmont?"

"Ah, don't get up, Frank. I just need to tell Choy that Mr. Hillmont is ready for a breakfast. I presume Choy knows what to get for him, after an evening of drinking?"

Still standing, he said, "Indeed he does know, by now. I'll get him for you."

"I'm always thanking you for one thing or another, Frank. I feel the relationship is lopsided, if I may use a country expression."

"You may, indeed, Mrs. Hillmont. Excuse me for now, please?"

"Of course. I'm stalling against having to go back into the car where Brad is, awake, and drinking again. Is this something I have to put up with all the time?"

"Pretty much. Come along and see where and how Choy manages to prepare meals for five people, in small quarters."

"Five?"

"Choy is the fourth one; his wife, Lai, is the fifth. And Lai is a maid, making beds, cleaning, dusting, and so on."

"Ah, yes, of course. I'd like to meet them both. Choy last evening announced dinner and served. A quiet little Chinese woman cleaned up after dinner. She would have been Lai?.."

"Indeed. Right this way, Mrs. Hillmont."

* * *

Choy and Lai were delighted to meet the young bride formally. They had seen how pretty she was, and she proved to be as gracious as she was pretty. They both felt better about working for the unreasonable and unpredictable tyrant, Mr. Hillmont. Thank goodness, they thought, the journey would soon be over, and Choy and Lai would be released. This had been a grand opportunity to return to San Francisco where each had relatives to visit and to assist in their getting other jobs.

Frank gave instructions for Choy to make breakfast, quickly, for Mr. Hillmont. Frank and Emily went to the private car. Brad had puked into the jardiniere for the second time while they were gone. His mood was thunderous. Choy entered with Brad's breakfast. Brad took one look at the coddled eggs and dry toast and roared.

"Dammit, you slant-eye! Take that garbage away! I can't stand the sight of it!"

Choy departed hastily with the food, sufficiently chastised . . . again.

"Damn chink!" Brad muttered under his breath.

Emily did not know what to make of all this unbecoming behavior. Her father had a drink perhaps once a month, but nothing like this. She was bewildered. She suggested, "Brad, why don't you go back to bed until you feel better?"

"I don't need a woman to tell me what to do! What are you, my mother?"

"I was only trying to be helpful, not domineering," she said.

"Oh, so now my mother is domineering!"

Frank intervened. "I hardly think that's what Mrs. Hillmont meant, Mr. Hillmont. . . ."

"And now you're taking *her* side! Get out of my sight, both of you!"

Frank and Emily looked at each other. She thought, and just where am I supposed to go, from a private car? Into the baggage car?

Without further words to anyone, Frank took Emily by the elbow and steered her to his office alcove in the next car. "Sit here, Mrs. Hillmont, in my desk chair. I'll fetch another from . . . somewhere."

Emily was too stunned to comprehend yesterday's unplanned-for marriage, the disappointing evening and the disastrous morning.

When Frank returned with another chair, they sat and tried to carry on a meaningful conversation, but it was as good as impossible.

"Frank," she said. "You must have work to do. Let's exchange chairs so that you can at least be in a position to take care of business."

"Thanks, Mrs. Hillmont."

"Really. I am growing weary already of being called 'Mrs. Hillmont.' It's no honor, from what I've seen, unhappily."

"It'll be different in Philadelphia."

"And how long will it take to get there?"

"More than a month, I'm afraid."

"I'm afraid, too, of other things–unknown things."

264

He looked at her sympathetically. He thought, she should never have to go through this hell.

* * *

By lunch time, Brad had slept through what remained of the morning. His mood was better. He was almost civil toward both Emily and Frank. And he was prepared to eat a hearty lunch. Everyone, Choy and Lai included, breathed a silent sigh of relief.

The afternoon passed pleasantly enough, Emily taking a nap herself in the single-bed compartment. By the time she awakened, Brad had begun drinking again. One stiff drink after another. At dinnertime, he was barely sociable. Words were slurred. Thoughts were hazy. He switched to wine with the evening meal. Then back to the hard stuff. He was insufferable.

Emily excused herself and retired to the single-bed compartment. Frank noticed that, but Brad did not. He wasn't noticing anything. Uncomfortable with Brad while he drank so heavily, Frank also excused himself and retired to his "office."

Later, Brad decided to go to bed. When he entered the double-bed compartment, he was conscious enough to realize that Emily had not gone to bed there. He went to the other bed compartment and opened the door. She was in the bed but not asleep.

"All right, my pretty little bride, it's time to consummate the wedding vows. Get out of there and come with me to the other bed."

This was the moment she dreaded, at the end of those wedding vows. A vow was a vow. A duty was a duty. And that's exactly how she measured it–a duty.

He grabbed her by the arm and, crazily, dragged her out of the compartment. With red bleary eyes, he looked at her lasciviously. Wanting to ravish her as quickly as possible, he grabbed the top of her nightgown and ripped it downward, past her waist. She tried to gather the two loose ends at the top, but he pulled her arms apart to look at her nakedness. He was so drunk, again, that he passed out on the floor, between the two bed compartments.

"Thank heaven," she breathed.

* * *

San Francisco was an exciting city to visit, in any century, but Emily was concerned about her disastrous marriage–a forced one, at that. She did manage to shop for clothing suitable for the month-plus voyage that lay ahead. Again, dread took over her being. Had it not been for Frank's occasional cheery and polite greeting, she would have expired, she was sure. This marriage burden was too much to bear.

After one week in the city, the ship was loaded with its cargo, a new crew had been engaged, and the tide was right. The Hillmont party--Brad, Emily, and Frank--boarded in the afternoon. Shortly afterward, the ship left the harbor.

Emily took one look at the various crew members and realized they were all Chinese men. All except for Captain John McGrady and his First Mate, Mr. Edward Hart. Captain McGrady was a craggy old seaman, beginning his life's work as a cabin boy. At least, he seemed old, weatherbeaten face and hands belied his real age, which was considerably younger than he appeared to be. Mr. Hart, the First Mate, was a young man, trained by the Captain since Edward's teenage years. This was the First Mate's third voyage under the tutelage of Captain McGrady.

While Emily puzzled over the strange crew of the two American officers and all the Chinese deck hands, and below-deck hands, she did not have to wonder about the odd arrangement for long. Brad came sauntering up to her, out on deck, looking at the city's becoming more and more distant. He said, "You like the accommodations, my dear?"

"Yes, thank you, it's small but cozy enough to be tolerated for the voyage."

"You noticed the deck crew?"

"Yes, of course I did."

"Well, my darling," he said oilily, "it's all for you! To help remind you of your Chink boyfriend back in Stoney Ridge."

She stiffened. "And why would you do that, Brad?"

"Because I'm sure you do not want to forget the slant-eye, do you?"

She was so enraged at the very idea of arranging to taunt her in this manner, she was speechless. She turned away from him and went below to their cabin.

At dinner, Emily ate in almost total silence. Frank noticed it. Brad ignored it. When she finished the last bit of dessert, she excused herself to go below and prepare for the night. She washed up and put on a new nightgown (to replace the one that had been ruined by Brad). The saleslady insisted she choose this one, a very attractive nightgown, beautifully trimmed in lace and embroidery. Pale blue chiffon seemed miles away from her choice, a flannel nightie with long sleeves and high neckline. It was bound to be cold when they were to sail around the Horn. Because of limited laundering facilities on board, she chose several nightgowns for the journey.

Emily went to bed in the three-quarter bed in the compartment, a tad bit larger than a single bunk. Brad, meanwhile, lingered at the dinner table, getting drunker and drunker. Frank tried to get him to retire early, after all the sometimes complicated arrangements had been made in San Francisco. "Surely," Frank said, "You are dead tired?"

"Not in the least! I do wish you'd have a drink with me, to celebrate our shoving off tonight."

"No, Mr. Hillmont, and thank you. I prefer not. If you'll excuse me, sir, I have considerable paper work to do."

As Frank left the dining area, Brad muttered under his breath, "Damned stubborn ingrate! A good man, though, and a hard worker, too. Oh, well." And he poured himself another drink.

Still muttering, Brad said, "Fine thing. A man's woman goes to bed, and his friend won't drink with him." He began to feel sorry for himself. He had another drink. "Dammit! I don't remember doing it with Emily! I must have, though. Just can't remember it. He gulped the drink and poured still another. He was going blind with the rot gut, he decided. He couldn't see straight. "Better call it a night. Nobody to talk to; nobody to drink with me."

Brad left the dining area and headed for the sleeping compartment. When he opened the door, he saw her asleep on the bed. He dragged her out of the bed by one arm. She awakened suddenly, wondering why she was being dragged out of bed. It was Brad, of course.

"You little chippy!" he shouted. She wasn't sure what that meant, but coming from Brad Hillmont, she could make a reasonable guess. "Get off the bed and watch me undress," he shouted. The deck was unsteady, she was wobbly on her feet. He reached for her, just as before, grabbing her nightgown (the frilly thin one) and ripping it down the front, almost all the way. Then he lost his footing because of the moving deck and fell to the floor. He lay there, in a sprawl, not moving a muscle.

Emily assumed he was drunk, as usual.

There was a soft knock on the door. She reached for her dressing gown and put it on, looping the tie at the waist, holding it close to herself at the top. "Come in," she said.

Slowly, Frank opened the door. "I heard some shouting. Is everything all ri . . ." He saw the heap of Brad on the floor. "Never mind. I see everything is not all right. I'll just pick him up and . . ."

"No," she said. "Leave him there. It's too disgusting to even think about going to bed with him!"

"As you wish, Mrs. Hillmont." He wondered why she was clutching her dressing gown so savagely at her neckline. He had an inkling–a memory, really. In some other place in the world, he had dragged Brad away from a house of prostitution, but not until he had seen that the woman's garment had been ripped from top to bottom. She had exposed herself to Frank brazenly.

He asked himself, "Did Hillmont really do that, too, to his *wife*? Good Lord. This is a vile state of affairs." His heart went out to Emily. He truly felt sorry for her and her future, if one could call it a future.

Frank said, "As you wish, Mrs. Hillmont," he repeated. He started to add 'good night,' but instead asked, "Will you be all right?"

"Yes. I'm sure he'll be out until mid-morning, as you have said in the past."

"Good night, Mrs. Hillmont."

"Good night, Frank. And thanks."

He closed the door and shook his head, as he left, wondering, "Thanks, for what, my poor Emily?"

Chapter Five

The Chinese ship's crew were everywhere, everywhere she went: out on deck, below deck, dining area–everywhere. It was Brad's way of taunting her and reminding her that she had given up Hue Lee for him. Changing the crew to Chinese men only was a cowardly ploy. What's more, she recognized it as such.

Early in the voyage, another personage seemed to be everywhere, the First Mate Edward Hart, except, of course, when he was on duty. That would be essentially 12 hours a day.

About Emily's age, Hart noticed her comeliness and admired it. It seemed to him that the honeymooning couple was a bad match. His boss, next to the Captain, was Hillmont. And he was such a lout!

Edward wondered why on God's earth did they ever tie the knot? Such a mis-match!

"Good afternoon, Mrs. Hillmont," said the First Mate.

"Good afternoon . . . Mr. Hart, is it not?"

"Yes, ma'am. I hope you are enjoying the voyage." Immediately, he wished he had not said that. She obviously was *not* enjoying the voyage.

She replied, "Perhaps not so much as I should, Mr. Hart. I am a landlubber at heart, you know. This is my first sea voyage."

"Have you experienced seasickness?"

"Not yet! Thanks be to God!"

"Just as a warning, watch out for rounding the Horn. Fierce winds. Fierce waters. But do not be alarmed. Forgive me if I did alarm you. I can assure you that the Captain and I will see us through it all safely."

"I don't know anything about the sea and its traditions, but, sir, you do seem to be a bit young for your position on the ship."

"The Captain has groomed me from early on. He told me some time ago that he was going to make me his First Mate. And here I am."

She smiled. She didn't know where to go next with the conversation. "I'd better go below," she said. I do take an afternoon nap every day. Helps pass the time."

"Of course, Mrs. Hillmont. I go on duty shortly, anyway. So nice talking with you, ma'am. I hope to encounter you out on deck again soon."

"Indeed."

The voyage to New York took longer than a full month because of heavy storms at the Horn, setting their timing back by two weeks or more. A good week into the voyage, Brad had managed to stay sober enough on exactly one afternoon and evening so that he could finally consummate his marriage to Emily.

She was devastated. All she could think about during the act was Hue. Hue, and how it surely would be different with him. The two men were two entirely different people, thank heaven, she thought! Such thoughts were dangerous and disabling, she realized. But Emily could not help herself. That was her situation with Bradford Hillmont: helpless.

The voyage dragged on.

The news passed around the crew and to the Captain and First Mate, as well. The news was that their boss, Hillmont, had ordered a cot to be placed in the main cabin, which was his cabin. Speculation ran riot. Whatever the officers and crew thought, it was the truth. Mr. And Mrs. Hillmont were not sleeping together. It wasn't difficult for everyone to figure out why. Hillmont was an ogre! Seemingly all the time.

What they didn't know was, which one of the Hillmonts slept on the cot?

Frank was not a speculator along with the others, because he knew exactly who slept on the cot. After all, he was having to tend to his duties every night when Brad passed out, as usual, and Frank had to haul him to the main cabin, undress him, and dump him into the bed compartment. Emily had always retired earlier to the cot.

First Mate Hart didn't know what to make of the shipboard gossip. Mostly because he was relatively inexperienced in the affairs of the heart. One girlfriend, from childhood, was all he had to draw on. He had asked her to marry him, but when she realized that he would be absent most of the time, at sea, she refused. She did not have the stomach for such a chopped-up marriage. She did get married, though, to someone else, a banker, an older man.

"Good morning, Mrs. Hillmont."

"Good morning, Mr. Hart. Brisk winds today."

"Yes, ma'am. Strong enough to give us good speed. It's blowing us in exactly the direction we want to sail."

"How fortunate!"

Their milky conversation continued briefly, every day. Edward began to notice more than ever just how pretty she really is. He began to think she was the nicest young lady he had ever met, even nicer than his old girlfriend. He began to feel sorry about Emily's unsatisfactory marriage, for that's how he saw it, plain and simple. Then he began to feel that, as a gentleman, he should do something to relieve her of the onerous union.

He caught himself up short. "What am I thinking?" he asked himself. "I must be mad. That's it. I'm madly in love with Emily. If only I could tell her that, bring her some bit of peace. If only I could just address her as 'Emily.'"

* * *

Frank noticed the young couple, meeting on deck every day, morning or afternoon, and having the briefest of brief conversations. Why did that bother him? he asked himself. After a few weeks time had passed, it dawned on him why. He, Frank Owens, was jealous.

* * *

In time, Emily did become "seasick." Or so she thought at its beginning. However, remembering the thousands of old-wives tales she had heard in her younger years, she knew that she was having morning sickness, and that meant that she was pregnant. She knew it would happen, eventually, but the realization made her feel sicker, not happy. The life with Brad was impossible. If she were lucky, in Philadelphia, he'd spend his days working for his father and his nights carousing the supper clubs or, worse, drinking at home.

Maybe it would be a good thing to have a baby to occupy her mind and put Brad into a separate compartment, to deal with only when absolutely necessary, and to do it with as much grace as she could muster.

* * *

The evening before the ship's putting in at New York, First Mate Hart came out on deck only minutes before he was to go on duty.

"Good evening, Mrs. Hillmont." His heart was racing wildly.

"Good evening, Mr. Hart."

"The voyage is almost over," he said.

"Yes! And I'm so happy for that!"

He thought, I can imagine so. Aloud, he said, "I have mixed feelings, myself. In one part of my heart, I'll be glad to set foot on land again. In another part of my heart, I will hate the world for separating us."

"You what?"

"I'm sorry," he stumbled for words other than that. "I mean, Mrs. Hillmont, that with all my heart, I have the strongest of feelings for you. I have wished that you were not married to that despicable excuse for a man! I would court you aggressively!"

"Mr. Hart, I don't know what to say!"

"Surely you have been aware of my attentions to you–every day–whenever I've been off duty."

"I am. And thinking so, I was aware that you were approaching me only when you were off duty. I looked upon our encounters as purely accidental."

"No, ma'am. In no way were our meetings accidental. They were all carefully planned."

"I see."

"I hope you do see, Mrs. Hillmont. Seriously, if you were not married–to anyone–I would be your swain." He grabbed both her hands and brought them to his heart. He didn't care who saw him. Hillmont, himself was probably having a departing drink with the Captain. "Farewell, Mrs. Hillmont. Farewell. I hope that sometime in our lives we may meet again."

"Farewell to you, Mr. Hart. That seems unlikely. However, it's a lovely thought."

He left abruptly, keeping in mind that he did not want to be late in relieving the Captain. At any rate, it was a naval courtesy to relieve the watch ten minutes early.

* * *

Emily greeted the arrival in New York with some trepidation. She was glad to be able to step onto solid ground again, but she had terrible misgivings about what lay ahead. There would be times to meet again the family members of the Hillmonts, get accustomed to having servants around again (after the Aunt Hilda experience), perhaps renew friendships from the finishing school, somehow make new friends, and, at the prescribed moment, give birth to her baby. Furthermore, Emily was not sure how she would greet her Aunt Hilda, after what had happened to Emily's and Hue's letters to each other. To say it would be awkward for her was an understatement.

At last they alighted from the now-familiar sailing ship, spent an overnight in a New York hotel, and took the train the next day to Philadelphia.

This time, there were Brad's parents (whom she had met at numerous parties) to greet them. At least it was not a servant. But that had been Aunt Hilda's doing. Not so with the Hillmonts. Remembering Emily from her two-year stint in Philadelphia, the Hillmonts extended their best manners and personae to Emily. And, Emily was grateful for that much.

At the Hillmonts' home (Brad and Emily would live there temporarily while they searched for a suitable house), Emily was introduced to the servants, one by one: Roland, an English butler; Melanie, a downstairs English maid; Thelma, an upstairs maid; and Mrs. Aldrich, the cook in charge of the rest of the kitchen staff.

Mrs. Aldrich, a substantial Scotswoman from the Chesapeake shores of Maryland, took one look at Emily and drew her into her ample arms, murmuring, "Bless my soul, Miss Emily. You are with child, aren't you?"

"How on earth did you know that?" asked Emily, astonished at the woman's perspicacity.

"Never mind, my dear. I know."

After that, Mrs. Aldrich took Emily under her wing, hovering over her every free moment she could manage from her kitchen duties. She made certain that Emily ate the right foods, denied her desserts, fed her milk–lots of it. If it weren't for her, Emily would have been desperate for a mother-figure such as Mrs. Aldrich. She leaned on her heavily for all kinds of support. It was forthcoming, gladly, for Mrs. Aldrich knew Brad well–perhaps better than anyone else in the world knew him.

Mrs. Aldrich was Emily's rock.

* * *

It was time to get re-acquainted with Aunt Hilda, much to Emily's dismay. She still had very bad feelings about Aunt Hilda's deception of the past.

Before Emily was confined to the Hillmont house with her advancing pregnancy, or to a house Brad would select, she took one of the Hillmont carriages to Aunt Hilda's. A note to Aunt Hilda had asked if Emily could visit her soon. Aunt Hilda's response was to invite her for tea.

It was a meeting fraught with distrust on Emily's part. Aunt Hilda, on the other hand, acted as though nothing in the world had changed since Emily left Philadelphia, months before. Emily was strained and distant. Aunt Hilda seemed oblivious to that. She chattered on and on. She never knew that Emily and Hue had figured out how the delivery of their letters was manipulated so cleverly. In spite of Emily's desire to confront Aunt Hilda about the letters, she remained silent on the subject and let Aunt Hilda go on blithely about her busy life of one nonsensical tea, party, or ball after another.

Emily tried to forget about Aunt Hilda, but of course, she was frequently in the Hillmont mansion attending one of those inane teas, parties, or balls. Tiresome, was all Emily could think of when she looked at their lives in the wealthy Philadelphia circles.

* * *

The baby was born before Brad and Emily found a house for them to move into. The last two months of the search was up to Brad himself, who was usually hung over, or tying on a big one. Emily spent the last two months of her confinement in seclusion. That rule for mothers-to-be was in full force in those times.

Mr. and Mrs. Hillmont made a big fuss over the baby boy, named Bradford Hillmont III. Emily had no say in it, of course, and she acceded to their wishes. It was more than their wishes being satisfied, Emily thought. More like a takeover. But, that was all right with her. It was her baby, and she had no say in naming him. However, she pondered, what in the world would I have named the child? Rupert? I don't think so. Daddy never liked his name, so that would not be a choice.

Face it! she demanded of herself. What's done is done, and I can't do anything to change it. Get over it, Emily, she scolded herself.

* * *

The baby thrived beautifully, growing and developing rapidly. It seemed so to Emily. She had to chase away the servants to have him to herself.

The search for a house continued. And Brad continued to be in an afternoon fog every day and into getting drunker by evening. He barely saw the baby. He barely saw Emily, not that he cared one whit about that. He had done what was expected of him–marry the Johnson girl from Stoney Ridge. Although he had pursued her while she lived in Philadelphia, she kept refusing him. She went back to her home out West. He lost interest in her until, somehow, as if by magic, forces beyond his control pressured him to do a forced marriage to Emily. Those forces working on him were his parents and the widow Hilda Franks.

The house search was an amusing pastime for him, totally without regard to actually finding a place for his little family. The drinking got worse, if such could be said about the drinking habits of Bradford Hillmont II.

Indeed, one night when Frank rescued him from the home of a charming widow, weaving and careening in all directions, Brad, with assistance from Frank, stumbled into one of the family carriages. Upon their arrival at the Hillmont mansion, Frank could not rouse

274

him.

It turned out, after one of the male servants and Frank's trying to carry him into the house, that Brad was not only dead drunk. He was dead.

The family doctor had been called out of his warm bed to pronounce Brad dead–from drinking. No surprise to anyone who knew him well enough. And certainly no surprise to Emily.

After the funeral, her in-laws tried to persuade Emily to stay with them forever. But Emily had other pressing plans. She promised the Hillmonts she would stay until the baby was walking, then she would board a west-bound train and return to Stoney Ridge.

* * *

Frank Owens was now out of a job. He had stayed on long enough to assist the family law firm to close up Brad's estate. On his last day of employment, he sought out Emily, who had taken the baby outside in the gardens at the back of the house. The baby was asleep in a pram, and she had just settled on a bench near the wisteria with a book to read.

"Emily," he said to her.

She looked up, startled. She recognized the voice, but he never before had called her 'Emily.' She looked at him briefly and said, "Sit with me, Frank, please."

He sat next to her and took one hand in both of his. "Emily," he began again, "I have distressing information to pass to you. Brad left you and the baby nothing–absolutely nothing."

"And why does *that* not surprise me? Never mind, Frank, I'm returning to my father's house. We shall be cared for."

"Im sure you will, but not in the style of what you have here in Philadelphia."

"I care not one tinker's curse for this kind of life, Frank. Surely you know that."

"Yes, but . . ." He paused, wondering how to carry on. "You also need to know that my strongest desire in my life at this time is to ask you to marry me and let me care for you and the baby." He paused again, recalling what he had decided to say next. "But first of all, I have to look for another job. Second, I have to make other arrangements for my mother. I certainly cannot afford the amenities for her that the Hillmont family have provided all these years. And third, and this is the real reason I cannot ask you to marry me– I know all about Hue Lee and how you had planned to marry him."

"You knew about Hue?"

"Everything."

She sucked in her breath suddenly. "Incredible how much Brad had inserted himself into my affairs."

"Yes," he said. "I had a large part in the investigations. So, I know what a terrible sacrifice you had to make. Brad even used your father as a weapon. I was in charge of manipulating everything he was going to do to Lee and to your father. I was poised for it. But it didn't happen. You had to agree to marry him. That bastard!"

She looked at him sharply.

"I'm sorry, Emily. That's exactly what he was. Not supposed to speak unfavorably of the dead, I guess. But Bradford Hillmont II was a huge exception to such a rule as that!"

She nodded slowly in agreement. Then she said, "You know, too, perhaps, that I have not been in contact with Hue Lee and know nothing of his whereabouts nor of his life since I left Stoney Ridge."

"I am reasonably sure of it."

"But my plan is to go back home to seek him out, to learn if he has married someone else. And to see if his new-found wealth has changed his situation in any way."

"I wish you well, Emily. But let me leave you, if you please, with this thought: I came to love you very much. I felt sorry for you in the beginning, of course, but in time it turned into love. Know that, Emily Johnson Hillmont!"

He squeezed her hand he was holding, almost to the point of being painful to her. She had suspected for many months that he was in love with her. He had been so gentle, so understanding of her dismay and despair. "In some small way, I knew it, Frank, for a long time now."

He let go of her hand and stood. "Goodbye, Emily. I'll never forget you, my dear."

"Goodbye Frank. God go with you."

He smiled, turned on his heel, and disappeared through the garden. He left the next morning. Each believed in his and her heart that they would never see one another again.

* * *

When the time came, Mr. And Mrs. Hillmont expansively gave Emily a sendoff that overshadowed all of Emily's misgivings about this unfortunate segment of her life. They also gave her the Nanny whom they had provided when little Brad was born.

Emily protested the human gift with, "Mrs. Hillmont, I simply cannot accept Lizzy as a Nanny. I will never be able to afford it!"

"Tut, tut," Mrs. Hillmont scolded. "We shall provide all that Lizzy needs while in your service. Now, do not argue with me, young lady. We want to make sure our grandson has the best possible care. Not that you wouldn't provide it on your own. But Lizzy's aid will make it easier on you. Lord knows, you've had a bad time, being married to our son."

Emily was surprised to hear Mrs. Hillmont say that about Brad II. In the end, she accepted the generous aid in the form of Lizzy, the Nanny.

Amid tears, both Mr. And Mrs. Hillmont rode with Emily, Lizzy and little Brad to the train station. They really liked Emily. A lot. Aunt Hilda managed to squeeze in a good-bye to her, at the train station, between appointments. Holding little Brad, Emily waved to them all from the observation area of the Hillmont's private car. Yes, they had provided that for her, too. "Bless them," she thought. She departed Philadelphia with a blend of relief, thankfulness, and . . . she struggled for another word: love.

Chapter Six

The train pulled into the platform at Stoney Ridge. Finally. Baby Brad had turned out to be a good traveler. He was allowed to sleep when he rubbed his eyes, to play in between, and to continue nursing. Emily thought that she would begin weaning him after she got settled in her old home.

Mrs. Weathers, Rupert's neighbor, was at the platform, waiting for Emily's arrival. She thought she could provide assistance with the baby and all. Emily was grateful, even though she did have Lizzy in tow to take over much of the needs of the baby.

Rupert greeted Emily warmly and chucked the baby under the chin. Little Brad looked at him with wonder. His grandfather was a stranger to the young Brad, but not an unfriendly one.

Knowing that it would be an impossible urge to ignore, Emily gave in to it and scanned the platform for another carriage, or horse, and any sign of Hue Lee. The platform was empty beyond Rupert's two carriages for passengers and a wagon for baggage.

After they were in Rupert's house, Lizzy prepared Brad for his afternoon nap. Emily went downstairs to speak to her father. She thought, no point in delaying the matter—just come right out and ask him. "Daddy," she began, "Put aside your feelings about Hue Lee forever, for me, and tell me all that you know about him as of today."

"Well, Honey, you're not going to like this. Word around town is that he has sent for a man who is a tailor, and the man's two sisters, all from China. The tailor from China will become the husband of Lee's older sister. The tailor's older sister will become the bride of Lee's brother, the next one in line. And the younger sister from China will become Lee's bride."

Emily was not altogether surprised at this bit of news, true or false. "*Will* become Hue's bride?"

"Yes. They're not here yet. They're on their way."

Emily breathed a slight sigh of relief. "Good. That'll give me time to contact Hue and change his mind!"

"Emily! Surely you're not going to marry Hue, after what you've been through?"

"Oh, but I certainly am going to try my best!" She had an afterthought. "And please, Daddy, do *not* try to interfere this time. Do I make myself clear?"

Rupert regarded his daughter. Never had he seen her so strong-minded. Perhaps she had good reason. "I won't interfere, Emily. I swear." Yes, he thought. She did have good reason. An enormous feeling of guilt overcame him. Would she ever forgive him for past interventions?

* * *

Emily was determined. No simpering female wiles for her—not in this case. The problem of winning back Hue was intimidating. She would crawl on her knees and beg him to take her back, if need be.

Not waiting for Friday's laundry pickup and delivery day to see Hue, she rented a carriage first thing the next morning and rode straightaway out to the Hue Lee spread. She had no idea if he would be at the house. She had no idea if he would be in the orchards or gardens or mining on the mountainside. Didn't matter. She would simply wait for him. It was the least she could do.

Emily had a fairly good idea of how to approach Hue, verbally, but nothing after that. She had not an inkling of what his reaction would be upon seeing her again. She had no idea what he would say to her. There was the matter of a mail-order bride, already on her way.

Hue Lee was at the main log house, going over accounts. The sisters were laboring in the laundry-tub house; the brothers were pruning in the orchards. Hue answered the insistent knocking on the door. The knocking surprised him because the entire family never had visitors at their home. He got up from his desk and went to the front door. He opened it. What he saw, or rather, whom he saw shocked him into silence. He was utterly surprised to see Emily standing before him. He was also confused.

"What on earth are you doing in Stoney Ridge, Emily? A visit?"

"No, Hue. I've come to stay. With you, if you'll have me."

"Emily, I don't know what to say. What has happened that you've returned to Stoney Ridge?"

"It's a long story."

"Then, please come in." He led her to the large kitchen with a long table down the center. He indicated to her to take a chair near one end of the table. He brought down from a cupboard two cups and two saucers. He placed tea leaves into a porcelain teapot. He took a steaming kettle off the range and poured the hot water into the pot. He waited for the tea leaves to steep, the two of them waiting in silence. At last he poured the tea into the cups. "Sugar?" he asked her.

"No, thank you."

Hue said to her, "Please, Emily, begin at the beginning."

She told him about the disastrous train ride to San Francisco, the busy time in that city, shopping and waiting for the tide to be right for sailing out of the harbor. She told him that Brad had hired an all-Chinese ship's crew, everyone, that is, under the Captain and the First Mate. She told him about Brad's loutish behavior on certain evenings, leaving out no details, shocking as it was to her as well as to Hue. What was puzzling to her was the fact that there was only one time that Brad had touched her intimately, throughout the entire journey.

"By the great gods, Emily, tell me no more! This is awful!"

"No, Hue. You have to hear the rest. There's more."

Then she told about the voyage around the horn, lasting for about a month and-a-half. The young First Mate who gave her some carefree moments out on deck, almost every day. The solicitous and sympathetic Frank Owens. The meeting with Aunt Hilda.

"You saw and talked to *her*?"

"Yes. She said nothing about the letters. I did not confront her about it. Perhaps I should have."

"No, my dear, now that I think of it, it was best not to bring it up. You did the right thing."

She continued with what it was like to live with Brad's parents, prestigious living, it was, with a servant for every little whip-stitch of a chore that needs to be done in a mansion. She told about Brad's continued brutish ways, the drinking, the carousing, having little or no regard for her.

"Then," she said, "came the baby."

"The baby!? Emily, on top of everything you went through, you have a baby?"

"Yes, Hue. A boy named Bradford Hillmont III. He's 15 months old and is walking now."

"I . . . I cannot visualize . . . I cannot even begin to imagine you with a child. Unless it were mine!"

"Hue! Do you mean that?"

"Of course I do, dear Emily. But, alas, you are still a married woman, and in time, I will be taking a bride, from China."

"No, Hue!" He looked at her with alarm.

"You have to hear the rest. Brad, my husband, died while the baby was still a tiny infant."

He took both her hands in his. "But that means, Emily, dearest, that you are free?"

"As a bird, Hue."

"Now let me tell you," he said, "about what I've been going through."

"Oh, please do, Hue!"

"When I called for you the next day, after our last meeting, your father told me what had transpired. That the Hillmont man had threatened to ruin me, even have me deported! Then, about a month later, he spoke to me during a laundry delivery day and told me he had a letter from your Aunt Hilda who explained further that Hillmont had also threatened you with the fact that he could cause your father to lose his newspaper business and to lose his house!"

"And then you knew, too?"

"Yes, my darling."

"Can you ever, ever forgive me, Hue?"

"Of course, darling! You were in a terrible fix. You had to protect your father and, thankfully, you also protected me." He seemed preoccupied for a moment. "All this news means that we are free to marry, Emily! Free to marry!" He could not contain his excitement.

"Wait," she said. "My Daddy told me about the tailor and his two sisters coming here from China."

"Yes, the plan was for me to marry the tailor's younger sister; the tailor would marry my older sister; and the tailor's older sister would marry one of my brothers, Ho. But that's all changed now. I will not take the Chinese woman as my bride."

"But surely you would not send her, nor the rest of her family, back to China, would you?"

"No, my dear. As soon as you asked me to forgive you, I began to think of a solution for my future plans. This is it: my once-intended bride will marry my youngest brother. That leaves only my younger sister without a mate. I must think on that, soon. Then he smiled grandly. "Yes, Emily, darling, we can be married after all."

"But what must the intended bride who is promised to you think of such a change in arrangements already made?"

"Do not fret over that, Emily. I have more than enough money to assuage hurt feelings. If I need to use money for that, she will be well compensated for her trouble. She will be free to return to China, if she chooses. Or she can stay in San Francisco (I would arrange for her a sponsor). Or she can accompany us back to Stoney Ridge and marry my younger brother. She will have more than one option. The money will come in handy, whatever she chooses to do."

Emily shook her head in amazement. "How quickly you think, Hue. I just hope, if the intended bride does come to Stoney Ridge, that she will not look upon me with great disfavor."

"Not to worry about that, either, Emily. The money will take care of everything. I guarantee it!"

"Well," she said, "you know the Chinese culture intimately. I know nothing!"

Hue needed a distraction. It came to him instantly. "Come, Emily. Let me show you your new home. It is entirely furnished now, while you were gone. I did not furnish it with a Chinese bride in mind. I still made it for you, even when I knew you were gone for all time." He paused. "Even when I knew it was hopeless, that you were gone forever, a small part of me prayed to your God to bring you back to me. That is why I furnished 'our' house with you in mind. And if I were to take a Chinese wife, she would just have to put up with it!"

Walking to the new house, he said to her, "I am so proud of you, Emily, coming through that distressing life with the Hillmont monster! It is unseemly to be glad that a soul has died. But I am glad your husband killed himself in the way he did. Such a life as he led was bound to come to an unsavory end. Yes, I'm glad he died. He left you in death so that you could come back to me.

They arrived at the front door of the larger, newer and better house behind the log house. When Hue opened the door and stepped back to allow her to enter first, he followed her. Then he pulled her into his arms. She melted into them. They kissed slowly, at first, and then with intense emotion, both of them enveloped with warm affection and love for each other.

* * *

Emily and Lizzy were not completely unpacked when Emily and Hue made their intentions to marry known to the pastor. They wished to marry soon. Later, and privately, the pastor asked Hue if he had told Emily about his plan to become a Christian. He said he had not. "Tell her! Now!" the pastor commanded.

Hue went immediately to Emily to give her the good news.

She was overwhelmed. "We'll be married the same day you do the ritual of becoming Christian!"

"A wonderful plan," he said.

* * *

The good ladies of the church were at a loss for planning a wedding feast for the happy couple. In the first place, they could not understand why a white girl would marry a yellow man. Whatever possessed her? They consulted with the pastor on what to do with this dilemma. He assured the ladies that Hue Lee would be a full-fledged Christian moments before they would be married. The ladies were to treat them as they would any other happily joined couple.

Still . . . some had doubts. . .

That small storm swirled around Emily and Hue. But they were oblivious. All they could focus on was their upcoming wedding day, their eternal happiness to continue.

* * *

They arranged for their wedding day to coincide with the day the train came through, going west to San Francisco. There was no time for a reception. Emily boarded the train in her wedding dress. There was no time for a feast in Stoney Ridge, for which the confused ladies were truly thankful. It relieved them of what they had perceived to be a major problem.

Little Brad was left behind in the care of the faithful and diligent Lizzy. Rupert enjoyed the playful times with Brad, but felt a disturbing unease with the presence of Lizzy in his house. She made breakfast, she made dinner, and she made supper. She took good care of little Brad. Running Deer's appearance to do the housecleaning three days a week was a big help for Lizzy. She was grateful for that.

* * *

"Good Lord, Emily!" Hue shouted, once they entered their hotel suite in San Francisco.

"What?" she asked.

"What was I thinking? I brought you to San Francisco for a honeymoon, and surely this city will have unpleasant memories for you! I'm so sorry, darling!"

"Yes, it could be. But I won't let that happen. And it'll be easy not to let that happen because this time, I'm with you, Hue. My love. My only love."

He clasped his arms around her, and she returned the gesture. They kissed longingly and lovingly.

Hue was a patient lover, a resourceful one, as well.

Emily entered the gates of divine bliss that was beyond description. This had not happened with Brad! There was no comparison.

She bared her soul and her body to Hue. He took her proclamations as any good man would: graciously.

* * *

Three weeks into their married state, Hue returned to San Francisco, where the tailor and his two sisters awaited him. He went from the train station directly to their hotel suite. After much smiling and bowing to him, the tailor and his sisters welcomed him into the suite and offered him a chair of importance and tea.

Hue had rehearsed how he would break the news to the intended bride, Suun. She was stunning. The real problem, he decided, was not whether his younger brother would be pleased with her, but rather the other way around: would she be enamored with him?....the youngest brother in Hue's American family hierarchy.

He needn't have worried.

With everyone speaking in Chinese, Suun exploded at the turn of events thrust upon her. "I am not pleased with this plan, Mr. Lee!"

"I understand, Suun. If you wish to return to China, I will provide the means for you to do so, plus a remuneration for your trouble."

"Return to China? Never!"

This young woman had a mind of her own and, once in America, she exercised the right to express it, loudly. Hue was impressed. And dismayed. It would take more negotiating, it seemed.

She asked him, point-blank, "And why, Mr. Lee, is there a need for such a change in the already made arrangement?"

Hue thought for a moment, forming the words in Chinese to the best of his ability. "I address all three of you in this response to Suun. I was married three weeks ago."

This was too much for Suun and her brother, Ton. The other sister, Wu, remained passive.

Ton, enraged, said "We demand an explanation, Mr. Lee. This is a serious breach of contract!"

Suun recognized that her brother was her superior family member and would take over the exchange from here on out. She knew when not to protest further.

"I realize that, Ton," said Hue, and I will try my best to make amends for the new arrangements. Not only can Suun return to China, if she wishes, you and Wu may also, if you wish. I will furnish all expenses incurred for your return. And I will extend to you remuneration for all your trouble."

Ton wanted to know, how much? When Hue gave him the figure, he paled. He never before had that much money in his life! But what he wanted more, and desperately, was to stay in America.

"Mr. Lee, Wu and I will accompany you to your home and carry out the rest of the contract. Suun is free to do as she wishes."

* * *

At the end of the visit Hue made in Ton's hotel suite, Suun had decided to accept the "remuneration for her trouble." Hue had produced a photograph of each member of his family, for Ton's benefit, primarily. And, later, for Suun's benefit as well. She found Hue's younger brother Tao to be a comely young lad, indeed! A good sign, she thought. Except, the young Tao was not in her future, she decided. The promise of the money gave her other ideas. She had a great desire and . . . almost a need to stay in America, where, with her new-found money she could establish a fine restaurant and become a successful business woman. A romance and marriage with a Chinese man could happen in the future. She was content with her new prospects.

Hue offered a silent prayer of thankfulness for this stroke of good luck. He was coming out of it well. In the back of his mind, however, he remembered Emily's question about Tao's new bride's attitude toward Emily, if she had elected to come to Stoney Ridge. She had a good point, but now it was moot. He had hoped for the best. He had done what the roving cowboys in Stoney Ridge often said: "Keep your fingers crossed!"

* * *

It was four more days before the train headed out of San Francisco to go back east. Meanwhile, Hue introduced the entire family of Ton's to a good friend of Hue's. He was a former fellow railroad laborer, and he had done well in San Francisco. A solid citizen, married and with five children, he would sponsor Suun.

At the hour of boarding the train, they all bade Suun a heartfelt farewell. The stoical Wu shed a tear or two, reminding Hue of his own sister Ah Ming. Wu was not very much unlike Ah-Ming's public image.

Hue had informed his brothers and sisters, by a very long telegraphic message, what day he would return, and the estimated time. And he instructed that all of them come to the train platform with two carriages and one wagon in tow--for passengers, and for baggage.

Hue had further instructed them to arrive dressed in Chinese clothing—their finest! He was determined to have them make a good impression. Ah Ming was a plain-looking woman, but when she wore her favorite jade-green chong-sung, she would be more than presentable to her promised bridegroom. By all standards, the younger Bahn was the more interesting—if more fiery—and certainly the more attractive sister. He could hope only that her appearance at the platform would not derail all other plans, now well in place.

Hue, being a shrewd observer of life, as he knew it, did notice, in San Francisco, Wu's reaction upon casting her eyes onto the photograph of young Tao. Hue wondered about that. She was easily six or eight years older than Tao. Ton's reaction to the photograph of Ah Ming was studied and controlled. Hue read nothing in his demeanor. It was not exactly a worry, but it was a mild concern for Hue.

Then he thought of Bahn, the youngest of all of them, and her need to be paired with a husband before too long. She might be too old at 20 or 21. He did hear her declare one night, not knowing that Hue could hear her, that she would just marry a round-eye, if need be! It gave Hue a start to hear that. It also gave him the kernel of an idea. Perhaps she was on the right track!

* * *

The two weddings would be performed together, Ton to Ah Ming and Wu to Ho. However, as the plans began to form, Wu sought Ton for a private discussion.

"What is it, Wu? You do not have your heart in this arrangement. I can tell."

"That is correct, honorable brother. I cannot tell the honorable Hue what is in my heart. It is for only you, my brother."

"And? What is in your heart, first sister?"

"I do not wish to marry Hue's brother Ho."

"But this is insane! It is all arranged! You, yourself, agreed to the terms, long before we left China. What in the name of the gods are we to tell our benefactor, Hue?"

"Tell him, dear brother, that I am enamored with the younger brother, Tao."

Ton sucked in his breath. "But Wu! You are much older than he!"

"That does not matter. If he will have me, then I will beg the honorable Ho a hundred pardons."

"I doubt," said Ton, "that a *thousand* pardons would relieve you of your part of the agreement!"

She retorted, "But the honorable Hue married someone else before keeping *his* contract with our sister Suun!"

Ton winced. Then he said, "Unfortunately, dear sister, the honorable Hue was in a position to buy her off. You and I are not in such a place in life."

Lowering her head, she said, "Will you plead for me, my brother? Plead with the honorable Hue to ask the beautiful Tao if he will marry me?"

"But a woman *never* asks a man to marry her!"

"That may be so, but Ton, we are in America now. Could it be that this has never happened before, in America?"

"Probably not!" He sighed heavily. And thought ponderously. Finally, he said, "I will try, for you, Wu, to see if it is agreeable to the young Tao, and to the brother Ho--after I get permission from the Honorable Hue, to approach both Ho and Tao on this matter."

"I cannot ask for more than that, good brother. A thousand thank yous for your assistance!"

* * *

When Ton approached Hue as Wu had asked him to do, Hue was as surprised as Ton had been, learning that Wu favored Tao instead of Ho. "My future brother-in-law," Hue said, "This is a most unusual request. Surely you are aware that the older brother, or sister, should marry before his or her younger siblings?"

"Yes, of course, Honorable Hue." He waited respectfully.

Hue had so much on his mind, this request left him stunned. Always quick-thinking, however, he made this proposal. "Let us take this problem to my next younger brother Ho and ask for his feelings on it."

"As you wish, honorable Hue."

They had been talking in the office. All the others were in the large kitchen, eating leftover desserts from the evening meal. Hue went to the kitchen and asked Ho to come into his office.

When they entered and Ho saw Ton, he was nonplussed about what looked like a meeting coming up. "Yes, Hue?"

"Ho. Please sit." He indicated a vacant chair , all three men facing the center. "Ton has come to me with a problem that involves his sister Wu."

"And?" asked Ho, wondering what this was leading up to.

"Wu begs to be excused from marrying you because she would like to marry Tao. What say you about this?"

"Well! I don't know what to say!" He looked from Hue to Ton and back to Hue, again, gleaning no additional information from them on the subject at hand.

Hue asked gently, "Do you want a few days to mull it over? We can postpone the double wedding until this is all settled."

Ho regarded the two men again, then looked upward at the ceiling. He was remembering that he was a bit disappointed that the Chinese ways had stayed with them in America. The idea of arranged marriages had always left him feeling . . . what? . . . incomplete. The Americans were much more forward in the man-and-woman undertakings.

Hue and Ton waited patiently. Ho stood and drew himself up, ready to make an important announcement in Chinese. "I concede to the lovely Wu. She is free to marry my younger brother Tao, if he so pleases to have her for a mate. She is not to feel obligated to me in any way whatsoever."

Hue was astonished. He had never before heard his brother Ho speak such a long sentence, not even in Chinese. Ton breathed a soft sigh of relief. Addressing Ton, Hue said, "You may have the privilege to announce this event to your honorable sister Wu."

"A thousand thank yous, Honorable Hue. I shall tell her immediately." There was a pause, then Ton continued, "Never having had this kind of experience before, I must know: is it my duty to approach the young Tao with this request? Or yours?"

Hue had never had this experience, either. As always, he made a quick decision. "Ton, since we are in this country, America, and manners and mores are different from those of China, I shall say to you that you may approach my brother Tao and explain this unexpected turn of events."

"Indeed. And thank you again, venerable future brother-in-law."

Ton left the room. Hue and Ho stood looking at each other. Neither speaking for awhile. Finally, Ho spoke. "I hope Tao goes along with all this."

"Tao is young and impressionable. He misses his mother yet." Hue stroked his chin thoughtfully, then went on, "Perhaps the quiet Wu will be wife and mother to him."

Ho listened in amazement. How could his brother be so wise? He asked himself.

* * *

Tao was armed with the entire background and information leading to his being asked to marry the older woman, Wu. Tao then came to Hue to tell him that it was altogether agreeable for him to take Wu as a wife. She had been so kind toward him since their arrival on the train. He liked her instantly. He looked forward to having a companion in his bed. He said to himself that she reminded him of his mother. Comforting thought. Then he said aloud to Hue, "She isn't the most beautiful woman in the world, but she is surely the kindest." He enjoyed his good fortune.

The two Hue Lee family weddings were performed together—a double wedding. Ton to Ah Ming and Tao to Wu. When Hue introduced his future relatives to the pastor in English, he added, "Pastor Smith, these relatives of mine, and their about-to-be-mates, are all heathens–in the Christian world. Do the best you can, for the conduct of the ceremony. And I promise you, I will bring them all, one at a time, to you for instruction such as you gave me so willingly in the months and years past.

The pastor was delighted at the prospect of adding to his flock. Up to now, it had been so flexible, families pushing on to the west coast of California, a few scattered families arriving from the East to find their destinies in Stoney Ridge.

After the ceremony, Hue and Emily accepted, with genuine grace, the reception the good ladies of Stoney Ridge arranged for the two newly-weds. As an afterthought, the ladies realized they had done nothing like this for Emily and her husband, the Chinese laundry man, the supplier of fruits and vegetables. They had talked about it, but at the time, it didn't seem quite the right thing to do. However, the reception for the two newly-wed couples of today was to include its being a reception for Emily and Hue.

In spite of the strangeness to have the Chinese family in full force mingling with the round-eyes, everyone seemed to have a good time. Ton and Ah Ming sat silently, looking at each other, trying to determine what good qualities he or she should expect; and what bad qualities he or she should watch out for.

Tao and Wu were cautious as they approached the married state, but at least they put on their smiling faces for the occasion. A fortunate thing, the ever-observing Hue mused, while balancing a teacup and saucer on one knee, a snowy-white napkin on the other; and a hearty oatmeal cookie about to be devoured. He was pleased to see that Tao and Wu were apparently well matched. The cooky reminded him of Emily's oatmeal cookies, which she had baked in the past, and which he had enjoyed before they were married. Was it Emily's cookies he was eating today?

Emily's little Brad was allowed to attend the reception, with Lizzy 's presence to keep him corralled. Rupert tried not to stare at the very active Lizzy, tracking Brad everywhere he went. He hated to admit this, but he actually missed the little boy's running through his own house. Emily and Hue's return from their San Francisco honeymoon had ended all that. And, of course, he missed Lizzy's presence, as well. . . he had to admit. Missed her more than he *cared* to admit.

The crowd was generally marked by merriment, Emily was relieved to note. Only her sister-in-law Bahn seemed to have a sour look on her face.

Chapter Seven

The ladies of Stoney Ridge had rarely seen Tao, one of the bride-grooms of the wedding party. He was a sight to see, they decided, quite handsome, really. His bride looked to be a tad older than he. A wrinkle here and there on the face; red, wrinkled hands; and–is that a gray hair streaked at the front? No matter. They were foreign people, after all.

Then they noticed the quiet and unassuming other Chinese brother of Hue Lee. This brother was the same size and stature as Hue; same blue-black hair and same dark eyes. The ladies did not know his name. They did not know if he spoke English. The daughter of the town's blacksmith took the bull by the horns and asked him, "Hey, Mr. Chinese Man. Do you speak English?"

To her amazement, not only did he speak English, but he spoke it impeccably. Better than she did, she had to admit to herself. Maybe she'd admit it to the rest of her family. Maybe.

"So, what's your name, Mister?" asked Coralee Burt.

"I am called 'Ho.' And you are?"

"I'm Coralee."

"So pleased to meet you, Miss Coralee."

Ho thought she looked familiar, but without a surname, he couldn't place where he had seen her. He asked, "And you are Miss Coralee what?"

"Burt. I'm the blacksmith's daughter."

Immediately, Ho knew that he had not seen her at the blacksmith's, but rather at their home. She had, on two occasions (and he did remember that), answered the door when Ho had assisted his big brother Hue to make laundry deliveries to the townspeople. Again, he said, "So pleased to meet you, Miss Coralee Burt."

"Well, y'all can call me Coralee. No need to use the Burt."

They conversed some more before moving on, Ho joining his new relatives, Coralee charging through the gathered crowd to find her girl friends and tell them about the Ho brother.

The Stoney-Ridge ladies saw the exchange between them, and tongues began to waggle. "What?" they asked one another. "Do we have another white woman chasing after a slant-eye?" "Disgraceful!"

Coralee was not unmindful of the whispering behind her back. In fact, she was pleased with herself to be so daring as to speak to a nice-looking, well-dressed, well-spoken Chinese man. He was all those things . . . and more, she was to learn later on.

* * *

After the reception that honored the two newly-weds as well as Emily and Hue, the Chinese families retired to their complex while the Westerners cleaned up the fellowship hall of the church building and wound their way back to their homes in the community.

Hue allowed the newlyweds one day to grow accustomed to their new surroundings and to the manner in which the household was operated. Then, everyone to work!

Ho and Tao were busy in the orchards, removing weeds from between the trees. And Ah Ming and Bahn showed the ropes of the laundry house to Wu. Wu was not very attentive. She had other ideas for her contribution to the family's resources.

Taking Ton into Stoney Ridge, Hue drove the carriage straight to the bank. They were going to look for a place to install a shop. It had been discussed on the train, as they traveled from San Francisco. Hue, with Ton's input, would rent or lease or buy a building in town to house Ton's new tailor shop. Nothing suitable was found.

Hue then made arrangements with a crew of builders to construct a building to Ton's specifications. In the meantime, Wu had expressed a desire to start a dressmaking business. Hue then concluded that one building could be designed and constructed to accommodate both businesses: the tailor shop and the dressmaking shop. Excellent combination, Hue decided.

The ambitious plan took time. An architect had to come from San Francisco. Building materials had to come from a California lumber company. Wu had to seek advice from Emily on what fashions were preferred in the small community. She asked Emily through Bahn–for the English language. And Emily sought further advice from the ladies of Stoney Ridge who had lately emigrated from Philadelphia, Chicago, and Kansas City. Ladies' fashions catalogs were ordered from New York City.

Wu could look at a picture of a dress, make a pattern, and put together a decent costume.

While all that was being arranged, Hue looked to his own housing situation. It would not do. The added members of the family was getting out of hand. It was time to build more houses–separate houses for the two separate newlyweds. He had a pang of guilt, realizing that he and Emily already had their house, fully furnished. The least he could do was to build and furnish similar houses for

Ton and Ah Ming and for Tao and Wu.

Hue had a conference with the architect and the crew chief of the builders. Two homes were designed and materials were ordered. The building crew could move from the double store structure, upon its completion, straight to the two homes on the Lee ranch.

As if there were not enough activity with all the building going on, Hue had reason to pause and rejoice–at the news. Emily presented him one day with the information that she was with child. Hue did an extraordinary thing: he picked up little Brad, swinging him through the air and down again, saying, "Brad! Brad! You are going to be a big brother!" Then Hue hugged the little boy as if he were his own child.

Emily was so pleased to see her husband take her son into his heart so readily. She tried very hard not to let her bad feelings for little Brad's father come through to the boy–her boy. It looked as though little Brad were now *their* boy. Again, she offered up a silent prayer for Hue's compassion and seemingly total acceptance of their boy.

* * *

Ho, meanwhile, was acting strangely, beginning with the end of the double-wedding reception, so it seemed to Hue. He thought he would question Ho about his change in behavior–more rash, somehow, and more charming, as well, treating his sisters and new in-laws with great respect. Ho began day-dreaming literally in the middle of an otherwise busy day.

First, Hue discussed the matter with Emily.

"You didn't notice, did you?"

"Notice what?" said Hue.

"That Ho had a fair conversation with the Burt daughter, Coralee. It was at the wedding reception."

"Coralee Burt? What nonsense!"

"No, for sure, my dear.

"What could they possibly have in common, my sweet?"

"Well," she said, "perhaps it could be the same thing *we* have in common: a genuine high regard for each other . . . that blossoms into a romance."

"Ho? Impossible!"

"No, darling, I think not."

Hue looked at her carefully, trying to read her mind. "I am going to have to consider this further."

She said, "You do that!"

The next thing Hue noticed about Ho is that Ho, one Thursday evening, asked Hue if he could make the laundry deliveries and pickups the next day.

Hue almost came out with an automatic "no," but caught himself before saying it. "I see no reason why you can't. You've done the route for me before, whenever I was gone to San Francisco."

"Yes, big brother. I have done so. And I remember the route well. So?"

"So, do it! I can use the time at the big house to work on the books."

"Thank you, oldest brother."

"And I thank you, younger brother."

The next day, Friday, Ho set out to make the laundry deliveries and pickups. He had carefully mapped out the route. The Burt residence would be toward the end. He would have liked to make it at the beginning because he was vastly interested in seeing Coralee again. But he took great pleasure in looking forward to such a meeting.

What if, Ho thought, Mrs. Burt comes to the door? I must think of something clever but not too forward . . . to see Coralee.

There were three houses left to make the dropoffs and pickups. Somewhat nervously, Ho rapped on the Burt household front door. What seemed to him to be an eternity, the door finally opened.

"Ah, good day, Mrs. Burt. Here is your fresh laundry, and may I be permitted to enter your home to pick up the clothing and linens to be laundered?"

Mrs. Burt was not about to allow this Chinaman come inside her house! "Just a minute. It's not quite ready. Coralee!" she shouted. "Come down here and bring your dirty clothes with you. The laundryman is here to pick up!"

Coralee's voice could be heard, faintly, from upstairs. "Not now, Ma. I'm still stripping my bed!"

"Well," shouted Mrs. Burt back to her, "hurry it up. It ain't Mr. Lee that's here. One of his brothers has come today."

Suddenly Coralee came rushing down the steps and to the front door. She saw Ho immediately. "But Ma, this is Ho Lee. He is a Mr. Lee, like his brother. Oh, hello, Ho. So nice to see you. Come on in, and I'll finish putting my things in the laundry bag."

Her mother almost had apoplexy! But she stood aside to let her daughter lead the way for the Chinaman. Merciful heavens, she thought. What will the neighbors think? We let a Chinaman in our house! What must that girl be having on her mind? Shocking, whatever it is!

But Coralee chatted on with Ho, as if she had known him all her life.

Ho tried not to watch her as she opened the laundry bag and stuffed her personal clothing and linens into it. What did it matter? He asked himself. I may see it as it tumbles onto the floor to be sorted and into the tubs in our laundry house. Sometimes, he assisted his sisters in those chores. What makes her smell so sweet? I wish I could be by her all day! Just to smell her sweetness . . .

Suddenly, Ho realized she was addressing him with a question.

"Would you like to go on a picnic next Sunday, after church, on the church grounds?"

Ho was at a complete loss. That word 'picnic' had not yet entered his already well-expanded English vocabulary. He faked understanding the word and had a moment of indecision, but only for a moment. He replied, "Yes, indeed, Miss Coralee. I believe I would like that very much."

Mrs. Burt glared at her daughter, disapproving of her asking the Chinese man to come to the church picnic. Imagine!

* * *

Soon afterwards, Ho's route was finished, and he was on his way home. He found his older brother in his house, doing exactly what he said he'd be doing—working on the books.

"Honorable brother," Ho said, "what is a 'picnic'?"

Hue pushed aside the accounting books, leaned back in his desk chair and said, "Wherever did you hear that?"

Blushing slightly, Ho said, "Miss Coralee asked me to go on a picnic after church on the church grounds. I have no idea what a picnic is. And I can only guess what 'church grounds' are!"

Hue was startled to hear the explanation from Ho. Coralee Burt? Asked him to a picnic? But, of course, it would be with all the church members in attendance. Not a private picnic. Aloud, he said to Ho, "Well, now that would be a spread of a feast upon the ground, perhaps on quilts or sheets."

"On quilts or sheets? A feast? How curious!"

Hue then said, with a twinkle in his eye, "Of course, a picnic can be for just two people at other times."

"Two people?" Ho asked. "Just two people?" He could not fathom such an arrangement, but it sounded intriguing to him. He asked himself if Coralee would ever invite him to a private picnic. Better yet, could he ask her to go on a picnic for just two people?

"Yes," Hue answered, "just two people." As an afterthought, Hue added, "It would be very gracious of you to take a dish of food as a personal contribution to the picnic on Sunday."

"What in the world would I take?"

"Ah Ming can make a fine chicken and rice and vegetables dish. It should be received very well, I think."

"Thank you, oh honorable brother, for such a fine suggestion. I will go to Ah Ming this very moment and make the request."

Hue smiled inwardly as well as outwardly, to show his brother Ho how pleased he was to know that Ho is showing an interest in a white girl. Hue could never, never show displeasure at such a turn of events. He himself, after all, has married a white woman!

* * *

The picnic was a success for all who attended. Ah Ming's rice dish was a huge hit. Ho's standing in the community had risen markedly.

While Ho and Coralee sat at one corner of her mother's "old" quilt, which was used only for these occasions, they chatted quietly. Ho said, "Miss Coralee, may I be so bold as to ask you if you and I could have a picnic, just the two of us?"

"Ho, that would be real nice."

"Any day but Friday, our laundry delivery day. I could call for you in our one-seater carriage. And I know just the place for us, on my brother's spread."

"'Way out there?" She seemed apprehensive, but only a bit."

"Not so far, Miss Coralee. We would be on private property, my brother's. All very safe."

She wanted so very much to agree to it, but there were reservations, in spite of her otherwise forward ways. Suddenly she became coy. "Well, Ho, I just don't know about that."

"What's to be shy about? I like you very much; I sense that you like me, at little, at least."

"Oh, I do like you, Ho. A lot!"

"Well, then? A picnic it is. You choose the day, other than a Friday."

* * *

The spot was made for lovers: a babbling brook, cottonwood trees growing at the edges, blooming mustard plants and dandelions, tall green grass for spreading the quilt that was borrowed from Mrs. Burt.

Ah Ming had prepared a tasty sauce into which they dipped chicken strips. They nibbled on diced fresh vegetables. A small loaf of bread was also provided by Ah Ming. And Mrs. Burt had baked a small cake for two. They drank warm tea that had been made in the sun all morning. To top off the outdoor meal, they ate pears and peaches, contributed by Hue.

Coralee, being the high-spirited young woman that she was, kept the conversation going steadily. She told stories on the ladies of Stoney Ridge and their daughters and what they did and what they said. Ho had never heard such stories before in his life. He was interested in the stories. He was enchanted by her cheeriness.

She was shorter than Ho, with blonde hair that had a reddish tint, especially in bright sunlight. Her green eyes complemented her hair. Sitting next to Ho, who had a darkened complexion, her white skin appeared to be very pale. Her mouth was small and a lively pink. She looked so demure and shy. But shy she was not!

Ho was quite taken with her presence. Almost in awe that she showed him so much attention in public and in this private place. "Coralee," he said, taking her hand. He said no more but leaned in toward her and gave her a warm kiss. She withdrew her hand and put her arms around his neck, bringing him closer to her. She kissed him with real passion, leaning back against the quilt on the grass, taking him with her. He thought his head would explode, he was so worked up about what she had done.

He rolled off to her side, and onto the quilt. His pulse was racing, out of control, it seemed to him. What should he do now? He asked himself.

"Aw, Ho, Honey, you gonna dump me now?"

"Dump you? I don't understand, exactly. You are already on your back on the quilt."

"No, Honey, I mean you gonna stop seeing me?"

"Again, I don't understand exactly. Of course I am seeing you. You are, after all, lying here on the quilt beside me. Yes, Coralee, I can see you." It struck him boldly: he had omitted the 'Miss' as in 'Miss Coralee.' She said nothing but smiled to herself. Still, she had doubts.

Frustrated, she sat up and looked back at him. "Ho. What I mean is, are you going to stop calling on me? Same as seeing me. Are you going to let me go for some other girl? That means dump me."

"Ah," he breathed. "Now I understand 'dump' and 'seeing'. Many thank yous for the explanations. No, my dear, I am not going to dump you. And yes, my dear, I am going to continue seeing you."

"That's a relief!" she breathed.

She was so appealing! Ho's head was swimming with visions of what he dared not think about. A wild dialog took place in his head: Stoney Ridge, small community; Chinese man rapes a helpless girl; "Tar and feather him!" Raging inside, he put his arms around her, while she was seated next to him. Again, she lay back down onto the quilt, taking him with her. They kissed passionately. There was no ending it. Once more the imagined dialogue entered his head. And again, he brought himself up shortly, sitting up this time, beside her, who was still lying down.

"Honey," she pleaded. "Please."

"No, Coralee, I cannot do this. I am sorry I let my feelings be shown so vulgarly."

"But darling," she begged, "you were not vulgar. You were wonderful. I could be wonderful for you."

"You are wonderful, dear Coralee." He stood up and reached for her hand to help her up, too. "I shall never forget this afternoon picnic."

"Oh, sweetheart, I'll never forget it, either."

Ho said, "I should take you home, I think."

"Oh, no. Do you have to? I could stay here like this with you forever!"

"I know."

"Do I have to drag it out of you, Ho?"

"Drag out what ?"

"Don't you want to marry me?"

"You are impetuous!"

"Now I gotta ask you what's impet-chew-us?"

He began gathering up the picnic leavings. She helped him. She was getting impatient about his not answering her right away. Why is he stalling? she asked herself.

Finally, Ho said to her, "Coralee, you are my heart's greatest desire. And you have to realize that I must confer with my brother Hue, who is the patriarch of our branch of the American-based family. All matters, both personal and public, must be brought to the head of the household and discussed at length ,and a decision to be arrived at between the head of the family and the lesser member of the family."

"You gotta ask your brother if you can get married?"

"Of course!"

"Well, I never!"

After Ho dropped her off at her house, Coralee ran upstairs to her room and threw herself onto her bed and began to sob softly.

Mrs. Burt opened the door quietly and saw that her only daughter was distressed. "What's the matter, Honey?"

"Oh, Mama, I love him so much it hurts!"

Her mother stiffened. "You mean the Chinee man, don't you?"

"Oh, yes, Mama. It's Ho I'm so crazy about. The other boys in town can go fly a kite, as far as I'm concerned!"

"You know," her mother said, "that you can have any young man in town, just by giving him a sign."

"Yes, I know, Mama. But Ho is the only one I want. He has to talk it over with his brother, for heaven's sake!"

"And you know, your Pa and I both have a say-so in this craziness you're going through. We say you have to forget the Chinaman. He's no good for you!"

"Oh, you and Pa have it all wrong, Mama. He's so right for me! I love him!"

"Pshaw! What does a snip of a girl like you know about love?"

"You wouldn't know love if it came up and bit you on the nose," Coralee retorted.

Mrs. Burt could only stare at Coralee with her mouth agape.

Coralee continued. "I know what I'm talkin' about, Mama. I seen you and Pa snarl at each other and heard you growl at each other all my life. Ain't no love in all that snarlin' and growlin'!"

Mrs. Burt threw her hands into the air and said, "I don't care what you think. You and that slant-eye ain't gettin' married! And that's the end of it!"

When Ho presented his case in the matter of Coralee to Hue, the head of their household, Hue was thoughtful. He said, "What do we know about this Coralee Burt, daughter of a blacksmith?"

Ho replied, "Well, venerable brother, she is a 'diamond in the rough,' as I read somewhere recently."

"Meaning?"

"Meaning that she does not speak her own language well. A bit of tutoring here and there, and she could be polished at English."

"And who would do the tutoring, next brother Ho?"

"Why, you would, of course! Just as you taught all of us in the branch of our American family to do. You are, after all, the best English speaker of us all!" Ho was trying to be emphatic as well as persuasive. He would do anything and say anything to pave the road to eternal unity with Coralee Burt.

Hue, still thoughtful on the subject, was beginning to warm to the whole idea. I, a yellow-skin, teach a white-skin how to speak correct English? It was almost laughable! But he did not wish to injure the dignity of his own brother. Hue said, "My good next brother, I shall take your request into consideration. I must think on these matters some more. And, by the way, what about the expected resistance from Mr. and Mrs. Burt themselves?"

"Honorable brother. I have given that problem some thought, as well. I will approach them personally (after the tutoring is completed) and petition them to allow their daughter to marry me. I will appear in the most acceptable clothing; speak in the most respectable manner possible; leave nothing to chance!"

"Another thought comes to mind, Ho. *Where* will the tutoring take place? Certainly not here, and most certainly not in her own home, with a dissenting mother breathing down our heads!"

Ho was inspired. He said, "What about the pastor's church building? It has a classroom, I noticed."

"Capital! Let's do it!"

* * *

The pastor was most helpful with the arrangements. Hue and Coralee could conduct their business in the classroom, leaving the door open, while the pastor practiced his sermon, and his wife would be in attendance, directing and helping the good ladies of the congregation clean the building and the pews at all times during the tutoring.

The tutoring took place once a week. After the first two or three tutoring sessions, Ho asked his brother, ever so politely, how Coralee was doing. Hue reported that it was a shaky beginning, but he thought he saw some improvement. He saw that Coralee had promise. Whenever Ho and Coralee met on laundry days, or at church (for Ho began attending the Sunday services), he looked for her eagerly so that they could talk. He noticed, gradually, a change in her diction, as well as her vocabulary. Very good progress, he thought.

A few weeks later, Ho asked Hue, "Most venerable brother, I wonder if you might introduce another book to Coralee."

"What kind of book, next brother?"

"A book I have seen on your office shelves."

"Which one?"

"I am not sure how to pronounce it–even after looking it up in the dictionary: E-tee-ket?"

"Ah, yes, the book on etiquette. And, while you looked up the pronunciation, did you look up its meaning?"

"Yes, indeed, oldest brother. It means the manners and mores of a polite society. However, I saw pictures that puzzled me."

"Yes, the pictures. They are diagrams, so to speak, of how to set a table."

"Set a table? What is 'set a table'?"

"It means setting up a table for eating a meal. Sooner or later, as this humble family becomes accepted by the families of Stoney Ridge, and we, the Lee family, can exchange dinner appointments with each other, all of us, with the exception of Emily, will need to know how to set a table–to accommodate Western manners." Hue had an afterthought. "Do you perceive that Coralee does not know how to set a table?"

"I'm not sure, brother Hue. Not a 'perfect' table, anyway."

"Excellent idea, brother Ho! Therefore, since you will need to be knowing the ways of the Western culture, as well, you will be the first in our family to read the book on etiquette . . . with Coralee!"

* * *

And so the months went by with Hue's teaching the finer points of English and with Ho's learning proper etiquette in America, along with Coralee.

The months went by so quickly for Hue. His overseeing the orchards, the laundry business, and the accounts, and teaching English to Coralee, suddenly paled. His daughter was born!

When Emily had rested from childbirth, Hue came to her to see if she were still sleeping. She was awake. "Darling!" he said, "are you all right? Has the terrible pain you went through abated? I could hear your pathetic moans and straining in the next room, while Wu and Ah Ming assisted you. Are you all right, Darling?"

"Oh, yes, Hue, I'm fine. There's no more pain. It's all gone. I want to get up!"

"Should you, Sweetheart?"

"Of course! Child-bearing women in Stoney Ridge stay in bed for two weeks after the birth and do nothing but eat and nurse the baby."

"So, should you be getting up so soon?"

"That's for white women. Wu assures me, through Ah Ming, that Chinese women go back to their usual work right the same day the baby comes. I fail to see why I should not do the same!"

"You are an amazing woman, Mrs. Lee!"

She beamed at him her best and winning smile. She got up and picked up the newborn infant. "I hope you don't mind, dear, the baby's name should be my mother's, Della. And her middle name should be your mother's name: Lu."

"Della Lu," Hue said reverently. "Darling, it's a beautiful name!"

* * *

Rupert came to the big house as soon as Tao came to his door to inform him that Emily had given birth to a baby girl.

Entering Emily's room quietly, even reverently, he asked her, "Did you send for the midwives in town to help you birth the baby?"

"Of course, not, Daddy. I had Ah-Ming and Wu to do that."

"What? The Chinese women?"

"Of course, Daddy. They know all about birthing, even though they have no children themselves, yet."

"Are you sure you're all right, daughter?"

"Of course, Daddy! Settle down. And come introduce yourself to your little granddaughter!"

After Rupert's formal self-introduction to little Della Lu, Emily asked him to stay for dinner, to stay for the night, and wait until after breakfast to return to Stoney Ridge.

"Well, I don't see why I can't do that. Thank you, Emily." As soon as he offered the appreciation for her invitation, he excused himself with, "I'm going to look for little Brad. He hasn't seen his grandpa for awhile." And, Rupert said to himself, I haven't seen Lizzy for just as long! Where could that young woman be?

With Brad, of course! Look for Brad and find Lizzy.

Rupert Johnson, graying to white, found the two of them in Emily's backyard flower garden. He approached, and when little Brad saw him, he ran from Lizzy and straight into his grandpa's outstretched arms. Lizzy came running after him until she spotted Mr. Johnson.

She stopped in her tracks. She asked herself, should I disappear while the grandpa and grandson enjoy each other? She turned to take another path from the flower garden to the back porch.

"Miss Lizzy! Where you going in such a hurry?" Rupert called to her.

"Just to the back porch, Mr. Johnson, while you enjoy the company of your grandson."

"But I also came to see you, girl. Didn't you realize that?"

"No, sir. Of course not." She felt flustered and hoped her face didn't show it.

He saw her discomfort and said, "Yes, dear Miss Lizzy. I came to see little Brad, his new little sister Della Lu, and . . . . you."

"Really, Mr. Johnson?"

"I do wish you'd call me Rupert, dear Lizzy."

"I'm not sure I should do that, Mr. Johnson."

"You can because I wish you to do so. I could demand you to do so, as a friend, of course."

"You would demand me to call you . . . . Rupert?" It felt strange on her tongue. "And why would you demand me to do that, Mister Johnson?" She drew out the "mister."

"Because, my dear Lizzy, forget what I said about 'as a friend.' I would like very much to court you, privately and publicly."

"Rupert . . . . . ."

Chapter Eight

At last Hue was able to pronounce Coralee to be well versed in the English language. He had taught her everything she needed to know, and she seemed to have retained it well. Hue was pleased. He was delighted. Ho and Coralee had meanwhile finished the etiquette book. They had learned it together.

Coralee had even shared the strange book with her mother who pooh-poohed the whole idea. Until she heard her daughter reading aloud a phrase that caught her fancy. Mrs. Burt decided on the spot that she herself needed schooling in the art of entertaining. It sounded real nice, putting the bread-and-butter dish in a place of its own. "Pshaw!" Mrs. Burt said aloud. "What's a bread-and-butter dish?"

And so began the daughter's tutoring her mother in the manners and etiquette of a society largely unknown to them, except to hear others talk about it. Society? "Pshaw!" said Mrs. Burt, partly disgusted, partly intrigued.

Coralee had a new life, it seemed to her. She felt a confidence that the old flirtatious, brash, and forward girl had turned over a new leaf. She viewed life with more certainty than she had ever known. Nowadays, Ho spoke frequently and eloquently about marriage–their marriage. She was excited, waiting impatiently, to be in a hitherto unknown heaven with her beloved Ho.

Coralee had to return the etiquette book to Ho for him to give back to his family, one at a time, to read and learn. Ah Ming would read it first, then Bahn, then Ton, then Tao. That way, Wu could have time to learn more English before she undertook the etiquette book. Both Ton and Wu needed to learn the Western ways since they would be interfacing with the population of Stoney Ridge in their new businesses. Members of the Lee family, other than Hue, taught English, day-by-day, to the newer members of the Lee spread.

* * *

When Emily and Hue showed up at church the next Sunday, with little Brad, Lizzy and the new baby, the ladies of Stoney Ridge went crazy over the new member of the Lee family. They thought Della Lu was the sweetest infant they had ever seen. Of course, they said that about all the newborns. It was a given.

The time came for Emily to reciprocate for the wedding reception the community had given her and Hue and the other two newlyweds, almost a year before. With help from Ah Ming and Bahn and Wu, she planned and prepared a high tea for the visiting community families. Those families had never set foot inside the Lee house. Most of the ladies were too scared, not knowing what it would be like to hob-nob with the heathens. Of course, Emily and Hue were not heathens, but what about all those others? And what, pray tell, they asked each other, is a high tea?

For the most part, the ladies had to get unfrightened and had to swallow their pride. Their curiosity overshadowed the fright and the pride. They came to the Lee house in droves, sipping tea, nibbling little cakes and cookies and delicate sandwiches. Emily herself had learned only recently about the sandwiches because Ah Ming had come across a recipe in the etiquette book.

The women of Lee's family, Emily included, dressed in Oriental clothing. The men of Lee's family opted to wear western clothing, to make the men feel more comfortable. As it turned out, the townsmen were all thumbs when it came to handling the teacups and saucers and white linen napkins and the delicacies. But the truth was: they, too, like the women, were curious about the Lee family and its ability to entertain white folks.

The tea was a success. With Hue and Emily's permission, Ho and Coralee used the event to announce their engagement. The members of the community were not surprised. The women knew (and therefore their husbands also knew) that Hue and Coralee were busy every church-cleaning day with English lessons. Not that Coralee didn't know English! For some reason, she was being groomed to be a "lady." They also were aware that Ho and Coralee had been studying another book, each week after the English lesson. The ladies had no idea what the book was about. Much later, they would learn about that mystery.

* * *

It was baffling that Ho had become a Christian early in his courtship of Coralee because she was only a sometime Christian, as others viewed her. Oh, she came to church with her Mama and Pa every Sunday, but she never took part in the "good works" of the church ladies, preferring to spend time with the Ho "boy," learning better English and keeping her nose in another book all the time. What they didn't know was that Coralee was a changed person. The fieriness was subdued . . . a lot. If it were going to surface, Ho had better watch out!

Well, Ho had his ways and means of calming the formerly quick-tempered Coralee. One adoring look from him, and she would melt. She was out-of-her-mind crazy about him. He was entirely devoted to her and her well being. Ho looked forward to the day he could carry Coralee over the threshold of their new house, the one Hue had built just for them. How did he know about carrying the bride over the threshold? He had read it in a book. What else?

After a decent period of engagement for the times, almost a year, Ho and Coralee were wed. Everyone in town turned out for the wedding of Ho and Coralee, wishing them happiness, but wondering how this Chinese "boy" would handle the fiery Coralee. The pastor performed their Christian wedding ceremony.

The townspeople teased Coralee mercilessly! "Coralee Lee? Ha-ha-ha-ha-ha-ha!" Coralee took it in stride, for she was extremely proud to be a member of the successful and now-popular Lee family. She laughed with the tears streaming down from her eyes, heartily, thereby deflating the sting of the teasing.

The fact was, Coralee Lee thought the name had a nice ring to it. She went on to enjoy the reception to the fullest.

Ho carried her over the threshold, as was his dream, and as was his next dream, spent a night in complete wedded bliss. Coralee, at last, had reached the heaven she knew was there, waiting for her. Ho unleashed his built-up passion, at last. He was exhausted. She exhausted him. Far into the night, she still wanted him over and over and over.

* * *

Bahn felt like a complete outsider. Both her other brothers were married and beginning their lives with their new mates. Ah Ming was married, as well she should, before the younger sister married. Bahn also felt betrayed. Wasn't her brother Hue supposed to be looking for a mate for her? Hadn't he promised such a quest? Well, Bahn fumed to herself–and sometimes to Ah Ming, when they labored together in the laundry house--Hue had better get busy! Or, she remembered, she would look for a white-eye and marry him and show her big brother a thing or two!

She fumed on. It did no good. Hue was so busy getting buildings and houses constructed, helping Ton and Wu start their businesses, keeping the books for all of it together.

It occurred to Hue, one day, that he needed professional help with the bookkeeping. The paperwork was mountainous! It would take years, literally, to have Tao or Ho trained to do that. And besides, Hue needed both of them to run the orchards and gardens.

Over the years, those orchards and gardens grew so much that Hue had to bring in outsiders–Chinese men who were former laborers on the railroad, as he had been. He found them living and scratching for work in San Francisco. He brought them to his spread, built a bunkhouse for them, hired their own cook, and built a mess hall, adding to his ever-growing "empire."

Dressing up like a western businessman should dress, in his opinion, he took a carriage to town to make inquiries. First, he visited his father-in-law Rupert Johnson.

"Good morning, Hue!" Rupert greeted him. "How are you? And how is my Emily and my little granddaughter and grandson?"

"Good morning, honorable father-in-law! They are all very fine today and always."

And little Brad? Is he as active as ever?"

"Indeed he is."

Rupert wanted in the worst way to ask about Lizzy. Should he or should he not? In the next moment, he threw all caution to the wind and said, "And Miss Lizzy? Is she well?"

"Miss Lizzy, sir?"

"Well, yes. I ask only because she seems to be a part of the family. Don't you think?"

Hue mentally squinted his eyes and replied, "Well, yes, sir, If you say so, sir. And, I suppose she is also well, along with everyone else!"

A mischievous idea occurred to him, as he addressed Rupert with, "Honorable father-in-law, should I convey your inquiry to the comely Miss Lizzy?"

Rupert was taken by surprise by the impudence shown by Hue. But he answered, "By gum! Of course, my good Hue. Of course!"

Having recovered from his astonishment, he asked Hue further, "And what brings you into town? We don't see you very much since your brother Ho has taken over the laundry pickups and deliveries."

"I do hope my next younger brother does a good job for you and the other citizens of Stoney Ridge."

"Indeed he does. As good as you always did."

"A thousand thankyous, oh honorable father-in-law. And to answer your question, I am in town today to find out if there is a person among the citizens here who could do bookkeeping work for me."

"Well, I do my own. Isn't much. But why don't you ask Mr. Hudson, the general store owner?"

"Very good! I will start there. Goodbye, honorable father-in-law.

And thank you."

"Goodbye Hue. And when are you going to start calling me Rupert?"

Smiling, Hue said, "In good time, Mr. Johnson. In good time."

Hue then departed the newspaper office and walked across the street to the general store.

"Ah, good morning, Mr. Hudson."

After their friendly greeting, Hue presented his need to Mr. Hudson.

"Well, Hue. So far, I do my own books. It's only a small store. Expect some Easterner to come to town any day now and set up real competition. Then I might have to make some changes. Big changes!"

"In the meantime, "said Hue, "I have a need for a bookkeeper. Do you know of anyone here in town, or in these parts who could do that job? The pay would be more than adequate."

"In the next town, Cork, 'bout five miles east, is a boy who went away to college in Chicago for a couple of years. You might ask him if he can do that kind of work. Name's O'Donnell. Richard, I think."

"A thousand thankyous, Mr. Hudson. I will call on him this very morning. Good day, Mr. Hudson."

* * *

Hue had no trouble finding the O'Donnell boy. The town of Cork was much smaller than what Stoney Ridge had grown to be. One inquiry, and Hue was directed to the O'Donnell home just two farm houses away.

Richard O'Donnell was working in the fields with his father. Other boys and one girl were in school. Mrs. O'Donnell, however, invited Hue into her kitchen and made a cup of tea for him.

"Tea?" asked Hue, amazed.

"Yes. Tea. She said. We always drank it in Ireland and continue to do so here in America. Sweet roll, Mr. Lee?"

They chatted in a friendly way. News of the Lee family and their ranch and Hue's wealth spread to all the surrounding communities. Daisy O'Donnell instinctively knew it was Hue Lee at her door when she had answered his knock. She was impressed. He looked so nice in such fine clothing, and driving a handsome one-seater carriage. Eventually, she learned why he had come to her house.

"Stay for dinner with us, Mr. Lee. My husband and son are due to come back to the house any minute now. It's about noon, isn't it? Dinner's already prepared. I just have to put it on the table."

"So very kind of you, Mrs. O'Donnell. But I do not wish to impose upon your generous hospitality."

"Tut! No imposition a-tall!"

The men came into the kitchen shortly afterwards. Hue noticed the very tall Mr. Michael O'Donnell and the even taller Richard. A fine looking young man. Who was calling him a boy, anyway, he wondered. Red hair? What a curiosity! thought Hue. Coralee's hair is not *that* red!

During dinner, Hue presented Richard the idea of his need for a bookkeeper. Did the young O'Donnell have any experience in ciphers?

"Oh, yes, sir," replied Richard. "Mathematics was my main subject when I was in Chicago. A little science, too. But mostly mathematics."

"Well, then," said Hue, "if I show you how to maintain the books for my extensive enterprises, I would be pleased to hire you and train you. Would you be interested in such a job?"

"Well, sir, I must discuss this with my father. I feel as though I owe him an obligation, here on the farm."

"Of course, Mr. O'Donnell," Hue said to Richard. "If your obligation to your father entails money, I can advance whatever you need to satisfy the obligation."

"Take it, boy!" exclaimed the father, Michael.

"You mean it, Pa?"

"Of course I do!"

Addressing his mother, Richard asked, "And you, Ma? What do you think about all this?"

"Dickie, m'boy, I'll miss you somethin' awful, but ye are a man now. Ye got to find yer own way in the wor-r-rld. Sounds like a real good opportunity to me!"

Richard turned to Hue and said, "When do I start, Mr. Lee?"

* * *

Hue stayed until the meal was finished and until Richard could wash up and change clothes and pack a bag. Richard accompanied Hue to his new job, and his new home.

On the long carriage drive back to Hue's property, he and the man Richard, no longer a boy, discussed where he would stay. Bahn was now living in the original log house, alone. It would be the most feasible place for him to stay. Hue certainly did not want to throw him into the bunkhouse with the Chinese men, eating the strange Chinese food, listening to the strange language. But Bahn and Richard in the same house, alone? Unthinkable!

By the time they reached Hue's ranch, he had decided what to do for Richard's housing. Bahn would move into the big house with Hue and Emily and Brad and Della Lu. Plenty of room. They expected to have more children in the near future. Hue would move his office from his house to the original log house, and Richard would stay there, for working and for sleeping. He could take his meals at Hue's house with that family. Satisfied with his plan, Hue thought it to be a very good arrangement.

Upon entering the log house, Bahn was absent—working in the laundry house. Hue had Richard bring in his bag, took him to the second bedroom and left him to get settled. Hue returned to the big house. Then Bahn showed up in the log house to make her supper. Heretofore, Emily had stopped inviting Bahn to take her meals with Hue and Emily. Bahn would have no part of it! She preferred to stew in her own juice, being left as the unmarried sister, but not enjoying her status at all, at the outset. Privately, she admitted to herself that she did not want to intrude upon her big brother's happy state with Emily and the baby and Brad.

Suddenly her thoughts were interrupted with the arrival of a very tall young white-eye walking into the kitchen where she was preparing her supper. She screamed and ran from the log house, making a bee line for Hue's big house.

"Brother! Brother! " she screeched at the top of her lungs. "Hue! Come quick!" forgetting to say quickly instead of quick. "There's a strange man in the house!" She took a breath. "Hue? Hue!!!"

Instantly, Hue ran to her to calm her. He realized, too late, he reflected, that he had left the O'Donnell young man getting settled in the second bedroom. Of course, he would walk into other parts of the house, possibly looking for me. How stupid of me! he thought.

"Calm yourself, Bahn. It is all right."

"It is *not* all right, big brother!"

He sighed heavily. "I owe you an apology, little Bahn." That was his endearment for her from time to time. He hoped it would help settle her back to normal. It worked, partially.

"Don't call me 'little Bahn.' What exactly is the explanation? And I hope you do have an explanation!"

"Of course. The young man is our new employee. He is going to be our bookkeeper."

Although Hue's enterprises were all his, he frequently referred to them as "our" or "ours."

"Come," he said. "It's time for proper introductions."

They rushed back to the log house. Hue purposefully; Bahn reluctantly, except for one thing: she did have enough time to notice that not only was the new bookkeeper exceptionally tall, he was quite nice looking. Red hair! The closest red hair she had ever seen was her new sister-in-law's, Coralee. Bahn settled down instantly, when she thought about the nice young man. She guessed he would be nice because he was so nice looking!

Upon entering the log house, they found Richard looking at them through the kitchen window. Hue immediately apologized for his lapse of manners, not being here to make proper introductions when Bahn saw the stranger in her house.

Bahn and Richard looked at each other as if they had known each other for a lifetime. Suddenly, the sassiness of Bahn turned into mellowness. Hue was amazed. He had never seen this younger sister behave so ladylike!

"How do you do, Mr. O'Donnell?" Bahn said with a little curtsey!

"I do very well, thank you, Miss Lee. And how do you do?" He bowed to her slightly.

Bahn was almost tongue-tied. He was so beautiful, his voice was so beautiful, his manner was so beautiful. She thought she'd died and gone to heaven.

Hue breathed a silent sigh of relief. This was going to turn out much, much better than he could imagine! He decided that his long carriage ride to the O'Donnells was very fortuitous, indeed. And certainly worth the effort!

* * *

With Richard's help, Hue moved the office from the big house to the log house. Bahn, who was disappointed but relieved, moved into Hue and Emily's house. She did so meekly, much to the now amazed Hue. Never before had Hue seen such a pliable and humble Bahn. It was not unlike a small miracle. Thank heaven for small miracles, thought Hue. Could the arrival of the O'Donnell young man have *anything* to do with it? Perhaps, mused Hue again and again.

Bahn was obliged to return to the log house on a regular basis, to do housework, except on Saturdays when she labored with Ah-Ming in the laundry house. The young Adonis now residing in the log house, could not be expected to do his own household chores. Could he? Bahn reasoned.

Shyly (another trait never before noticed by Hue), she approached her big brother on that subject. Should she continue running the household in the log house? With the Richard person installed in a bedroom and in the office, taking all his meals in Hue's house?

"Of course, youngest sister! The O'Donnell young man will be so engrossed with his ciphers, I doubt he will even notice your puttering around the house, keeping it in order."

That comment gave her pause to think: The Richard person will not even notice me? She said, aloud, "Well, then, I guess it would be all right, if he's not going to notice me!"

"And," said Hue, "is that going to trouble you? His not noticing you?"

She drew herself up sharply. Her old self came back into play. "Of course not!"

"Then, all is settled. You may return to the log house each day, make his bed, pick up his laundry, clean his room, clean the whole house!"

Suddenly shy again, while she thought about doing such personal chores for the new bookkeeper, she said, simply, "Yes, honorable brother. I shall do all that . . . for you, of course."

"Of course!" he said, smiling to himself.

Chapter Nine

In the next moment, Hue reflected on another subject that had recently occurred to him. With the changes in households' happening seemingly too fast, he realized that the women in the complex will be needing, if not already needing, outsiders to come into their homes and help the women with the child-rearing, housekeeping, cooking, and whatever else needs to be done. Laundry chores, of course, did not present a problem in each household. The Lee spread owned and operated its own laundry facility. A need for extra help also existed in the laundry.

Tao and Wu were hoping that Wu was not too old to reproduce. They were trying. On their wedding night, Wu gently led the innocent Tao into a realm where he had never been before. Afterwards, as they lay in their bed, Wu told Tao that when she was younger, she was married to a man in China, and she became a widow in six months. Her new husband was a victim of a local cholera epidemic.

She could not tell Tao, before their wedding night, that she was experienced in matters of the bed. She suspected that he knew not precisely what to do, on their wedding night. With great care, she indicated to Tao what is to be first, what is to be next, and on to the magnificent conclusion.

It was the first time in Tao's young life that he felt he was a man. He loved Wu more than he ever could have imagined possible. He was transformed on that night.

Ton and Ah Ming had the same hope for a child, the same attempts.

Time would tell if either couple were successful.

* * *

Hue went to the Chinese laborers' bunkhouse one evening after their supper was completed. In Chinese, he explained what he was looking for and asked them for suggestions. One laborer said he had a female cousin in San Francisco; another said he had two sisters in China; still another had an aunt, same age as he, in Seattle. And on and on until Hue had enough names and addresses to begin writing persuasive letters.

Hue decided that even if all of them mailed him positive answers, he would send for all of them, finding work for everyone here on his ranch. He could breathe more easily, while he waited for responses. He told Emily of the plan, already implemented. She was pleased until she realized they would all be Chinese-speaking, lucky if some of them could speak pidgin English.

"Not to worry, Emily," said Hue "We will simply school all of them in their new language."

Then Hue turned his attention to the construction of a dormitory for the women, including messing facilities.

* * *

Hue made another decision: As soon as the laborers' relatives and friends arrived at the Lees' complex, Hue allowed Ho to spend whatever part of the next two years he wished to spend at the gold mining site. And Tao would take over the full management of both the orchards and vegetable gardens, plus the Friday deliveries and pickups. After those two years, Hue would allow Tao to do the same, with Ho's taking over what Tao had been doing for him. Whatever amount of ore each of them could pull from the mountainside in a two-year span would belong to each one.

That would take care of his own brothers. What he could or would do for his two sisters' fortunes was yet to be determined. In Hue's opinion, the women in his Chinese/American family were entitled to the same rewards. The sisters have labored just as hard as the brothers. He said to himself, I must think further on this matter.

In another month, Hue had come to a conclusion about furnishing his two sisters their share of the gold fortunes still available on their property, in the mountainside. While he himself was still hale and hearty, his two younger brothers were far more able to work the goldmine, each one for another two years. After Ho finished his two years of mining for himself and Tao finished his two years of mining for himself, Ho would return to the mine to do another two years–for Ah Ming. And after that, Tao would return to the mine to do another two years–for Bahn.

Hue could manage the spread with one brother in residence while the other did the mining. And again, the brothers traded places. Each one would mine for four days, then return to his home for resting for three days. He would, the next week, repeat the process and doing so until his two-year term was completed.

Hue breathed a big sigh. That problem was solved.

* * *

Bahn, meanwhile, was able to be relieved from the laundry house work a few hours each day. The arrival of more Chinese women made it possible–they began to work in the laundry house, too.

316

Bahn dawdled over her chores in the log house, making many unnecessary trips back and forth in front of the office's open door, stealing a peek at the tall, redheaded round-eye. One time, she got caught in the act. Richard had noticed the many trips back and forth, back and forth that Bahn was making each day. Surely, he thought, she is not doing that on purpose. Or is she?

He determined to say something the next time she slipped past the door. He could have sworn that each time she passed the door, she paused ever so slightly.

The time was right: "Miss Lee," he said, as he turned to face her. "Would you be so kind as to show me how to get a drink of water?"

"I'd be delighted to show you, Mr. O'Donnell. This way."

They walked to the kitchen area. Bahn remembered how the etiquette book taught her to drink water not from the dipper but from a glass. She removed a glass from the cupboard. She took the dipper from a peg on the wall. She put it into the bucket of water next to the pump. Then she poured the bit of water from the dipper into the pump, beginning at the same time, to pump the pump handle up and down swiftly until the water began to flow from the well. Putting down the dipper, she picked up the glass and let the water pour into the glass.

"There!" she said, handing him the glass of water. "That's how you do it."

"Thank you so much, Miss Lee." Richard felt a pang of guilt. He knew perfectly well how to extract water from a pump. But he smiled grandly after he drank most of the water.

"Will there be anything else, Mr. O'Donnell?"

"As a matter of fact, there is."

"And what might that be?" she asked, wondering what he was going to request.

"I invite you to call me Richard, or Dick, if you prefer."

"Dick?"

"Yes. It's a nickname for Richard."

"Dick," she said softly, looking off into the distance. Then she straightened herself and said, "My brother Hue would be most insistent that I not call you Richard, nor Dick. Too familiar!"

"Of course it's familiar, Miss Lee. And I would hope that you would permit me to call you by your first name. Bahn, isn't it? And, by the way, how do you spell 'Bahn'?"

Before she thought about it, she blurted out the letters.

He smiled his engaging smile again. She nearly swooned. He was so beautiful. She caught herself daydreaming even as he stood next

317

to her. So closely. Really closely. She said, "I must be getting back to work, Dick. . . I mean, Richard. . . Oh, I don't know what I mean!" She fled into the farthest part of the house to do some pretended chore. What is the matter with me, she asked herself! I truly like this Richard, or Dick, I truly do. And I ran away? I must be under the influence of some ill-begotten devil! A foreign devil, no doubt!

Richard, still smiling grandly, went back to the office to work on the books. It was a job he enjoyed immensely. He felt as though he were cut out for it. Bookkeeper? Sounds impressive. I Hope Bahn thinks it's impressive. Stop thinking about that girl, he scolded himself. I've work to do!

* * *

Working with numbers required Richard's close attention to details. Thoughts of Bahn kept intruding upon his work. He put down his quill. He got up from the chair and stretched. He sat down again. Bahn had never left his thoughts. He sat, musing about her. He adored her blue-black hair, usually pulled back into a bun; he pictured her almond-shaped eyes, so black and piercing, they seemed to penetrate his very being. He wondered what she looked like without the Chinese laborer's 'costume,' he called it—loose top with semi-long sleeves, baggy pants, hemp sandals, with a single thong on each sandal. As she walked, the sandals slid over the highly polished floors of the log house.

Richard need not have wondered too long about what she looked like in a dress, any kind of dress, because at a birthday celebration for someone in the extended family (he knew not all the members—couldn't keep them straight), the women wore Chinese dresses. Bahn wore an embossed pink satin chong-sung, a slit up to the knee on the left side; high stiff collar at the neck; two frogs coming down at an angle from the left shoulder. She was dazzling in it. And he was dazzled by the very sight of her!

During that birthday celebration, he not-so-shyly approached Bahn. "My little flower," he said to her. "You are looking more beautiful than I thought possible!"

"Mr. O'Donnell! You are too, too familiar!" she rebuked him.

"And what happened to 'Richard' or 'Dick'?" he asked.

Bahn was flustered. Part of her wanted to keep the role of the quiet, unassuming Oriental woman, expected of her. Another part of her wanted to flirt with the red-haired Adonis. Oh, how she wanted to call him "Dick," wanted him to call her "my little flower" again. And again, and again.

So, what did she do? She ran away!

Richard was not puzzled by her action. Sensing what the real Bahn is like, he was aware of the personal war going on in her mind. He smiled at the thought of it. He knew he was affecting her in a way that was not unflattering to him. He continued smiling, at the birthday party, giving the other family guests a good feeling about him. In fact, they all were delighted with him, even infatuated with the O'Donnell person.

Before the birthday celebration was over, Bahn waited for the right moment to approach Richard. The women were beginning to remove the remains of delicacies, distribute them among the other households, and do a cleanup in general. Bahn was expected to help, but she disappeared mysteriously, hoping no one would notice. They didn't, so preoccupied they were with the cleanup.

She found him in Emily's formal garden at the back of the big house. He was admiring a rose, the same pink shade as her dress. Then he was fondling the rose. He suddenly sensed that someone was watching him. He turned. And there she was, on the back porch. He smiled at her. She smiled back.

Then she walked toward Richard and stood there, speechless. He let go of the rose and picked up her hand and kissed it.

"What nonsense is this?" she demanded.

"I am kissing your hand, a fine old-world custom. A gentleman always kisses a lady's hand in greeting. The moment is right."

"Well," she said, "I have to admit that it is rather nice."

"Permit me to kiss your hand again, my little flower." She let him. "When I saw you on the porch just now, I had been admiring the pink rose here. It is exactly the same shade of pink in your dress, which, if I may add, is very, very lovely on you, Bahn."

She stiffened. "I must remind you, Mr. O'Donnell, my brother does not permit such familiarity!"

"Really? I have never heard it from his lips!"

She stammered. "No one need hear it, but everyone must know it!"

"You are so enchanting when you are riled, Bahn."

What is he doing to me? she asked herself. I scold him, and he continues to flatter me! Foolish girl! she said, still talking to herself. You *know* you want to call him Dick!

He smiled all through her thinking crazy thoughts. She was enchanted with him.

"Oh, all right!" she said, finally. "Thank you, Dick!" A pause, then, "Are you satisfied?"

Dick laughed out loud, throwing his head back.

"And now you make fun of me!" she shouted.

"No, my dear Bahn. Never. You are too delightful for words!"

His smile was infectious to the point that Bahn could not, in all good conscience, keep from smiling with him.

* * *

Emily, looking out the kitchen window, saw the couple exchanging their charming smiles. She was moved to smile with them. Hue approached and put his arm around her waist. "What are you smiling at, dear one?" Hue asked.

"Look," she said, nodding toward the window. "In the garden, by the roses."

He followed her gaze and discovered what was amusing her. "A good sign," he said.

She turned to look at her husband and said, "You planned this eventuality all along, didn't you?"

"Well . . . . I'm not so sure, Emily, darling. But it looks as though hiring the O'Donnell boy/man . . . . was a marvelous thing to do." Then, thoughtfully, "Yes, I believe so."

* * *

The very next evening, after supper at the big house, Bahn assisted Emily with the removal of dishes from the table. When Bahn returned to the dining room alone, Richard was there and said to her, "Bahn, would you do me the favor of walking with me toward the sunset, on the path outside the log house?"

Walking toward the sunset, Bahn mused to herself. How romantic! "I would be pleased to do that, Dick. After I've finished helping Emily."

"Of course," he said. "I'll await you on the back porch of the log house."

The wisteria was resplendent all across the top of the log-house back porch. There was just enough light to give it a mysterious aura. Richard reveled in it. He felt a pang of homesickness, but only for a moment. And then it passed, for he heard a door close, and he turned to see Bahn approaching from the big house.

Reaching out with both hands, he said simply, "Bahn, my dear."

"Dick," she replied, letting him take her extended hands toward him.

"Let's walk," he said.

Hand in hand, they walked around the log house then toward the sunset. The mountains in the distance gave them an early sunset every evening. They said nothing. Just before the sun disappeared completely behind the mountain range, Richard stopped and pulled Bahn back toward him. He placed one hand behind her head, onto the bun. He kissed her gently.

Bahn was neither surprised nor outraged. She was thrilled. She put both arms around his neck and pulled him toward her, kissing him with greater emotion. Ending the second kiss, they were breathing irregularly.

By then, it was almost dark. "Let me walk you back to the big house, Bahn."

"Yes, do that, Dick."

Picking their way back to the big house, in the darkness, Richard held her closely by putting one arm around her waist. When they arrived at the big house, Richard accompanied her onto the back porch. He kissed her again, whispering, "Good night, my sweet Bahn flower."

"Good night, Dick. "She backed away from him, still holding both his hands. She said, softly, "I love you, Richard O'Donnell."

When she entered the big house, Emily was just coming down the steps, after first putting little Della Lu to bed, then little Brad. Hue stood at the door of the office, now a library, book in hand. Bahn gave both of them a guarded glance, then, with head down, ran up the stairs to her room.

Emily and Hue looked at each other and smiled. "A clear case of amorous embarrassment," said Hue.

Emily said, teasingly,"I can't imagine why!"

Together they smiled knowingly.

Chapter Ten

Rupert Johnson, owner and editor of Stoney Ridge's only newspaper, made a heavy decision. He decided to ask Lizzy to marry him. Lizzy, somewhere in her late thirties, pale gray eyes, mousey hair, mousey personality. What could he possibly see in her? he asked himself. There must have been something, but he could not, for the life of him, discover it nor describe it.

Perhaps it was the way she dealt with little Brad (getting older and bigger every day). His only grandson. It was plain to see that she was totally engrossed in little Brad's every move, whim, and word. Rupert decided he needed to marry her so that she would have somewhere to go other than another child-caring job. Of course, with the advent of the new granddaughter, Della Lu, Lizzy had plenty of work on her hands, helping with the baby, still keeping Brad in tow.

What to do? Rupert asked himself over and over, never coming to any solid conclusion.

After putting the weekly edition to bed, Rupert rode out to the Lee ranch and asked Emily straight out, "Where is Lizzy?"

"Lizzy?" Emily asked. "She's probably with Brad, out in the flower garden, or the log house . . .he adores his 'Uncle' Richard. . . or, at the stables . . . "

"At the stables?! Whatever for?"

"For his riding lesson," said Emily, so sweetly. "Ordered by his new father."

"Isn't he a tad young for that?"

"Hue doesn't think so. And I trust his judgment, Daddy."

"Of course you do. And why in tarnation is Brad calling the O'Donnell boy his uncle?"

"It is a bit premature, Daddy, but Richard and Bahn are very sweet on each other. Leave it to a small child to perceive these kinds of things, early on. Thus, he calls Richard his uncle."

"I've lost track of why I came here, girl! No, I remember. Where can I find Lizzy?"

"Come with me, Daddy. I've just put the baby down for her nap. I'll help you find Lizzy."

No one was in the flower garden. Richard was alone in the log house. They found Lizzy sitting on the board fence of the corral, watching Brad's riding lesson. Rupert saw her watching Brad. Or, he wondered, was she watching the riding instructor, a very young and very handsome Chinese man, born in this country, on a horse ranch on the Coast, Emily had told him. His father had labored on the transcontinental railroad, as did Hue.

Fie! Rupert scolded himself.

"Good afternoon, Miss Lizzy." She turned to face him and smiled.

Lizzy then said to Emily, "Miss Emily, (a form of address that Emily suggested Lizzy use instead of Mrs. Lee) how nice of you to come watch Brad do his riding exercises!"

"I don't want to disappoint you in that, Lizzy, but my father here was looking for you, and I helped him find you. I'll leave you both to talk." Shouting across the riding corral, she called to Brad and waved to him. He smiled broadly, proud of his newest accomplishment, and waved back.

Emily then departed to return to the big house.

Lizzy said, "And a good afternoon to you, too, Mr. Johnson."

"I can't get anyone to call me Rupert. Even Hue Lee still calls me his honorable father-in-law when addressing me!"

Lizzy regarded him quizzically. "And why do you wish to see me . . . Rupert?"

He thought, now we're getting somewhere. "Lizzy, I want to talk to you about your future . . . and mine."

"I'm not sure what you mean, sir."

"Consarn it, girl, now you're calling me 'sir'! Back to the Rupert!" Instantly he regretted his outburst. Between Lizzy and all the Chinese folks, he's "Mr. Johnson this" and "Sir that." Aloud, he said, "Ah, forgive me, Lizzy. An old man [wishing he hadn't said *that*!] like me doesn't want to hear so much bowing and scraping words!"

Lizzy said nothing.

A bad sign, he thought, and he was picking up on a well-used phrase by Hue, his son-in-law. Oh, well, here goes. "What I mean, my dear, is that I am proposing marriage to you, and I sincerely hope you will accept."

She dropped down from the fence top, gathering her skirts around her demurely. Then she walked back to the gate to open it and leave the corral and to close the gate again. He faced her. She walked up to him. She said, "Rupert, I cannot give you any children, if that's what you're wanting from me."

"How do you know this?" He regretted what he asked. "Begging your pardon, Lizzy, it's none of my business."

"I'm making it your business. When I was very young, I was married to a boy I was so much in love with, it drove me crazy. Two years later he was killed by falling off a scaffold for a building he was working on. We never had any children. And that drove me crazy, too. In the next year, I found employment taking care of two children. They grew up. Then I took care of one child. Then three children. Brad is my latest charge, and so is Della Lu, at times. It's my life, Rupert, taking care of other people's children. "

"Should that stop you from marrying again?"

"There would be no children, Rupert." She lowered her head.

He reached for her, brought her toward him, and lifted her head by the chin until she could look him in the eye. "Yes, there could be, Lizzy. Adoption comes to mind. I would be happy if you would marry me and accept some fatherless and motherless child into your home—our home."

"Rupert. I dare not ask if you really mean that!"

"Dare to ask, Lizzy. Dare to live again."

* * *

"Dick," Bahn said shyly, uncharacteristically, "can we see the sunset together again this evening?

* * *

A week later, Bahn approached Hue. "Oh, Honorable Brother?"

Hue replied, "Bahn, when you address me as 'oh honorable brother,' I have come to know that it means trouble!"

"No, Hue. Not trouble. I hope it is good news for you."

Hue heaved a big sigh. His youngest sister was the most troublesome of all his Chinese family in America. She looks at you in a certain way, and it's trouble. But, he indulged her with, "Well, youngest sister, what is it now?"

"I want to marry Richard O'Donnell."

"Well, now, that is an admirable ambition. Has he proposed marriage? He has not asked me if he may marry you. So, what is to be done about this predicament?"

"You don't understand, Hue. We are Americans, and I am willing to take certain liberties . . .

"What certain liberties?" Hue asked with suspicion. No telling what this girl-woman is up to.

"To begin with," she said, "*I* want to ask *Richard* to marry *me*!"

"By the great Father above! And the devils below! What are you thinking, girl?"

Hue's outburst was not exactly unexpected by Bahn, but his explosive language left her feeling insignificant, insecure. She began to have second thoughts: who was she to go about telling anyone that she was going to ask a man to marry her? She ventured a response. "Dear Brother Hue, if you cannot accept this ploy, then *you* ask him for me!"

Hue answered her as evenly as he could. "Surely you are not serious about this . . . this travesty!"

Bahn looked at her patriarch of this branch of the Lee family and said, "Dead serious, oh Honorable Brother."

"I will not ask him, and I forbid you to do the asking! And that is final! You have gone far too far this time, Bahn. It is unthinkable!" He thought for a moment, then added, "However, the boy-man is a comely and polite, respectful, and diligent person. Like Chinese. " He paused again, noticing his speech had lapsed into pidgin English. "No, I will not do the asking, and neither will you. You are dismissed, youngest sister."

She knew when she was beaten. She also knew that the other side of her brother had a propensity for thinking more and more like an American–a result of living with his pretty American wife, no doubt. And that gave her an idea. "Can you, Hue, at least, tell Richard that I'm smitten with him?"

"I cannot and will not!"

She decided not to tip-toe around her big brother any more. She charged back at him. "Very well, then, Hue, oh honorable but pig-headed brother! I will do whatever it takes to get him to ask me to marry him!"

Hue was now alarmed. He asked himself, she will do whatever it takes? God forbid! Not that! "Wait! Bahn! Let me think. Do not speak to me for the next few seconds while I think!"

She waited, impatiently, but respectfully. He was, after all, her patriarch in this branch of the Lee family.

Hue heaved a huge sigh and said, finally, "All right, Bahn, I will do as you ask: put in a kind word about you to the Richard boy-man. Hint largely how much you like him. Anything to keep you from disgracing yourself and from disgracing the entire family."

* * *

The result of Hue's talk with Richard was that Richard, willingly and happily proposed marriage to the beautiful and ardent Bahn. Bahn, meanwhile, had no idea what Hue had said to Dick. But she didn't mind; she didn't care. His talk got results, and that was all that mattered!

* * *

The conversation between Hue and Richard went something like this: Hue went to the office and greeted Richard and plunged directly into the subject at hand. "Richard, my boy. . . .a thousand pardons . . . . my man, I have serious business to conduct with you."

Richard began to pale, thinking, What have I done? Or, what have I *not* done?

Hue continued. "My sister Bahn thinks very highly of you, Richard. Indeed, she admires you, she is enamored with you, and she would be very happy if you were to propose marriage to her." Without giving Richard a chance to react, he turned to leave, paused, and said, "And, to relieve you of any doubts about this information, I tell you this: I would be pleased and honored to have you as a brother-in-law."

He left the office, abruptly, leaving Richard totally bewildered. But not for long. That evening, Richard requested Bahn to join him in another sunset walk. She accepted.

That was not all that she accepted that night.

* * *

To find a replacement for Lizzy was Hue's next project. She would be leaving his employ when she and Rupert were married. He thought: Another letter to San Francisco? Another visit to San Francisco? Hue considered the possibilities and discussed them at length with Emily. It was her bailiwick, after all. After discussing the matter for a few days, Emily came up with the possibility of finding a baby/child helper among the women already brought onto the ranch.

To assist in the choosing, Hue sent for Fu Chou, his longtime and faithful laborer, his fellow railroad worker during those hard years. Hue put big faith in the natural abilities of Fu. Immediately upon hearing the problem Hue and Emily faced, Fu suggested they try out the niece of one of the laborers, very bright, very industrious. Perhaps these qualities in the niece would be of use to them?

Emily sent for the designated girl, interviewed her, and gave her a one-week trial period to see if she would work out satisfactorily. Fu's suggestion had been on the mark. The niece, Roh Tan, was petite but fast on her feet when it came to keeping up with the active Brad and the now-crawling, almost-walking Della Lu. It was settled: Roh (pronounced row, as in row the boat) would work with Lizzy until Lizzy left to order her trousseau from Wu's dressmaking shop, to include a traveling costume for the train to San Francisco and return.

Then came the fittings and the alterations, and the second and third fittings, the packing before moving into Rupert's house, the pre-wedding party given to Lizzy by the ladies and daughters of Stoney Ridge. The activities left her breathless. Lizzy was heady with excitement and, dare she say it to herself? and with expectation!

* * *

Hue hosted another double wedding: Rupert and Lizzy; Richard and Bahn. The tables groaned under the weight of American food and Chinese delicacies. Hue managed to end the party at a decent hour so that the two sets of newlyweds would be free to go their own ways. Rupert and Lizzy spent their wedding night at his house, catching the train to San Francisco the next day.

Richard and Bahn chose to have the wedding night in the log house, where they would take up permanent residence. The next day, they traveled to Richard's former home for him to introduce his new bride to his parents. They seemed delighted with her, albeit they had unwanted misgivings about their son's marrying a slant-eye. Oh, yes, and Richard had respectfully, specifically, and without reservations, requested them never to refer to his bride as a "slant-eye." It would take some getting used to. In the short span of time of the visit with the elder O'Donnells, Richard's parents came to love their new and first daughter-in-law.

Three days later, Richard and Bahn climbed aboard the carriage, and the horse trotted the long way back to the Lee Ranch. There they made their home in the log house, where they had met, where they had courted, where they came to love each other unfailingly.

Chapter Eleven

The idea of a medical clinic for all ranch hands and residents took form while Hue searched for a schoolmaster in San Francisco. The school, serving both adults and children, was getting to be more than Hue could handle alone. He passed a clinic, while walking to an interview appointment. After the appointment, in which he hired the new schoolmaster, he returned to the clinic and went inside to make inquiries about the availability of a doctor.

Dr. Thomas Meadows met him for dinner that evening, and Hue presented his plan for a clinic and his need for someone to operate it. Would Dr. Meadows be willing to do that? And would the good doctor have knowledge of a nurse to assist the doctor and who would be willing to go into such a primitive workplace?

The conclusion of the meeting was that Dr. Meadows would draw up plans for his needs for a clinic. Hue suggested an addition at the back of the clinic: two sitting room/bedrooms, one at each end of the addition; and a kitchen with dining space between the bedrooms. Upon the medical team's arrival, Nurse Arabella would have the privilege of selecting a Chinese woman from the labor pool to work at the clinic's living quarters as a house cleaner and cook.

Hue would engage his construction laborers to build the clinic with the living quarters. Dr. Meadows and Nurse Arabella would arrive soon after the clinic was finished. The doctor and nurse would travel by train with the packed clinic supplies to be hauled in the baggage car of the train.

Six months later, the clinic was opened—for all to use: field laborers, houseworkers, and family members. Schoolmaster Charles Sweeney arrived the day the clinic was opened. He was put to work the next day. The assistant schoolmaster that Hue hired would arrive from San Francisco the next month. She was to be the teacher of the Chinese language.

While in San Francisco, Hue hired two more office helpers for Richard. Hue had a separate building constructed for the office so that Richard and Bahn would enjoy complete privacy in the log house.

Before the year was out, Bahn was expecting her first child. It would be born in the new clinic. That child would, at school age, join all the other children at the ranch school. Brad was in school now, leaving Della Lu's having the run of the house—Roh in hot pursuit.

The Lee clan was enjoying immeasurable success in agriculture, businesses, scholarliness, and medicine. The clinic alone became known county-wide, for Dr. Meadows was a well-liked man by all his patients. He had a sideline to do research, albeit a primitive research. Family members of Stoney Ridge made the long ride out to the Lee Ranch just to have the good doctor follow them to their homes to treat the sick--their ailments and their broken bones.

* * *

Schoolmaster Charles Sweeney was temporarily housed with Hue and Emily in the big house. There were plenty of extra rooms, all bedrooms. And he took all his meals with the family there. Emily pondered on the complicated logistics for when the schoolmaster's assistant should arrive. She knew she could put her up in another bedroom, at the opposite end of the second floor. Was it wise? All things considered? Putting Mr. Sweeney into the laborer's bunkhouse was out of the question. Putting his female assistant in the housing for the female household and laundry workers was also out of the question. They both deserved better, was Emily's thinking. Hue's ambitious plans were taxing her ingenuity. What, exactly, was Emily supposed to do with the two teachers?

All too soon, for Emily, Miss Shi (pronounced shee) Wong arrived and was ensconced in the bedroom at the opposite end from Mr. Sweeney's room on the second floor. She came in on the train that arrived mid-morning. Shi had time to unpack and settle in before the mid-day dinner..

Shi came downstairs, found Emily, and offered to help with the meal preparation. She had already smelled the delicious aromas creeping into the upstairs. She was hungry!

Emily thanked her profusely and explained that the household was staffed with kitchen workers and cleaning workers. They would go to the drawing room. Emily asked Shi to tell her about herself and her background.

Shi Wong was born in San Francisco, learned English from the neighboring children, at the same time speaking Chinese in her home. Two years at university (the only woman student), and taking courses in education, she was well prepared for such an assignment that Hue hired her to do. Indeed, she was working at the university when Hue visited there, doing his search for an assistant to the schoolmaster.

Hue had been assured by Shi's professors that she was most competent and should fit into the mixed population of Hue Lee's ranch.

He hired her on the spot. She had asked for a short period of time to prepare for the journey and her new life.

* * *

At precisely noon, Charles Sweeney walked into the front door and heard the voices coming from the drawing room. He recognized Emily Lee's voice, but not the other. He paused at the door and looked inside. As Emily rose and approached him, he was drawn to the other occupant. She was so beautiful, he took a fancy to her instantly.

"May I introduce you, Charles? This is Miss Shi Wong, your assistant. Miss Wong, Mr. Charles Sweeney, the schoolmaster."

Shi, was equally attracted. Demurely, she too rose and walked toward Sweeney. Holding out her hand, she said, "A pleasure, Mr. Sweeney."

Dumbstruck, the not-too-tall but sturdily built schoolmaster managed to mumble a "Charmed, Miss Wong." He thought he had just spoken to a queen, black hair in a crown at the top of her head, the almond-shaped dark eyes gazing at him almost brazenly, slim as a reed, dressed in a strange form-fitting dress. He asked himself, dressed like that? On a ranch? He was accustomed to seeing the women in the Chinese work clothing–baggy pants and loose-fitting top with three-quarter length sleeves, or like Mrs. Lee, and her daughter-in-law, Coralee Lee, in long, swirling skirts, nipped-in waists, long sleeves puffed at the shoulders, tightly fitting at the wrists.

While he appraised Shi Wong, in great detail, Shi herself was doing the same thing about him. Her exposure to the round-eyes (she thought she must stop thinking in these peasant terms) in San Francisco was merely to see them at the university, in an academic way, or on the streets, but not in a social way. Charles Sweeney had medium brown hair, medium height, medium hazel eyes. A ruddy complexion was the only thing about him that was not "medium."

Emily waited patiently while Sweeney and Miss Wong looked over one another, deciding things about each other before they got to know each other. Emily finally broke the silence and said, "I believe dinner is ready for us now. Come."

Charles offered his arm to Shi, who, although a bit puzzled, took it and walked with him to the dining room. Never in her life had she been treated so politely. Never in her life had she been exposed so familiarly to a white-eye . . . white man, she corrected herself.

Emily seated them around a corner from each other. Then, making her excuses–to look in on the children, a trumped-up excuse at best–she left the two alone. Hue was in Stoney Ridge, conferring with Ton about the future changes to his and Wu's combined shops to be enlarged.

"Miss Wong," said Charles, "I welcome you to the Lee Ranch. I hope you like it here. I look forward to working with you in the schoolroom."

She smiled demurely, wondering if she should say what was on her mind. "Oh, Mr. Sweeney, I like it here already!"

* * *

Fu Chou of the laborers came to the big house and asked to approach Hue Lee.

"What is it, Fu?" asked Hue.

Fu explained the purpose of his visit. He suggested that Hue build and stock a store for ranch residents to shop in, exclusively.

"My dear Fu. I cannot, in all good grace, become a competitor for Mr. Hudson and his General Store in Stoney Ridge."

"But it is a long distance for us poor peasants to go when we have personal needs. A store here on the ranch would be a huge convenience."

"This is true, Fu Chou. I must think on it and give you an answer later."

* * *

The next week Hue rode on his horse into town and paid a visit to Mr. Hudson. "Mr. Hudson," he began. "I wish to make an honorable proposal to you."

Mr. Hudson said, "I'm listening."

"You have been very lucky that no one has come to Stoney Ridge from the East to establish a store similar to yours and become your competitor."

"That be right, Mr. Lee. Why do you mention that?"

"Well, Mr. Hudson, I would like to propose that you open a branch store on my humble property. I will have a building constructed, and you will pay a very small rent. You will stock it with the kinds of things you know what my workers, male and female, like to buy from you when they come into town. And do you not have a son who could run the store?"

"What? MY son? Mr. Lee, you must be daft! My son could not add two items together and get the right answer."

"Ah, but Honorable Mr. Hudson, I have made inquiries from the delightful schoolmistress in Stoney Ridge's one-room schoolhouse. And she has spoken glowingly of your son's true ability!"

"My Denny? The schoolmistress must be daft, too! I swear!"

"It seems, Mr. Hudson," Lee persisted, "that your firstborn . . . Denny? . . ."

Mr. Hudson nodded.

Hue continued, "It seems that your Denny is an extremely bright young man who simply has no real challenge to use his capabilities . . . according to the schoolmarm, Mr. Hudson."

"I never heard of such nonsense!"

"Trust me, Mr. Hudson, I urgently wish to build a small store on my property, rent it to you, have you stock it, and have your Denny operate it."

"Well, I'll be hornswaggled!"

* * *

After much cajoling and promising that Denny would be more than a satisfactory clerk for his father in the branch store, Harold Hudson finally agreed to the arrangement. Shaking his head in disbelief, he could not for the life of him understand what the Lee fellow saw in his son Denny!

When the branch store was finished and stocked, Hue held a celebration for the benefit of all members of the ranch. A program was put together with Hue's making a speech at the end of the program.

During Hue's speech, he collapsed on the store's front porch. Dr. Meadows took charge and had four laborers carry Hue into the clinic. He then pronounced the trouble to be a heart attack, but Hue would live for a few more years.

At his bedside in the clinic, Hue sent for Ho and Tao. He said to them, "Faithful brothers, it is time for me to pass the torch to you. Ho, you will oversee all the businesses; Tao, you will take charge of the orchards and gardens. Both of you will retain Dr. Meadows, Nurse Arabella, and Schoolmaster Charles Sweeney, along with his assistant Shi Wong. Let them run their own activities. They are the professionals. And do not forget the fine new store. Help the young Hudson boy with his new-found responsibilities. He will do well, I predict. Richard O'Donnell must be in charge of all accounts. It is his special talent. He will be responsible for his aides' performance and deportment.

* * *

While Hue languished in bed in his home, there was a trail of visitors from morning til evening, each one seeking advice and direction from the venerable Hue Lee.

Before his heart attack, Emily discovered she was with child again.

At the boy's birth, Hue rejoiced from his bed and held the baby for long periods of time, looking at him, wondering once more at the miracle of birth, the miracle of life.

Emily kept Hue abreast of the ranch gossip. Denny and Roh met each other the day Roh took Della Lu into the Hudson branch store to make a small purchase. Secretly, Rho had made up the errand so that she could get a good look at the boy she heard the house workers babble about. Yes, Roh said to herself, a pleasing personage, indeed.

Denny was not unmindful of her appraisal, so he appraised her in return . . . with great pleasure. He noted her long black hair falling freely around her shoulders, her soulful dark eyes, her exquisite figure. He had no idea a young Chinese woman could be so beguiling. He was bewitched.

That first meeting, in the store, Roh approached shyly and said to the brash young Denny, "Please, sir, do you have ladies' handkerchiefs?"

"Yes, indeed, Miss . . .?"

"I am Roh Tan. Please, sir, and you are called Denny? Denny Hudson?"

"Yes, Miss Tan. I am very happy to make your acquaintance."

"As I am yours, kind sir."

"About the ladies' handkerchiefs?" he asked

"The what?" she seemed flustered, this young man was so polite, so nice, so good looking! "Oh, yes, the handkerchiefs. Something white, with lace."

"I would expect you to request exactly that–a white handkerchief with lace, to match your delicate beauty."

Roh was flattered far beyond anything her expectations might be, meeting this fine young man. She blushed, in spite of herself. "This plain Chinese person does not deserve such praise . . ."

He smiled as he retrieved the box of handkerchiefs.

* * *

Emily also told Hue about the schoolmaster Charles Sweeney and his aide, the beautiful Shi Wong. Their working together had given each one a rare exposure to the wiles and peculiarities and charms of the other.

"Miss Wong," Charles began one afternoon when school had been dismissed. "Will you walk with me toward the sunset this evening after supper? I've been told it is a magical experience."

"A walk toward the sunset? It sounds invitingly romantic."

"And that is what I mean it to be–romantic."

While they strolled in the direction of the sun setting behind the mountain range, Shi said, "Mr. Sweeney, you know all about me, as a result of Mr. Lee's briefing you before I came here. But I know nothing about you beyond your name. Please, kind sir, tell me all about yourself."

He blanched at the request to reveal *all* about himself. But he made a start, trying to keep his autobiography short and to the point. "I was born in Detroit, Michigan."

"Excuse, please, Mr. Sweeney. What is a Detroit, Michigan?"

He explained the city and the state and where in America they existed. "I attended a small college in Detroit. Then I was a merchant seaman, sailing from the port of New York City . . . "

"And, please, kind sir, what is a New York City?"

Again, he interrupted his story to explain the location of New York City. Continuing, he said, "from New York City, around the Horn, to San Francisco. . . ."

"You've been to San Francisco? My former home?"

"Yes, an enchanting city–as enchanting as your lovely company."

He took her hand nearest him. They talked like that for the rest of the way and return. He, telling more of his life's story; she, marveling at the wondrous experiences he related to her.

At the big house, Shi said, wistfully, "I do not want this evening to end, Mr. Sweeney. Your stories are most entertaining. I have enjoyed the walk enormously. Thank you, kind sir, for inviting me to join you in the sunset walk. And now it is dark."

"The only reason I want us to enter the house is so that, in the light of the lamps, I can see you more clearly. You are a beautiful woman, Shi Wong."

"You are a beautiful man, Charles Sweeney."

He smiled at the intended compliment. They entered the house together and walked up the stairway. Before he turned to the left and she turned to the right, he took her hands in his and said, "Good night, my lovely Oriental Beauty."

Shi was too overcome to answer. She disengaged her hands and fled to her room.

He stood smiling after her, watching her enter her room.

* * *

Shi and Charles had come to Emily first, with due regard and respect for Hue's condition. They announced that they were to be wed. Emily passed on this news to Hue, who, predictably, was not at all surprised. He was, after all, the first one to meet the very attractive Shi, in San Francisco. No, he was not surprised.

* * *

The romance between Denny and Roh flourished. Again, Hue was not surprised. He had put much faith into the Dennis Hudson boy, barely knowing him personally. And, he depended upon Emily to supply glowing reports about Roh's work with the fast-growing Brad, the toddler Della Lu, and the infant boy Rupert Rhee Lee.

Of course those two young people, Denny and Roh, were attracted to each other. In time, the young couple approached Hue and Emily together at Hue's bedside. They asked permission from them to get married. Hue and Emily gave them their blessing.

Mr. and Mrs. Hudson, Denny's father and mother, became apoplectic at the news. With a benevolent smile, Emily broke the news to them—Denny's special request. Emily took Della Lu along with her so that the forlorn parents could see the beauty of a mixed-parentage child. They were somewhat mollified. But only somewhat.

Hue began to make plans—again—in spite of his bedridden state—with occasional outings in a makeshift wheelchair. Plans this time were for having a house built for the Sweeneys-to-be.

Until Hue and Emily's children were old enough to need less and less supervision, Denny and Roh would live in the big house. Then, their own house would be built. There was no questioning about Denny's not wanting to live in Stoney Ridge. He was enjoying his freedom from parental put-downs. No way would he consent to live in Stoney Ridge again! Roh was just as happy with Denny's decision.

In the end, Hue, from his sick bed and wheelchair, orchestrated still another double wedding at the ranch: Charles Sweeney and Shi Wong; and Dennis Hudson and Roh Tan. Emily put it to work, the plans, fussing like a mother hen, checking all the arrangements that others were performing for her. The two weddings took place on the ranch, an outdoor double ceremony. Hue had been trundled, in the makeshift wheelchair, outside to watch the ritual. A beneficent smile on his face.

* * *

Brad's exposure to the Chinese children, playing with them every day and his Chinese lessons in school helped him to pick up the language quickly. And when he played with Della Lu at the big house, he dropped Chinese words and expressions right and left.

The little girl absorbed it all like a sponge.

Chinese children, exposed to English from Schoolmaster Sweeney, learned rapidly how to speak something other than pidgin English. Chinese adults also benefitted from these classes. Children of mixed marriages went to both classes, for English and for Chinese. Reports of this progress were passed on to Hue by both Charles and Shi, much to his great satisfaction. All was going well on the ranch, it seemed to him.

* * *

Then a disaster occurred. During an unusual thunder-and-lightning storm one violent night, the main barn was struck by the lightning and burned to the ground.

Fu heard the crashing noise and, in his sleeping garment, rushed outside to see what was happening. The flames were already leaping into the sky from the barn. He awakened the entire compound and organized a bucket brigade. Every water pump on the ranch was engaged to supply water, constantly, for the fire in the barn.

They managed to save all the horses, the four cows, and a wagon and a carriage. But everything else was lost, including the straw for bedding the animals and the hay for feed. Most of the chickens were lost, with some running for their lives and clucking and squawking all the way. Sheep were not barn animals, penned outside the barn. Two goats resided with them.

With Fu's and Ho's combined efforts, those few items and animals were saved. Hue had been apprised of the catastrophe by Richard, running through the big house, warning the house workers, reaching Hue's and Emily's bedroom breathless and sweating.

Emily grabbed a dressing robe and accompanied Richard downstairs. She began manning the pump in her kitchen. Richard returned to the burning site to form another bucket brigade from the big house to the fire.

By daylight there was only a charred place on the ground. Before everyone retired to clean up themselves and to get well-earned rest, Fu and Richard went to the big house to report to Hue. They bundled him up, at his request, and carried him downstairs and into the wheelchair. The sun was just appearing in the East. Hue surveyed the terrible damage. His gaze passed on to the few animals and equipment that escaped the fire.

He raised his head and said aloud, "Thank God it was the barn and not a domicile!"

* * *

A month or so later, Hue's father Rhee passed on. Neighbors had sent one of the new-fangled telegraph wires to Hue. It was a stroke, the wire said. One week later, Hue's mother Lu died of a broken heart . . . as was reported by friends and neighbors in still another telegraph wire.

Rhee Lee's store was sold. Hue, having inherited the store, donated the entire funds from the sale to his parents' community. With those funds, the townsmen built a park of grass, flowers, shrubs, and trees. It was a living memorial to Rhee and Lu Lee.

Chapter Twelve

In good time, the barn was rebuilt, lost chickens were replaced, straw and hay replaced. The horses and cows, grown accustomed to outdoor living, were herded into the new barn. Fu oversaw the entire project. Hue was wheeled outside the big house daily to watch and offer a suggestion here and there. Fu was glad there was something useful for Hue to do. His body may be wasting away, but not his mind.

To demonstrate that Hue's mind was still at work, he designed what would be called the fire house. It was a building equipped with buckets and hoses and three water pumps, using water piped in from the nearby creek. Other farms did not include such a building on their properties. It was pure folly according to the area farmers. It was innovative, according to the Lee ranch population.

* * *

Dr. Meadows and Nurse Arabella were relieved, as was Hue, at the end of the barn fire, that no one was harmed. Burn treatment had always been an especially difficult task for Thomas Meadows. Broken bones? . . . . Easy!

Nurse Arabella seemed to have no last name, everyone's calling her 'Nurse Arabella.' She was tall, gaunt, somewhat masculine. Not the most lovely face to look upon, with hazel eyes and streaked blonde hair. But she was kind, especially with the children–they needed the most care, in her opinion, their being helpless against the ravages of disease and various bumps and scrapes. Arabella (a romantic-sounding name), was never referred to as Arabella Kenton, the remainder of her name. She did well, however, to bring esteem to her chosen life's work. Nurse Arabella was a fitting term and name.

The dining/sleeping arrangements at the back of the clinic were most satisfactory to both Thomas and Arabella. The Chinese woman who kept the place neat and clean and who cooked and served, and who washed and dried all the dishes and pots and pans, left the clinic quarters as soon as all was spick and span in the kitchen. She would retire to the women's barracks.

Dr. Meadows was a literate man, as well as skilled in medicine. He read constantly and voraciously everything he could get his hands on. Hue's library supplied him many times over with new and different books. Hue was happy to lend them out to someone who was so eager to read, read, and read.

Thomas stood almost 6 feet tall, just barely as tall as Arabella. His head was covered with only a wisp of light brown hair; his eyes a gentle brown. Large hands hung from the ends of his arms. But they were capable hands, administering his skills smoothly and competently. He was totally devoted to his chosen profession. Like Arabella.

The days were usually hectic, with first one patient and then another coming in. On some days, two or three, or five or six patients would show up altogether. The good doctor and the empathetic nurse, practiced good medicine for the Lee Ranch members.

Their evenings, quiet and sedate, found Thomas in his quarters, reading, of course; Arabella in her quarters, sometimes reading, sometimes doing needlework. Each retired to his or her bed without a "good night" between them.

The only time of the day they spent conversing socially, as it were, was at the supper hour at the end of the day. Breakfasts were separate, catching a cup of coffee and a piece of toast on the run, trying to get into the clinic to begin seeing patients. Noontime dinner was also on the run, each taking turns to see the patients. Then, as the work-day ended, they relaxed, having suppertime together.

"Nurse Arabella, thank you so much for seeing patients with coughs and sniffles today. There seemed to be a lot of them."

"True, Doctor Meadows. I don't think it was at the epidemic stage, however."

"Oh, I agree, Nurse Arabella."

And so their watery conversations proceeded throughout the evening . . . evening after evening.

* * *

In time, Arabella became restless. She was 32, unmarried, and not a chance in Hades of ever being married! The thought of it made her almost morose, cheerless. Then she would get hold of herself and scold herself for such impossible thoughts. And, to take her mind off the whole subject, she would think about the sick children she had nursed back to health, and she would feel very good about herself again.

A year later, Dr. Meadows began to think in the same cheerless way as Arabella was wont to do from time-to-time.

* * *

A few more years went by. Brad grew to be a strapping young man. Hue and Emily agreed that he should be educated beyond the ranch schoolhouse. They gave him a choice: university in the East, or college in Chicago? Brad chose Chicago–where Richard O'Donnell had matriculated.

Della Lu blossomed early and was the object of affection of every Chinese boy and mixed Chinese/American boy in the ranch school, cousins included.

Emily fretted about that. She came to one conclusion: Della Lu must be enrolled in a girls' school (much like what Emily had attended in Philadelphia so many years ago). Aunt Hilda had long ago passed on. And, Aunt Hilda's being childless, her entire estate was handed down to Emily, who was now a wealthy woman in her own right.

When Aunt Hilda's attorney finished disposing of all her possessions (some things to dear friends; remaining items to charity), he packaged two small bundles into a box and mailed it to Emily, no note, no letter of explanation. Upon receiving the box, she was puzzled about it. Then she recognized the attorney's name on the return address of the box. She went to the room where Hue now spent most of his days--in the library.

"Whatever in the world could this be? From Aunt Hilda's attorney?" Emily posed the questions to Hue, who was equally curious about the box. She opened it. She picked up two separate packages from inside the box. "Good Lord!" she exclaimed.

"What? What is it, Emily?"

"The letters . . ."

* * *

They looked at each other, mute, stunned, absolutely unable to speak or move. Finally, Hue wheeled himself to his desk. She followed him, walking as if in a trance; she sat on a chair, stiff-backed. Carefully, he took the two packages from her. After examining their contents, he handed one package back to her, and he retained the other.

At last, she shook her head to clear her mind and inspected the letters in her package. They were the 24 letters that Ho had written to her. His package held the 24 letters she had written to him. They took turns, Emily's reading aloud the first letter written by Hue, and then Hue's reading aloud the first letter written by Emily.

They read all the letters, one at a time, aloud. They wept from joy and from relief, each knowing for certain that the other had not failed to write every month, as promised. Heartache was evident in each letter. Heartache from their being separated for two years and

341

from the doubts that ravaged their souls.

The readings took nearly two hours. "Bless Aunt Hilda's attorney for mailing these to me," said Emily. "He knew exactly what to do!"

Hue said, "I wonder how much he knew—about us?"

"Probably everything, darling. Probably."

* * *

A few days later, Mademoiselle Dubay's Finishing School for Young Ladies became Emily's focus for Della Lu. Emily wondered if the venerable Miss Dubay were still alive. Perhaps her school continues on. Something to look into, soon. Very soon, she decided.

Rupert Rhee Lee, Hue and Emily's second child, was given that name, after Emily's father and Hue's father. Emily's earlier thinking that her father (who hated his name) would object to having a grandson named for him--turned out to be erroneous thinking. When she told him what she would like to name the new baby, Rupert was pleased as punch to have his new grandson named for him. He now regarded his intensely disliked name as a very distinguished name. He was downright honored to have the new baby named for him.

The young Rupert had exactly the same upbringing that Brad was exposed to, including the horse-riding ability, the bi-lingual learning, and developing a healthy attitude toward improving the mind as well as the physical body. The young Rupert was a delight for everyone on the ranch.

* * *

Hue's latest project embraced the church by having a chapel built on the ranch. The pastor of Stoney Ridge, now ageing rapidly, moved onto the ranch to supervise the construction and to assist Hue's engaging a young pastor, preferably already married, to take over the duties of ministering to the spiritual needs of the population of the ranch. Upon the arrival of the new pastor and his little family of a wife and three small children, Hue had still another house constructed, a parsonage, next to the church building.

* * *

With Ho's report to Hue, Hue learned that the gold vein he had discovered so many years ago was still in evidence. And its location was still a secret to Hue, Ho and Tao only. Emily knew it was in or on the mountainside of the Lee property, but she never knew exactly where. The Lee sisters were told this much: their new wealth was from a vein of gold on the property. That was their share. They knew only that Ho and Tao had worked the vein for two extra years each, and they had brought the money to the sisters, after assaying the gold and converting it into money.

The sisters, Ah Ming and Bahn, were coached by Hue on how to invest their wealth so that it grew and grew. They were impressed by their oldest brother's golden touch, whether it was on the vein or in the investment realm.

* * *

Fu Chou visited Hue as often as he dared, not wanting to tire the failing Hue Lee. Hue always insisted that Fu stay longer, he valued his visits so much.

On one visit, Fu announced to Hue that a small child in the laborers' compound, a very bright child, being schooled early for his age because he showed so much promise, had come up with a name for the Lee property.

Normally, they spoke Chinese. But for now, Fu spoke in English. He said. . . . . . "Leesville."

Hue, propped up with pillows while lying on his bed, closed his eyes. A contented smiled appeared on his face. He was at peace with his world. He spoke no more, but closed his eyes with that smile still on his face.

Fu Chou could not rouse him.

Dr. Meadows was summoned from the clinic. He pronounced the venerable Hue Lee to be deceased. Thomas's heart itself seemed to skip a beat. He had come to appreciate and honor Hue Lee with great respect.

Nurse Arabella was almost as grieved as Emily. She teared up when Thomas told her that Hue Lee had died. Upon seeing her distress, Thomas put a strong arm around Arabellas's shoulders, speaking softly. "There, there, Arabella. He was a good and generous man. Everyone will miss him."

She wiped her tears with a hanky. "Thank you, Thomas."

* * *

Indian Agent Jeremy MacGregor (also known as White Elk–he was "half-breed") was stationed at Spider Leg, Wyoming. His partner, Frank Owens, was a law clerk from back East. Owens was an assistant, actually, but was considered MacGregor's partner. MacGregor conferred with Owens when MacGregor needed certain advice, knowledge, and general information on procedure or a point of law. Owens also acted as a secretary to MacGregor, maintaining office files, writing letters and memos, and completing mounds and mounds of bureaucratic paper work.

The two men together were to be transferred to a newly opened Indian Affairs post at Stoney Ridge, California.

When Frank Owens opened the letter informing them of their upcoming transfer, he turned pale and began to shake–inside his gut–he was so excited.

"Surely I will get to see Emily . . . again, after all these years," he said aloud but to an empty office. No one else was present. Jeremy was at the Reservation, attending a pow-wow with the Chief.

Jeremy's wife, Mary Lou, was upset at the prospects of leaving Spider Leg, her home town. They had been so happy in their old haunts, where she had grown up, and where they had met each other under unusual circumstances. She had saved his life by shooting a stalking puma, ready to pounce on the unsuspecting White Elk.

But, she reasoned, since she and their two children would be moving with White Elk (she preferred calling him by his Shoshone Indian name), there was no need to look upon the transfer as the worst thing that could happen to them. They would rent out their Spider Leg house and save it to return to at retirement time, if they could find a renter.

* * *

Stoney Ridge! Frank hadn't recalled any memories of that place for such a long time, even though crazy thoughts had entered his head from time to time about Emily Johnson Hillmont. He asked himself, "I wonder if she ever connected with the Lee fellow?" His thoughts wandered: "I can make discreet inquiries about Emily Johnson Hillmont around town . . . . " "I can ask at the newspaper– if her father is still alive." "I can't wait to see Emily again!" "I just hope she remembers me."

The thoughts and ideas swirled around inside his head, as their small caravan (not really a wagon train–only one family involved) made its way south and west. He was almost dizzy, thinking about seeing Emily again. He never dreamed the opportunity would show itself so easily, so naturally. It was heady.

* * *

Two months later, the MacGregors and Frank Owens came to the end of their journey in a caravan of three wagons. A team of mules pulled each wagon. Jeremy and Frank rode their horses. They had hired three wagon drivers to manage the cross-country trek and to assist in the whole moving process, at Spider Leg and at their destination.

At last the three wagons and two riders beside them entered Stoney Ridge. Mary Lou was impressed at how large and prosperous the town seemed. Jeremy was surprised to see very few Indians on the streets. Only a handful, at best. Different from Spider Leg, Wyoming, at the end of his tour of duty there. The two children squealed with delight to see all the stores and a nice-looking school and a grassy park in the middle of town!

Frank cast a searching eye left and right, hoping against hope for the impossible: to see Emily Hillmont again.

* * *

Mary Lou and the children spent only a few days in the hotel while White Elk and Frank looked for lodging for the family. Frank would remain at the hotel until he might find a boarding house to provide a more home-like environment.

A suitable house was found for the MacGregors, and the wagon drivers helped Jeremy and Frank move most of the goods from the wagons into the house, The remaining goods were moved into an office space that had been arranged for in advance.

Jeremy had sent for, by messenger, one of the owners of the office space, Ho Lee. Ho came into town. Jeremy identified himself so that he could collect the key to the office. Frank was with him to make the transaction. And when Frank heard the name "Ho Lee," his heart did a flip-flop. He recognized the Lee name, of course, as well as recognizing Ho Lee to be an Oriental. However, he did not recognize the name "Ho". He could have sworn that Emily's love was "Hue Lee."

"Excuse me, Mr. Lee," said Frank. "Are you perhaps related to a Hue Lee?"

"Yes, sir, Hue Lee , my brother."

Frank was relieved. He *had* remembered the correct name. But what to do about it? Not here and not now. He thought, "I must ask around elsewhere."

Frank's heart pounded thunderously. He was sure the other two men could see what was happening to him.

Ho Lee said to the two new men in town, the two Indian Agents, "I hope your office space will be adequate and comfortable. There is a clear view of the main street. If you need anything further, please come to Leesville to contact me, and I will do what I can to take care of your needs."

"Leesville?" asked Jeremy.

"Yes, sir. It is the name of our ranch, not too far from here. But it is strictly an unofficial name. It does not appear on a map of this area. You can ask any one of the businessmen how to get to Leesville." He paused. "Will there be anything else, Mr. MacGregor?"

"No, and thank you, Mr. Lee," said Jeremy. "Good day to you."

"And good day to you both." Ho Lee left the office.

Frank was too tongue-tied to say anything to the brother of Hue Lee. Not even what he wanted to ask–if Emily were living in Leesville or here in Stoney Ridge. Surely the Ho person would know that much!

* * *

When the MacGregor family was settled in their "new" house, and Frank had found an attractive rooming-and-boarding house, Frank took it upon himself to do some serious inquiring around town about Emily. Where to start? He decided to see if the newspaper were still owned and run by Rupert Johnson. Or, would he be too old to do that now? Or, is he dead?

He said to himself, "Stop delaying! Get to it!" And so he went to the newspaper office. A young Oriental-looking man met him at the door. "Good morning, sir. What can I do for you? You're new in town, aren't you?"

Frank nodded.

"Welcome, sir."

"Thank you, young man. Is Mr. Rupert Johnson still the owner of the newspaper?"

"No, sir. He died a few years ago. I am now the owner. I am his grandson, Rupert Rhee Lee."

"Rupert Lee? . . . . I don't understand."

Rupert asked, "Did you know my grandfather, sir?"

"Not exactly. I knew *of* him." Get to the point! Frank scolded himself. "And I knew his daughter, Emily Johnson Hillmont."

"Ah yes, sir. That is my mother."

Wheels spun throughout his head. He was thinking as fast as he could: "If Rupert Johnson were this fellow's grandfather, and Emily his mother, then Emily must be Emily Lee? Do I have that right? He thought. And in the next moment, his hopes fell. He said, still to himself, "Then Emily *did* marry Hue Lee! Good Lord! I've lost her again!"

Aloud, he said, "Thank you so much, Mr. Lee. I am distressed to hear of your grandfather's passing."

"Thank you, sir. Will that be all?"

"For the moment, young man. For the moment."

Frank left the newspaper, heart pounding heavily. "How can I present myself to her? She's married to Hue Lee. But I *must* meet Emily, sometime, somehow. I must!"

* * *

While Jeremy MacGregor was the field man for the Agency, Frank Owen was the detail man, in the office. He spent most of his daily work hours at the office. He dared not day-dream because day-dreaming would cause errors. He was disgusted at himself for spending long periods of time thinking about Emily and how much he wanted to see her again. He needed to devise a plan, any kind of plan that would lead him to her. But what? he asked himself.

Frank and Jeremy's monthly pay vouchers came by mail on the westbound train. Frank went to the bank to cash his voucher. At the conclusion of the transaction, he turned to leave the bank. He approached the door, holding it open for a lady to enter before he exited.

She stopped in mid-step. "Frank Owens? Is that you, Frank?"

He had lowered his eyes while he waited for the lady to enter, but that voice–it shook him to the core! "Emily?" he asked shyly, softly. Then, loudly, he exclaimed, "Emily!"

* * *

My God, how he wanted to sweep her up into his arms! Her beauty had not faded one whit. He was dazzled by the sight of her!

Softly, he said, "Emily, for weeks I have been trying to work out a way to see you again."

"What on earth are you doing in Stoney Ridge, Frank?"

"I have so much to tell you, so much to ask you. Can we go somewhere to talk?"

She stepped inside the bank and said to him, "You can accompany me back to Leesville. As soon as I do my banking errand, I am on my way home."

"I'm sorry, Emily, it would be unseemly of me to ride with a married lady, unchaperoned, as it were."

"But, Frank. I am not married. I am widowed. . . . ."

* * *

Frank's horse was tied to the back of the carriage. Once they passed out of Stoney Ridge, Emily turned the reins over to Frank. They chatted on their way to Leesville. He told her about his employment at the Indian Agency, about his associate, Jeremy MacGregor. She told him about Hue Lee's remarkable life and accomplishments and how he died.

Frank asked, "Emily, do you by any chance remember the last things I said to you before saying goodbye to you in Philadelphia?"

"Every word," she replied.

"I still mean what I said . . . . that I love you and that I'd never forget you."

"Yes, I know."

* * *

The carriage with Frank's horse following had reached the narrow path that led to the mountainside's secret gold-mining site. Frank brought the carriage to a halt. He took off his hat. He put an arm around Emily's shoulders and drew her into his embrace. They held each other comfortably for long moments. Then he found her lips and kissed her sweetly, deliciously.

The kiss and the embrace ended gracefully. Frank put on his hat again and picked up the reins. They smiled at each other as he urged the horse to continue on down the road.

For both of them, it was a new beginning, the turning of a page in each story of their lives. Frank knew in his heart and in his head that after all, he had *not* lost Emily again.

# # #

THE CAMP

It began on December 7, 1941. The Japanese bombed Pearl harbor. An island in the Micronesian Group, Tataya Island, was taken by Japanese Marines on January 27, 1942.

Tataya had a native population of about 800; its foreign population (Australians, New Zealanders, Canadians, Americans, and British subjects) was close to 1,500. Two Japanese cargo ships were used to haul the human cargo, all non-native people of Tataya, to internment camps in the Philippines.

Suffering humiliations, meager rations, and non-existent toilet facilities, approximately 150 internees did not survive--most of them small children, a few elderly persons. Disease was rampant; medical care was absent.

Among the internees on the "transports" were an American, Mr. Anthony M. Newlon, gaunt and very tan; his wife Beatrice, with brown hair, hazel eyes, nice figure after three pregnancies; and two boys, Tony age 6 and Donald age 5. The younger boy did not survive the sea voyage. He became a victim of pneumonia. He was buried at sea.

Mr. Newlon was a construction engineer and had been working on a project for a Canadian construction company: roads, bridges, water-purification plant, sanitation plant, and a power plant. The Japanese took over all these facilities, importing an engineering unit of the Japanese Army to utilize what was already completed and to finish other engineering undertakings.

The Newlon family, father, mother, and one surviving son, were offloaded at a port unknown to them. All they knew was that it was in the Philippines. There, Anthony and his son Tony were separated from the mother. They were marched to a camp for men, and Beatrice, with the other women and small children, was marched to a camp for women.

* * *

There were 275 women (three of the women were each carrying a baby), some teenage girls, and a number of very small children, marching to the women's camp. The distance from the pier was three miles. They all managed to trudge through the gate in a ragged double line. The Japanese prison guards prodded the women, young and old, forward, making sure there were no stragglers nor escapees.

The women were allowed to drop off their paltry possessions in the two barracks buildings, known as Barracks 1 and Barracks 2. Then they were forced to make their way to the parade ground, where they stood in long lines, each line widely spaced from the other.

A Japanese clerk-soldier who could read English--sometimes not knowing what he read--shouted into a microphone, "All persons in lines will bow low when camp commander arrives. He is Colonel Hichio Itara. Memorize name: Hichio Itara! Hichio Itara! All say Hichio Itara! Hichio Itara. Remember bow very low to Colonel Itara!"

The women looked at each other, some shrugging their shoulders, some with raised eyebrows. The children were, thankfully, quiet with awe. The colonel approached the microphone.

"All bow! All bow!" screamed the soldier.

The women complied. Beatrice strained to look at the colonel, barely missing the cue to bow. Then she bowed very low. Colonel Itara spoke much better English than his clerk. He said to the women, without notes, "I will conduct an inspection of the new arrivals. You may now stand erect. Please do not speak to me nor look directly at me. Look straight ahead, only. Maintain silence."

He left the microphone and began his inspection, with the clerk, clipboard in hand, following the Colonel. He strode in front of the first line, pausing only to look at each internee in the face as he passed her. Then he inspected the back of each line, as well as the front. Having the clerk following behind him seemed to be unwanted baggage. The Colonel said nothing about anyone, giving no instructions to the clerk. Until . . .

When he looked at Beatrice Newlon, he stopped. He spoke rapidly and authoritatively to the seemingly afflicted clerk. The clerk wrote something furiously on his clipboard, and then he scrutinized Beatrice for one interminable moment.

It took a long time for the Colonel to finish his inspection. The women and children were hot and tired and hungry--always hungry. At last they were dismissed, the clerk bawling at them, "All go to barracks now! Mark your bunks! Quick, quick! Small children will sleep with Mother in bunk. Quick, quick!"

The Colonel disappeared into a small building that served as his quarters in one section and his office in the other. One soldier named Koshi, short and squat, was the Colonel's steward. He was a private in the Japanese army. He kept the building clean inside, made the Colonel's bed every morning, laundered his uniforms and underwear and socks, polished his boots, cooked his tea and rice for his breakfast and lunch meals. Other breakfast and lunch items for the Colonel were delivered from the officers' kitchen. For the dinner hour, the Colonel usually ate with his officers in their dining room.

Colonel Itara was a man of medium height, very black hair, and equally black eyes. A sensitive mouth with a delicate nose above it, and a sturdy chin and jawline gave him a complicated appearance: the aesthetic with the brutal.

Jiro, a sergeant, was the name of Colonel Itara's clerk. He kept all records of the Japanese military on the post, was supposed to begin keeping records on the newly arrived internees. They were the camp's first "guests." Jiro wore a perpetually worried expression. He was wiry, and, like the Colonel, of medium height.

* * *

Colonel Itara strode into his office and called for Koshi to bring him his lunch. Hichio had a fleeting thought. He had yet to instruct the clerk to direct the women to their own lunch, such as it was. He printed on a letter-sized paper the instructions in English.

The colonel was concerned, but not worried, yet, about how he was to feed 275 Anglo women and children on the skimpy rations that the higher echelon of the Japanese army had meted out to him for the internees. His staff and non-coms would fare much better.

It was a bitter pill, though, for the Colonel, and the staff and non-coms, to be assigned to this god-forsaken place in the Philippines, guarding......women and their offspring! Outrageous! None of them, from colonel all the way down to the lowest private, liked being stuck out in the boonies, babysitting 275 women and squalling youngsters. It was insulting! Degrading.

He gave Jiro the mess-hall instructions. His lunch was served. He ate it. He sipped his tea. He waited.

* * *

Jiro entered each of the two barracks buildings. The voice noises were disagreeable to his ears. He blew a whistle to bring them to silence. The women flinched. They gazed at him diffidently. When the big room became silent, he announced, reading from the clipboard, "All women go to eat! Follow me!" He led the way for all the women of both barracks to their mess hall. He stationed himself at the door, watching each woman, some with child or children, and some without, some young, and some old.

After ten minutes of eating their rice and a banana, Jiro blew his whistle again. Then he shouted, "All go back to barracks! Quick!

Quick!"

They filed out silently, Jiro searching their faces again. He put his arm in front of Beatrice as she started to pass through the doorway. She stopped. She had an inkling of what was going to happen next but said nothing.

Jiro spoke to her gruffly, still reading from his clipboard, "You! Come to Colonel Itara's office. You follow. You bow very low to Colonel when you see him!"

She nodded. She followed him to the Colonel's office.

She entered first, not because Jiro was being polite, but because he was a guard. He needed to ensure her arrival, always to be alert against an escape.

Beatrice was temporarily blinded by having walked in the bright sunlight and entering what seemed to be a darkened room. There he was, Colonel Hichio Itara, seated at a desk directly in front of her, his back to the far wall, a window behind him.

The clerk entered, saluted stiffly, then took his place at his desk at the left side of the room. A second, unoccupied desk was across the room from his.

She bowed. Very low. The Colonel stood, speaking softly, "Mrs. Newlon, please stand upright. You do remember me, yes?"

Standing erect, she said, "Yes, I remember you, Colonel Itara, very well. But you were a university graduate student when my husband and I last saw you, in Tokyo. We had engaged you to be our tour guide of Tokyo and environs during one weekend. I congratulate you on achieving the rank of colonel at such a young age!"

He quirked a tiny smile. "Please, Mrs. Newlon, sit." He pointed to the one straight chair facing his desk at an oblique angle. She approached the chair and sat on it, stiffly. He sat behind his desk again.

He said, "I have the rank of colonel not because of long years of military service. It is only because I had so much education. I am an accountant, equivalent to a CPA in your country. The Army, in its infinite wisdom, made me an instant colonel!"

She nodded. He continued. "With my accounting background, the Army could give me no real command in the field. That, I presume, is why I am assigned to this women's internment camp." He indulged in a small moment of self-pity. A women's camp! It was hard for him to swallow that! He proceeded.

"I, too, remember you very well, Mrs. Newlon. And how are your husband and the two boys?"

"My husband and Tony were marched away from the pier in a

different direction from where we women and small children were marched. I haven't seen them since."

"Yes. That would be to the men's camp, not far from here. And the other boy, Donald?"

Bea swallowed hard. The tears brimmed in her eyes. The Colonel noticed it all. "Mrs. Newlon, is something wrong?"

She told him the circumstances under which little Donny died and was tossed into the sea. He folded his hands on the desk in front of him. He was silent for an eternity, it seemed to Beatrice. Finally, he said, "Mrs. Newlon. I cannot tell you how very sorry I am to hear that."

"Thank you," she croaked.

He gave her some time to recover from her renewed grief before he spoke again. "I promise you this, Mrs. Newlon. I will make inquiries at the men's camp and try to find out if Mr. Newlon and Tony are all right."

"Oh, Hichi.....I mean Colonel Itara......I would be so grateful for news of them. After losing Donny, I'm worried sick that some other disaster could happen to either or both of them!"

"Do not worry, Mrs. Newlon. I will find out everything possible."

Now it was her turn to eke out a smile of sorts.

The Colonel cleared his throat. "Well, there is one more thing I wish to discuss with you, Mrs. Newlon. I sense that it was you who typed the letters from Mr. Newlon and you, which were mailed to me from America and from Tataya Island. Is that correct?"

"Yes. But what has that to do with anything?"

"Oh, a great deal! My clerk, you see, can read English and pronounce it, but he cannot understand it. And, he does not know how to use the typewriter at the other desk." He nodded toward the unoccupied desk.

"So?" She didn't have a clue what he was leading up to.

"So," he continued, "I need your help. I ask you, as a friend, to assist me by typing all the records and memos and letters in English that I will need from time to time. There are 275 women and children in the camp today. That's a lot of record keeping. Can I count on you to work here for me, every day?"

She was too stunned to answer.

He filled in the silence with, "You would, of course, be exempt from the ordinary labor to be done in the rice fields every day. Hard work. Backbreaking. Tedious! All under guard."

"I'm really sorry, Colonel, because I would feel guilty doing the easy work here in your office while my barracks mates are toiling in the rice fields."

"Bea." He stopped. "I'm sorry. That's what your husband calls you, isn't it?"

She nodded and said, "Yes, but my friends call me 'Bea' as well."

"Bea," he said, almost under his breath. "I'm begging you to do this. For me. Please."

She continued to look at him, saying nothing, thinking.

He tried another ploy. "And, you know that through you, I can arrange certain amenities for the other women and their little ones --three babies and numerous toddlers, I noticed at the inspection. All you have to do is put it into my ear what they need, and if it is in my power, I will get what they need, allow what they want. Within reason, of course."

She smiled again. "Your offer is attractive, Hichio." She looked down at her hands. "I'm sorry. I really should always address you as Colonel Itara. I'm sorry I took that liberty..."

"It's all right. Let us put it this way. You may call me by my first name, and I may call you by your first name whenever we are in the office alone."

"Agreed, Colonel Itara." She looked covertly toward Jiro.

"Excellent, Mrs. Newlon."

Jiro interrupted with words to the Colonel, in Japanese, of course, and the Colonel answered him. Jiro left the office.

"And so, do you agree to do what I have asked?" he said.

"Agreed, Hichio."

"Excellent, Bea."

* * *

When the women had made their new surroundings as comfortable as possible, most of them flopped onto the bare wooden bunks and rested.

Beatrice's bunk was next to a woman with two toddlers. She offered to sleep with the older one in her bunk, remembering the strange instruction that all small children will sleep with their mothers in her own bunk.

Bea's bunk neighbor was Susan Lancer. She looked at the world under long ash-blond bangs. But her hair was short. She was tall for a woman, but not robust. Her husband, an Englishman, had been a tea plantation owner on Tataya. When the Japanese arrived, Andrew Lancer resisted his arrest; he was shot immediately. Susan had to leave her husband's body there as they took her and the two children away in a truck.

Susan's older child was 4 years old. His name was Arthur. The younger was Bennie, for Benjamin, age 3.

She ventured a question to Bea. "What went on when the soldier escorted you away? Are you all right?"

"Oh, yes," Bea answered. "I'm fine. I was taken to the Colonel's office and asked to do all the record-keeping of the internees and to type letters and memos in English, as the Colonel needs them."

"What on earth will the rest of us have to do?"

"Work in the rice fields. However, I don't know what you'll be doing between the end of a harvest season and the next planting season."

Susan almost made a crack about Bea's getting a favored job but decided against it, in view of the fact that Bea had offered to share her bunk with little Arthur.

The thought was not wasted. Beatrice guessed what Susan must be thinking. She said to her, "I can only imagine what you're thinking, Susan. And you're right, it *is* favoritism. I can't help that. My husband and I met the Colonel, when he was a university graduate student in Tokyo three years ago. The Colonel wishes to extend some sort of courtesy because of the friendship. He is not the enemy, Susan. He is a friend."

Susan shot back, "He may be *your* friend, but his army killed my husband. He is *my* enemy!" As soon as she said it, she regretted what she said. "I'm sorry, Bea, but I can't help thinking this way."

"I know, Susan. I understand. It's okay to feel what you feel."

* * *

The days began to run into each other. It was December 1942. The women, with babies in arms and toddlers hanging onto their dress skirts, all went to the fields to work all day, every day, taking only one break for a so-called lunch. It was rice three times a day, with a banana or mango or papaya. Rice was cooked in huge pots at the camp, then hauled to the rice fields for the women and their children. By noon, it was warm rice, maybe. Not hot rice. Water was the only liquid for the internees to drink.

Life was not easy. It was a drudge.

Bea fared better, by far. Colonel Itara was surreptitiously solicitous of her needs and continuously asking if the other inmates had any requirements. She occasionally mentioned a medication, and always inquired about bed sheets and mattresses because neither was furnished. Since there were no mattresses, they had to spread a thin wool blanket onto each bare bunk bed.

Sheets were out, the Colonel announced, after looking into the matter; mattresses, a maybe. "This is not the Waldorf," he said, hoping to inject some humor into the situation. It didn't work.

"Isn't there *anything* else I can do for you and your compatriots?"

Stealing a look at Jiro's empty desk, she said, "Well, yes, there is, Hichio. A week from today is the Christian world's Christmas holiday."

"And," he said, "what is it you want from me?"

"Only permission for us to be able to make ornaments and decorations for a make-shift Christmas tree in the barracks."

"Make-shift," he said half aloud. "Explain, please?"

She answered, "Make-shift means to use one thing instead of something else; create or fabricate something out of something else; make-do; make-shift."

"Ah so. And what would you use for a tree?" he asked.

"There are bushes along the road to the rice fields. One or two of the women, who have no baby nor child, could wrest a couple of bushes from the ground on their way back to camp—one for each of the two barracks buildings."

He thought about it, frowning. "Make certain the bushes are not on someone's personal property. Make sure it's in the countryside."

"They can do that, Colonel."

"Then, you have my permission."

She managed to smile at him. "And thank you, Hichio. May we also gather up your waste paper for making some of the decorations?"

"Upon my soul! Yes, of course!"

* * *

By summer of 1943, the war was still raging. That much Beatrice learned from Colonel Itara. And she passed each tidbit on to the barracks population. She could not discern, however, who had the upper hand in the conflagration. She surmised that the situation was pretty close to being even.

But there were signs to the contrary. The Colonel made a passing remark one day about not having enough protein in the internees' diet. Bea wondered if that meant Japanese shipping were suffering some adversities, thus affecting cargoes coming onto the island.

However, the women, one day, upon returning from the field, reported an amazing incident to Bea. Susan was the spokeswoman for everyone else.

She said to Bea, "You won't believe what we had for lunch today!

Beef! Looked like and tasted like roast beef. It was all cut up into big bite sizes. Even Colonel Itara was present. We got the feeling he was guarding the guards, to keep them from taking the beef for themselves."

Beatrice pondered about it. She knew that the Colonel had had beef for lunch and had even slipped some of it onto her plate of rice when she wasn't looking.

The next day, Bea approached Hichio with the subject of the beef. Jiro was in the office, so she said to the Colonel, "Colonel, the women told me yesterday about how you and the guards brought them large portions of roast beef. And I remembered also seeing some on my plate here in the office. What's that all about? It's so unusual."

"Oh, yes, it is. As I've said before, I'm worried about the lack of protein in your daily meals. So, when we got this strange and large shipment of beef, and since we have very small refrigeration facilities, I decided to have all of it cooked in one morning so that officers and men would have their share, and the rest of it could go to the fields."

She said, "That was most generous of you, Colonel. I must tell you how pleased the women were with such a precious treat."

"Precious," he said half to himself. "Explain, please?"

"Precious is something rare...and superior," she replied.

"Ah-h-h so!"

* * *

The Colonel instituted a new routine to break up the old routine for the internees. He had scouted the area all around the camp and found a natural waterfall with a medium-sized pool of water at the foot. Water from the pool then ran off into a stream through the jungle and out to sea.

He did some calculating. With 275 women and children, he could take them to the pool in groups of approximately 34, a truckfull. That would mean that each group could go to the waterfall once every 8 weeks.

The first group was trucked to the jungle waterfall site. The pool was surrounded with fairly smooth rock formations. The women could splash in the pool with the children, then sit or lie in the sun on the rocks to dry off.

Each group was well guarded. The captain of the guards maintained a very strict discipline among them because the women, it turned out, were bathing in their underwear! Who would have packed bathing suits during the short times they had before being forced by the Japanese to leave the island?

When it was Bea's turn to be in a waterfall group, the Colonel announced to Jiro that he would be in charge of the office during the Colonel's absence--camp business at the port headquarters.

Hichio did, indeed, go to port headquarters on some trumped-up business, driving his own military vehicle. Then stealthily went to the waterfall site, bumping and weaving through the jungle, on a route different from the truck's. He stationed himself well away from the guards and the women, at a higher level. He removed his field glasses, adjusted them to his eyes and found her.

After staring at her for a solid ten minutes, he put away his field glasses, took one more look at the scene below. He decided that Beatrice Newlon was a lovely sight to behold. "What a shame that I am the enemy," he said half aloud.

Something caught his eye, however. While the Captain of the guards was sitting in the truck, waiting, a guard made an obscene gesture toward one of the women.

A sudden, loud gunshot filled the air. Everyone stopped whatever he or she was doing and looked around, wondering where the threatening sound came from.

Hichio put away his weapon. He returned to camp.

The incident was never reported; it was never repeated.

* * *

One morning, after the women had been transported to the fields, Bea heard two trucks pull up at their barracks buildings. She went to the front door of the Colonel's office to see what was going on. In amazement, she watched four Japanese non-coms unload stacks of . . . mattresses? Mattresses!

She turned to Hichio and said, "Colonel Itara, they're unloading mattresses outside the women's barracks!"

"They are?" He left his chair and raced to the door to look with her. Instantly, he turned to Jiro and rattled off rapid and forceful-sounding Japanese to him.

Jiro sprang from his desk chair like a man demonized and ran to the four men unloading the mattresses. After much gesturing and shouting at them, the four men began to haul the mattresses to the inside.

Bea turned to the Colonel. "What's going on, Hichio?"

"I sent instructions to the loaders to take the mattresses inside and put one on each bunk!" He snorted. "Leaving them on the outside. Were they born in a barn?"

Bea began laughing. "Oh, Hichio, I never thought I'd hear *you* say an expression like that!"

He grinned. "I had a roommate at Berkeley who was straight from a farm in Nebraska."

"That explains everything!" Still beaming, she said, "Hichio, this is so grand, getting the mattresses. I can't thank you enough for the effort. I feel it was not easy."

"Don't thank me too soon," he replied. "They're hardly real mattresses--thin pads, actually, stuffed with some kind of grain chaff. Not the Waldorf!"

This time the attempt to be humorous worked. They laughed together. She said, "We don't care what they're stuffed with--they'll be better than the bare bunks!"

They returned to their desks in good spirits. Bea gradually turned thoughtful. She felt that Hichio must have had to move heaven and earth to find anything *resembling* a mattress. Somehow, she thought, she must spread the feeling among the other women that these pads are truly a bonanza--all Colonel Itara's doing. She resolved to do that.

Then she recalled that she must also mention the Christmas permission and the trek to the pool every six or eight weeks. All in all, she thought, there was much to be thankful for, under the circumstances. Yes, every woman must realize all that.

* * *

The Colonel received a phone call one morning in late 1943. He seemed disturbed. He put down the phone and looked at Beatrice. She was aware of his eyes upon her. She stopped filing the cards and looked up.

Hichio had a well-defined frown across his brow.

"Something wrong, Colonel?"

"Yes. I've just been issued a very strange and worrisome order. The Commanding Officer of the men's camp, a colonel who outranks me by date of rank, demanded that I send to his camp's Officers Club by truck 25 women--unattached young women, with no children. It will be an entertainment. I'm afraid to think how this will play out. But you will be one of the 25."

It made her skin crawl. How could he do this to her? If he had any regard for her--and she long ago suspected he did--then why would he send her to the men's camp on what appears to be a mission of some suspicious enterprise? She was speechless.

He read her face. "Do not be dismayed and do not be frightened.

359

I will see to your safety. Just make yourself presentable. Do you have a best dress?"

By now she was appalled.

She did have a best dress. She took off her shift (no slip) and her thong sandals. After a spit bath, she put on the "best" dress and slipped into the only pair of shoes she had, shoes she had worn when they left Tataya. She lined up at the truck with the other 24 selected women. Colonel Itara had specified, for the selection, that no young girls, teenagers, would be chosen--only women aged from 25 to 45. He hoped that most, if not all, in such a group would have been experienced women.

There were mixed feelings among the chosen women. Most of them suspected what was in store for them, and they faced it stoically. A few who were naive were simply petrified.

At the Officers Club in the men's camp, a group of Japanese officers waited. When the women entered the club, the officers began to mingle with them.

Suddenly, Bea felt a presence near her. She didn't see him approach. A voice from behind her said, "Do not register any surprise. Just turn to face me, and smile, please."

It was Hichio Itara, resplendent in dress uniform. He was smiling grandly; she, in good faith, could manage only a weak smile. His uniform was impressive. Taking her by the elbow, Hichio escorted her to a table in a secluded corner. They sat down, next to each other, not across from one another. He spoke once more. "Relax, Mrs. Newlon. You will not be subjected to whatever happens to the other women. Some of them will come out of it unscathed. Others . . ."

He didn't have to finish. By now Bea had the full picture. She lowered her head.

"No, no, my dear," he spoke gently. "We both have to look as though we're having a fantastic time!"

"I don't want to believe what will be going on!"

"This is the only way I could think of to protect at least one of the women of the 25 from our camp. You."

She swallowed hard, understanding the significance.

"Shall we dance, my dear?" he asked.

Slowly they worked their way around the dance floor. She was taken back in time, to the first time she had danced with Hichio. It was a nightclub with a Latin ambience: Latin music, Latin dancing, Latin costumes. Latin food. She remembered that for the first few moments of their first dance, a rhumba, back in Tokyo, he was

360

nervous, never having danced with an American woman before--not with any western woman. And now, it was she who was nervous.

Gradually, she lost her stiffness, her body becoming more lithe, more attuned to his body's moving slowly, slowly, sensuously. She took a deep breath and asked herself, "What is going on here?"

The dance band played three more numbers, all American tunes, then took a break. Hichio and Bea sat once more. Drinks had been left at their table. She didn't want any part of it.

Neither did he. He knew he had to keep his wits about him, to protect her . . . and to protect himself.

* * *

The next morning, back in Colonel Itara's office, Hichio reported to her that he had made another inquiry, the day before, about Mr. Newlon and little Tony. He saw for himself that they were all right. Mr. Newlon had made friends with one man, Sam Jeffreys, who had lost his wife during the ships' journey to the Philippines. And he had no children.

"The friend has taken to Tony, watching out for him along with Anthony. Tony looks at the friend as though he were an uncle. The two men scrimp food from their rations to give extra food to Tony. "He's a growing boy, after all," they reasoned.

"Oh, Colonel, I'm so grateful for all the news you bring me. I'm mystified, though."

"About what?" he asked.

"Why is it you didn't tell me all this last night?"

"I didn't want any of the officers, who might understand English, to overhear."

"Of course," she said. "I never realized." She was thoughtful about another matter. "The women coming back in the truck last night were awfully quiet. I hope nothing disastrous happened to any one of them."

"On that, I cannot report. Because I have no knowledge. We can hope only for the best, and time will tell. I regret the whole evening's tawdry ramifications, except for one thing."

"And that is?" she asked.

"And that is, I have no regrets that we were able to talk cheerfully and . . . to dance together. I was half afraid one of the officers would press for a dance with you. I had a speech made up, if I had to."

"I don't dare ask."

"Just as well. However, if Colonel Kajimoto, the camp CO, had asked to dance with you, I don't know what I would have done, his outranking me. I would have been obliged to agree to his request. I would have been outraged, at first. Devastated. And I would have been apprehensive, hoping against all hope that you would not be invited to . . . " He couldn't go on.

"Thankfully," she thought, "the other Colonel did not ask me to dance." A small shudder ran up and down her back. She began to look at Hichio with a different set of eyes.

* * *

The Colonel did a survey of his 275 inmates and found one nurse and two nurse's aides. He established a modest clinic in one of the camp buildings, a small one. The nurse was Clara (named after Clara Barton, she claimed) McBride. She established a working schedule and assigned duties for all three of them.

An occasional bad scratch, a skinned knee, and some allergies dogged the children. Those were fairly easy to treat. The women's problems were more complicated.

Clara had to report to the Colonel each problem that she could not handle. He, in turn, contacted the one Japanese army doctor for both the women's and men's camps. The doctor chose to maintain his infirmary and office at the men's camp. But he did come to the women's camp upon the occasions that Clara deemed absolutely necessary.

* * *

The same survey produced two school teachers: Miss Lavinnia Stockwell, a tall and stalwart woman, in her 40s, able to exact strict obedience from her elementary-school students (when she was actively teaching, before the internment); and Mrs. Rose Lesh, as delicate as her first name, honey blond and blue-eyed, still childless at 28. Her husband was an internee at the men's camp. She had been a junior high school teacher.

Hichio interviewed them separately, then together. He assigned Lavinnia to teach the five- and six-year-old boys and girls as well as the girls through age 12. When a boy reached his seventh year, he was transferred to the men's camp. Rose was assigned to teach all girls from ages 13 through 19, primarily math and English.

When Bea learned that boys could stay with their mothers until age seven, she remembered that Tony was only six when he had to go with his dad to the men's camp. Probably, she thought, because he was as tall as a seven-year-old boy. Probably, she thought further, the records were inadequate; perhaps even nonexistent. Their leaving the island was on such short notice.

She had an idea, from all this thinking about seven-year-olds and a six-year-old looking like a seven-year-old. All confusing. All confusion. The idea took shape. Bea decided to do some creative book-keeping in the records of all the six-year-old boys' of the women's camp.

Searching out the six-year-old boys in her records, she surreptitiously altered their birth dates to make them one year younger. That resulted in postponing their being transferred to the men's camp by one year. Who's to notice this crop of "seven-year-olds" looking taller than usual? Some of them, yes; the others, no.

Again, working furtively, she had to make a list of those boys with altered birth years. And after she consulted each mother about the changes, secretly, she destroyed the list. She had a few days–and nights–wondering what made her cheat like that. She herself had lost one boy in the system that was inadequate. So why not take advantage of such a system and make it possible for a group of boys to stay with their mothers an extra year? Then she promptly forgot all about it.

Once the school classes were established, all the school-age children were exempt from working in the fields. School was in session six days a week. Lavinnia taught her group in Barracks 2; Rose taught her group in Barracks 1.

On a regular visit to the men's camp, Colonel Itara visited the supply officer. The visit yielded a virtual goldmine for Colonel Itara. He found that the men's camp had no school for the boys interned there but that the supply officer had stacks of pencils, rotting away in their boxes. Itara pleaded for them . . . and got them. The supply officer was glad to get rid of them. They had cluttered up his storage space.

Hichio also arranged for all uncrumpled waste paper from the men's camp to be picked up by him each week. His two schools in the women's camp would use that paper, along with the paper generated by his own office, for doing their school assignments on any page that was blank on the back.

Bea noted these two more projects, the clinic and the "school" that Hichio had initiated. She vowed to use the next opportunity to mention these to the other women--make them think--maybe make them appreciate. She sincerely hoped they would be appreciative.

* * *

In the month following the party at the Officer's Club in the men's camp, Hichio made his routine weekly trip there to check on the well-being of Anthony and Tony. He listened to the Provost Marshal's story. He listened with clamped jaws. He had to take time to believe what he was hearing. He made other inquiries about Tony--who was looking after him? Sam Jeffreys, he was told. He then requested that he be permitted to speak to Jeffreys in the boy's presence. He was allowed to do that.

Having seen for himself that Jeffreys was indeed caring for the boy, he left the men's camp. He raced in his beat-up vehicle back to the women's camp, cursing aloud and beating his hand on the steering wheel. He tried to calm himself before going into his office.

He saw her there, typing and typing and typing. He sat at his desk, waiting for her to finish. He barked an instruction to Jiro who immediately left the office on some bogus errand that Hichio had dreamed up.

He stood up. Slowly he walked to Bea's desk. He brought his visitor's chair with him. He placed it next to her at the typewriter. He sat down. Her hands had left the keyboard and rested on her lap. He took her right hand in his. He began.

"Beatrice, my dear one, I do not know how to tell you this."

She stiffened, sensing something foreboding, by the way he was regarding her. "Hichio, what is it? Something's dreadfully wrong. I feel it."

"That is correct, my dear. Something horrendous. Beatrice, your husband Anthony is dead. It was an accident. The CO of his camp had singled him out to do construction work. Anthony fell off a scaffolding made of bamboo. The bamboo was strong enough, but the vine lashings at the 90-degree joints disintegrated. He hit his head on a pile of rocks. He died instantly. I'm so sorry, Bea. First, you lost a son and now your husband. This is a terrible thing to bear."

She looked across the room, disbelief covering her whole being. He released her hand. put his arm around her shoulders. She began to tremble that turned into uncontrollable shaking. He put his other arm around her. She wept quietly. The shaking would not stop. He held her more closely.

Finally, it all stopped, suddenly. She registered grief as she faced him. He dropped his arms to his sides. "What about Tony?" she wailed. "What's going to become of him?"

"Do not worry, Bea. I have an idea for what to do for him. The Provost Marshal told me, when I arrived in the camp, that Tony is being looked after by your husband's friend, Sam Jeffreys. I'm working on a plan. A plan I cannot reveal to you because of the secrecy involved. Take off the rest of the day, Bea. The work can wait."

"I know that, Hichio, but it's just not right to the other women, my wandering around in the barracks, while the children's classes are in session, and while the rest of the women are sweating in the fields. I just can't do that."

"Yes, you can. Because I say you can. Go. Come back tomorrow. Meanwhile, I have things to do. Go!"

* * *

A monumental idea began to take shape in his head. During a normal work day, in the morning, he asked Bea an off-the-wall question: "Mrs. Newlon, I was thinking, if you were ever to be repatriated from here--no matter who wins or who loses this war--where would you request to go? Back to your island, Tataya?"

"Oh, no, Colonel. There's nothing left on that island for me to return to. Our house was torched as the truck pulled away. Anthony, a civil engineer, would normally finish a project, and then we'd move to the site of the next project. No one place has been a permanent home. And now, with Anthony gone . . . "

"So," he said, slowly and quietly, "where would you go? To America?"

An answer came to her quickly. She said, "Yes. To my aunt's house in San Francisco. My parents are gone; they were killed in a car accident just before we went to Tataya."

"And, what is your aunt's name, Mrs. Newlon?"

There was a distinct pause in her response while she wondered why he was asking *that* question. Then, she said, "Mrs. Rita Dutton. She's widowed. Lives in a big house, rattling around in it all by herself. She never had any children." To herself, she said, "I gave him a lot more information than he asked for. Why did I do that?"

It didn't matter. Hichio questioned her no further. He turned back to his work. She turned back to hers.

That night, from his bed, Hichio listened to the quietness of a camp gone to sleep, except for the guards on duty. Koshi and Jiro slept in the enlisted men's barracks. He was alone in his building. He got out of bed and went into the office. He debated over the ethics of what he was about to do. Setting aside that quandary, he went to Bea's desk, opened drawers, probed, and found what he was looking for. A small Red Cross packet of letters rested in the bottom of the lower right drawer.

The Colonel pulled out the packet, sorted through the letters, and came across a certain envelope: an envelope with a return address for Rita Dutton of San Francisco. He wrote it on a scrap of paper, not trusting himself to remember it accurately. He made his way back to bed, crossed his hands behind his head, and planned the next step. Having ironed out that in his mind, he was free to fall asleep.

The next morning, Hichio drove himself again to the men's camp and paid a visit to the commanding officer, Colonel Kajimoto. Although Itara really wanted to check on Sam Jeffreys and the half-orphaned boy Tony, he covered up his real intent by asking Kajimoto if he could "inspect" the men's camp for ideas on how to conduct the operation of the women's camp. Greasing the CO's ego, Itara then complimented Kajimoto on his smoothly running camp.

"By all means, Colonel Itara," Kajimoto said grandly, pleased with the praise. "I am delighted that you find my camp an example for yours."

Hichio wandered among a group of men involved with painting a building. He saw the Jeffreys fellow. Tony was nearby, playing a game of "Kick the Can" with other boys.

Hichio said to Jeffreys, "Do not stop painting. Do not look at me. Just listen." He introduced himself to Sam, covertly, explaining in part why he was here. He asked, "How would you like to return to the States?"

"What! Are you kidding me?"

"No, Mr. Jeffreys. Not at all." Sam kept on painting.

A Japanese guard approached, and the Colonel pretended to watch the others who were doing the painting chore. When the guard passed the Colonel and Jeffreys, Hichio continued, "I'm working on a plan that will entail a bit of cloak-and-dagger on your part, with the boy Tony."

"Well, I don't know what you have in mind, but I'm game. What's the plan?" Brush, brush.

"Can't give you details because I haven't worked them out yet. It's only an idea, so far."

"Just keep me advised, Colonel. I'm ready for anything!"

"Good."

Colonel Itara, stealing another glance at Tony, departed. The painting continued without interruption. Jeffreys' chore for the day took on a spark of enthusiasm.

* * *

That night, Colonel Itara entered his own communications hut, now buttoned down for the night, the radio operator sound asleep in his bunk in the next room. Normally, the communications hut would be manned 24 hours a day, but restraints had been imposed upon the number of personnel allowed for the camp. There was only one radio operator; there should have been at least three, preferably four.

The Colonel furtively turned on the gear, sat in front of the radio equipment, and sent in Morse code and in English, a complex message to sea. Three hours later, a U.S. submarine in nearby waters contacted him. He requested the ship's captain to present himself to the radio room.

While Hichio waited for the sub to re-establish contact with him, he listened to the light snoring of his radioman. Then the message came to inform him that the sub's captain was present.

Hichio outlined a simple plan. The captain agreed, eager to help a couple of escapees, but he was also wary. Would this be a trap? The captain asked, through his radioman's using code, for Colonel Itara to send him a sign to allay his fears.

The Colonel gave it some thought, then sent the following message back: "America America God shed his grace on thee."

After considering the strange response, wondering how a Japanese army colonel would know those lyrics to America the Beautiful, he assumed that the Japanese colonel may have grown up in the States, or had spent some time there. The Captain accepted the message and decided the sender to be valid. Then he ordered the Colonel to stand by until two nights later, at 0100, and he would give the Colonel his coordinates and method of communicating from the sub to shore.

Meanwhile, a Japanese radioman at an outpost on the island began to copy the messages he heard in Morse code. It made no sense whatsoever. He tried to trace the sender's location, but the connection was broken. "Well," he said aloud, alone in the communications room, "I'll ask my supervisor about it tomorrow." The supervisor was as baffled as the radioman. Neither of them knew how to read nor speak English. Neither of them even recognized the message to be in English. Sheer gibberish, they thought. It became a forgotten incident, not being carried to a higher echelon.

* * *

Hichio had only 48 hours to put together the rest of the plan from his end. He needed to visit Sam Jeffreys again.

Continuing his "inspection" of the men's camp, with Colonel Kajimoto's eager consent, Hichio found Jeffreys, with a small crew of inmates, pulling weeds at the base of the camp's perimeter fence.

Acting furtively again, Hichio outlined how he would assist Sam and Tony to escape the camp. It was fortuitous that Sam was at the fence, doing his weeding. That very spot was established to be the Colonel's meeting place with Sam and Tony. The place to meet that night lined up perfectly with an unmanned tower near the camp's one gate, easy to find in the dark.

That night, Hichio, in fatigues with no insignia, slipped out of the women's camp, unnoticed. He was carrying in his hand a heavy-duty wire cutter and there was a powerful flashlight attached to his belt. He walked into the jungle for a short distance, turned left and walked a few miles farther, until he arrived at the back side of the men's camp.

Hichio waited at the spot where he told Jeffreys he would be. Waiting for the next patrol to pass and continue on its rounds, and waiting for the searchlight to complete its next sweep, he pressed his body against the fence with a force loud enough to be heard a few yards away. Then he lay down on the ground, next to the fence. Soon afterwards, Sam Jeffreys, with Tony by the hand, arrived. They lay on their bellies while Hichio cut enough wire of the fence, at ground level, for them to wiggle through. Together, the two men placed wisps of weeds at the site of the wire fence where Hichio had cut.

Then the two men and boy walked three miles through the jungle, away from the men's camp, to the beach. Upon their arrival, they watched in both directions for a roving beach patrol. They had to dive into the jungle only once during Hichio's search for his marked location. Finding it later, he removed vines and leaves that had covered a rubber life raft.

The life raft was another device of ingenuity "engineered" by the Colonel. He filched it from a nearby Filipino quay.

They waited for another beach patrol, and after it, too, passed by them, Hichio, signaled toward the sea with the powerful flashlight. He waited, holding his breath. After agonizing seconds had passed, there it was: a pale blinking signal from the ocean, blink, a long pause, blink, a long pause, blink .

It was a beacon for Sam to follow while he oared the raft toward the light, with Tony as his passenger. As soon as Hichio signaled for the flashing to stop, he and Sam dragged the raft onto the beach down to the water's edge. Another flashlight signal by Hichio to the sub, and the sub began the blinks again.

Last-minute instructions, and a scrap of paper were passed from Hichio to Sam before he and the boy shoved off.

Hichio, with a bush twig, brushed away the tracks of the raft and feet. Then he hid at the edge of the jungle again, remaining still as a statue, never taking his eyes off the flashing light. When it stopped, he breathed easily. It was a sure sign that the man and boy had arrived and by now were safely aboard the sub. Just in time; another patrol appeared from farther up the beach.

Colonel Itara heaved a great sigh of relief. The approaching patrol would not have been in position to see the sub's blinking light. So far, the escape had come off splendidly.

Back in the women's camp, he left his fatigues on the floor, falling onto his bed and sleeping soundly for the first time in three days.

Koshi, rising later that morning, and arriving at the Colonel's quarters, looked at the sweaty fatigues on the floor, wondering what in the world his Colonel had done the night before. He picked up the fatigues, washed them with everything else, and rejected the matter entirely.

* * *

Bea noticed the Colonel was looking a bit haggard the last few days. He did not drink alcohol, at least not when they met him in Tokyo. Nor did he drink alcohol at the Officers' Club in the men's camp. So possibly it was not a hangover. Whatever it was, he looked as though he hadn't slept for a week.

Should she ask him, she wondered?

Finally, after giving the situation much thought, she said, "Colonel, are you feeling all right?"

"Of course! Never felt better!"

She let it drop.

* * *

Hichio needed to pretend to inquire about Sam and Tony, for Beatrice's benefit. Also, Hichio needed to appear at the men's camp --to make a one-time phony inquiry about Sam's and Tony's welfare. On Hichio's next visit, the Provost Marshal reported to him that Jeffreys and the boy had disappeared off the face of the earth. If they had escaped, he said, no trace of them has been found.

"But rest assured, Colonel Itara," the Provost Marshal said, "We will find them. And we will punish them severely."

Hichio nodded approvingly.

Then he was faced with the problem of *not* coming to the men's camp each week to check on the now-absent Sam and Tony. He needed an excuse just to go to the men's camp to satisfy his legitimate need to make a pretended report to Bea each week. The escape, executed so perfectly, was beginning to produce all kinds of complications for Itara--entanglements--and lies. He would worry it through, somehow.

As it turned out, Colonel Kajimoto had, a few weeks before the escape, invited Hichio to join him in an occasional chess game. Hichio jumped at that opportunity by eventually accepting the friendly invitation. The games began, weekly.

The reports about Tony continued. Hichio was noncommittal in telling Beatrice that the boy was okay. Only basic information was forthcoming.

Six weeks after the escape by submarine, Bea received an anonymous hand-printed page in an envelope addressed to her. In capital letters, the message said,:

"MRS. NEWLON, PLEASE GIVE THIS MESSAGE TO COLONEL ITARA.

M.A."

"What on earth?" she asked, after reading it. "Colonel," she said to Hichio. "This came in an envelope addressed to me, but look at this cryptic message. It's for you."

The Colonel looked up from his tedious paper work. Neither perplexed, nor surprised, but tense inside his gut, he took the message that she handed him while he sat at his desk.

He read the message. It took enormous effort on his part not to show any emotion whatsoever. "Maybe some kind of prank. I'll look into it. Thank you, Mrs. Newlon." He set it aside, treating it carelessly.

* * *

The next week Hichio made his usual trek to the men's camp to play chess with Colonel Kajimoto. Upon his return, he said to Bea, "Mrs. Newlon, your son Tony is doing very well, indeed. Skinny, of course. But he's doing well."

"Oh, Colonel, thank you so much for your going to the trouble regularly, to see about him."

"My pleasure, Mrs. Newlon."

She wondered why he seemed so jubilant these days. Was there news of Japan's having an edge in the war?

* * *

Three months after the two schools began, Colonel Itara was able to view his efforts, and the teachers' efforts, with great pleasure. The children were learning! He enjoyed a smug bit of satisfaction from that reality. That was one thing he could crow about, and he did so when talking to Beatrice. He was immensely proud of the children's learning and the teachers' endeavors.

* * *

Another Christmas came and went. Once more the purloined roadside bushes served to be the decorated Christmas trees. Then 1944 arrived. Early into the year, it was Bea's turn to do another pool outing. The women and their children were hauled off in a truck. The Colonel disappeared in his vehicle. He made his way through the jungle by a route different from the truck's route, as usual. And, as usual, he watched only Bea with his field glasses. And, as always, he marveled at how good she looked, skin and bones aside. She was still a stunning woman, with her brown hair and hazel eyes. Eyes that made him melt, when they looked at him.

He thought about the two women who were impregnated on the night of the party at the men's camp Officer's Club. One, a woman 42 years old, had lost her baby at 8 weeks. The other, age 31, was still carrying hers.

Good Lord, he thought, what am I going to do with another mouth to feed--and no milk for the mother, either!

He gazed at Bea again, now drying off on the rock formation in her underwear. He put the field glasses into the case. He stole one more look at Bea without the glasses. Didn't matter to him. She still looked ravishing, up close or far away. He thought he must be the worst kind of voyeur, spying on her every time her group was eligible to come here.

He thought, for the hundredth time, about the man and the boy. He could not tell Bea about them because of the need to maintain secrecy--again, to protect her, and to protect himself.

One more longing look at her, without the glasses, before he made his way back to the vehicle and then back to the office in the camp, thinking about her constantly, wondering if and when this war would end, wondering what is to become of them all. Wondering.

Whether at the pool or simply working in the office, the very sight of her ignited a multitude of feelings--feelings he dared not act upon nor even contemplate. But they were there, the feelings. He could not negate them, no matter how he tried.

* * *

Beginning in 1944, shipments from Japan, as well as from nearby larger islands, were becoming fewer and further apart. Local farmers could supply some of their food needs, but only under duress. It was a duty of distaste for the Colonel. But he had to do it--if they all were going to survive.

It was his brutal side, coming to the fore only when it was necessary.

No, the war was not going well for Japan, he conjectured. He did not share this assumption with Beatrice. He dared not. It could breed trouble from the barracks, had his thoughts become known throughout the camp.

He wished he could share it all with Beatrice, however. If the war should come to an end, in favor of either side, separation from her would be inevitable. And that would be the most excruciating part of it. He wished he could share many things with her. He was even beginning to think about her all day, all night. Dangerous.

* * *

Even as Colonel Itara stared through his field glasses at Beatrice Newlon, and she lay on the smooth rock, letting the sun dry her off, her thoughts wandered: from worrying about Tony (in spite of Hichio's assurances) to worrying about the war's progress. No news about the war was maddening. Hichio was very close-mouthed on the subject. Unsettling, as well.

Thoughts of Anthony were fading. She realized she was thinking about Hichio a lot lately. Why, she couldn't imagine--except for the fact she saw him every single, solitary day, day in and day out. They worked in the same office seven days a week, no Sundays off. Japanese culture did not observe a Sunday off.

With the daily exposure, she noticed how methodical he was in his work, how preoccupied he seemed most of the days. Was he worried about the outcome of the war? Hard to say. He said nothing about it. He did grouse now and then about the shortages of just about everything.

Aha, she thought. The shortages had become worse and worse. Could she draw upon that as a clue about the progress of the war? Why not?

Then she asked herself, how come I think about the Colonel so much? No, it's not the Colonel, it's Hichio, the man. The man. What kind of man? That's it. Kind. And thoughtful. And caring. She liked him for all those traits.

Oh, yes, he had to act stern now and then. But that was expected from a Japanese commanding officer of an intern camp. And it definitely was just an act.

Oh, yes, again, she thought, I like him for all that. I like him a lot.

What am I saying? Of course I like him! He was our friend, for heaven's sake!

Wait. Wait a minute. Friend. I wish . . . . I wish it could be more.

She was shocked at herself. This kind of thinking is getting out of hand! She got up from the rock, put on her dress, and made her way to the truck, leaning against it, pondering, wondering, turning herself into a tingling mass of nerves.

* * *

It began in early 1945, the spread of a flu epidemic in the camp. Officers and men alike were stricken. Little Bennie Lancer, Susan's younger boy, was one of the first victims. It was touch-and-go for the boy, but he pulled through and finally recovered.

The next day, Beatrice went to work at the Colonel's office, feeling very tired. She had stayed awake, late every night, along with Bennie's mother Susan. They took turns looking after him, and sitting up with him, for several nights. No wonder she was so tired, she thought. She hadn't slept well at all.

One hour later, the Colonel noticed Bea's typing had slowed to a deliberate cadence. She was normally a fast typist--and accurate, he added to his thoughts.

He got up from his desk and walked to hers. He stood beside her. She looked up at him, smiling wanly, eyelids lowered. He put a hand on her forehead. She was burning!

"Mrs. Newlon, you must report to Miss McBride in the clinic. You surely have a raging fever."

"Oh, Colonel Itara, I'm fine. Really."

"No, you are not fine! I *order* you to go immediately to the clinic!" He barked something at Jiro, who jumped up from his desk, partly from habit, in response to an order from the Colonel, but mostly from fright. The Colonel seemed close to be losing it!

Then, more gently, Hichio said to Bea, "Jiro will accompany you. I can tell from your typing that you are weak, as well."

He took both her hands and pulled her out of the chair. She made it out of the building and down the three wooden steps to the ground. Jiro walked behind her, his shouldered weapon in place. He noticed, halfway to the clinic, that she was faltering. He reached forward to catch her. Then he had to carry her the rest of the way. Although Jiro and Beatrice were the same height, picking her up and carrying her was no problem for him--Bea was thin as a rail, weighing a pittance by any standards.

The Colonel stood at the window, watching. Flinching when he saw her stagger. Slitting his eyes when he saw Jiro pick her up and carry her into the clinic. Now his jaws were clenched to the point of pain.

He sat at his desk, unable to do any paper work--there were mounds of it to read, analyze, and apply to his intern camp situation. The bureaucracy would be the first to capitulate in the event of a lost war, he thought bitterly. Serve them right, was his next thought.

He waited fifteen minutes. Jiro returned. Colonel Itara decided he must not ask Jiro about Bea's condition. He picked up his telephone and rang for the clinic. Speaking English, the Colonel knew that Jiro would not know what he said. "Miss McBride. Colonel Itara. What is your report on Mrs. Newlon?"

He listened carefully. Clara McBride had a peculiar accent that he had not been exposed to while he spent his one year at Berkeley. He remembered, then, that Bea had told him Clara's accent was southern. Whatever that means. His mind was wandering. He tried to concentrate on the odd accent from Miss McBride.

She assured him that Mrs. Newlon had been put to bed, and they would use cold wet cloths to try to bring down the fever. "Is there any way you could get aspirin again, Colonel? It'd be a big help."

"Sorry, Miss McBride, no." Another thing they were not even short of, but out of completely. He thought about that. Another sign--that things were not going well for the Japanese. Another sign.

Bea's condition remained unchanged for four days. Hichio was, frankly, worried beyond reason, near panic. He thought long and with agitation. Should Miss McBride ask for the Japanese doctor to come here to see Bea? Is it just the flu? People in WWI died from it, all over the world. Should he go to the clinic and see for himself just how seriously ill Bea is? Should he phone Clara McBride, with the weird accent, and inquire for the second time about Bea? He vacillated between making a visit or a second phone call.

* * *

Clara finished cold-cloth bathing Bea for the eighth time since early in the morning. Bea had not awakened for four days, had not eaten. Sipped some water. Elimination was limited. Clara was beginning to worry. She wished time and time again that an aspirin supply would materialize.

Just before Clara turned away from Bea to bathe the next patient, Bea stirred. She opened her eyes and saw Clara. Bea said, in a small voice, "Clara? I just had the strangest dream."

"Welcome to the world!" said Clara. She put her hand on Bea's forehead. It was cool. The fever had broken. She heaved a silent sigh. "What was your dream, Honey?"

"Well," said Bea. "It was the darndest thing. I dreamt that Colonel Itara came to see me. He stood at the foot of the bed, just looking. Not saying a word. Then he disappeared."

"That was no dream, Doll. The Colonel *was* here. At the foot of your bed, just looking at you. Left without saying a word. No, Honey, that was no dream."

Bea closed her eyes, a faint smile on her face. Then her eyes flew open, and she said, although weakly, "I'm starved!"

Clara quickly brought some rice broth. Then she telephoned the Colonel, to give him the good news, sensing that he would want to know that Bea is okay.

He had never before come into the clinic.

* * *

When the flu epidemic subsided, 1945 plodded along wearily and drearily. One day was exactly like the previous day and the next day and the next. There was no variation except that food was scarcer and medicine was a distressing non-entity. Women's clothing and soldier and officer uniforms were all shabby. The women's shoes wore out altogether. Many were barefooted all the time.

Beatrice continued her typing and filing; filing and typing. The office chores never ended.

The Colonel was so weary of the old instructions from the higher-ups that he would nearly fall asleep while reading them. "Old" instructions because there had been no new bulletins for many weeks. He had to look busy; thus, the reading of old bulletins. It was a mockery.

Food rations decreased at an alarming rate. Adults could weather the shortages, but the mothers worried constantly that their children were becoming gruesomely malnourished.

How would they ever survive these appalling conditions?

* * *

One morning in August 1945, Colonel Itara and Beatrice were alone in the office. Both Koshi and Jiro had been strangely occupied with packing--mostly personal items. It was curious, Bea said to herself.

While the two soldiers hauled knapsacks to a truck, Hichio spoke quickly to Bea. "Beatrice. I have something to tell you."

She listened, carefully.

He said, "We are ordered to report to the harbor to defend it. An American invasion is inevitable. You must take charge of the women after my staff and men and I leave the camp. Today. Moments from now. You can do it. Maintain order. Be calm. Have Miss Stockwell take charge in Barracks 2. She's a strong and competent lady. And

Mrs. Lesh can assist you in Barracks 1. Use the mess halls and kitchens wisely. My officers and men have to use army ration kits from now on."

She looked at him, disbelieving. The Japanese are going to have to *defend* the harbor? This is an insanity, she thought.

He continued. "The end is about to take place, my dear."

The 'my dear' did not go unnoticed. She held her breath.

"Before I leave, Beatrice, do you have my Tokyo address?"

"We did, but the house was burned to the ground--your address, along with everything else."

"Take it down as I dictate it."

"Yes. It's a long address, and I could never commit it to memory. Is that a home address? Your parents?"

"Only my mother. My father has died since I left for this intern camp duty." He told her his Tokyo address. "We must be in touch with one another when all is settled between our countries. I don't know where you'll be, for sure, but you have my address. *I want to hear from you! Do you understand me?*"

"Yes, Colonel. I hear you, and I understand you."

"One more last thing I need to tell you--something I wanted to tell you . . . long time ago . . . but couldn't. Tony is safe, in San Francisco."

"He's what?" she asked, not sure she heard him right. "What kind of nonsense is this, Hichio?"

"No nonsense. The truth. A truth I could not reveal to you until now, at the eleventh hour of my commanding this camp. The man Jeffreys and Tony were taken onto a submarine offshore on the other side of the island. A message from Jeffreys--that came addressed to you--confirmed their safe arrival in San Francisco."

"Oh, yes," she said, the truth beginning to sink in. "I remember the mysterious message. But the initials, 'M.A.' were not Sam's initials. What did that mean to you?"

"Mission Accomplished."

"Good lord," she breathed. "And thanks to the Lord." She wanted to hug him, she was so relieved. "How on earth?"

"I can't go into any explanation for now. Just know that Tony is with your aunt in San Francisco, waiting for you to join him."

"Oh, Hichio, how in the world can I thank you for whatever part you had in their escape?"

"Seeing the relief in your eyes and hearing it in your voice is enough." He gazed at her longingly. "God," he said to himself, "I want to kiss her so badly . . ." He came to his senses.

"I must say goodbye, dearest Bea."

He picked up his sheathed weapon and buckled it around his waist. He took one last look at her. She was so vulnerable! And would be more so, once he departed. He wanted to scoop her up in his arms and take her with him. Madness! Sheer, unadulterated madness! Madness all around them.

He left.

She whispered, "Goodbye, dear Hichio."

* * *

Standing outside the two barracks buildings, the women watched, stolidly, as the last of the trucks pulled out of the camp. Colonel Itara was in the passenger seat of the last departing truck. Everything was eerily quiet. The women looked at one another, questions in their heads. But one thing was for sure. They had been abandoned. And in a hurry.

Beatrice, rushed out of the office and toward Barracks 1, where all the women from both barracks had gathered. Bea was the first to speak.

"Listen up, everyone. They've gone to defend the harbor. Depending on how long this battle lasts at the port, we should be liberated afterwards. The Americans are going to win, ladies. Win, I tell you!"

A faltering cheer rose up from the crowd. Bea led them to the mess halls and kitchens. They had a feast, but not too much so. The food that was left still had to be rationed, based upon how long they might have to wait for the Americans to rescue them.

Bea was forceful in her instruction to them all to be calm and to remain in the camp and wait for . . . whatever was to be. No one believed, however, that the Americans would not be able to take the port.

* * *

Only two days later, the Americans entered the camp and celebrated with the internees, now freed. "Stay put, ladies, until we get a transport ship into the harbor and send you all back home," said the U.S Army Captain Morris. "One is already on the way."

Then Captain Morris broke the wonderful news to them. "The Japanese have surrendered." This was followed by a stunned silence. Gradually, they began the cheering, laughing, hugging, crying, and dancing crazily in the camp streets.

After the joyous celebration, the American liberators maintained order and dispensed level-headed direction.

"What about the men in their camp?" someone asked. Others

joined in with a chorus of questions. The Captain explained that they would have to wait for the transport to arrive before joining the men. "It's not fair! We want to be with our husbands and sons!"

The Captain answered, "There are no facilities nor means to unite you now and house you all together. Just stay here and be patient! Food is on its way!"

Another cheer went up from the crowd.

* * *

It was nine days before the ship arrived. The women and children had no baggage. There was nothing left after the rotting process of the tropics took over their possessions, their clothing, everything.

They were trucked to the pier. A line of the men from their camp was already in place. There was a separate line for the women. But husbands and wives, fathers and children were all united in a most untidy manner. It didn't matter. What mattered was that they were together again and boarding a ship that would take them home.

The women from the camp took no notice that Bea was not looking for her son, Tony. They were too involved with their own reunions and embraces and tears of joy and unrestrained laughter.

And so the two lines became intertwined as one larger and longer line. Meanwhile, more trucks arrived, along with ambulances. Those occupants formed another line to board the transport. They were the wounded and infirm--both Americans, the conquerors, and Japanese, the conquered.

Bea gave that line a passing glance. Then, something made her turn back. The line was not far from where she stood. She saw something that forced her to take another hard look, closer.

It was Hichio Itara on a stretcher, his left leg heavily bandaged, eyes closed. She ran to him. She grasped his hand that was hanging over the side.

"Hichio! It's me. Beatrice! Hichio, speak to me!"

He opened his eyes slowly, recognized her instantly. He thought his heart would burst through his chest. The line was stopped. She stood next to his stretcher, hanging onto his hand for dear life.

"Oh, Hichio, what happened to you?"

"My leg got in the way of a passing bullet. Nothing serious, so one of your Army doctors told me."

"Oh, darling," she said. "I thought I'd never see you again. your information was right. Tony and Sam are not among the men internees! My darling, how can I ever thank you for what you've done for them--for me!"

Hichio smiled faintly and said, "'Darling.' Explain, please?"

"Explain what, darling?" she asked.

"That's it--explain what darling is?"

"Hichio! How can you jest about something so frivolous at a time like this?!

"Ah so, my darling," he said, now with a grin. "Frivolous? I think not!"

"I can't believe we're having this conversation! I'm trying to tell you, Hichio, how much I appreciate what you did for Tony and ultimately for me."

"Please, Beatrice, enough. I did only what I thought was best--for everyone." The sun was bright and making his eyes squint. "It *truly is* you, Bea, isn't it?" Did she really call him 'darling'? Was he hearing things? "You are the dearest person I've ever known, Beatrice. Believe me when I say that."

"It's something I wanted to hear, Hichio. For a long time."

He nodded in agreement. "Remember. You must write to me. I want to meet with you again, after my rehabilitation. We must, my dear, focus on our meeting again. Dearest Bea."

The line began to move again. She walked alongside. Just before he was taken onto the gangplank, the line stopped once more. She leaned over him and kissed him soundly on the lips.

He closed his eyes completely, savoring the taste, the thrill, the swelling of a love entirely encompassing his being, such as he had never before experienced.

He had kissed her back. The stretcher moved again, onto the gangplank. She released his hand. She blew him a kiss. While he continued smiling, she watched his being taken into the ship.

And he was gone.

* * *

Once the ship was loaded with its precious human cargo, it left the harbor. San Diego was its destination. Beatrice tried to get to wherever the wounded were berthed on the ship. She was informed that their area was restricted. No visitors. She had been hopeful but was disappointed. She felt let down.

There was so much she wanted to say to Hichio, so much to confess--all her warm feelings for him, for starters. Patience, she realized, was the only course to take, under the circumstances.

* * *

The ship arrived at San Diego, and Beatrice was debriefed because of her former internee status. She took a train to San Francisco. A month had passed since the ship had left the Philippines. She found Tony at Aunt Rita's in San Francisco. Their reunion was joyful, and tearful.

She wrote to Hichio, giving him her Aunt Rita's address and phone number. Just before she relocated in Montecito, California, she had not heard from him yet. She wrote him again from Montecito. And she waited. The postman's arrival meant that perhaps there would be a letter from Hichio. But it did not happen. It was all very perplexing. She simply could not give up on him.

* * *

In December 1946, Beatrice said goodnight to Tony after he had gone to bed. She told him not to forget a prayer. He assured her he would not forget. She went into the living room.

The doorbell chimed. She turned on her porch light. She opened the door. And there he stood, a crutch under each arm. He placed them against the outside wall. He took her into his arms. She surrendered to his embrace. Then they kissed one another, deeply and lovingly.

Again, she was his prisoner, emotionally. But this time, as he stood on her porch, *he* was *her* prisoner.

# # #

THE GRYMWADE COLLECTION

OF

ARTICLES

AND OTHER TRIVIA

Having been brought up in the Midwest's Bible Belt, I learned at an early age not to smoke or drink, not to cheat, lie or steal, and not to have intimate relations before marriage. My parents told me all of that except not to have sex before marriage. It was implied but never spoken. In those days, the word sex was never mentioned.

I obeyed all the rules.

It wasn't until I was nearing retirement age, in my early 60s, that I learned something I wish my parents had passed on to me at an early age.

One of my co-workers, a young woman in her 20s, made the casual remark one day that when she was beset with a lot of problems, most of them seemingly unsolvable, she prayed and put them all at Jesus' feet.

It sounds simplistic and childlike, I know. But that's the beauty of it--it is simple and childlike. Her advice was a marvelous revelation. I tried it, too, and it worked. At once, I felt a great sense of peace. Letting someone else worry about my problems was also a relief. I slept better. The days passed more serenely.

Some may say that in putting my problems at someone else's feet, I shirked my problems. Not at all. I am reminded of the old story that goes as follows: A man on his deathbed called his children around him and said, "I've had a lot of troubles in my life, but most of them never happened!"

And so, most of our problems never happen.

Of course, one could accomplish nearly the same result by going to one's favorite psychiatrist or to the neighborhood psychologist. But praying will not cost $75 per hour.....or more.

This praying method will not work without a belief in God and without faith (the simplistic part), and without implicit trust (the childlike part).

Parents are correct to tell their children all the "thou shalt nots"; parents fail their children when they do not tell them what they can do to live a more productive and fulfilling life. That is, pray to God for Jesus to take on their problems, troubles, trials and tribulations.

I shall be eternally grateful to the young woman who put me on the right track. It was something I should have known years ago--something that had slipped through the cracks.

<u>Trusting in Lord builds on 'can do'</u> - Guest column, 1996

In the 1980s I attended a prayer breakfast at the Seabee base in Port Hueneme, California. The head nurse from the clinic was the speaker. She pointed out that the apostle Paul was the first Seabee because he wrote, in Philippians 4:13, "I can do all things in Christ which strengtheneth me."

The Seabee motto is "Can Do."

Today, as I recall the nurse's remarks, I remember some times in my life when I said, "I can do that."

When I was 13, my best friend, age 16, talked about her typing class. She said to me, "Billye, you'll never learn to type because you're so slow."

Three years later I sat in a typing class: "r-u-g space, f-u-r space, j-u-g space," and so on. I said to myself, "I can do this!" The next year, we had daily three-minute speed tests, and one day I typed 113 words per minute.

At age 20, I investigated the possibility of enlisting in the Navy. The recruiter painted a black picture of how difficult life would be struggling through boot camp, living in a barracks, dealing with homesickness, etc., etc. I said to myself, "Shucks, I can do that." And I did.

When I was 52, my boss, the editor of a semi-technical magazine published by the Navy, sent me to a military-civilian school in Indianapolis for a three-week course in news writing and editing.

The director of the journalism department told me up front that he didn't think I could hack it. I said, "Yes I can!" He called my boss to tell him that he was sending me back to California because of my age and inexperience. My boss talked him out of it, and the director relented. He let me stay.

It was a rugged course. In three weeks, we had to read two textbooks, write five papers, do homework assignments in a workbook every night, and for our final, we had to write an 18- to 20-page mini-thesis.

It was a Pass/No Pass course. I passed, and on graduation day, the director handed me an envelope. Inside was a letter of commendation.

At age 59, I went back to school by taking night classes at the

Learning Center of LaVerne University, Point Mugu. Upon completing the first class, I realized I really could do it. After three years of classes, five CLEP exams and challenging a course at UCSB, I received a bachelor of science degree with a major in psychology.

In the middle of all these events, there was a divorce, and I made it on my own.

However, making it on my own was not altogether "on my own." Neither was the typing, nor serving six years in the Navy, nor completing the difficult three-week course, nor earning a degree. There was help from above. Trusting in the Lord helped me to accomplish these feats.

What's important is that you, too, *can do.*

# # #

<u>Was his soul lost, being an atheist?</u> - Guest column, 1997

During my marriage, I met a man who was a friend of my husband's family. I shall call him "John." John was a dyed-in-the-wool, hard-shell, card-carrying, certified atheist.

Throughout the years, when we visited John and his family, or they visited us, he made my life miserable by taunting me about my religious beliefs. "Did you go to church today, and did you see God?" "Did you tweak his beard?" "Do you really believe in an anthropomorphological God?" And so on.

One day, John asked me, "Just what is the meat of religion? And to give you time to think about it, I'm going to the kitchen to fix another drink." I said that I didn't need time to think about it, for I had a ready answer. I said, "The meat of all religions is the same. Each one states it a trifle differently, but it's all the same. It is the Golden Rule: Do unto others as you would have others do unto you." (See Luke 7:31.)

John stopped in his tracks and said to me, "You get an A."

It was noticeable to me, after some years, that whenever we had a religious discussion, it was always John who initiated it. I avoided bringing up religion, for I knew the taunts would begin again.

The fact that John always initiated talking about religion made me think God was on his mind more than he would have us believe. Nevertheless, the teasing and ridiculing continued.

Some years went by, and after John and his wife moved to the East Coast, he died of cirrhosis of the liver and lung cancer; he had been a heavy drinker and a heavy smoker.

I often wondered, after his death, if I spent too much energy and time defending myself and my religious beliefs. I felt as though I should have spent time attempting to instruct John so he could have a personal relationship with God, and come to accept Jesus.

I am saddened that I shall never know, and I am guilt-ridden that I may be responsible for John's lost soul.

It teaches me that one must take advantage of the opportunities to spread the word--by example, if nothing else. But "example" might not have been enough--in this case.

I once heard a minister of the gospel say from the pulpit, "You have not lived as a Christian until you have been persecuted in some way." Being ridiculed for believing in God was my persecution.

That is small comfort, however, knowing that John's soul may be lost, for I do not know if he ever accepted God as a living, omniscient, omnipotent force.

If he had, it would have been a comfort to him, a source of inner peace.

# # #

Don't repay kindness; pass it on - Guest column, 1998

In chapters 19 and 20 of 1 Samuel in the Bible, we learn that Jonathan, son of Saul, befriended David by saving his life on more than one occasion.

Later, in 2 Samuel, chapter 9, we see that King David desired to repay the kindness in some way, so he sought out Jonathan's son, Mephibosheth, to pass another kindness on to him. David restored to him all the lands of his grandfather, Saul. Further, David told Mephibosheth "...and you shall eat at my table always."

In 1947, my husband and I were in the Navy, living in a rented room in a private home. Every morning, we walked from the house, onto the highway and to the main gate of the base. There we caught a station bus that took us to the hangar where we worked.

One morning, during our trek to the main gate, a Navy chief in a big Cadillac stopped to give us a ride. He took us all the way to the hangar. The next day, the same thing occurred. And the next and the next.

After a few weeks of riding to work with the chief every weekday, we said to him, "Chief, how in the world can we repay you for your giving us a ride every morning?"

The chief said, "You can't. Just pass it on."

Thirty-five years later, I was out of the Navy, divorced and working at the Seabee base in Port Hueneme. One of my co-workers broke his foot while playing baseball and was on crutches for a considerable length of time.

As soon as he was permitted to go back to work, he called me on the phone at home and asked if I would pick him up every morning to go to work and then take him home each afternoon. He explained that both his automobiles were out of commission, and that his wife had only a bicycle to go to the supermarket each day. I said that I would give him the ride, because it was on my way, anyhow.

After two weeks of this arrangement, he called me again at home, on a Saturday morning, and asked me if I could give him a ride to the auto shop where he would buy a part that would enable him to fix one of his cars so that his wife could drive him everywhere. I said I could and would.

On our way back to his house, he said to me, "How in the world can I ever repay you for your kindness?" I said, "You can't. But what you can do is...pass it on."

# # #

On turning disasters into assets - Guest column, 1998

Many will remember "The Donna Reed Show" in the 1950s. Donna Reed was the female equivalent to Robert Young in "Father Knows Best." She solved all the family's problems, large and small.

I remember one episode in which the teenage daughter planned to throw a party for her friends. On the day of the party, her brother drove home in an old and decrepit, beat-up bus and parked it in front of their house.

The daughter was appalled. How could she give a party with that ugly bus parked in front of the house? She would be embarrassed, she would be humiliated. It was all unthinkable. She begged her mother to demand that her brother drive the terrible eyesore to some other place.

But Mother had another idea: "Let's take some crepe paper and decorate the outside with festoons and decorate the inside with streamers coming down. Let's take the sodas and snacks out to the bus and have the party there."

Needless to say, the daughter was aghast at the proposal. She was reluctant to have the party in the bus. Not in a million years! Mother, however, was firm; the brother need not move the disreputable old heap; they would have the party in the bus, and that was that.

So the guests arrived, the party was held in the bus, and the daughter's friends were delighted. They had a ball. They loved the idea and all went home glowing with the good time they had.

When mother and daughter finished tearing down the crepe paper and bringing the empty soda bottles and platters into the house, the mother told her daughter that she had learned a lesson that day. The daughter wanted to know what that was. Mother said, "You learned to turn disaster into asset."

An interesting account of turning disaster into asset is found in Genesis 37-50. Those chapters tell the story of the treachery Joseph's brothers did to him: they threw him into a pit; they made it look as though he had been killed by an animal; and they sold him into slavery. As a slave, Joseph moved to a position of responsibility in his master's house. Later, after being falsely accused, he was thrown into prison. There, he functioned as a caretaker of the other prisoners, a job entrusted to him by the keeper of the prison. Joseph, in prison, made a series of accurate dream interpretations. The pharaoh was duly impressed, and Joseph eventually became a man of power, second only to the pharaoh.

Through all these trials and tribulations, Joseph, with God's help, according to Genesis, managed to turn his disasters into assets. How much easier our lives would be if we could learn to change our daily, inconsequential disasters into assets. And how much we could reduce our suffering if we could change our major disasters into assets, as well.

If we need the kind of help Joseph had, we have only to pray to God to see us through each "disaster-to-asset" cycle.

#

Is that all there is? - 1999 (Unpublished)

Eartha Kitt and Peggy Lee, in their separate recordings, sing a song entitled "Is That All There Is?" The lyrics are somewhat discomfiting because their theme is so negative. What a downer! The song begins with a soliloquy (the woman is talking and not yet singing) about when she was a little girl, and the house caught on fire. Her daddy took her outside, and they watched everything go up in flames. She says to herself, "Is that all there is to a fire?" Then begins the chorus, and she sings that part: "Is that all there is? Is that all there is, my friend? Then let's keep dancing. Let's break out the booze and have a ball. Is that all there is? Is that all there is?"

The soliloquy continues. When she was 12 years old, she went to the circus, watched the clowns and the elephants and the dancing bears, and when it was over, she asked if that is all there is to a circus. Then she sings the chorus again.

Back to talking, she tells us that she fell in love with the most wonderful boy in the world. They took walks by the river, and they gazed into each others eyes. He went away, and she thought she'd die, but she didn't. "Is that all there is to love?" The chorus is sung once more but with an interruption.

At that point, someone asks her why she just doesn't end it all. She says that she's not ready for that final disappointment--breathing her last breath--while saying to herself, "Is that all there is? Is that all there is? If that's all there is."

My first impression, at the end of her song, is that she has never known God. In the letter of James to the twelve tribes in the Dispersion, it is written in chapter 1, verses 2 and 3, "Count it all joy, my brethren, when you meet various trials, for you know that the testing of your faith produces steadfastness."

She, in the song, can't find a positive side to the various happy highlights of her life. She doesn't recognize that her experiences, both good and bad, are a part of living. She isn't tuned in to the nature of things. She has met trials without joy, without faith. She faces the end of life with the same old question: Is that all there is? Obviously, the dancing and the booze and having a ball is not the answer.

388

I'm asking her/him (Kitt or Lee or the author of these lyrics), with regard to her life's attitude, "Is that all there is?"

And, I repeat, what a downer!

# # #

Classroom Assignment, Defense Information School - 1974

If I were to be confined to a bed in a two-bed hospital room for six months, and I could have a choice for a room mate, the individual I would choose to occupy the other bed is nameless and faceless. Hospital regulations being what they are, my room mate would have to be female--a fifty-percent choice limitation right from the beginning!

She, of no name and no face, must be intelligent but not too smart, able to talk interestingly but not so much as to show me up to be inferior to Her.

She must be an excellent listener, hearing every golden word I say when I am talking to Her, chuckling and chortling and laughing uproariously whenever it is appropriate and timely. (Of course, if She is a surgery patient, I will allow the chuckling and chortling and not demand the uproarious laughter . . .)

My marvelous Female room mate will never wake me up when I am catnapping although it will be perfectly all right for me to awaken Her when I have thought of some fascinating story to tell Her--and it cannot wait until later. After all, I may forget the fact that I have remembered a fascinating story, and it will be lost forever.

If She has visitors, they must obey the visitors schedule religiously, and they must not ask me surreptitiously, "Do you mind if I smoke?" She, of course, will be a non-smoker.

Further, She will never, but NEVER, flirt with my male visitors. I, however, can take a second look, and perhaps a third and fourth look at her most attractive male visitors, and She will not be offended.

She will have read the same books I have read and will have seen the same movies I have seen so that we can discuss them thoroughly and enjoyably.

If She does not have a broken arm, wrist or thumb, she will be able to do needlepoint, embroidery, crocheting and knitting so that

She can teach me new stitches and encourage me when my fancy needlework grows stale and tiresome during our confinement.

My room mate will not have any children (so that I do not have to listen to the unending tales of what cute thing this one said and what darling thing that one did). However, because She has no children of her own, she will be inordinately curious and interested in what <u>my</u> children said and did while they were growing up. After I have exhausted my source of reachback material, She will still be thirsty for more and ask questions upon questions about <u>my</u> children and beg me to tell Her more clever anecdotes.

It is a good thing that my prospective room mate has no name and no face and indeed does not exist, for by the time She would have completed Her six-month confinement, She would expire from the effort of pleasing me, catering to my whims, and filling my needs.

Therefore, if I must be confined to bed in a two-bed hospital room for six months, I earnestly hope the other bed will be empty because I do not wish such a tortuous death for anyone, not even for someone who is nameless and faceless.

# # #

"....<u>no one takes care of me!</u>" - from *The Navy Civil Engineeer*, circa 1975

R&R--Rest and Recreation. That's what every overseas military family looks forward to, especially if they've been cooped up on a rock in the Pacific for a year or longer.

And that was the case for LCDR Clyde Hawley, MC, USN, and his wife and children in 1961 as they prepared for a ten-day cruise aboard a Military Surface Transport Service (MSTS) vessel from Guam to the Philippines and back. For Doctor Hawley, R&R would mean rest and <u>relaxation</u> and freedom from the daily grind of sharing the care of about 700 infants and children in the Pediatrics Clinic of the Naval Hospital on Guam and from having to stand the duty in Obstetrics every fifth day.

On the morning of the sailing date, all the passengers assembled in the dockside warehouse. Their passports and visas were examined for validity, and their baggage was tagged and accepted for delivery onto the ship and into the cabins. The last transaction for each passenger before boarding the ship was to pass a final inspection by the medical team whose station was located at the end of the baggage check-in counter.

Mrs. Hawley and her children, with passport and immunization cards, passed through the medical team. They were all found to be free from visible symptoms of contagious diseases, their immunization cards were up to date, and the Medical Officer-in-Charge stamped and initialed their boarding passes.

Dr. Hawley, following his wife and children in line, also proved to have a valid passport and visa and passed the visual examination for the absence of communicable diseases. But the Medical Officer-in-Charge of the medical inspection team refused to sign his boarding pass.

Dr. Hawley did not go to the Philippines . . . his immunizations had expired and had not been updated.

"I take care of nearly everyone on this island," Dr. Hawley wailed to the medical team, "but no one takes care of me!"

# # #

Unsung heroes ignored - College paper editorial, 1976

The term "unsung hero" is one we hear and read about infrequently. A recent television program about Edwin E. ("Buzz") Aldrin, second man to walk on the moon, reminded me of some unsung heroes from the Apollo missions of NASA's space program. [Neil Armstrong was the first man to set foot on the moon. Aldrin followed him from the LEM on the same mission.]

In the television story, Buzz Aldrin was pictured as a super hero-- a hero's hero. Indeed, that is what he was, at the time of his famous moon walk.

All astronauts who enjoyed the glory and fame connected with their achievements gave full credit to the teamwork of everyone who supported them on the ground--all the way back to those who first planned the missions and even to those who first dreamed of them.

In spite of that, I always felt during each Apollo mission, where men walked on the moon, that there was an unsung hero. Each of those missions had one--the man who stayed in the command module, orbiting around the moon, ready to connect with the LEM when it returned from the moon's surface and subsequently to return to earth.

While the moonwalkers planted their personal and national trophies, collected their rock samples, surveyed their assigned regions and gamboled in the moon dust, hardly anyone mentioned the command module pilot (Michael Collins)--the one maintaining his all-important vigil around the moon. If the television camera were ever focused on him, I was not aware of it and certainly never saw the orbiting astronaut doing his dull, mundane, but vital job of maintaining readiness for the heroes to come back to the command module.

The nation suffers from chronic, misplaced, hero worship. Without the orbiting astronaut, none of the moon-walk missions would have had the success each one enjoyed. Those indispensable orbiting astronauts from the Apollo missions are today's American Unsung Heroes.

[Apollo-11 was launched July 16, 1969. Its mission was to perform a manned lunar landing and to return the mission safely. It was achieved. The command module spent 59.5 hours in lunar orbit, with 30 orbits.]

# # #